THE PRINCE

LAS VEGAS MAFIA SERIES

FALCONE FAMILY

AMBER ALLEE

Cover Design: Graphics by Stacy
Full Content Final Editing: Kristen Portillo @ Your Editing Lounge
Edit: Christi Price @ Essential Edits
Formatting: Stacey Blake @ Champagne Book Design

To Kevin, who pushed me to chase this dream.
Your support is *everything*.

THE
PRINCE
LAS VEGAS MAFIA SERIES

PROLOGUE

Luca

Age: 30

May 2023

MY SHOULDER CONNECTS WITH THE FRONT DOOR, bursting through it. I'm met with two things—silence and the barrel of a gun shoved into my face.

My entire life, I've had to deal with guns and pussy-ass wannabes who thought they could take me down. Right in front of me is the last person I'd hoped to ever see again. The one who taught me everything I know in the world I grew up in when my pop was occupied with other business.

"It's time to come home now, Prince." Giovanni Mossimo Barone's deep voice commands the room.

I take in my surroundings, knowing I don't have the option of taking him down. He'd expect it after all. Five men stand in the room behind him, waiting for instructions. These men were assigned to me years ago to make sure I survived, and they've followed my every move despite my efforts to evade them.

The house is quiet—too quiet, and that worries me. She's supposed to be home right now, but I'm hoping that, by some miracle, she went over to her friend's place or out to the grocery store. *Anywhere but here.* Why the fuck did I decide to meet up with a new guy at work instead of coming straight home to my woman.

The moment the silent alarm at the house alerted me, I blew out of the meeting to my car and raced home. That alarm was put in place in case the unthinkable were to happen. I also have cameras situated around the house, and for some reason, I couldn't access them on the way over. It was the longest twenty minutes of my life. I'm panicking inside but refuse to cower or show any sign of distress. I was brought up to not show any emotions. Even when your life is ending, you are to show no signs of weakness.

"Emotions will get you killed, Son," Pop always insisted.

"Ask me, Prince," Gio taunts, and I hate that he knows I'm hanging on by a thread. I hate that he calls me that still, to this day. It gets under my skin, and I want to rip his throat out.

In an instant, I block the gun aimed at me, knocking it out of his hands and taking him by surprise. I've got him shoved up against the wall, my forearm up against his throat with just the right amount of pressure.

"Where's my wife?" I grit out. My teeth grind and my jaw ticks.

Gio's lip twitches a fraction, knowing that I've just given him the satisfaction of showing my weakness, but I don't give a fuck. She's my world, and I'll kill a hundred bastards with my bare hands if harm is ever brought on her.

"She's on a plane headed back to Vegas," Gio informs me. "Mr. Falcone wanted to make sure your arrival was immediate. Thought this was the best way to get you there."

My body stills and a million thoughts run through my mind. Will Pop hurt her to get me back home? Does she have her EpiPen and inhaler on hand? I've always made sure all the people around her carry them just in case something happens and they have to intervene. Did she go quietly or is she scared? Fuck!

"She put up one hell of a fight," Cassio, my best friend and right-hand man, interrupts my internal thoughts and points over to Carlo, who's sporting a swollen eye and busted lip.

"I'll gut you like a fucking fish if you laid a hand on her." I twist and pull the metal from my waistband pointing it at Carlo while still holding Gio on the wall. My voice is deadly, and there is no doubt I could drop his ass dead with a bullet between his eyes. I don't care if we were friends growing up or not. I'd get two shots off before they could restrain me, but I think better of it. They have the one possession that matters the most to me, and I need to keep a clear head and focus on her.

I go to take a step toward him, but Gio stops me, grabbing my shoulder.

"Easy, Luca. No one touched her but me. She put up a struggle, but I sedated her quickly before she could hurt herself." His words don't bring me any comfort. "She was able to get the upper hand on Carlo when she was cornered though." He chuckles, as do Cassio and Bosco.

"Laugh it up, fuckers," Carlo sneers as he touches his lip.

My head is about to explode. This was what I'd worked so hard to get away from, and now my two worlds have collided. I was born into one and walked away from it. But I *chose* the other and never looked back.

"Mr. Falcone said it was time to come home. Our plane is ready to board now, and all your"—Gio looks around the room before settling back on me—"things will be packed up and shipped to the house on the compound."

"I want proof she's safe," I growl.

Cassio comes over with his phone and plays a video. It shows my beautiful wife taking Carlo down. A sense of pride fills my chest as I realize those awkward and hard sessions at the gym paid off, but then rage takes over when I watch Gio sink a needle into her. Moments later, she goes limp while Gio cradles her, laying her on the living room couch. What really surprises me is the person who comes into the video—a person who's been in our house many times over the last year and who we consider a friend. They gather my wife's sedated body and leave the house, ending the video. How could I have not seen them coming? How could I have let my guard down even for a moment and allowed them to snake their way into our lives undetected?

Resigned to my fate, I mentally prepare myself to head back to Las Vegas. I'd left for good reason—to be with the one who truly became my world, the one I love more than my own life.

"If one hair is out of place or there is even a scratch on her skin, I'll torture you in the worst way before I kill you."

I kick Gio's gun out of my way and head back out the door to the waiting SUV that I hadn't noticed parked across from the house. It takes a few minutes for everyone to pile in, but once the crew is loaded, we head out in silence. It takes us twenty minutes to get to the private jet on the runway, and all I can think about is my wife.

We exit the SUV, but Gio grabs my upper arm, holding me back while the others board.

"She'll be fine Luca. Trust me."

I shrug him off. "You don't know shit!" My jaw ticks, and I really want to lay him out. He doesn't know how hard it was to get her out of her shell, to make her feel secure and safe. How my very breath depends on her. He has no idea the lion's den he's sent her into.

"I know more than you think." His eyes are hard, reminding me that he's still the same man who trained me since I was a little boy. "Mr. Falcone has known your whereabouts since the moment you left the state of Nevada." Well, shit. "Changing your last name and living a different life didn't hide you from him. He let you leave and have your fun. Now, it's time to come home and get ready to take your position in the family. Though, he has no idea you're married." Gio nods at my wedding band. "I'm sure Mrs. Falcone will be ecstatic to be adding a daughter to the family."

I brush past him, knocking shoulders, and I can't help but think about what Gio just said. Had my father truly known about where I was this entire time? Had he kept tabs on me, despite my efforts to stay off his radar? Was I deluding myself to think walking away from my family was even possible? Probably.

My wife has no idea what my family is or does for a living. She'll have a heart attack once she learns what I've done in the past. I'm clueless as to how I'm going to tell her. Will she accept me for who I really am? Accept my family? Christ, what if Pop tells her before I have the chance to explain? She'll think I'm a monster and run.

No, I won't let her have a choice. She's mine and has been from the moment I laid claim to her. She has no other choice but to accept it. I changed for her, but deep down I always knew this day was coming. I was just hoping to have a little longer before she found out about me and my family.

I'm the son of and future Don of the Falcone family. One of five mafia families in Las Vegas.

CHAPTER ONE

Luca

Age: 23

2016

WE MAKE OUR WAY THROUGH A BACK WINDOW undetected. The fool didn't lock a single one. Careful not to alert him of our arrival, we creep through the small laundry room and down a short hallway. We're here to follow through with orders from the head of our family. Most call him Mr. Falcone or Boss, but my whole life, I've called him Pop.

"Check those rooms," Gio whispers his command as he points in the direction of where I'm supposed to go.

Gio is Pop's second-in-command, or underboss, and my handler. He's here to make sure everything goes smoothly. After tonight, Pop wants me to do more by taking a bigger role in our organization. Gio has taught me everything I need to know about guns, knives, fighting, and women from a young age. My pop was always too busy when it came to anything other than making money and keeping his territory secured. He has Las Vegas at his feet, and everyone bows to him. He has the police in his back pocket and on payroll, along with many state and local officials, making him untouchable.

We are one of five families that own Las Vegas, and we each have our own territory in the city. Every family runs their territory how they see fit. Our family, the Falcones, is run by my father, Arturo Falcone, and only deals in guns, drugs, and prostitution on the illegal side. We own the waste management business and real estate on the outskirts of town, and we are the only Italian family in our group.

"Clear." I keep a steady hand on my weapon as I incline my head toward the ceiling.

The sound of water moving in pipes reaches us from the second floor. Bingo. Our target is getting into the shower. He won't have a clue what's about to happen until it's too late.

"Just because he doesn't know we're here doesn't mean he's not prepared," Gio scolds when I lower my gun slightly. Gio has done nothing but lecture me since a young age, and the older I get, the more his nagging annoys me.

Getting back in position, I slowly start to ascend the stairs. The walls are covered in family photos of a woman with a small girl, and the higher we go the older the girl becomes. Reaching the top, there's a picture of the three of them—my target, the woman who I suspect is the dead wife of the target, and the daughter. The pride and joy of the mother's eye. Our target gazes back at me with a bored expression, as though he doesn't belong with this family.

The picture had to have been taken within the last three years or so because, from the intel we received, the wife is deceased. The daughter is sitting between her parents. Long, curly brown hair frames piercing blue eyes and stark, pearly white teeth beneath plump lips. She's gorgeous like the mother, but evidence shows she doesn't resemble the dad at all. I'd say she's around the middle of her teenage years in the photo. She looks as though she should be gracing the covers of magazines or on billboards.

I glance over my shoulder and catch Gio mesmerized by the family photo I was just gawking at. His eyes are all over the dead wife as though he knows her. Ever since I was old enough to understand fucking, I've known Gio was the biggest man-whore there is. '*My life wasn't meant to include a family,*' is what he told me once when I asked him when he would settle down. Ma said that Gio had been seeing someone before he was sent away for a few years, but he'd kept her identity a secret. I was about seven years old when he returned from prison, and I remember noticing a complete difference in him. He was cold and hard, but his eyes always had a hint of sadness.

Pop said that prison will do that to a man—make you turn off all the compassion you once had. Pop had his stint. He was locked up right after I was born. He was sentenced to eighteen months for money laundering, which was all they could get him on. Of course, with Pop being who he is, he got out a lot sooner than that. After that, he put people in place who valued their lives enough to ignore his criminal activities.

The floor creeks beneath my foot, and I freeze in place.

"Breathe," Gio instructs from behind. "Now, move." He gives my back a shove to get me going.

"Don't rush me!" I grit my teeth. This is far from my first time, and I don't need to be pushed. I've never failed any task I've been given, and I don't need him rushing me. That's when mistakes are made.

The water from the shower shuts off, and my adrenaline starts to kick in. My biggest fear in life is disappointing my pop. My whole life, I've always wanted to make him proud of me, so I've always gone above and beyond to impress him. My grades were better than everybody else's, my bullets always hit the target, and I even changed my wardrobe halfway through high school to match his. There's nothing I wouldn't do for Pop.

The bedroom door opens, and Mario Ricci stands there in his boxers and tank top. From the look on his face, we've surprised him completely. He quickly tries to slam the door, but I'm on him within seconds.

I work out every day and have honed my body to be a deadly

weapon. My size might hinder some, being that I'm well over six feet tall and have solid muscle, but I'm quick.

"Not a chance, Mario." I've got him by the front of the tank, hauling him into the hallway so he's not able to reach for anything.

"What the fuck do you want?" He looks over my shoulder at Gio as if I'm not even there. "I've paid my loan this month already."

"We're here for something much bigger than that," I state, slamming his back against the wall and releasing his shirt, bringing his focus back to me.

"I've got nothing here of any value."

"Oh, but you do." I grab the front of his thin tank again when he tries to be sneaky inching back toward the room. "We have it on good authority that you're trafficking again."

There's a twitch in his left eye, but other than that he's as stoic as ever. A pathological and practiced liar for sure.

"No idea what you're talking about. I've kept my nose clean, and I pay my dues like everyone else," he defends. If I'd been anyone else, I might have bought it, but as someone who's been taught to read tone and body language, I know he's full of shit.

"Then you won't mind coming with us to clear this up, right?" My hand is by my side, but I'm always on guard. You never know what a person will do when backed into a corner.

Mario tries to shove off me, but thanks to my size, he's not getting anywhere. Both Gio and I manhandle him down the stairs and into the living room. Gio grabs a wooden chair from the breakfast area, and I shove Mario down while pulling out the rope from my back pocket. With his hands behind his back, I bind them to make sure he can't get loose.

Mario must realize that he's been caught and the game is over because he starts to plead his case. I always hate this part—they'll do anything to save their miserable lives.

"Mr. Falcone has ordered us to remind you that nothing happens in his territory that he doesn't know about. You've been trafficking children within his territory for months under his nose."

"Please, I have a family."

"So do all those children that you've abducted."

"I'll do anything, please."

"Mr. Falcone demands and expects loyalty."

Without another word, I raise my gun and fire once. Perfect aim, right between the eyes. His head snaps back, and his body slumps as blood flows out of his head.

"Should've made it last longer," Gio comments. "That fucker deserved to be tortured." He moves toward the stairs and stops again at another set of photos on a table, admiring them. "I'll get his electronics."

Gio disappears upstairs, and I'm left there with a dead body to add to my growing number. Everyone always says that you remember your first. Not the second or fifth, not even the hundredth but only your first. To me, he's some scumbag who stole kids from families.

The backdoor handle jiggles and it paralyzes me for a split second. The first floor of the house is dark except for the dim lamp Gio turned on in the corner. Is someone else here for backup to make sure it goes smoothly? Gio would've told me so none of our crew members got their heads blown off.

The door opens, and from the outline of the invader by the street lights, I know it's not one of our guys. Whoever it is drops the keys clumsily on the ground, and I'm on them in a heartbeat. Gio made sure to teach me how to surprise someone.

"Don't make a sound." I take a deep breath of a flowery scent as I haul them into the pantry. I've had this house mapped out for days and could probably move around the place with my eyes closed.

The girly fragrance lets me know exactly who it is, and she couldn't have shown up at a worse time. From our intel, the daughter has been placed in an all-girls private school since her mother died. She doesn't come back often, if at all, which is why we didn't foresee any trouble tonight. How wrong we were. What is she doing here?

She whimpers, as whatever scent she's wearing invades my nose and fills it with sweetness. She's tiny compared to me, almost as if I could put her in my pocket. From the dim light of the corner lamp, I can see her pictures don't do her justice. She looks like a beautiful life-sized fairy with her silky hair and small stature.

Our orders have always been to leave no witnesses. Even though Pop has the police in his pocket, we still don't chance it. Our business is all about survival of the fittest, and Pop didn't get where he is by leaving loose ends.

Is that what I need to do now? Do I kill her so that she can't rat me out? She hasn't seen my face, so how much could she tell someone? If Gio sees her, she's dead. *'Wrong place, wrong time,'* is what he'd say to justify her demise. But even though I've been brought up to kill, I've never taken an innocent life. I don't even know if I can. She's young and has her whole life ahead of her. There's no reason to punish her like her scumbag father who kidnaps and traffics children. Hell, she could be a victim too.

I'm behind her as she faces the shelves of canned vegetables. Her small frame makes it hard to whisper directly into her ear, so I bend my knees a bit. Opening my mouth next to her ear, her head whips forward hitting my gloved-covered hand in quick succession.

"AHCHOO! AHCHOO!"

Did she just sneeze on me?

There's a murmur against my glove as I feel her cheeks move, and I swear I hear her apologize. I'm about to tell her, *'bless you,'* but stop myself. I can't show any empathy or kindness to her. I've been taught that showing mercy is a sign of weakness, and our kind can't afford any of that. Yet, for some reason, I don't want to be the harsh killer I've been trained to be all these years. Why is she so different? This little slip of a girl has me checking my brutality and ignoring nearly everything I've been taught.

There's a creaking coming from the stairs, and I know Gio is headed back down.

"You are going to stay right here and not make a sound, or my partner will fill you full of bullet holes," I whisper with my lips near her ears. "Ten minutes, then you can come out and call the police. Tell them that your piece of shit father, who kidnaps kids and sells them to the highest bidder, is dead in the living room."

I let that sink in, and her body starts to tremble even more. Her tears are soaking my gloved hand, but she stays quiet. She's probably in shock, but at least she's following my command.

"We know all about you and where you go to school. If you don't do as you're told, we'll come up to your private school and do the same to you." This is the first time I've had to strongarm a female, and I hate it, but it's necessary if she wants to live. "Are you going to be a good girl and follow instructions?"

She nods frantically.

Gio is in the next room coming this way and I've only got seconds before he starts calling out for me.

"Ten minutes. Don't disappoint me." I remove my gloved hand from her mouth and exit the pantry, getting the door closed just as Gio comes in with a laptop in his hands.

"Ready?" he grunts.

I nod, and we head out the back door that was left open when I surprised my little invader. I'll check in on her in a few days to see if she's doing what she was told. I've never kept anything from my family before, but I don't feel the need to tell them this. She's innocent, and hopefully, she'll be able to have a good life now that she won't have to deal with her asshole of a father.

The intel from our guy said the mother had divorced the father years before she died. He was a conman who drank too much and wanted to live off his wife's large inheritance. She put a stop to it and left him, taking the daughter with her. He and the daughter never had much interaction until the wife passed away. She was sent to a private school in accordance with the wife's will, and the father got a minimal number of supervised visits.

So, why is she here? The private school is over an hour away. How did she get here?

"Looks like the neighbors just got home," Gio interrupts my thoughts.

I look over to where he's nodding, and my steps falter slightly. I know it has to be the daughter's car parked in the street. Of all the nights to make a home visit, she sure picked the wrong one.

"So, are you paying for dinner after a job well done or what?" I nudge him as we turn the corner and locate our vehicle down the next street.

"You're paying. I had to babysit your ass when I could've been out finding a woman to bed."

As he gets behind the wheel my mind drifts back to the tiny invader I let slip through the cracks of my armor. *Never show weakness.* I'd like to think that maybe it wasn't a moment of weakness but rather a good deed for an innocent person who has their whole life ahead of them.

I just hope this good deed doesn't come back to bite me in the ass later.

CHAPTER TWO

Luca

Age: 25

May 2018

Don't do it. You shouldn't be doing this, I chant in my head as I make my way across campus toward the commons area of the little school, trying to blend in the best I can. My size always draws unwanted attention, but when your job is to kill for a living and not get caught, you learn ways to fly under the radar. My expensive suit makes it easier to fit in here with the elite rich people who shove their daughters off to be brought up by someone else, and I've mastered the art of adapting my body language to suit any purpose.

I've kept tabs on this girl for the last two years, ensuring she adjusted after what happened that fateful night in her house. To this day, I still don't know why she was there and not at her school. I know I should have made sure all witnesses were flushed out, but something was needling me; I just couldn't bring myself to kill an innocent girl. Her father? That bastard had it coming, but something had kept me from doing the same to her.

After we finished the job that night, I've snuck off every so often to see how she's been doing and if she'd mentioned what happened that night to anyone. She hasn't. The police report turned into a cold case and was labeled as a home invasion/murder. There were no leads, and nothing in her statement proved useful to the cops. *Good girl.*

Gemma has gone on with her life the best she could. That's her name. *Gemma.* Her mother left her with a large inheritance but being only sixteen at the time had made things a bit complicated. She was considered an orphan, and the state tried to come in and place her in foster care. Thankfully, one of her teachers stepped up, and she was under their guardianship until the school helped her get emancipated. That same day, she changed her last name from Ricci to Barone, though her mother's maiden name had been Amato. I'm not sure how she came about the last name. I checked, and there wasn't a single Barone among the faculty. *Mystery.*

Gemma Barone.

So, here I am on the day Gemma graduates from preparatory school. I know how big of a day it was in my family when I graduated, and since I'm part of the reason she has no family member alive to celebrate her big day, I feel like I need to be here. So, here I am. Hiding in the back, a pillar keeps me concealed just enough to avoid being seen by anyone of importance.

She looks absolutely stunning. I'm not mentally or physically ready when I see her walk across the stage to receive her diploma. Her long curly locks hit the middle of her back and bounce with every step she takes in those killer heels. She turns slightly to look at the professional photographer while standing next to the dean of the school, and her brilliant blue eyes set her apart from everyone else. She takes my breath away.

Geez, she is gorgeous. How is it possible to be even more beautiful than she was two years ago? She's taller now and has definitely filled out in areas that should be illegal for an eighteen-year-old.

The reception is packed, and I'm able to go unnoticed easily. We actually stand next to each other at the drink station, and she is none the wiser. She speaks with fellow students and their families about going to a college out of state. I quickly make a mental note of the college and store it for later. Her getting out of the Las Vegas area is best for both of us. She can move on with her life and never look back at the horrible memories she's been carrying for all these years. And I won't have the guilt and betrayal of not following my father's orders constantly hanging over my head.

I watch from afar as she awkwardly stands off to the side of the reception while families converse. I wish I had the balls to walk over to her and help with her seclusion. I know this must be hard, not having any family, but there's nothing I can do without revealing myself to her and putting both of us in danger.

When she goes to take a bite out of her cake, the entire thing falls off the plate and splats on the floor by the table. It never fails. Every time I've ever come for a visit, she does the clumsiest things. She's a walking insurance claim and should be clothed in bubble wrap. I just wonder what happens when I'm not here to witness the debacle that is her life.

Gemma scrunches her face, which is absolutely adorable, then looks around to see if anyone else saw her fumble. With a huff of justifiable frustration—because the cake is amazing, and there's no more left—she takes the side of her silver heel and nudges the cake beneath the tablecloth with all the grace she can muster. The move has me looking away and biting back laughter in an effort not to make a scene, but my body betrays me, and my shoulders and stomach shake with mirth.

This girl.

For some reason, my heart constricts every time I think about her and what she might be doing. I know it's unhealthy to have those thoughts after what I did to her father. I'm a monster, and she's this innocent lamb I'm trying to save from the slaughter. Although, some might thank me for putting the disgusting asshole six feet under. It just goes to show that not all horrid traits are genetic.

Before I risk bringing any more attention to myself, I slide my way out the side door of the reception area and away from her. I told myself that I'd check in on her to see how she was doing, and I did. Mission accomplished. My phone vibrates again in the pocket of my suit jacket, and I pull it out to see the name of the caller that I've sent to voicemail each and every time for the last two hours.

Gio.

Once I'm in the car, I press the button.

"Yes, dear!" I sing to my pop's right-hand man and my handler.

"You better be dying for not answering your damn phone!" Gio growls and I can just imagine the steam shooting out of his ears.

"My phone was dead," I lie smoothly.

"This isn't the time to get your rocks off, Prince." His snide tone angers me after he uses the nickname to rile me up, like I'm some kid. "Pay the slut and make your way over to the warehouse—that shipment we've been waiting for came early. Your birthday isn't until next month, so hurry the fuck up and you might live to buy pussy then."

"I'll get there when I get there," I say calmly into the phone then hang up. I've got one hell of a drive back and can only imagine the hell I'll catch when I do show up to help with the product.

My phone vibrates again, but I toss it over to the passenger seat. I'm sure Gio has a few choice words for me for hanging up on him, but I don't care. The good mood I was in after seeing Gemma has now vanished, and the cold-hearted dread has taken its place.

Back to the grind.

One more glance in the rearview mirror has a small smile pulling at the corner of my mouth. She's still just as clumsy as she was when I first got ahold of her. I know in my heart that I did the right thing that night. She is alive and seems to be flourishing. Pop would likely think it was a weakness to let her live, but you can't always reign with an iron fist. She'll go on to college, find a great guy to marry, and have babies. That night will be but a blip to her, and she'll never look back.

My mind wanders the entire drive home. I envision a white

picket fence with a large backyard for a son to play with our dog. I come through the backdoor after a long day at work only to be greeted by my family. My son runs over with a football, ready to play, just as my wife walks up and kisses me long and hard.

By the time I'm pulling into the warehouse, my little fantasy for the future is constructed down to the last tiny detail. Every time my eyes settle on my future wife, I see *her*.

I see Gemma.

Can I have her? Is that even remotely realistic? She's just starting her life. Could we make this work? Am I seeing her as the only option because she's a little forbidden and my biggest secret?

My heart does a flip at the thought of building a life with her but sinks as I watch my crew load up eight hundred pounds of drugs to be distributed. Is it right to bring her into this world?

I could marry her and protect her from the wrath of my father and Gio if they ever found out about her. She'd be family, and if there is one thing my pop loves more than his organization, it's his family. Maybe I'll just continue to stalk her a little longer and see if maybe I've grown a vagina to go with my bleeding heart since I decided to develop a conscience. There's nothing wrong with keeping an eye on her and making sure she's adjusting to college…

Cassio knocks his knuckles against the hood of my car, bringing me out of my rambling thoughts and back to reality. With a long sigh, I open the car door and get back to the grind, pushing her out of my mind so I can work.

CHAPTER THREE

Luca

Age: 27

September 2019

I DECIDED TO TAKE A FEW DAYS AND FLY TO SAN DIEGO FOR a quick weekend trip to check up on Gemma. No one knows I've left Vegas. They all think I'm holed up in our local brothel binge-fucking after the long-ass street war that left a few of our crew dead and the Canadians completely obliterated. I needed some fresh salty air to take my mind off of everything and regroup after the months of bullets flying and sleeping with one eye open.

A few months after Gemma's graduation, things started heating up with the Canadians who use us to procure guns and drugs. It went back and forth for months as the new leader of their organization tried to make a name for himself. Pop was more patient than usual, but after one of our businesses was leveled by explosives, he pulled out all the stops. We hardly had time to change underwear as we took out the entire organization. The streets of Vegas were flooded with blood for weeks on end. Things were on shaky ground, and I was unable to break away for a visit to Gemma, but

I thought about her a lot and I'm glad she was away from all the destruction and chaos.

So, I've snuck away to watch my little secret. A dirty, gorgeous little secret that is still known only to me. I've had more than enough opportunities to confess my sins about what happened that night, but for once, I want something that is all mine.

The moment I leave the hotel after getting settled, I roam the campus in my college gear in search of the brown-haired, blue-eyed beauty. The campus is buzzing with talk of a rival football game happening the next day. All the students are in spirit shirts with crowds chanting and cheering on every surface of the college campus. My chest feels a bit hollow at the reminder that I was never able to experience something like this. From the beginning, I was groomed to take over the family business, and college was never even an option for me to consider. No, I was always the one who would step up and take the throne when Pop decides to retire or when a body bag claims him. I was sent over to Italy to train and learn from my grandfather and uncle on how to become the next in line. They run Italy like Pop runs Las Vegas. He was sent over here when he turned seventeen to establish roots and move product throughout the U.S.

For a brief moment, the outpouring of school pride has me wishing I came from a different family. A normal one. To be so carefree and only worried about what party to attend on the weekends. Of course, it's not like I can't get alcohol and pussy on demand, but the vibe here is different. Like a rite of passage or something.

This is my first time on campus, but I made sure to study the college map on the flight down. She might not even be on campus right now, and all this could be for nothing, but I at least have to try. If nothing else, I appreciate the opportunity to stretch my legs after the flight. Just when I'm about to give up and head back to the hotel, I see something to my left in the common area right in front of the library.

Gemma.

It's as if the universe is trying to pull us together. My eyes are drawn to her like iron to a magnet. Her curly brown locks sway as the balls of her feet bounce in time with the band fight song. She's wearing the shortest shorts that display her toned and tanned legs. Her college jersey is cropped and shows off her midsection. She's a walking wet dream.

Her freshman and now her sophomore year have done her well. Most gain the freshman fifteen and have to work hard to get it off during their sophomore year, but she's rocking that body. My dick immediately strains against the zipper of my pants, needing more room. My mouth waters as she twirls in a circle with her hands raised in the air, letting the jersey lift even further north so that I catch a peek of her black lacy bra.

Down boy, she's just a kid you saved. Woman. There's no doubt in my mind that she's all woman.

Even though it's been a while since I saw her last, she still reminds me that you can't change a leopard's spots. Right as she finishes her twirl, she stumbles over thin air and almost topples over. My feet make their way on instinct, but I'm stopped as a lame-ass joker sweeps in and saves her from falling. He tucks her into his side with his muscled arms circling her body. It's almost a protective hold. *Familiar.* He leans in to tell her something in her ear because the noise out here is too loud to have a conversation. Whatever he says makes Gemma throw her head back and laugh. She leans in and pecks him on the cheek as he steadies her then releases his hold. Even from this distance, it's clear that he hesitates to let her go.

For some unexplained reason, my blood boils. I flew here with no heavy metal or lead because this is just supposed to be a quick visit, but if I had my gun on me, I'd shoot him where he stands, right between his pussy-ass manicured eyebrows. Who in the hell does this joker think he is touching what's mine? My hands ball into fists.

Mine?

No…She's not mine, just someone I saved.

She could be mine.

I shake those thoughts out of my head immediately. No way could that ever happen. She's just some girl I decided to show mercy to because it was the right thing to do. I had a moment of weakness and spared her life. That's all.

Then why have I been checking up on her all these years?

Why do I always see her in my future plans? I shake my head, knowing that I made the right decision not to bring her into my world. Even if I wanted to be selfish, I refuse to let her become a pawn for one of my enemies to use against me.

Disgusted with where my thoughts have gone and the pushy college kids, I watch her for another moment and decide right then and there that this will be the last time I go out of my way to see her. This is it. No more visits. None. She's fine and living the life she is meant to have, and I gave that to her. This is the one good deed in my life that I can look back on and say I helped someone. When I'm standing in front of my maker, at least I'll have a little less blood on my hands. This feeling in my gut is not going to sway me to continue to stalk this poor girl.

Tonight, though, the college is holding a Midnight Madness gathering to celebrate the big game tomorrow afternoon. After hearing Gemma and her friends make plans to attend, I decide to go too. I'm leaving in the morning, anyway, so why not enjoy this one last thing before having to get back to the grind?

She and her friends are all congregating on the lawn with blankets, as are all the other students. After a little while, I watch as Gemma puts down her book and stands to make her way to the bathrooms nearby.

My little bookworm.

Why is she going by herself? Doesn't this chick have any type of self-preservation in her body? Some psycho-stalker-rapist could be waiting to snatch her up, never to be seen again. Or some human trafficker like her pansy-ass father could snatch her up and have her in a shipping container halfway to the Middle East before anyone could blink.

I follow slowly behind her to make sure she isn't kidnapped. There's a bit of a line for the women, so I discreetly duck into the men's side and do my business to kill some time. As soon as I walk out of the bathroom, I'm knocked into by a flash of brown curly hair.

"Oh, sorry," chimes a voice I haven't heard from this close in a long time.

Once I'm able to gather my wits, I realize I'm holding her so that our chests are touching. That in itself sets my body ablaze. *None of the women I've bedded have made my body react like this.* The air around us is thick and electric. Gemma seems to bring all these emotions out in me, and I'm not so sure how to handle it. I shouldn't even be here to begin with. I'm too fucking old to even be thinking these thoughts.

"Um, thanks for catching me," Gemma speaks again, and it brings me out of my stupor.

It's then that I realize I've just been holding her and staring and not saying anything, like a total idiot. Never—and I mean never— have I had a problem sweet-talking a woman or laying it on thick with my charm. She seems perfectly fine with being in a stranger's arms though, and the thought of her being touched by someone else, like the scene I watched earlier today, makes me tighten my hold on her.

Get a grip, you fool. Next, you're going to toss her over your shoulder and then bang on your chest from the nearest rooftop. How the hell are you going to justify having someone from your crew come bail your ass out of jail for kidnapping? And being in a completely different state.

Easing up the strained muscles in my arms, I release her slightly, giving her a chance to take one step back away from my chest.

"You barrel into people often?" A growl of frustration leaves my throat at my failure to keep my mouth shut and let her walk away. Way to act like a douche instead of just soaking up all the attention I'm being given right now.

What if she recognizes my voice from that night?

She obviously doesn't hear me though, because her eyes are

roaming all over me as she blatantly checks me out. My hard body instinctively flexes under her gaze. A sense of pride fills my chest as I see her eyes light up, taking me in. My tattoos are on display in the short-sleeved shirt, and she's like a kid in a candy store for the first time, big eyes widening and trying to decide where to start exploring first.

Go ahead, baby, take in all that I have to offer. I bet the sight of my dick will make you pass out.

"Huh?" she finally answers when her eyes sweep up to mine.

It makes me chuckle, but it's short-lived as her palms come up and rest on my pecs. She's exploring as if I'm a unicorn. The laugh is caught in my throat, and my dick pulses at the same speed as my heartbeat under her contact. Her heat and pressure around us could turn coal into diamonds.

As though someone kicked her in the shin, Gemma flinches and removes her hands from my body, and I feel a cold shiver where her warmth was only seconds ago. *Does she know I'm the one who killed her father? Does she feel the same connection I'm feeling?*

"I…I'm," she tries to speak, but she's tongue-tied. Her cheeks pinken like she's thinking dirty thoughts. She traps her lower lip between her teeth, making me want to have a turn. With her eyes avoiding me, I can see she's shy, and her naiveté is pouring off of her in waves. As much as I want this, I can't do this to her. If it were a different time or place in our lives I'd sweep her right off her feet and never let her go.

Damn it.

I decide to put us both out of our misery and reach for her hands. My last touch of something pure. Her skin is soft and her fingers are so tiny in my large, callused hands. *Blood-stained hands.*

It's dark, and only the faint flicker from the flood lights on the buildings are on tonight.

"Th-thank you," she stutters just above a whisper and looks away to avoid eye contact.

I nod, not trusting my voice. Shit, I've become such a pussy. If

Gio saw the way I'm acting right now, he'd never let me live it down, or he'd just shoot me in the head for behaving like some limp dick. The chance of throwing her over my shoulder and heading back to my hotel room increases as the seconds tick by. I need to either make a move or end this.

I notice how her eyes sparkle in the light and her innocence shines through. I glance around to see if anyone is nearby. I could take her, and no one would notice. It'd be days before those friends of hers even started to seek her out.

That's when it hits me.

She deserves better than me. She has her whole life in front of her, and she shouldn't be strapped to a man who kills and tortures people for a living. Someone who doesn't have choices and lives by a certain code. She'd never be able to live in my world, and even if she could, Pop and Gio would eventually find out who she really is and kill her.

I blow out a huff, releasing all my frustration as I make my decision. It's better for the both of us that I let her go now. The smile on my face is fake as shit when I let go of her hand and make the hardest decision I've ever had to make in my life.

Goodbye, baby girl. Have a long and adventurous life.

Of its own accord, my hand reaches up and cups the side of her face, and I relish the touch and feel of her. The life I'll never have with her. With one last wink, I force myself to walk away. It isn't easy, but just like I did that night all those years ago, I give her the chance to live and not be put in a cage—or worse, six feet under. I might be strapped to a life full of death and destruction, but she doesn't have to be. She is what is good in this world, and I'd be an asshole if I tried to snuff it out.

I keep walking down the cement path toward the main street where my rental car awaits. With every cell in my body, I know if I turn around to look back, I'd change my mind and steal her away. Away from everything that I've tried to give her since our first encounter.

Keep walking. Keep walking, and don't look back, I chant as I make the final turn into darkness and away from the only good thing that has ever touched my life. If I look back, and she's still standing there watching me, I think my heart would explode, knowing that I'm making the biggest mistake. On the other hand, if I looked and she's already walked away, I think my heart would crack into a million pieces.

Either way, I can't afford to put either of us in that kind of danger. *Keep walking.* So, I do what I've been trained to do all my life. I push my wants and needs aside and focus on what is best for the family, even if I die a little more inside because of it.

CHAPTER FOUR

Luca

"FORGET TO DO LAUNDRY?" GIO POINTS AT MY NECK, where I'd usually be wearing a tie along with my daily three-piece suit, looking like I walked straight off a GQ photoshoot and loving the attention I get from women. But not now. Nowadays, I couldn't give two shits if I even rolled out of the house in my running gear. I didn't feel like having a noose around my neck today, so I left the top two buttons undone instead. "Mr. Falcone isn't going to like it."

I shrug because lately, I don't give a rat's ass. Ever since I got back from visiting Gemma a few weeks ago, I've been in a mood. Things are different now, and what once used to appeal to me doesn't hold the same attraction as it once did. Bedding whores has become a chore. Getting out of bed each morning is like the beatings Alice, my baby sis, and I used to get from Ma. She'd wait until I was fully asleep before delivering our punishment with the wooden paddle. Geez, for a small woman, she really knew how to pack a swift hit. The older I got, the smarter I was, sleeping in extra clothing when I'd misbehaved, in case she'd come in the middle of the night. Except the older I got, the larger the paddle grew.

"Mr. Falcone has a few clean-up jobs on the list today." Gio continues to talk, but I tune him out.

"The usual, handsome?" Susie, the waitress, asks when she comes over to fill up our coffee mugs and take the same breakfast order we get every damn day of the week.

We're sitting in the same diner we meet at every morning before checking off the to-do list Pop has for the day. After what Gio just said, it seems like it's going to be a long-ass day.

"What's crawled up your ass and died, Prince?" he asks, and I want to scream my head off at his nickname for me. He's done it since I was little and knows it rubs me the wrong way. First, he started calling me Lulu, but since Pop made it clear that I'm his successor, Gio's been shoving that name down my throat any time we're alone. "What's going on? You haven't been the same for weeks." He takes my silence as verbal communication and as a green light for him to continue to rib me. "I told you for years to lay off the hookers and blow—one day it's going to catch up with you."

Thankfully, his phone starts buzzing and he leaves me the hell alone in my thoughts. I down the last of my blistering coffee, hoping to feel the burn. Hoping to feel anything. I've grown numb, complacent in my life, and nothing is helping. Especially not drugs or women. I stopped doing drugs years ago when that shit landed me in the hospital, and I had to have my stomach pumped because I thought I was invincible. Ma made me promise to never touch that shit again, and I've kept my word. The women, on the other hand, have been using a revolving door since I was thirteen.

A set of fingers snap at my eyes, jolting me out of my head.

"Pay fucking attention," Gio growls. "Jesus, I don't know how I got stuck with the likes of you. Let's go."

He stands, shoving his large hands in his back pocket to fish out his wallet to toss several large bills on the table for the breakfast we didn't get to eat. Without another word, he walks toward the door that leads out to the street. Like the good soldier I am, I pick up my black bag and follow him, but to just show I'm not a pussy, I take my time getting in the car.

Several hours later, I've delivered over half a dozen beatings after collecting the monthly dues, and my mind is finally right where it needs to be. I'm focused on the task at hand, and the physical aspect is therapeutic to my soul. Working out my aggression and anger finally loosens my muscles and gives me a sort of release. It's temporary, but at least I get some type of reprieve.

"Boss needs you to clean up over at Hoover's place," Gio says as he chews on an apple after I get into the car, wiping the blood from my battered and bruised knuckles.

'Clean-up' in our world means to wipe out the guy, exterminate him from this world, and make it look natural. We don't leave a trace unless Pop wants to send a message to someone.

The sun set hours ago, and Gio and I wait in the back of the house for the last of the lights in the house next door to go off before we make our move. The last thing you want is for someone to hear something and come over to investigate or to call the police for a noise complaint. Just as the switch is flipped, we're out of the car and jumping the small chain-link fence. I've got my bag secured and ready for when we have Hoover contained.

"I'll take the front," Gio grunts over his shoulder as he quickly makes his way to the side of the house, not giving me an option of what I want. Pop made Gio stay with me and set up a good crew ever since announcing me as his successor to make sure I'm protected and left unharmed in case someone wanted to take me down. I've known Gio my entire life and he's not a bad guy, but lately, everything seems so monotonous, like I'd rather be somewhere else.

My mind wanders back to all those years ago when I was creeping into the back window of Gemma's father's house. To this day, I can still describe every second and every action I took that night. Not because I can remember every kill I've had, but because she was there. She's been in my dreams ever since then, and I can't shake the feelings I have. No matter how hard I try to cleanse her from my thoughts or how many whores I've bedded, she still stays right there in the forefront of my brain. This last visit really did my head in, and I wonder if this is what a breakup feels like.

I lift the screen off the window and notice Gio is already in the living room, coming this way. The glass slides open and a hand snaps out, grabbing at my lapels and dragging me across the windowsill.

"What the fuck is taking you so long?" he sneers, checking his surroundings. "You've been off all day, and now is not the time to get one of us killed because you're sulking about something."

"Some of us just don't barge in like a bull in a china shop. I like to scope out our surroundings before I move." I adjust my suit jacket and move my hand to the back of my waistband for my gun.

"Get your head out of your ass and focus!" he whisper-shouts, then leaves the room in search of Hoover.

Shaking my head to focus on the task ahead, I follow through the same door he just exited and down a hallway. Gio is halfway up the stairs when I start to ascend. Not paying attention I step on something squishy as a loud squeak fills the house. My body stills as I look down at the offending noise.

A stuffed elephant.

"Christ almighty!" Gio murmurs.

Just then a door opens, and out steps a tall figure. Hoover. When his eyes adjust to the two figures in his house late at night, he quickly tries to make a run for it back into the room he just exited. Gio jumps into action, grabbing him and slamming him up against the wall with his hands behind his back. Gio is whispering something I can't hear, but the nod of Hoover's head tells me he heard just fine.

"Take him downstairs," Gio orders, then shoves him over to me at the top of the steps.

I give him a quizzical look, wondering why, but don't have a second to spare as he turns to continue down the hall. Once I've secured Hoover in the wooden chair, I bind his hands and feet with wire that'll cut through the skin if he tries to fight against it. I'm ready for this day to be over so I can start my nightly routine, so I pull out my hunting blade. I keep her nice and sharp, so sharp that she can slice through canned goods without any problem.

"I'm sorry, Luca, I thought I could get you all the money, but I came up short. Please, just give me some more time, and I'll have the full amount with interest," Hoover pleads. He has to know that if it's me or Gio who got called here, that's not going to be an option. I'm the last person people want to see. I'm the reaper that comes right before you meet your maker.

"You went to the Slater family and tried to trade secrets for money, Hoover." The words stop him from begging anymore. I hate having to listen to their excuses, like I'm going to say, *Sure, just one more chance.* Pop might be a lot of things, but he does give certain people chances to make it right, depending on the offense and how much money is at stake. "Arturo Falcone doesn't grant mercy to those who've betrayed him or his people. You're lucky we're only taking you out and not your entire bloodline," I threaten, not that we'd kill innocent children or women.

His eyes widen at the mention of his family then whips his head toward the stairs.

Tired and ready for this day to be over, I move behind him with my blade tightly in hand.

"Mr. Falcone demands and expects loyalty," I recite our pledge, then slice the blade all the way from one side of his ear to the other. The sound of blood gurgling in his throat fills the room as I hold him from behind. It takes a few minutes before all the blood rushes out and coats the rug as the life leaves his body.

The stairs creak as I watch Gio come down the steps with scratches and traces of blood on his arms.

"What the hell happened to you?" I ask as I wipe my blood-covered blade on Hoover's t-shirt.

Gio looks down at his arms and shrugs, "Killed the dog. Didn't want it to wake the others."

My brows pinch together. Why didn't I hear the struggle of any of it? Dogs aren't the quietest when being attacked, but my head isn't in the best mindset, so it doesn't surprise me.

"We done here? I've got somewhere to be." Gio adjusts the gloves on his hands and walks past me towards the back of the house where our car is parked.

Not wanting to be stranded, I make sure I've got all my equipment along with the wire I used to strap Hoover in the chair. His limp body hits the floor and I swing the bag over my shoulder, not thinking about what we just did.

I've come to terms with this life I'm destined to have as I step out into the night air and sullenly make my way over to the waiting car. I'm the first son of our mafia family and this is what I've been groomed to become my whole life. I need to start acting like the next boss and not someone who daydreams about a girl he'll never have. I can get any woman at anytime, anywhere. One chick is not going to mess up my plans to become the next mafia boss. My life is here, my family is here, and it's time for me to step up, take charge, and put my wants and needs aside.

So, why do I feel like I'm drowning?

"There's my baby boy!" Ma exclaims as I walk through the front door of my childhood home. "What took you so long? The food is cooling, and you know how I expect a call if you're going to be late."

Home is an understatement—more like a mansion or compound compared to other homes. The house is on the outskirts of Las Vegas, towards the mountains. Pop bought up all the surrounding acreage to build Ma the home of her dreams. My house is situated down a ways but still included in the fortress. We have guys who patrol around the clock to make sure no one tries to gain access to the property. Decades ago, a pissant group of wannabe mobsters tried to infiltrate our compound, aiming to take Ma to use her as leverage against Pop. Needless to say, it didn't end well for those fuckers and their families. Ever since, Pop has made sure to have the property secured so that the enemy would have to go through at least two lines of defense before ever getting remotely close to her or the house.

"I'm not a baby anymore, Ma," I try to defend, but she swats me on the arm with the dish rag in her hand.

"You'll always be my baby, Luca, I don't care how old you get. Now go and wash up, we waited for you. Hello, Giovanni."

"Good evening, Mrs. Falcone. It smells delicious," Gio sucks up to Ma but keeps his distance.

Every one of my pop's men knows not to make any contact with Ma or be placed on ice. One thing my pop has always said to me is that once you have the most prized possession, you make sure no one ever touches it. There are two things my pop holds as his most prized possessions—his business and my ma. He might be a cold-hearted bastard, but when it comes to Ma, he'd give everything up in a heartbeat if she asked. She never would do that, of course, but she does hold a lot of power over him. Some might call him pussy-whipped, but they are perfect together. Their relationship is what books are written about or what countries go to war over. Grandfather wasn't happy about their relationship at first because he thought Ma distracted Pop from the goals that were set for him, but Pop didn't care and went head-to-head with Grandfather over it. They were married six weeks after meeting and had me a year later. Alice came much later. I'm almost twenty-eight, and Alice, who is our little princess, is sixteen.

"Thank you, Giovanni." She leaves us and heads towards the kitchen telling Rosa, their housekeeper, to prepare to serve dinner.

Gio and I wash up in the hall bathroom then make our way to the dining room that could seat forty people. Ma loves to host parties with the men and their families. She's the social butterfly, whereas my father likes to isolate and rule from behind his office door.

As we enter, my father walks in from the south entrance where his office is located.

"Everything get handled today?" Pop greets us. He comes over and swallows me in a hug then holds me at my shoulders with his large hands.

"Yes, sir," I reply, and he gives me an approving squeeze.

"Good, good." Pop turns his attention to Gio and gives a nod. Conversation over.

"Dinner is served!" Ma comes in from the kitchen door carrying a plate of food and a tumbler of amber liquid.

We take our seats as Ma places a plate of food in front of Pop. For as long as I can remember my Ma has always served Pop first. We've always had staff who work for us, and even though it is their job to wait on us, Ma has always been the one who waits on and serves Pop, whether it be food, drinks, or even the morning paper, she makes the effort to be attentive to his needs. He has always suggested that she should be served first since she was the one who prepared it, but Ma never lets it happen.

"Arturo is the head of this family and should always be put first," Ma said one time when I asked her as a kid.

The one thing I know for sure is that Pop will always wait to take a bite until after Ma takes hers. She may not notice it, but I've watched them my whole life, and it's the little things that they do for each other that tell me how much they love and respect each other. Pop seems to always know just what Ma needs before she even thinks about it.

"Luca, honey, when are you going to settle down and give us some grandbabies?" Ma asks after we all tuck into the delicious meal. The bite I just took gets lodged in my throat, and I choke. Gio beats my back with his hand, thinking it's funny.

"Sweetheart, he'll find the right woman when he's ready. Let's not push him too soon, or it might not work out and then we'll have to deal with only seeing our grandbabies every other weekend." Pop places his hand on Ma's. "Besides, Luca is busy learning about the business and making sure our legacy will be strong for the next generation."

"I know, I just want him to have someone like I have you. He needs a woman in his life who will take care of him." They speak as though they're the only two in the room.

"He will, Tesoro." *Sweetheart.* The affection they show is such a contradiction to the cold-blooded killer that my pop is. He treats Ma as though she's the sun that lights up the world but handles the rest of the world with an iron fist. Only a select few have ever seen my pop interact with Ma in such a gentle manner. Most of our rivals have never seen Ma or Alice because Pop feels like it would place a target on them. Ma does help out at a local shelter for women and children once or twice a month. They just don't know her connections because of security risks.

"Where is Alice tonight?" I ask, hoping to change the subject from me to anything else.

"She's with some friends seeing a movie," Ma answers, turning her attention from Pop to me.

Gio eats in silence, like always. He is one of the only members of my Pop's business who eats with us on the regular. Pop trusts him more than anyone in the business, and they are as close as brothers. He has been a fixture in Pop's life since moving to the U.S. when Grandfather sent him over at seventeen. They are thick as thieves—or murderers.

After dinner, Gio and Pop head to his office and I start to make my way home. Ma always has me come at least four times a week to have a meal with her. Yeah, I'm a mama's boy, but when she starts the guilt trips about Alice being a teenager who's never home and never having her babies spend time with her, I know I'll give her anything.

"I just don't want you to be alone. You understand that, right?" Ma says as I pull on my suit jacket.

"I know, Ma." If she only knew the woman I want is unattainable. "One day."

She kisses me on the cheek, then pats it.

"I know this life can be hard, Luca. When I first met your father, I thought there was no way I could deal with what he did for a living."

"What changed your mind?" I ask, hope swelling in my chest.

"When you love someone like I love your father, there isn't anything that would stand in the way of being with them. You learn to love them for everything that makes them who they are—the good and the bad. I know he's done some terrible things in his life, but my life without him in it isn't a life I even want to imagine."

"I hope one day I'll find a woman who will love me as much as you love Pop, Ma."

"She's out there, honey. Just give it time. You'll be happy knowing that you waited for the right one."

I take my leave because if I don't, I run the risk of telling Ma all about Gemma. Ma and I have always been close. I've talked with her about nearly everything in my life. She listens and hears everything I have to say before she weighs in on what she thinks is the best direction to go—which is usually the right direction. Adele Falcone gives the best advice. The fact she's never judged my choices lets us have the best relationship. I don't know what I'd do without her.

"Thanks, Ma. I'll call you tomorrow." I kiss her on the cheek and walk out the front door to head to my house.

Even if Gemma accepted the life I live, could I bring her here to be locked away from the world so that she could never be used against me? She'd have constant guards around her. At any given time, she would have a minimum of five guards surrounding her, not to mention that when I take over, that number will increase.

Even though I'm headed to my home to stay on the compound, I know there are at least three men out of sight, watching to make sure I'm not taken out by an enemy. I grew up in this life, living it every day, so I've grown accustomed to it, but could she? I'm the next in line as the head of the family when Pop decides he's had enough or dies. Could she be like Ma and live this life?

My head hurts thinking about this. I've made the decision but why do I have so much regret in walking away from her?

Move on and let things be.

That's going to be my motto starting tomorrow, but for tonight I plan on savoring one last evening dreaming of my life with a curly brown-haired, blue-eyed woman.

CHAPTER FIVE

Luca

Age: 29

March 2022

Eight months ago, I made a life-changing decision and left Las Vegas and the family business behind. I'm still in a similar type of business just lower-key. The main thing that changed was the last job I did involved women being trafficked in our territory. We were supposed to go in, kill the assholes who were transporting them, and take the women to a shelter. Only, when we got there the men were actually women who were running the ring. Gio had come down with the flu and was two steps away from being hospitalized, so he wasn't with us to handle all the details which left me in charge. Once we saw that it was six women instead of men we faltered slightly. At first glance, they didn't look like they belonged there, and we started to think our intel had been wrong. Little did we know what would transpire next.

We had them cornered in the shipping container where they hauled the girls and other women, but we weren't planning on them being fully loaded to the teeth with ARs and AKs. They were the ones who shot first and we countered immediately. After ten minutes we'd finally gotten a foothold in and were about to take them down when the shooting started to erupt in the container. There was the sound of guns going off and then silence rang out. What we saw when we entered the container still gives me nightmares. All the girls and women were dead. The six women in charge had lined up all the captives and shot them dead then killed themselves.

I had seen a lot of bloody crime scenes in my life from a young age but seeing those innocent girls and women messed me up. There was one in particular that looked almost identical to Gemma and I knew then what I was going to do. Life is too short not to be with the ones you love. So right there in that tomb of a shipping container, I decided I was leaving and living my life with her. It also didn't help that Pop was pressuring me into some sort of arrangement to marry the daughter of one of his associates. He never outright ordered it, but his subtle hints were starting to make me tight around the collar.

The night I killed Gemma's father changed the course of my life. She changed my life. I'm glad we've had this time apart, though, because it made the decision to leave easier. I just wish I'd left on good terms with my family. Family has always been the one thing in life that I could count on, but this never would've been allowed if I approached Pop. He'd have expected me to marry someone he approved of or arranged for me. Pop was appeasing Ma by letting me date, but in reality, it is ultimately his decision who comes into our family. Even though Pop broke the mold marrying an outsider, he still has a business mind. What benefits our territory and our place in Vegas benefits the family. I shot myself in the foot a long time ago when I expressed no interest in marrying, and Pop made it clear I was to follow the family guidelines that have been in place for over a century.

After I left Gemma two years ago, I felt like a part of my soul was missing. At first, I tried to brush it off and push it to the back of my mind, but as time went on, I started to think more and more about her. I obsessed about what she was doing or who she was with, and it was making my focus shift. I tried having a relationship, much to my mother's joy, but all I could do was dream of Gemma. Think of her. I saw her face in every crowd and walking on sidewalks as I drove by. She was the ultimate deciding factor when I left Vegas and the family behind. Gemma was going to be my family, my love, *mine*. There wasn't anything or anyone who would stop me. I left a shitstorm back home, but I didn't give two fucks about it. My need to be with her overtook it all. This was about me and what *I* wanted for a change. It was time to do something for myself and not what was dictated to me.

I set things in motion long before I knew I was coming here. Now, I'm waiting for the right moment to approach my woman and make her mine.

I stare at the stolen picture on my phone and brush my index finger over her plump lips. I never thought that I'd end up here. After everything I experienced over the last two years, I thought that I'd be dead by now after being a good soldier for my pop. I had become reckless and out of control when I decided to change the course of my life. To have my own life. Maybe in a few years, I'll feel differently and Gemma and I can return to Vegas, but only if she can handle that life.

So here I am, in sunny Malibu, California, waiting patiently for the one woman who has taken up residence in my head for the past seven years. The woman I absolutely refuse to stay away from. The more time that goes by, the hungrier I am to see her. To feel her. To be with her.

The last time I checked in on her was over two years ago during her sophomore year. She had settled into college life here in California and seemed to have made a few friends. Little did she know that being so oblivious to her surroundings made it easy for me to watch her. She could be almost touching me and not even aware that the bad men of this world could snuff out her beaming light before she could even yell for help. I love her innocence but hate that she is putting herself in harm's way by not being more aware of the evil lurking around her. The world is anything but rainbows and sunshine, but Gemma can wear a set of rose-colored shades fixed over her eyes and mounted on her pretty little face as long as she is close to me. I'll protect her, even kill for her.

The time to make my move is approaching. I am sitting across from her at the pool in a resort in Malibu. She's wearing the tiniest string bikini; it barely covers her beautiful body. Those blue and white polka dots are wreaking havoc on *my* body. She's with a friend, laying out by the pool and drinking some girly drinks. Her friend is soaking up all the male attention and flirting with anyone who has a dick. Not my girl though. She has a book in hand and is ignoring all the male attention that's being thrown her way. *Good.* I'd hate for our first real meeting to start with me beating the shit out of some preppy college kid. When she finally falls asleep, I pay the waiter to move the umbrella to cover her sun-kissed skin so that it doesn't burn out here on this cloudless day.

I watch her the rest of the day, acting as though I've been doing work on my laptop all afternoon. When they finally decide to head back to their room, I follow. We share an elevator ride, and I stay towards the back of the packed car, out of sight. She has no idea her world is about to change. I listen in on their short conversation and learn that they'll be having dinner in the restaurant downstairs at seven.

Good. Me too!

What I don't like is the friend insisting that Gemma stop being so introverted and finally talk with the guys that come up to her. The *friend* is berating her for not throwing herself at the men who have tried to buy her a drink and not trying to pick up the hot guys at the pool. I'm tempted to speak up but bite my tongue. Gemma's shyness works in my favor, and this isn't how our first meeting will go. *Well, our first time meeting for her.*

They exit on the tenth floor, and Gemma sways her hips in that tiny fishnet cover-up as she makes her way to her room. I'm disappointed when the elevator doors close, and I can no longer watch her strut that sexy ass down the hallway.

I'm down at the restaurant before seven and sitting at the bar with a drink when I see them make their entrance.

Gemma is wearing a short, white dress that hugs her curves and sky-high fuck-me heels. She looks absolutely stunning with her tanned skin and curly brown hair. I swear watching her walk in with that white dress has me envisioning what she's going to look like on our wedding day.

Her friend is wearing a scrap of fabric that leaves nothing to the imagination and looks as though she should be working the corner later this evening.

I watch from afar, waiting for the right time to make my move. I've played this out in my head over a dozen times. I oddly wonder if she'll remember our last encounter during her sophomore year but shake those thoughts. Surely, she's been too occupied to remember that blip in time. It was dark, and our moment lasted less than five minutes. So much has probably happened to her in the last two years.

They are almost done with the meal when I bring myself to look over at their table. I quickly pay my tab at the bar and tell the bartender to pick up the bill for their table as well. He walks over and tells the waitress, which prompts her to stalk over and let them know that the bill has been settled as she points over in my direction. When they turn their heads, I lift my bourbon-filled tumbler in the air. *Come like a moth to a flame, baby.*

Gemma gives a shy smile as she gets up and starts to walk over to me, but she bumps into a waiter who's bent over a table collecting the dirty dishes. He drops several dishes on the table, making them rattle before snapping an angry glare her way. I can't hold back the chuckle from my throat. The coordination on this girl leaves something to be desired, but I'm on my feet in an instant, striding up to the douche who's about to make the biggest mistake of his life if his expression is anything to go by. But of course, one look at my woman and he's caught under her spell just like every other hot-blooded male on this earth. Before he can engage with her, I step right between the asshole and Gemma, taking away his view of her.

"You alright?" I smoothly ask as I caress her upper arm. It's been too long since I've felt her. The closer I am to her, the more my body craves her. I'm certain a doctor would find me certifiable if anyone knew how obsessed I am with her. Is this how Pop felt about Ma when they first met? Did he have these urges to constantly be near her or know her every move?

"Thank you so much for the meal," she says in the same angelic voice I've been longing to hear for over two years. Her voice isn't as hesitant as last time, and it thumps my chest to know she's found a little confidence.

"You're welcome, beautiful," I say before thinking.

At my compliment, she forms the most perfect blush that covers her cheeks and moves down toward her ample chest. I swear to God they've grown since the last time I saw her. *They'd fit perfectly in my large hands.*

"If you were going to pay for the food you should have joined us so you could've tasted what you paid for," she says.

I know she doesn't intend to make it sound seductive…but damn.

Baby girl, I'll taste whatever you're offering.

I give her my best panty-dropping smirk because what I want to tell her is not something she's ready to hear yet.

"I'd much rather taste your lips," I say boldly. She's going to have to get used to my bluntness. I've never been one to hold back, and I don't plan on it with her.

Just when I think she can't blush any more, she proves me

wrong and turns scarlet red. She pulls a loose curl behind her ear, exposing her jaw and neck to me.

"Gemma!" We both turn to find her friend making her way over with a guy on her arm and his buddy behind him. "Hey, these guys are heading out to the bonfire down by the beach and want to escort us there," she wags her eyebrows.

No way in hell is Gemma going with that fucktard. Gemma seems to agree when she turns to me with almost pleading eyes, clearly not sure how to get out of going, and I'm all too happy to save the day. "Well, she and I will meet you there. We're going to have a drink at the bar first," I state.

Her friend looks me up and down then leaves without a fuss. What kind of friend leaves her with a stranger? Didn't they learn about *'Stranger Danger'* in school? I could be a serial killer—or worse a kidnapper who's into human trafficking.

I shake those thoughts from my head and focus on my woman.

"Now I have to thank you for the meal and a night away from drunken idiots," she chuckles as I lead her over to my chair at the bar.

"Does she always do that? Leave you alone while she goes out with strangers?"

She gives me a one-shoulder shrug and gracefully sits down on the empty barstool that I was occupying. Well, as gracefully as she can in her tight dress.

"I'm Gemma, by the way," she offers me her hand.

"Luca Fontana," I say and accept her dainty, soft hand. I changed my name when I moved here. Pop and Gio could easily trace my moves if I'd kept Falcone, so as of eight months ago, my official name according to all my fake documents is Luca Fontana. "What brings you to Malibu?" I ask as I flag down the bartender. "Wait, let me guess—Spring Break."

She giggles in confirmation, and it knocks me for a loop to be the one who makes her sound that way. I have yet to release her hand and she seems oblivious to it.

She tells me they're here for the week and tries to explain her friend Jill to me. She sounds like a total bitch, but I decide not to comment or let my face show how much I don't care for the girl. They might be best friends, and I'll need to stay in her good graces until things progress a little further with Gemma before I really tell her how I feel about this *friend.*

"Jill's my roommate. The one I had in the fall left before Christmas because of some family emergency, so the college assigned her to me. She's a little different than Monica, but I think, deep down, she means well."

"She doesn't seem to mind leaving you behind with a total stranger though," I point out again and try to hold back my disgust.

Gemma shrugs and takes a sip of the fruity drink the bartender just set in front of her. She lets out a small moan and closes her eyes in appreciation. "These are so much better than the ones offered down by the pool," she says, more to herself, and I force my body not to lunge for her. She's not even aware of the war I'm battling right now. My instincts are telling me to throw her over my shoulder, haul her back to my room, and chain her to the bed for the rest of her life. "What about you? What are you doing here?"

I knew this question was coming and planned my response. "I own a business and was here for a conference over this past weekend. My week was free, so I decided to make it an extended vacation until Sunday."

"Oh, what type of business are you in?" she asks eagerly.

"I sell life insurance."

She cocks her head to the side studying me for a second. "You don't look like someone who sells insurance." Her eyes roam over my body in a seductive way that can only be her stripping me of my clothing. Does she even know what she's doing? Does she understand the need she's putting off? Is my sweet, sheltered woman hiding a little vixen in there?

A loud laugh a few feet over interrupts several conversations, including ours. I reach out and gently rest my hand on top of hers to get her focus back on us.

"What exactly do insurance salesmen look like to you?" I smirk. "I hope you're not picturing those weird vacuum salesmen?"

"Um…no, but also, not you," she answers innocently. "You look so familiar for some reason. Is it possible we've met before?"

"Maybe, but I'd remember a beautiful woman like you."

The return of her blush tells me I've caught her and a crisis has been averted for now.

Over the next few hours, we drink and get to know each other. I off-handedly mention visiting her college for a seminar, and she swears that must be where she's seen me. We have small touches throughout the night and hold hands while walking around the resort. When we finally meet up with Jill, she's heading up to the room. She looks terrible, like she's been ridden hard and hung out to dry.

"Can we hang out tomorrow? I've had the best time getting to know you and would love to spend more of my vacation with you," I ask as her friend insists Gemma come with her. I stifle the urge to demand to know why she'd left Gemma alone with a stranger in the first place.

"I'd like that. Here, let me put in my number," she says as she grabs the hand that holds my phone. Her fingers graze my dick, making it even harder than before. I use all my training over the years to suppress a moan.

"Oh my god, I'm so sorry. I was aiming for your bone…I mean phone." She smacks her palm to her face and flushes. We've both had several drinks, but I'm not the lightweight she is.

Is it horrible of me that I love to watch her be embarrassed? She is such a breath of fresh air.

I knew going into this I was going to have to be patient with her and go at her pace. Her inexperience and shyness are factors I can't ignore, but once I crack that shell, I know we'll be coasting along. It doesn't bother me though. I've waited this long, and it isn't going to deter me in any way. Tonight, I think we made huge strides. She opened up more than I expected, and we connected like I hoped we would.

"Don't worry, I'm sure my virtue is still intact," I say, hoping to put her at ease. I text her right away after taking her number.

She starts to turn away and head to her roommate who's slumped against the pillar by the door, but I grab her wrist, pulling her flush against me. I've never had to wait so long for something I wanted. We can go slow and I can be the gentleman she deserves after this. I capture her lips with mine, planting a soft peck, but again, my plans change the moment we connect, and I invade her mouth when she gasps. One hand steadies the small of her back as I push her toward my hard length. She needs someone who is going to take control, and that's exactly who I am. I end the kiss, leaving her wanting more, and push her towards an impatient Jill. I can tell she's dazed, as her legs wobble like a baby fawn. That'll give her something to dream about tonight because God knows I'll be thinking about nothing else until morning.

"You'd better tend to your friend," I nod toward her roommate when she stalls in getting her bearings, "before I take this past second base."

"Who?" she asks dreamily. "Oh, yes, yes. I'll…we…"

"Goodnight, beautiful." I lean forward slightly and graze her lips. "Dream of me, because I know I'll be dreaming of you."

With a soft push of my hands on her hips, I guide her in Jill's direction; the girl is swaying and barely able to stay upright.

"Goodnight, Luca."

CHAPTER SIX

Gemma

Age: 22

THERE'S A KNOCK ON OUR HOTEL DOOR AS I GLANCE OVER at the clock on the bedside table. Jill is passed out, and with how drunk she was last night I'm sure she's going to want to sleep the entire day. The clock reads ten in the morning, and I groan because after leaving Luca last night, I had a hard time falling asleep. My mind kept replaying images over and over again of the earth-shattering kiss we shared.

Another thud at our door brings me out of my daydream. I thought I remembered placing our 'no housekeeping' sign on the handle of our door. Scrambling out of bed before they wake the morning monster, Jill, I open the door only to come face to face with Luca. I smell the manly fragrance of him with a hint of aftershave before my eyes focus on him. He's wearing board shorts, a ballcap, and a white t-shirt that fits him in all the right places. How is it possible for someone to look so devastatingly gorgeous? Most men have a couple of attractive traits, but none have the whole package. Luca stands there with perfect hair, eyes, smile, teeth, height, muscles, and tan. I bet his feet are perfect too. My eyes immediately drop to his flip-flops, and, yep, his feet are perfect.

I watched him yesterday from across the pool and had never seen a more attractive man. He was so handsome with his tan, tattooed, built body. I swear, something in my belly flipped when he looked up in my direction. Sadly, it didn't go any further than that. He was on his laptop, appearing to work most of the day. Women went over to talk with him, but he kept his head down not engaging them at all.

"See something you like?" He smirks at me.

I nod, unable to speak a word. *Smooth, Gemma, way to get caught ogling the man. So embarrassing.*

"I tried calling, but you didn't answer, so I thought I'd check on you," Luca says with concern. He holds up his phone and gives it a wiggle.

"Oh. I must've let the battery die. Hold on."

Just my luck, as I'm walking quietly back over to my bed to retrieve my lifeless phone, my foot snags one of Jill's hooker heels, and I bump into the wall. Ugh, that's going to leave a bruise. I wish gravity and I got along a little better. Why is it so hard for her to pick her stuff up instead of having every article strewn across the room?

Luca is still in the doorway holding the door open to let some light in. I can see his eyes dance with mirth at my clumsy self, and I have to bite back my own laughter to not wake Jill.

"Sorry. I'm the world's worst at charging this thing. The nuns at my old private school and Dr. Collins are always getting on me about that." I shrug as I explain more than I'd intended.

"That can be dangerous, Gemma. What if something happened and someone needed to track you down?" he lectures me. His eyes bore into me, and I feel like I'm being reprimanded like a child.

"I know, I know. What are you doing here?" I try and change the subject. Did I give him my room number last night?

"I wanted to take you out on a boat, then to lunch and dinner if you're available."

"Oh. That sounds like fun." I happen to see my reflection in the mirror and gasp. Did I happen to push a finger into a light socket or turn into a raccoon last night while sleeping and didn't realize it? "Ugh, could you give me around thirty minutes, and I'll meet you down in the lobby?"

"Sure." His smile is soft, but then he follows it up with a wink that sets my insides ablaze. He could melt metal and set wildfires with that one gesture.

Luca leaves, and I hop in the shower, right after plugging in my phone.

Forty minutes later, I'm dressed in my little blue bikini with shorts and a white tank top. I have my hair in a French braid that hangs down my shoulder and is covered up with my fedora and a pair of sunglasses. My phone is only charged halfway, but I left Jill a note telling her where I'm going. After the conversation with Luca last night at the bar, I see his point about Jill leaving me alone with someone I just met. Even though I'm pretty sure Luca is safe, I still need to be more aware of others and not put myself in dangerous situations.

Once in the lobby, it doesn't take long to find him. He's reading the newspaper next to a group of people waiting for the shuttle. He doesn't notice me until I'm about to reach out and touch his arm, but when he looks up, his welcoming smile elicits a flutter in my stomach, as though I've swallowed a butterfly.

"Hey, baby girl. You look beautiful." Luca stands and greets me with a kiss on my cheek. Why does that sound so sexy on his lips? I'm starting to love his endearment for me.

"Thank you." I feel a rush of heat to my cheeks.

He gestures towards the exit. "Shall we?"

We walk down the short path to the dock on the beach, and they set us up with our boat and crew. Luca swiftly takes a life vest from one of the crew members and fastens it securely around me.

"I could have done that," I offer, but I love his hands on me. For once, it's nice to have someone take care of me after being on my own for so long.

"I know, but I'd much rather strap you in. Plus, this way I'll know you won't drown because I'm an expert with straps and knots."

He must've picked up on my constant clumsiness. I've always hated being a walking accident, but over the years I'd like to think I'm getting better. Or at least Sister Margret thought so. I hadn't had any major incidents since my junior year when I accidentally started a fire in the parish while trying to light the candles for a midnight mass.

"So, you were a Boy Scout?

He gives me a devilish smile. "Something like that."

"Oh. Well, if you are lucky, I just might let you strap me in again later," I tease, and he lifts his shades as something flashes across his eyes. There's almost a twinkle to them.

"Baby girl, you have no idea the things I could strap you to," he retorts with a wink.

I clench my thighs together at his words. Good thing we are getting into the water because I'm already wet.

This man is making me do and say things I've only read about in books. Jill has been pushing me to open up more and explore the male species, but I've always clammed up until now. This man seems to do things to put me at ease to talk and open up. It feels simple in a way, so easy, to share things with him.

The rest of the afternoon is a blast. We play out in the water for hours. My only near-death experience is when I get a cramp in one of my legs while we snorkel off the catamaran Luca rented for the day. While we snack on the boat, he makes sure to massage my leg, never letting me out of his sight. I feel better after resting, so we stay out longer on the water, enjoying the beautiful weather and company.

"You mentioned a Dr. Collins earlier. Who's that?" he asks, offering me some fruit.

"Oh, Dr. Allison Collins is my therapist. I've been seeing her since I moved down here. The nuns thought it would be a good idea to have someone to talk with because I've had a hard time coping since my mom died. She's great, more like a mother figure sometimes."

"It's good to have someone to talk to." He holds my hand in his like he's trying to give me strength. "Feel free to use me as a sounding board anytime."

"Do you have someone?" I pry.

"I decided to cut off my family and came out here to start a new life on my own. Everything is going great, and I think I found the perfect girl to tell all my woes to." He smiles and squeezes my hand. "What are your plans after you graduate?"

"I want to be a teacher. My plans are to find a public or private elementary school and help kids—not just in the classroom but in life."

"Having summers off has a nice ring to it, but I hear the pay sucks," he says as he continues to massage my calf with the hand that isn't holding mine.

"It does, but I'm not in it for the money. When both of my parents died, I struggled for a while. I had the nuns at my school, but none had children of their own, so it was hard to feel the love and connection with an adult. They knew how to teach, but the tenderness and bonding weren't there. Like a lifeline. I want to be that for the kids. A place where they can come and be loved and know that I'm there for anything they might need."

"I'm sorry about your parents. I can't imagine what it was like not having them while you were growing up."

"It was difficult, but I've come to terms with it. It's hard knowing that I'm alone and don't have even one relative, but I'm adjusting." I begin to fidget with my fingers and look down at them in my lap. This is not the heavy conversation I wanted to share on this date.

My stomach growls loudly enough that makes him chuckle, and the heaviness lifts.

"You ready to head in and grab some lunch?"

"I'd love to."

We find the perfect spot to eat lunch on the beach after hitting a food truck. We stay on safe topics of conversation, and it's the best day ever. I feel a close connection with him, even after only knowing him for a day. There just seems to be something more with the two of us. Like we've known each other for years.

We decide to meet up for dinner, and I can't wait. His room is on the top floor, and we planned to have room service and watch a movie. Hopefully, there will be a make-out session or two involved. The way his body looks in those swim trunks should be illegal, not to mention how his muscles flex when he moves. I'm not even sure how I'm able to breathe without my inhaler when he's nearby. He truly takes my breath away. Sister Margret would be scolding me right this minute if she knew all the dirty thoughts that were running through my mind. There aren't enough 'Hail Marys' to make up for all the sins I've committed in my head, and it's only been a few hours with this Adonis.

When I get back to the room, Jill tells me she plans to stay in the room for the rest of the night to recuperate after hitting the nightlife scene pretty hard the last two nights. I don't know why she's pushing herself so hard to have a good time, finding random hookups. She just started dating a guy back home before we left. I can't remember his name, but he looks much better than any of the guys she's been trying to hook up with here. He's the total surfer package. Yes, he's older than she is by a few years, but I think they're good together.

I finish up my second shower of the day and dress in white shorts and a thin pink t-shirt with matching flip-flops. Luca told me to dress comfortably since we'll be lounging on the sofa.

After checking the room number on my phone from his text, I leave my room and head to the elevator. My mind plays so many scenarios as I walk down the long hall and stand in front of his door. Once I give myself a small pep talk I give a timid knock, Luca answers the door with only a towel around his waist. Good lord, he looks even better than he did earlier. The sun definitely agrees with him. He must have just gotten out of the shower because water droplets are still all over his body. His tattoos are on full display, and I can't help but wonder what they all mean. His chest is covered, along with both arms, but if he were in a dress shirt, you'd never know he had any ink on him.

My tongue darts out on its own accord and licks my now dry lips.

"Sorry, got caught on a business call." He opens the door a little wider to let me pass. "Let me throw on some clothes and then we can order up some room service."

He starts to make his way to the bedroom.

Or you could stay just like that all night, I joke in my head, watching as he walks away.

I watch him stop mid-stride and turn back to me. Shit, did I say that out loud? From the smirk that is playing on his perfect face, I did.

Oh. My. God! Kill me now. He's going to think I'm a slut.

"If you wanted to have a *'clothing optional'* sleepover, then you should have said it sooner." He moves his hand to the twist on the towel as though he might release it. "I was just trying to be a gentleman."

Sweet Jesus! I think I might pass out.

My knees practically give out, but he makes his way over to me in three long strides, catching me mid-fall. How did he do that so gracefully? Our bodies are locked together and only the thin material of my shorts and panties, along with his towel, separates us from the waist down.

His head bends down and his lips take mine in a scorching kiss. Our tongues dance with each other as our hands explore every inch of our bodies. Every trace of his fingers sends a tingle throughout my body. For such a big man, he's so gentle when he handles me.

"I want to feel your skin pressed on mine," he says and edges back, waiting for me to consent. He puts me under a spell when his voice is lowered and we're so close to each other.

I nod and remove my hands from his hard chest.

"It's only fair if you drop your clothes too," Luca says and lifts the hem of my shirt over my head before I can register what his words and hands are doing.

I stand there in a daze, watching him undress me. When my senses finally resurface, I'm standing there in only my bra and lacy panties. Our heavy breathing is the only noise in his suite.

Did someone turn the heat on or open a window to let the humidity in?

His eyes rake over my practically naked body. When his gaze meets a bruise, there's a slight tension in his jaw, but he says nothing. He only feathers his fingers over the purple spot and continues on. I've learned to live with the marks my entire life because I seem to bump into things all day long.

"Baby girl, if you want me to stop, tell me now. I won't be able to once I wrap you around me," he says giving me a chance to back out. "We can order food and watch a movie if you still want to." His voice is strained as though it pains him to say those words.

"No," I say firmly.

Why would any living, breathing female turn him down at this very moment?

What is wrong with my brain? I don't hook up with guys. Ever! I'm a virgin, for goodness sake! This man weaves some sort of magic over me, and I become putty in his hands. He could tell me to jump out the window right now, and I think my brain would be okay with it. I'm pretty sure this is not what my therapist had in mind when she said to make a new friend this trip, but God help me if I'm going to back out now.

He takes a step closer.

"Wait!" I say stopping him from wrapping his arms around my waist. "I've never done this before," I rush to say. Warning him is only fair, right?

"Amore mio, it's okay. I'm not some random hook-up. I've been waiting for this for what seems like an eternity."

He's about to realize that makes two of us.

"No, I mean, I have never done *this* before." There's a moment when the words finally settle in his brain, and he realizes what I mean. His cute, confused expression is priceless. "Like sex," I elaborate, just in case I've stunned him too much.

His eyes widen in disbelief.

"You're a virgin?" he asks as if I've just blown his mind.

"True story."

"But how?" He sounds even more confused now that I've spelled it out.

I shrug. How do I explain to him that it's hard to let people in? That he's the first one I've even started to let myself open up to.

"But you've done other things? I mean college is the breeding ground for exploring and experimenting. What about sophomore year when—"

He stops before finishing the question, and I'm not sure what he's talking about. There were no guys my sophomore year unless he means Travis. He was a study partner for a class who tried to include me with his friends. He also wasn't batting for my team. Travis transferred after that year and moved to UCLA to finish his degree. But how would Luca know about him? I don't think I've even thought about him in over a year. Luca must be in shock that I have no experience. This is probably a major turnoff to most men, and he might be trying to find a way to get out of this situation. Jill is always saying to just fake it and not let on about my inexperience.

I shake my head. It's not like I haven't had offers, but I've never felt comfortable enough to try it with anyone. Being shy tends to put a damper on quickies at frat parties. Besides, shouldn't you want to lose it to someone special or someone who at least makes you feel special? Having sex in a bathroom at a frat house doesn't give me all the feels. Maybe all those romance books have ruined me for men. Travis always thought I was too picky and should sow as many oats as I could before we hit the real world.

"God help me," he says under his breath. "You were made for

me." He seems to mull over something in his head, but I can't decipher what he's thinking. "Are you on birth control?"

I nod. "Sister Margret and Sister Bethany insisted when I was graduating high school. She thought I'd be in the one percent to get pregnant using condoms with how many incidents kept occurring over the years and strongly advised not having sex until marriage because with my luck, I'd be pregnant right out of the gate."

All the nuns agreed that sex was for marriage, but Sister Margret knew most of the girls were already having sex by the time we graduated. She told me that things happen and we should be prepared for them just in case. I was to never speak of it to anyone when we left the doctor's office and headed back to the school because she would have lost her job if anyone found out.

Luca's smile makes him seem so much younger, and I know he's fighting back a laugh, but in reality, it's probably true. If an accidental pregnancy is going to happen to someone, I'm the most likely candidate.

"I'm clean. I just had a physical done last week, and I haven't been with anyone for almost a year." He has this gleam in his eyes that almost looks loving. "Do you want this, Gemma? Truth be told, I want this and much more. I just knew you were meant to be mine in every way."

He sounds so genuine in the way he speaks to me, and I know it should scare me, but for once, I feel no trace of fear. I think I've finally found someone who could be mine. It's as though he's known me for a long time and has simply been waiting. A feeling of peace settles in my chest as I think over one of the biggest decisions in my life thus far. It could change my life forever. With determination and hope for a future, I look right at his beautiful face.

"Yes. I want this."

CHAPTER SEVEN

Luca

I'M PRETTY SURE I'VE DIED AND GONE TO HEAVEN.

How is it possible for a woman like her to never have been touched before? I lost my virginity when I was thirteen to some twenty-something-year-old lady who worked at one of my pop's businesses. Gio was getting his dick wet and told me to stay put when he went to collect the dues owed to Pop. Being the little shit I was, I'd never have missed the chance to see naked women at titty bars, so I followed him in. Granted, I didn't look thirteen at the time. Most thought I was pushing eighteen since I was tall and built for my age and Gio had me on a strict weightlifting schedule. Names weren't exchanged, and after we left the hall bathroom, we never saw each other again. To be truthful, I'd never be able to pick her out of a line-up. Much of that night was a blur, but I do remember using a condom that was in a basket on the counter.

My eyes rake down Gemma's beautiful body in only a bra and skimpy panties. She puts my dreams to shame. She looks so much better than I ever pictured in my head. Her tits are more than a handful, and the soft curves of her body have my mouth begging for a taste. My dick hasn't gone down since early this morning, and only releasing in her is going to satisfy his need. I don't think she completely understands what is about to happen when she finally lets me have her in every way. I've never been a possessive person in my life, but when it comes to her, I'm all types of psycho. I grew up trained to kill, and I wouldn't hesitate to murder some bastard who looked her way. The captain of the boat we rented today almost died when he looked at her in her bikini. My gun was packed away in the backpack I had with me, and if she hadn't gotten that cramp in her leg, he'd be a fixture at the bottom of the ocean.

"Anima mia, once my dick claims this perfect body, I'm not giving it back." *My soul.*

Her muscles tense, and I curse my mouth for not shutting the fuck up. It's like my brain and mouth can't get on the same page. The plan was to take things slow and ease her into the relationship. To woo and charm the shit out of her until she's just as invested as I am. But the moment she stepped over the threshold of my hotel room, it's like all my plans went out the window and I'm jumping from point A right into the happily-ever-after stage.

"You're not going to cut me into little pieces or wear me as a coat, are you?" Her voice suddenly sounds hesitant for the first time since we made contact yesterday at the restaurant.

She's nervous. She should be considering how intense I get when I'm around her. Shit, if she knew I've been stalking her for the last seven years, she'd run screaming from the room. Not that I'd let her get far from me. Still, it would be a lot harder for us to move forward without coercion. That's not the route I want to go, but if it comes to it, then so be it. There is no other option but for us to be together.

Before I can reassure her that no harm will ever come to her on my watch, someone knocks on the door to my room, and we hear a guy's voice from the hallway.

"Room service!"

"Shit." I forgot I'd ordered for us before I got a call from Carson at the business.

My eyes shift downward at our nearly naked bodies. My dick is really hating me right at this moment.

"Head to the bathroom and wait until I come get you," I demand, the words coming out a little sharper than I intended. The thought of some other man seeing her in this state makes me want to break the guy's neck. "Please," I add quickly to soften the heat vibrating off me.

Gemma's mouth turns down into a frown, but she turns toward the door that leads to the bathroom, and I give her juicy ass a good swat. She yelps in surprise, then lets out a playful giggle that makes me want to forget about the knocker who has our dinner waiting.

"Put it over there." I point to the couch as the young kid rolls in the food cart. I fish out a few bills from my wallet and hand them over to him before practically slamming the door on him. Just to make sure we aren't interrupted again, I swing the door back open and hang the *Do Not Disturb* sign on the handle as the poor kid waits by the elevator, then I slam the door again for good measure.

After taking several deep breaths to collect myself after one of the most important moments of my life was interrupted, I knock lightly and open the bathroom door at the same time. I chuckle as I watch Gemma rifling through my bathroom travel bag. She's so focused on her mission that she doesn't even hear me or notice that I'm leaning against the doorframe.

Damn, she is adorable.

After letting her spray my cologne in the air and sniff it, I clear my throat. "Find what you're looking for?" I joke letting her know she's so busted. "I hide the good stuff under the bed."

She really must not be aware of her surroundings because she jumps and nearly drops my toothbrush in the toilet when her hands whip up in the air. It's a good thing I keep my gun in the nightstand or she might've shot the ceiling. The errant thought reminds me to put my gun in the room's safe. I can only imagine her reaction if she found it, and I'm not ready to answer those questions yet. To her,

I'm just an owner of a life insurance business; she doesn't need to know how I really make my money yet.

"I—" I can see the wheels turning in her head, trying to come up with an excuse for going through my stuff, but she's at a loss. "Just checking the name of the spray that makes you smell so good."

The words travel straight to my dick, and once again I'm harder than cement under my towel.

"Is that all?" I raise an eyebrow, then bend down to retrieve my toothbrush off the floor.

"Mmhmm," she hums but doesn't elaborate. "You ordered food already?" She changes the subject and tries to walk past, but my arms reach around her waist pulling her flush with my chest.

"Yes, and once we're done, we'll pick up right where we left off before we were so rudely interrupted." I nip at her ear, making her breath hitch. "You can go through all my things if you want. Feel free to investigate all the drawers—I've got nothing to hide."

Except a mountain of information about her, you liar.

We walk back out to the living space, and I sit her on the sofa while I sort out the food. A thought pops into my head, and I decide to hand-feed her while seducing the last few articles of clothing off that delicious body of hers.

"I want to try something," I state. "Lie down on the pillow and close your eyes." I place a napkin across her eyes so she can't peek.

She obliges and it rocks me to the core how easily she seems to trust me after only meeting me the day before. I can't even imagine what she'd do if she knew I was the one who held her in that pantry all those years ago.

Taking the shellfish platter from the cart, I reach for the oysters first.

"Open your mouth and swallow once it hits your tongue. Don't chew," I instruct while squeezing some lemon on it before lifting it to her plump lips.

Gemma seems hesitant at first, but when she feels the shell against her lips, she opens immediately. I give her a few seconds, then tip the slippery food into her open mouth. She does as she's told and swallows without chewing.

"What do you think?" I ask as I prepare the next one after I tip one back and swallow it whole. This is one of the best things about living near the coast—the fresh seafood is amazing.

"Umm, it's different. I've never had much seafood before," she admits as she continues to lie there.

How is it possible for this gem of a woman to live on the West Coast and not relish in the fresh delicious seafood it has to offer? She's blowing my mind at every turn. I knew she was a tad sheltered, but I'm loving the fact that it'll be me that shows her the world and all the treasure it has to offer.

"Want another?"

She nods but then clamps her hand over her mouth. Gemma shoots up from her prostrate position, making the napkin fall away from her eyes as she looks wildly around. It's as if I'm not right in front of her. She scrambles over me like I'm a hurdle on a school track and races to the bathroom, leaving me to wonder what in the hell just happened.

The sound of heaving echoes from the bathroom and has my legs swiftly moving toward the door she left wide open. Did the oyster make her sick? I spring into action and grab a washcloth, dousing it with cool water before walking over to her as she curls herself around the stark white toilet.

"Is everything okay, baby girl? Did you not like the oyster?" I ask, placing the wet cloth on her forehead and then over the back of her neck.

As soon as Gemma looks up from hovering over the toilet, I know something is terribly wrong.

"Holy fucking shit!" I say, though I didn't mean for it to leave my mouth.

Gemma's lips have almost tripled in size, and her cheeks are all puffed out and splotchy.

"My mouth is tingling, and my stomach hurts really bad," she whines with a lisp—and for good reason. The girl looks like a cosmetic procedure nightmare, and I can tell her tongue is swelling by the way her words start to slur as she's talking.

"We need to get you to a hospital, baby. Like right now!" I bolt out of the bathroom and jet over to my clothes, grabbing anything I can reach for us to throw on while calling down to the lobby to see if they have an EpiPen on hand.

It feels like it takes forever to get her dressed and when I carry her out of the elevator, the manager meets us in the lobby to direct us to a town car waiting just outside. Luckily, he did have an EpiPen with the hotel's first aid supplies, and I injected Gemma in her thigh just as her breathing was starting to become a wheeze.

Less than ten minutes later, the town car drops us off at the hospital around the corner, and the medical staff gets her into a room right away. They start an IV and provide her with an oxygen mask to help her oxygen levels until the swelling goes down. They mention that they might keep her overnight, depending on how her body reacts to the medication, and it sends me reeling.

Will she be okay? God, I could've killed her. There's so much I need to know to keep her safe. Obviously, she has an allergy to shellfish.

"Sir," I hear from the doorway jarring me from my thoughts.

I look up from the bed and see a lady in business clothing gesturing me out to the hall. The last thing I want to do is leave Gemma's side, but I follow her out.

"We are going to need to get some information for our records," she states and walks me away from the room to a corner by the nurse's station.

I want to punch the bitch in the face for asking not even an hour after being brought in. This is the last thing Gemma needs to worry about right now. The lifestyle of being in the mafia is completely different. Dr. Fulton has been with our family since before I was born. He takes care of my family and all of our men in the organization. If someone has a cold, Dr. Fulton handles it. Got a gunshot wound? Dr. Fulton is there to fix it. So, handling all this insurance shit is foreign to me. I divulge all the information I know and tell her to put everything on my credit card. I notice a couple of doctors and medical staff walking in and out of the room but don't think too much of it while I wait for her to input all the info. Once a man in a security uniform walks in, I end my conversation and march back over to Gemma's room to find out what the hell is going on. Alarm bells are going off in my head.

The moment I'm in the room, I can sense the tension in the small area is thick. A nurse and doctor are standing at the side of the bed, asking Gemma personal questions about our relationship and where her bruises came from. It does look bad if you don't know how clumsy she is. She's got a few bruises on her hips and upper legs, along with her arms, but nothing that looks too bad. The security guard is standing by the door giving the nurse and the doctor some room to speak to Gemma.

The reality of the situation hits me like a ton of bricks in the chest. I've done a lot of bad things in my life. I've killed a lot of people, but the thought of physically hurting my girl is abhorrent to me. It's almost enough to make me lose the contents of my stomach.

Gemma's shaking her head, trying to speak but having a hard time since she's got the mask covering her mouth.

"This is a safe place, honey. You can tell us. We can help you," the nurse offers, and a growl pushes out of my throat as my hands ball into fists.

The noise alerts the three of my presence as they turn their heads toward me.

"I think it's best if you all get the fuck out and let her rest," I sneer, walking past them to be at Gemma's side. She reaches for my hand, and I lace our fingers together.

These assholes tried to lure me out so they could take her away from me. My mind goes into fight mode. They'll have to pry her from my cold, dead hands before I let any one of them remove me from her presence again.

The doctor clears his throat. "We're just getting an assessment and letting Ms. Barone know that she'll be released later today as long as she improves and she's able to pass some simple tests. She clearly has an allergy to shellfish that she wasn't aware of and will need to make sure to steer clear from here on out. It'd be in her best interest to carry an EpiPen on her person at all times. We'll get her a prescription for those before she's discharged."

"I'll make sure she has one available at all times." I grind my teeth.

This entire ordeal has put me on edge. Usually, when I need to release this sort of aggression, I spar with one of my crew or take on a few extra assignments and dial up the beatings. Doing strenuous activity always helps reduce my frustration and get my center back in place.

Before now, the idea of losing her had never crossed my mind, and it's all I can do to contain my emotions. There is no *me without her*, and *no her without me*. Period.

CHAPTER EIGHT

Luca

"Soooo, I stopped by to say that I'm heading back to San Diego," the bitch roommate has the nerve to say as Gemma is lying in a hospital bed.

"What?" Gemma says in disbelief. "I thought we were staying until Sunday?" She shifts in the bed and sits up a little, now fully awake thanks to Jill storming into the room. My first instinct is to slap the shit out of her and tell her to jump off the nearest bridge, but I stay silent, letting this unfold. Jill tests my patience with every word out of her mouth, but I have no doubt this is going to play in my favor. We've been here for several hours now, and nearly all of the swelling has gone down. The medicine has done wonders since we arrived here last night, and I'm itching to leave. They're in the middle of a shift change this morning, but then we should be good to go.

"Yeah, well, Elizabeth called and invited me to go out with her friends on her dad's yacht."

"But I'm—"

"The concierge has your bags and is holding them until you're able to get out of here." Jill waves her hands in the air gesturing around the room.

"Jill how am I—" Gemma starts again but is interrupted before she can even form a sentence.

"Listen, I've got to get going if I'm going to beat the traffic back home. Call if you need anything." She's out the door before another word can be spoken.

The look on Gemma's face has my jaw ticking. Before I can stop myself, I've shot to my feet.

"I'll make sure she makes it to her car safely," I lie, not wasting any time before heading out after this pathetic excuse for a person. Though I may make it seem like it's the gentlemanly thing to do, I plan on being anything but a gentleman.

I beat her to the parking garage by taking the stairs and wait. The fact that my obsession with Gemma is at an all-time high now that I've made contact has me roaring with rage at the thought of someone hurting her, and that goes for hurting her feelings too. The killer in me wants to pound this bitch into the ground and leave her for dead, but knowing I'm keeping a low profile makes me pause and go a different direction.

Just make your point and send the slut on her way.

Jill walks right by me as she passes a pillar, oblivious to her surroundings. Not wasting more time and wanting to get back to my girl, I step up behind her. I spin her around and shove her up against a white van. Her surprised gasp has my body humming, and I feel the adrenaline shoot through my veins. This is what I left behind in Vegas. The brutal man that had no empathy for others or remorse for causing them pain. A man who gives orders and takes action without any regard for the consequences.

"Oh my god!" She tries to yell, but I clamp my large hand over her mouth.

"You're a piece of work, aren't you?" I'm holding her up by the throat with my other hand, making it difficult for her to move or breathe. "This is what is going to happen." I shake her trembling body to make sure I have her full attention. "Once you get back to that shoebox dorm, I want you to pack your shit up and move the fuck out. I don't give a fuck where you go or who you stay with, but I want you gone." Tears are streaming down her cheeks now. "Write Gemma a note telling her that you decided to move in with a boyfriend or whatever the fuck, but it had better be done. I don't want to hear of you having any more contact with her after today. Block her number, change schools, I don't care. I'll know if you contact her, and you don't want to be on the receiving end if I catch you next time. Do you understand me?"

This bitch stares at me, and I think she's about to pass out when a small jerk of her head—as much of a nod as she can manage—moves my hand.

"Good." I check my surroundings before releasing her. I know all about her wealthy family and how her father came into that money. I never wanted to use my name after I left Las Vegas, but I will if it means this spoiled-ass bitch stays clear of my girl.

She must be having a hard time grasping the situation as she stands by her car in shock, but my patience is wearing thin.

"You have one minute to get this car outta here and on the road, or I'm going to make good on that promise. I know all about your family, and make no mistake, I'll kill everyone you're close to right in front of your eyes if you tell a single soul about me or what just happened," I threaten. It must shake something in her because she practically throws herself into the car, slams the door, and peels out of the garage.

Back in the hospital, as I enter Gemma's room, I can hear her muffled sobs, and for the first time ever, my heart hurts hearing someone cry. I swear this woman has done a number on me since I met her. The door makes a sound, drawing her attention to it, and I watch as she tries to hide her tears and put on a smiling face.

"And then there were two," I joke trying to lighten the mood.

A small watery giggle escapes her, and I think it worked, yet I'm still angry. It doesn't take me long to pinpoint the source of my frustration either. I've watched Gemma for years, and for most of her life, Gemma has been on her own. When her mother died, she was sent away to a private school. Then her piece of shit dad died and she was put in the care of a teacher. She's had to look out for herself through the most important years of her life.

But that changes right now.

She needs someone to take care of her, someone to be that stable person in her life. She needs a person who will lay the world at her feet and take a bullet for her. *I'm* that person. I've been connected to her for years, and I'm finally claiming what I've wanted for so long. I can be the person she leans on, the man strong enough to shoulder the bad times and celebrate the good ones. To love her with everything a person has and to help guide her into becoming the woman she wants to be. I'll be that person. I'm the right man for the job. I left my family and the business for her, so she can live the life she deserves.

"Do you mind if I use your phone? I'm not sure where mine is and I need to figure out how I'm getting home when they decide to release me..." she's saying and her voice trails off at the end. My frozen heart thaws as a frown forms on her beautiful face. Even without makeup, she's the most gorgeous woman in the world. Call me pussy-whipped, but I plan on making it my mission to see many more smiles than frowns in the future.

"Who needs a phone? Your chauffeur has already arrived," I exclaim with my arms held wide.

She has the most adorable look of confusion, and I think she's in need of more sleep.

"Me, Gemma. I'll be driving you home when you're ready to leave," I explain so she doesn't have to guess what I mean.

"Oh, no I couldn't ask you to do that. I mean, I'm sure I've already ruined your vacation." This chick has no idea that I'm only here for her.

"I'm not worried about my vacation. I told you when we met that I wanted to get to know you and see where this could lead. We'll call this the sickness and health times of the relationship," I joke, and it seems to relax her stiff posture.

Two hours after Jill made her exit, Gemma finally gets her discharge papers. I've contacted the hotel and instructed them to put all her belongings in my suite. We still have the rest of the week and weekend before heading back to San Diego. I plan to take advantage of every moment to solidify our relationship and have her tied to me—have her as needy for me as I am for her.

"Thank you for staying with me through all this craziness," Gemma says as we pull up to the hotel. My blue Maserati was delivered to the hospital by the hotel manager at my request.

"Hey," I turn to face her, taking her hand before the valet opens her door, "if you remember correctly, I was the one who fed you the shellfish. If anything, I'm the one who caused all this craziness, and there isn't anywhere else I'd want to be. I mean, how would it look if I left my girlfriend at the hospital when I'm the reason she was there?"

"Your girlfriend?" She chokes on the word.

I nod, and when she gives me that million-dollar smile, I know I've said the right thing. I might not know a thing about relationships, but I've watched my parents enough over the years to know how to navigate my way through this. The start of our relationship might not be perfect, but it'll end up being a fairytale in her eyes.

"Ms. Barone, I'm so glad to see you in better health," Bob, according to the hotel manager's name tag, says. He must be the one I've been dealing with last night and this morning.

"Oh, umm, thank you." Gemma bites her lip, embarrassed by the attention.

"She was given a clean bill of health," I cut in, tucking her against me as my possessive side kicks in. "Here's the prescriptions she needs. Make sure to note that no seafood is to touch our food at any point. Have the chef use new utensils and kitchenware." I order, making sure he understands.

"Of course, sir. Would you like to leave a breakfast order with me, and I'll make sure the food is personally delivered along with the meds?"

I turn toward Gemma and see her eyes widen as she stands

there listening to our conversation. She's going to have to get used to people waiting on her for the rest of her life.

"Baby, what do you want to eat?" I turn her to face me.

Is it possible to need physical contact with someone all the time? I'm sure a therapist would have a hay day with me.

She hesitates for a beat but replies, "Eggs and pancakes?"

We give Bob our order, then head up to our suite. In the elevator, I can't help but feel like she's a little distant.

"Do you always speak to others like that?" she asks, throwing me off as the doors close. It's just the two of us enclosed in the ascending square metal box.

"Like what?" I'm confused as I try to think back to the conversation with Bob.

"Order people around. Command them to do what you want."

I open my mouth to answer, but I pause for a moment. She doesn't know I was raised to give orders and commands for others to follow. I don't do that with her because she isn't someone I need to order around. She's the love of my life, even if she doesn't know it yet. Gemma is the most precious thing in the world to me—a delicate person who means everything to me. I'm reminded that Pop said when you find the one, you treasure her like the most valuable possession you have.

"I guess I didn't realize I do that. Owning a business is stressful at times, and taking control is something that comes with the territory." I pause. "Does it bother you?"

She blushes. "I kinda like it," she whispers like it's a secret, and the shade of her cheeks turns even more red. I can't stop the smirk on my face or the chuckle that leaves my throat. So, my girl likes to see me in boss mode.

I pull her to me, closing the small space between us. I look down at her as she gazes up at me. "Oh, baby girl, you really shouldn't have said that." I lean in, nipping the exposed skin of her neck, and work toward her luscious lips. I steal all the air from her lungs as

I consume her mouth with mine. She doesn't know the monster she's awakening.

Since she went to the hospital in little to nothing I had the manager buy her an outfit to come home in. After the incident with the nurses and doctors the night before, I refused to leave her side. I'd told him her size and what type of sundress she likes. Needless to say, he did well. With the amount I've forked over here to make sure our stay goes smoothly, I expect to have my ass kissed every time I turn around.

The doors of the elevator ding, but we don't move.

"This is us," Gemma's voice is breathy in my ear, and it takes all of my strength to move away from her.

Once we're in the suite, I try to cool my body down. Everything in me urges me to take her and make her mine right now, but that's not how I want this to go. She deserves better, more than a trashy quickie. She's taking in the spectacular view from our suite as the sun rises higher in the sky. I want the rest of the week to be complete bliss and an experience she'll never forget.

My hand sweeps her hair over her shoulder, exposing the back of her neck as I sidle up behind her. Both arms circle her midsection, pulling her back to my hard chest.

"Beautiful, isn't it?" Gemma asks. I know she's talking about the view, but my eyes never leave hers.

"The most beautiful thing I've ever seen," I say wholeheartedly.

"Thank you," she says as she turns in my arms. I refuse to move an inch, so she has to wiggle to face me, making my dick rage even more.

"Why are you thanking me?"

"For being so kind and for staying with me during that totally embarrassing episode." She buries her face in my muscular chest. I love how small she is compared to me; she really only comes up to my pecs when she's barefoot.

"Listen to me, baby girl, I don't know who you've had in your life before me, but I can guarantee you that I'll never abandon or hurt you." It's not the full truth, because I know just about every person who's been in her life. We haven't talked about her family fully, but I know by the end of our trip, she'll have told me. My curiosity is eating away at me over what she'll say about her piece of shit dad.

"Please don't make promises you can't keep." She places a small finger on my lips to stop me from continuing. "I'm not sure if I can handle one more person I care about leaving my life."

I swiftly grab her wrist and place the softest kiss to her knuckles as I look directly into her eyes. "There's nothing in this world or the next that will keep me from you," I admit and crush my lips to hers. She returns the intensity as I dominate her. She rubs against me, and my dick is on fire to shed these clothes and fill her up. My hands have a mind of their own as one arm hoists her up under her ripe ass and the other has a hand squeezing her plump breast.

A knock at the door interrupts our heavy petting. Regretfully, I place her down, only waiting until the knock comes again before my lips leave hers. When I open the door, Bob wheels in the breakfast we ordered and hands me her prescriptions. After tipping him and making sure to cover the cost of her medicine, I find my girl seated on the sofa in the living area of our suite already partaking in the food he brought.

"Before we continue, is there anything else I need to know about you? Medical history? Allergies?" I half joke, but it's definitely something I need to ask so I don't accidentally do something to kill her…again.

She sets her fork down giggling, and it's the most beautiful gift she could give me. It eases the knot in my chest. I could've lost her. The thought is sobering.

"They tested for other allergies, but shellfish seems to be the only thing I reacted to, but I do have asthma and have to carry an inhaler with me."

"Asthma? How often do you have attacks?"

Christ, this little slip of a woman is going to have me carrying a damn fanny pack if she keeps this up.

"I don't have to use it often, just when I work out sometimes." She shrugs. "But I don't do it as often as I should." She goes to pinch the underside of her thigh and it has me moving like a bullet to her side, grabbing her hand.

"You don't need to work out," I reassure her. "If you get any smaller, I'll crush you when I'm on top." She blushes as I lean in and steal a kiss. "So, working out…any other time I should know?"

Gemma starts to wring her fingers, a tell-tale sign she's embarrassed again.

"You can tell me, don't be shy." I nudge her.

"Well," she pauses before finally looking into my eyes, "I thought I might need it after kissing you in the elevator. I've never been kissed like that—ever." Her teeth bite down into her plump bottom lip, and I lose it. I attack.

My body stretches out over hers, pushing her back on the sofa as my mouth takes possession of hers. This girl just told me I stole her breath away, and the rope around my hardened heart loosens. She does things to me that I never thought possible.

Being mindful of her breathing, I let up after I ravish her mouth. I need this girl.

"Tell me you want me. That you want this." I thrust my dick right into her dress-covered pussy and she rewards me with the perfect moan. "You have to say it, baby."

"Yes. Yes, I want you."

I have her scooped into my arms before the entire sentence is off her tongue and headed toward the bedroom. The only way we are leaving this room is if the fucking hotel is on fire. I reluctantly set her down at the foot of the king-sized bed and start with my shirt. I want her to know she has free reign over me, so I guide her hands to the bottom of it and help her lift it over my head. Her hands go immediately to my pecs, and I'm thankful for all the workouts Gio has made me do over the years. She traces my tats but doesn't ask what they mean. I'll tell her one day but not now. Right now, I just want to bury myself in her and never come up for air.

My hands move hers down toward my belt and guide her to pull it out of the loops. Her breathing has picked up, and I listen for any wheezing. I'll never put her in harm's way again.

"Should we get your inhaler just in case?" I hate to ruin the moment, but I don't want us to end up back in the hospital because I'm too much of a bastard to stop and check on her.

"I'm good, just excited," she breathes.

This girl disarms me at every turn.

I know this is her first time, so I think me getting naked first will ease her mind and hopefully relax her. Together, we pop the buttons on my jeans, and I help her hands glide my pants and boxers down my legs. Her hands shake slightly, but she's not showing too much hesitation. Gemma's focus is on my throbbing, rock-hard dick, and he can't help but jump at her attention.

"He won't bite." I take her hands and wrap them around my shaft. Her dainty hands don't fit around him as I show her how to rub from root to tip, but I show her how tight to make her grip. "That's it, baby girl," I moan and can't help closing my eyes at the feel of her finally touching me. It makes me lightheaded with every caress and tug.

It's been well over a year since a woman has touched me, and I've been waiting for years for this moment. Even when I walked away from her years ago at her graduation, I still pictured this moment. Every time I was with someone else, I pictured her. All the others were only to fill a void.

The feeling of her hand on me is overwhelming, so I stop her before this ends sooner than I want. I'm not some teenage prick who comes before the main event.

"Was that okay?" She bites her lip, and I inch a little closer to the edge.

"Perfect, baby, but I want to play with you before I erupt too soon, and I'd rather come in that tight little pussy than in your hand." I give her a knowing look and hold her hand up, which has some precum on it.

"Oh."

My pants and boxers are around my ankles, and she watches my every move as I kick them off along with my shoes and socks. Fuck, her gaze makes me want to preen like a fucking peacock the way she takes me in. Not wanting her to be left out, I reach down and catch the bottom of her sundress, pulling it over her head. Her large tits sway when her arms come back down to her side. She's nervous but is putting on a brave front, trying to figure out where she should put her hands.

"Don't be nervous, baby. There is nothing for you to worry about. I got you," I say.

She tries to cross her arms in front of her, but I stop her from covering herself. My large, rough hands caress her tits and massage them as her nipples peak at my touch. They're hard as diamonds and the perfect dusty pink color. I guide her to lie down on the bed.

She has on sheer white panties, and I see a wet spot. I don't even try to quiet my groan at the realization that my girl is turned on by my body and jacking my dick. My eyes rake over her perfect, untouched body as I lean forward, and my nose runs along her seam, inhaling her scent. Heaven.

"Lay back for me. I want to see all of you."

She obeys and moves to the middle of the bed. I take this moment to appreciate what God created. She is perfection. There isn't a part of her body that isn't exquisite—even her clumsiness and naiveté make her that much more attractive.

She fidgets, and I worry I've been staring so long that now she's starting to rethink this. I stalk upward from the foot of the bed, taking an ankle in my hands and kissing my way up to her upper thigh. I can smell her essence, and it makes my dick throb harder. My head drops on her stomach as I try to cool down. Shit, maybe I should take a hit of her inhaler to calm myself. The last thing I want to do is let my beast out to ravage her for her first time and ruin everything. "You smell like heaven, and I bet you taste like it too." Slowly, I begin to pull her panties down her thighs. I plan on keeping these for my personal use at a later time. If I could, I'd frame them. They represent the beginning of my future, a symbol of what I thought I'd never have with the life and family I could never have. Unable to help myself, I bring them up to my nose and as I inhale, my eyes roll back and a moan leaves my throat. Her scent is like a drug.

I remember when my boys and I used to snort the good shit before I overdosed. We were only looking for that little piece of heaven to take us away from all the shit we saw and did. This is so much better than any of that. After I get my fill, I toss the prized panties on top of my clothes. She seems to bring out the freak in me, and I won't apologize for it. My beast is scratching at the surface, wanting to take charge, but the moment my eyes reach hers, I know I would walk through fire for her.

She's bare, and I love that nothing is going to be between us. I waste no time bringing my mouth down on her pussy. She's wet and I lap it up, my tongue exploding at her taste. I knew she'd be the best after inhaling her scent. Fuck! My dick is so hard it's painful. I reach down with the hand that isn't holding her in place and give it a hard tug, then squeeze, hoping for some relief. Never have I cared about any other woman's pleasure. My life has always been about me and my needs, but Gemma is different. My life is now about her and what she needs, so he'll have to wait until it's his turn.

Gemma's moans are loud, and if we weren't the only ones on this floor, I'd gag that pretty little mouth of hers so that no one else could hear her. My tongue hones in on her swollen clit, and her hips buck under my grip.

"Please," she begs as she doesn't know what she's begging for. Her hands grasp my hair, and she pulls me even closer. *Yes, ma'am!* Her hips are moving as if we're fucking, and I can't wait for her to ride my dick like this.

I work my tongue over her clit again and again as I push a finger into her tight-as-fuck channel. Holy shit, I have never felt such a tight snatch. I swear to God, I could come on the spot right now at how tight she is. I feel her hymen but decide to leave it be and let my dick have the honor of breaking through it. I add a second finger and scissor her to try and loosen her up, but even with that, I know she's going to bruise the shit out of my dick. And I couldn't be happier. A little pain to reach heaven is completely worth it. My focus goes back to her pulsing clit, and I know she's close to losing it. I devour her as I move my fingers in and out, sucking on her pearl until she tips over the edge.

"Oh, Luca!" She screams my name as her body locks up and jerks. I revel in it and lick her clean as the juices flow out of her.

In an instant I'm up on my knees, towering over her with my elbow by her head. There's no easy way to do this, so I decide to make it quick, but it's like shoving a paint can in a pencil sharpener—it's going to hurt; there's no way around it.

"Hold on tight to me, baby."

I place my arm behind her back, and she wraps her limp arms around me, still reeling from her orgasm as I guide my dick toward heaven. She's dripping and it lubes my dick at her pulsating entrance. Without hesitation, I spear my thick cock into her and push all the way home. Gemma is still coming down from her orgasm when her hymen breaks, but I know my size hurts. She cries out, and I hold her tight to my body as her instincts kick in and she tries to move away from the pain.

"Luca!" she cries out, and there's nothing I can do to make it better but hold her still until it passes.

"It's okay, it's okay," I repeat over and over. Her nails dig into my shoulder with a sharp bite, but I kiss her to distract from the pain. "I got you, baby." I move a hand back down over her clit to help relax her a bit.

My hips start to move ever so slightly as the hold Gemma has on me loosens. *Lord, give me strength to not start hammering into her.* Her body is so soft against mine, and I have to be careful not to crush her. As time passes, my movements get smoother. She's starting to relax.

"How you feeling, baby girl?" I ask, breaking our kiss. Her lips are swollen. She nods, but that's not what I want. "Tell me."

"I…it's better. The stinging is almost gone."

"Good, that's good. Let me know if it gets to be too much."

She nods again, and I start to move my hips a little faster, bringing both hands up to frame her face. I'm not going to last very long with how great her pussy feels. I'll have to make it up to her later. She moans as I thrust, my hips slapping against her pelvis. My dick can only take so much before he shoots off like a rocket.

"Oh…oh…" Gemma moans every time my cock knocks into her G-spot. She'll be screaming from another orgasm soon, and that's all I can take.

My hand slips back between us and my finger finds her clit. Sweat is rolling down my back as my thrusts speed up.

"You feel so good, baby. You. Feel. That?" I punctuate each word with a thrust, hitting her in the right spot. "Take every drop, squeeze me good."

Her walls clamp down around me, and my fingers lightly pinch her clit. She comes with the scream of my name again, and I finally let go. My head falls to the crook of her neck as I call her name. I come long and hard, painting her walls and womb with my seed. Even after I have nothing left to give, I keep thrusting not wanting to leave my home. Gemma has gone limp beneath me, still moaning as I finally come to a halt.

"You were incredible," I praise as I brace my forearms on either side of her head.

A lazy smile is all she's able to give as exhaustion takes over her body. She's had a rough twenty-four hours, but my dick has taken over my brain since we made contact.

"I really liked it. I see what all the fuss is about," she giggles, and I chuckle along with her.

Not wanting to separate but knowing she's going to be sore, I slowly pull out, making her wince. The light pink color on my dick is all the evidence I need to know she's all mine. No other man will ever touch her like this. She was made for me, and as soon as I can, I plan to tie her to me in every way possible. The caveman in me wants to push a pillow under her hips and make her lay like that, not letting any of my cum drip out until the seed takes hold and puts a baby in her, but I don't think we are in the same place right now. She thinks we just met. No, we have to go at her pace, and patience is going to have to be my priority.

"Let's have a bath," I say and scoop her naked body up from the bed. A good soak will hopefully help soothe her muscles.

CHAPTER NINE

I'M STARTLED AWAKE FROM A NIGHTMARE. OCCASIONALLY, I dream of being back in the pantry at Mario's house. I can feel the man who held and threatened me. He's always in the back of my head, making me wonder if he'll come back and kill me like he and his partner killed my stepdad. Holy cow, it felt so real. My heart is racing, and when I move, my body aches. It's still dark outside, and I wonder how long I slept. A quiet snore brings my attention to the left side of the bed, and right away I tense.

Oh. My. God.

I did it! I really had sex. I'm sore as all get out down there, proof my virginity has left the building. I swear, I think I only said a few words during our lovemaking. Hopefully, Luca won't think I'm some weird mute who freaks out while being intimate. It truly was one of the best days of my life. Even after being so scared at the hospital, thinking I was going to die from eating shellfish.

My bladder is calling, but the death grip he has over my stomach is preventing me from getting up. Carefully, I maneuver out from under his arm and quietly make it to the bathroom.

This suite is so nice and fancy. The tub is amazing, and a handful of people could fit in it. We soaked in it after sex to help my muscles relax, and it felt wonderful. It also helped because Luca held me so close, as though his life depended on it. I'm not sure if all guys do this, but I felt pretty special. He has this way of knowing what I need before I even have to ask or think about it.

I was so lucky when Luca bought our dinner that first night. We hit it off and haven't spent more than a moment away from each other since. It turns out that he works and lives in San Diego too. It's like our fates are colliding, and I don't want this time to come to an end.

I flush the toilet, then turn the water on to wash my hands as a figure in the mirror catches my eyes. I gasp, startled to see Luca standing there in the doorframe. "You scared me," I say, clutching my soapy hand to my chest.

"I woke and you weren't there," is all he says before he comes prowling over to me. "You must still be sore." He picks me up bridal style, as though I'm no heavier than a basket of laundry.

"I can walk." There's no sternness behind the words because I love that he's carried me everywhere since we had sex.

"Not if I can help it. If you need something, you wake me."

My head rests on his bare shoulder as he makes his way to the bed. "Even to pee?" Even I hear the surprise in my voice as I blurted it out. The room is dark, but I can feel the heat in my cheeks. Why can't I keep my mouth shut? Just like when I told him how I liked his bossiness.

I feel him chuckle as he lies back down with me on his chest. He seems to like having me as close as possible. It's a good thing too because my hands and feet are always cold and his body heats them right up.

"You need rest. We've got a busy schedule ahead of us."

"We do?"

"Yes."

After a few beats, I can't stand the silence even though my eyelids are getting heavy again.

"What are we doing?"

The idea of sightseeing or driving up the coast runs through my mind. He turns his body so we're lying on our sides, facing each other. Luca takes my cold feet and puts them between his warm thighs.

"I plan to explore every inch of this delicious, sexy body of yours."

"Hmmm," I hum not protesting one bit.

I feel his lips kiss my forehead before I fall right back to sleep.

This has been the most amazing week of my life. Luca took me to a special place every day, then brought me back to the hotel every night and worshipped my body until the wee hours of every morning.

"Tell me more about your family," Luca asks as we sit at an Italian restaurant on our way back to San Diego.

I hate talking about my family. It makes me sad and angry all at once. I feel like I've been on my own since I was thirteen and hate it. But I can tell Luca isn't going to let up on this subject because he's asked several times over the last few days, so I figure I might as well tell him. Most people have no idea what really happened. I do try to keep it to myself or just skim through most of it because it's not something you talk about.

"My mom died when I was thirteen. She was in a car wreck on her way to pick me up from a friend's house. It'd been raining, and she was going through an intersection when a teenager ran the red light." I pause and cringe as I remember it. "I was told later that she died at the scene."

He reaches across the table and takes my hand in his large one.

"I'm sorry you had to go through that. I can't imagine what it was like to have a parent pass away." He squeezes my hand and I feel his empathy. "At least you had your dad to get you through it, right?"

If he only knew the Pandora's box that was.

"No," I almost sneer. "My mom had been in a yearlong divorce battle with the man who helped raise me. I hadn't seen Mario for two years before that whole mess started. Mom didn't think it was a good idea for him to be around me and left him. I was confused at first, but I listened in on a meeting she had with one of her lawyers. Mario was into a lot of dirty things. Things that he didn't want to become public. So he either kept his distance from me, or Mom threatened to expose him."

I finally raise my head to look over at Luca and he doesn't give me a look of pity but of understanding.

"I'm glad your mom protected you. Sounds like he wasn't a good guy."

I shrug one shoulder. "He really wasn't there for me years before. I can't even remember him ever being interested in anything my mom put me in growing up. He never made the school plays or met the teachers."

The more I think back, I can't remember him being that affectionate toward me at all.

"Mom was, though. She was with me for every step or milestone of my life until the accident happened."

"Then who did you stay with when your mom died?"

"Mom was a very wealthy woman. That's probably why Mario married her. When she left him, she set up her will to make sure that if anything ever happened to her, I'd be taken care of. I was sent to an all-girls school out of town and away from him. At the time I was still confused, but later I learned something that shook me to my core."

"What happened?" Luca leans in.

I try to think of the best way to tell this and still not say anything that would put me in any danger if it ever got out. That night still haunts me to this day.

"I received a call from Mario one afternoon, telling me I needed to come home, that he had to give me something. He was planning to leave the next morning and not come back. I was sixteen at the time, so I convinced one of the older girls at school to ride with me so I wasn't traveling alone. Ellen wanted to grab some supplies or something to stash in her dorm room." My hands are starting to sweat, but Luca refuses to release them so I can wipe them off. "We arrived later than we were supposed to because I'd tripped at the gas station and knocked over one of their displays. It took me forever to help the poor old woman pick everything up and clean the mess I'd made, and I guess I can be thankful for that."

"I feel like wrapping you up in bubble wrap every time we walk out the door," he says and chuckles as I do the same. I've been clumsy my entire life and am used to it by now. Hopefully, Luca won't get annoyed like Jill or others once they've been around me long. "It's one of the charming characteristics that draws me to you." He kisses my palm and I melt like butter. "Keep going, I can tell you need to get this all out."

"Ellen stayed in the car while I went up to Mario's house. It'd been years since I'd been there, so I wasn't even sure if my key still worked, but it did, and I went in through the back door. All the lights in the house were off but one. I thought about calling before I got there but didn't. The moment I walked in, I knew something was wrong. There was a smell at first, like iron, which I know now was the smell of blood."

"Blood?"

"Something had happened right before I got there, and I found Mario dead in the living room."

"Do you know who did it? Or what happened?"

This is where I follow my script—one that I've told too many times to count. The police, social workers, and the nuns at school all got the same transcript.

"I think it was a burglary or something. The cops were never able to solve it or find anything about what happened to him."

"That's insane, Gemma. You didn't see anything or anyone? What about the girl, Ellen, who went with you? Did she see anything?"

I shake my head. Technically, I didn't see anyone because I was forced into the pantry and it was dark. I'll go to my grave with what really happened that night and how I walked in while the two guys who had killed Mario were still there.

"Ellen didn't see or notice anyone either. She'd laid the seat back and fallen asleep, waiting for me to meet with Mario."

Luca looks thoughtful for a moment before he continues. "Where did you go to live after that?"

"I was considered an orphan because both parents were deceased and neither had any family. One of my teachers, Sister Bethany, became my guardian until I was able to get emancipated. My mother had put many plans in place for all scenarios if something were to ever happen to her, so money was never a problem. Sister Bethany helped me with the legal paperwork, and once the judge signed off, I was able to change my last name and live the best I could until I graduated. She was great—"

"Wait, you changed your name?"

"Well, the moment Mario died, the lawyer who handled my mother's estate gave me some letters written to me from my mom. It turns out that Mario was never my father."

Luca sits back in his seat, which breaks the connection of our hands. Thankfully, this gives me a chance to wipe my sweaty palms on my shorts.

"The guy who raised you wasn't your dad?"

"No."

"Your life could be a movie right now."

"For real."

We eat a few bites in silence, and I'm grateful because I could use a break, but I can tell he's got more questions.

"So, who's your dad, or do you not know?"

"My mom met a man who was on leave from the military. According to her letters, they had a two-month relationship before he got called back. She didn't realize until later, but she'd gotten pregnant with me during that time. They'd written letters to each other over the span of three months, but the day after she found out she was pregnant with me, she received a letter saying that he'd died overseas. She was devastated for months, and somehow Mario had conned his way into her life at her most vulnerable time. She married Mario right before I was born. He gave me his name and said he'd be the best dad to me and that I'd never have to know I wasn't his."

"Sonofabitch," I hear Luca mumble before he reaches for my hand again, holding it tighter this time, as if he fears I might bolt out of my seat. "What's your dad's name, baby? Maybe we can find some family members."

"Mossimo Barone," I say and Luca's eyes widen slightly as I continue. "I tried looking for him when I found out. Sister Martha helped me, but we couldn't find a single person who had died in the military—or anywhere else for that matter."

Tears clog my throat, and I can't help the sniffle. Luca wastes no time getting up and sliding into the booth with me. He holds me as I let the tears finally fall. I'm a mess. He's going to think I'm a basket case and never want to see me again after this.

"He probably gave her a fake name or had another family hidden away," I cry.

"Any man who does that should be dumped in a lake with cement boots."

Why does everyone in my life leave me? I silently ask the question I've asked myself over and over all these years.

"I won't. You're going to have to kill me to keep away," Luca admits, and I realize I've said it out loud.

"I changed my name because I found out that Mario did horrible things, and I didn't want to be associated with him, ever. Barone might not be my dad's real last name, but it was what my mother thought, and I can live with that."

The waitress comes over to leave the bill, and I recall where we are.

"Oh my gosh, I'm a complete mess!" I try to wipe under my eyes, hoping I don't look like a raccoon.

"You're the most beautiful woman alive." Luca grabs my chin

and forces me to look at him. "I wouldn't have you any other way."
He leans in and captures my lips, not caring that we're in public.

How does he do it? Just when I feel myself falling over the edge, he pulls me back to safety. Or at least to the surface where I can breathe again.

I need to change the subject.

"Can you tell me a little more about your family and why you left them?" I ask, wanting to learn about him as much as he knows about me.

Luca sits there for a bit lost in thought for a moment. "Pop and Ma have been married for over thirty years and are more in love now than they were when they met. I have a younger sister, Alice, who lives with her head in the clouds most days." He chuckles as if imagining his sister. "My family owns a lot of different businesses and has grown in wealth over the years. My grandparents are in Italy and sent my pop over here when he was seventeen for better opportunities."

"Thirty years is a long time. It's rare for most marriages to last these days."

"That it is. That's why I plan on marrying only once," he comments and has a look in his eyes as if looking into my soul.

"How old is Alice?" She can't be that young since Luca is pushing thirty.

"She's seventeen, and drama is her middle name. Alice was a late-in-life surprise gift for Ma and Pop, so she's the little princess that gets away with most things."

"I always wanted a sibling. Growing up, I dreamed of having someone to play dress-up or play outside with. Mom always said that once she had me, she knew that I was enough. I can understand why now. Once you find your soulmate, it'd be hard to continue that with someone else. I just wish I knew about all the secrets before she died so I didn't have to just read about my real dad through letters. I'd love to hear their story."

He reaches for my hand in comfort.

"Why did you leave and cut off contact from your family? I'd give anything to have some sort of connection to a living relative."

"I-my family is complicated. For years I was groomed to take over the family business, but as time went on, I wanted more. I didn't want to be strapped down and a slave to my father's orders. My plan is to give it a few years, live my life to the fullest, and maybe reconnect with my family."

"You don't have any contact right now. Like not even phone calls?"

"I needed a clean break to accomplish my plan, to have those dreams I've wanted for years, and I knew that wouldn't happen if I stayed," he says, then sits back in his chair.

"What are your dreams?"

"To come out to the coast and find a curly-haired, blue-eyed woman who makes me want to be a better version of myself." He smirks, and I blush.

Surely, he's trying to be charming, which is working.

"Let's get out of here." Luca pulls away and throws some cash on the table—much more than enough for our meal.

His phone rings as we wait for the valet to bring his Maserati around, making him tense up while the hold on my hand tightens.

"Give me just a second. This is business," he tells me and walks off down the sidewalk away from the crowd.

Ten minutes pass, and I wait in the car for Luca to return while the valet is getting impatient with having the car in the way. After another minute Luca makes his way over to the valet and palms something to the guy. From the smile on his face, I'm sure Luca just handed him a nice tip.

"Sorry about that, but sometimes work needs some attention," Luca says pulling out onto the street as we make our way home.

"It's okay, I understand."

"No, it's not. I want you to know that work will not be an issue in our relationship. You are my top priority. All that other shit can come later." He grabs my hand over the console and brings it with his to the gear stick as he shifts into a higher gear. "It's time that someone put you first, and that's what I'm going to do."

I have to turn my head toward the window to keep him from seeing the tears forming in my eyes and the smile that's about to split my face in two. Is it possible to fall for someone you've known for less than a week?

We arrive back on campus in the late afternoon. Everyone seems to be getting back from the weeklong getaway because the roads are packed as Luca pulls into a parking spot.

"Ready for the last few weeks of college?" Luca asks as I stare out the windshield toward my dorm.

I hate that our time has come to an end. Once I get out of the car, life will go on, and the bubble we shared over the past week might be over. All those words he said could be for nothing. He could leave, and I could never hear from him again. The thought makes my heart hurt.

"Hey. What's going on in that pretty little head of yours?" Luca tugs my hand making me turn toward him.

I hesitate—because how do I tell him what I truly feel? Will he think I'm crazy or clingy? Don't guys hate a clingy girl?

"I had such an amazing week, I just don't want it to end. Reality is setting in, I guess," I try not to sound petulant. Not only am I physically exhausted but also emotionally.

"It's not ending, baby girl. Our story is only beginning, don't you see?" He leans over the console and slants his lips over mine. "If I had it my way, you'd move in with me instead of going up there." He points toward the dorms.

I wish.

"You always know the right things to say. A true Casanova." I snort.

"I'll be whatever you want me to be."

I lean over and take his lips this time. I can't help but touch this man when he's near.

"If you don't stop, I'm going to haul you up to that tiny dorm room and break your small bed having my way with you." He holds my face in both hands. "I'm pretty sure your roommate wouldn't like being locked out while we christen every square inch of your room."

That sobers me quickly. I'm not sure I'd want Jill to see Luca naked.

"I guess we'll have to wait then," I say and unclick my seatbelt.

We climb out of the car, and Luca grabs my bags out of the trunk. Walking across the grassy knoll, I start to look around and see how out of place Luca really is. He seems so much more mature than all the guys here. I know he's way older, but just the way he carries himself is different. People part for him when he strolls by or duck out of the way to not come in contact with him.

We head up to the third floor, and I just hope I didn't leave my side of the room a mess before we left for Malibu. Even before unlocking the door, I know something is off. Jill's dry-erase board is gone from our door. She made such a big fuss about having one and made sure to bolt the thing in the door so no one would knock it off or steal it.

As I open the door, I see my side is perfectly clean and straightened. The nuns at my private school were always on us girls about having our rooms tidy and always making our beds every morning. What shocks me is the empty side that Jill claims. All of her things are gone. The smell of cleaning solution fills my nose as if it was just recently cleaned instead of the floral scent when she first moved in and the walls have been painted back to their original color. Her bedding is gone, along with all her belongings. What in the hell happened here?

Confused, I move around Luca and check the dorm number to make sure I'm in the correct room. Confirming this is in fact my room, I walk back in as Luca places my bags on the chair by my desk.

"I thought you said you and Jill shared a room," he says as he gazes over to the unoccupied side.

I nod. "We do." I wave my hand over to her side. "Or did?"

Is this the Twilight Zone? We saw each other not even a week ago.

"I think she left. Here." Luca holds up a piece of paper and hands it to me.

Right away I recognized Jill's elegant handwriting.

Gemma,

I've decided to move in with Courtney off campus. She's going through something and needs me close. I've had the room cleaned and painted so you didn't have to worry about my mess. I wish you the best.
Have a good life,
Jill

"What'd it say?"

"She moved in with someone else for the rest of the semester," I murmur. "She doesn't even like her." I'm super confused at this turn of events. Jill has always spoken so horribly about Courtney. She was always saying how poor she was, even though Courtney comes from a very wealthy family.

"Will the school assign a new roommate, or do you get the room all to yourself for the rest of the semester?" Luca asks.

"Huh?" I hadn't realized he was talking, lost in my own thoughts. "Oh, I think it's too late to get a new roomy. We only have about six weeks left, so I don't think they would."

Luca walks over to where I'm standing on Jill's side of the room and holds my hips. "You look so sad. I'm sorry she left."

I shake my head, ridding my loathing thoughts.

"It's fine. You should get going before someone dings that expensive car of yours." I try to change my expression to not let him see what is really happening inside of me.

"I don't care about the fucking car, babe. I care about the hurt look on your face. I don't like seeing you like this. How can I make it better?"

I give him the best smile I can muster. "I'm fine. I just have a lot to get together before classes start back tomorrow. And I probably need some rest, since a certain someone kept me from sleeping most of the week."

He bends down and encircles me with his arms, pulling me close. He rests his face in the crook of my neck and inhales.

"Do you want me to stay? We can continue our vacation one more night," he murmurs into my neck, placing kisses on my sensitive skin. It makes me smile and almost forget about Jill.

"I really need to get ready for classes tomorrow. Can I get a raincheck for another night?" I can't even believe I'm saying this. You'd have to be out of your mind to turn down this man.

"Okay, but I want you to call me before bed."

"I promise." I cross my heart.

He seems satisfied with the promise because he pulls back and kisses the tip of my nose.

"I'll set up lunches and dinners when I hear from you tonight, okay?"

"Okay." I can't help the genuine smile that spreads across my face. I love that he's planning for the future, and it makes me relax, knowing he plans on being with me a little longer.

At least you have one person in your life right now, Gemma.

"Don't forget to call, or I'll be knocking on this door at midnight." His playful voice has a hard edge to it. Almost threatening.

"I'll set a reminder," I tease.

He walks out of the room but not before telling me to lock up after he leaves. Of course, I comply.

Standing in the room alone has a sobering feel. Before I can stop the tears from falling as I take in the room, I crumble and I don't know why. I just had the best week of my life. I found an amazing man who has shown me what it means to care about someone else.

I gave him something so special; I'm glad I waited to give it to him and only him. We ate and laughed, and I've never felt so cherished in my life other than with my mom.

I know why I'm crying, and I hate it. It's only a matter of time before Luca decides to leave too. I can honestly say it will break me when it happens. The feelings I have for him are like nothing I've ever felt before, and I know without a shadow of a doubt that I won't survive it.

CHAPTER TEN

Luca

I'M A BASTARD.

I knew what was waiting for her at the dorms, and I couldn't help the satisfaction I was going to get from it. The moment I saw the sadness on her face, I knew she was going to cry, and I wanted to stop it, to tell her not to worry. But I need her to want me. To be so consumed with me that she can't see her life without me. Shitty, I know, but if she depends on me, and I give her the comfort and security she needs, she won't want to leave me once I tell her about my past and the things I've done to get us here today.

She's stronger than she thinks. No one who has been dealt the cards she has would come out on top if they were weak. She could've blown through her inheritance or snorted it like I did when I was in my early twenties. But no, she finished high school and went to college, wanting to become a teacher. To help others the way she needed help. She's a delicate flower, and I plan on preserving her petals to watch her bloom even more.

I move my car down the street but still have her dorm in sight. I've sat here in my car for the past two hours waiting for her to call. I need to be close to her now that I've got her. I'd have moved her things to my house if I hadn't thought it would scare her away.

My phone rings, and I immediately answer without looking to see who it could be.

"Hello."

"Boss," I hear my guy, Carson, through the receiver. "Tommy had a problem with a guy over at Lucky's."

Disappointment shoots through me, but I quickly shift into business mode. I've learned over the years that you must compartmentalize business and personal. My pop was good at it, and I learned from the best. Never did he bring the stress of the business home to his family, and I plan on doing that with Gemma. She'll never know what kind of stress my business causes me.

I know she believes I'm a life insurance business owner—and I do own it to be legit—but what she doesn't know is that I own underground casinos. They are illegal mini casinos around town that haul in a shit ton of cash. We host card games along with slots and craps tables. I've got six locations up and running smoothly. Once you make something illegal, people eat it up, coming to break the law just for the chance that they might hit a jackpot and win big money. Especially in the economy nowadays.

"Have James handle it. I'm in the middle of something and won't be back until tomorrow."

The phone beeps, and I see Gemma calling. Without a thought, I switch over to her, hanging up on Carson.

"Hey, baby, you heading to bed early?" I check the time and see it's almost seven.

"No." There's a pause, and the silence is killing me, but I need her to open up to me to let me in. "I just…are you already home?" she asks.

She's lonely and doesn't like to be alone now that we've spent every waking moment together. *I feel the same, baby girl.*

"No, I had a few errands to run to get ready to head back to work tomorrow. Why? What's on your mind?"

"Is it bad that I hate being here alone in the quiet after the amazing week we had?"

BINGO.

"How about I swing by and we have dinner? I can be there in fifteen minutes," I try not to sound too eager when I know I can be there in less than five.

"Only if you're not busy." She's trying not to come across as needy, and I'm loving every minute of this.

"I'm never too busy for you, baby girl."

We hang up, and I calm my heart rate. She's hooked on me just like I am on her.

Twelve minutes later, I'm walking in the dorms when a lady who looks like she's got a stick shoved up her ass tries to block me from heading toward the stairs.

"Excuse me sir, but you can't be here. No boys allowed after six."

Is this lady for real? Aren't we all adults here? My head swings left to right before I speak.

"Glad to see no boys are around." I start to move around her, but she blocks me again.

"And men. The opposite sex can't go up to the rooms; they must wait here in the lobby. You can use the phone and call up to whoever you're here to see, and they can come down to meet you out front." She plasters on a smile, and I'd like to wipe it right off.

"Listen Ms…" I wait for her to give me a name while giving her my best panty-dropping smile that used to get me any woman I wanted. Like riding a bicycle, it works, and her eyes start to roam over me.

"Amy. You can call me Amy." She's breathless.

"Ms. Amy, I'm here to pick up my girlfriend. She has no idea that I'm dropping in to see her and want to surprise her with dinner. Is there any way you could bend the rules just this once, and I'll make sure to follow them from here on out?" I give a wink and watch as she melts.

"I guess, this one time. Please be mindful of the rules after tonight though."

"Yes, ma'am."

She's still standing in my way, and I have to step wide to avoid touching her. I bound up the stairs two at a time and reach Gemma's door quickly. After knocking with three raps the door flies open and a surprised Gemma stares back at me.

"Luca! I thought you'd call and I'd come down when you got here."

"A gentleman never expects his woman to walk to the car without him." She giggles, and I've missed this side of her. Her eyes are a little puffy, but she tried to hide it with makeup. "Besides, I wanted to ask you something." She bites her bottom lip, waiting for me to ask, but the plump lips I've sucked on all week distract me. "Pack a bag and stay with me at my house. I'm not ready for our bubble to be popped just yet. The thought of waking up in the morning alone without you has me feeling miserable."

Her eyes light up, and it jumpstarts my heart.

"You sure you aren't tired of me yet?" She plays it off, but I know she loves the idea.

"Pack for more than one night, just in case," I say and throw her a wink.

I sit on her bed as she moves about her small room, packing a bag. She's apparently done some laundry as her suitcase is now empty and stored away. Once she's grabbed her clothing of choice, I add a few more items. She laughs as I sort through her panty drawer, but she has no idea that I'm slowly packing her things to keep at the house we'll be sharing from here on out. I plan on having her there every night, even if I have to tie her to the bed.

"Ready?" I ask as she gets her backpack in order for her classes in the morning. While she's occupied, I fill the overnight bag with even more clothes.

"Yeah." She turns after zipping up her backpack and grabbing for her purse. "Ready!" Her enthusiasm is infectious, and I can't wait to bring her home.

My stomach drops a little at the fact she might not like the house, but I tamp it down. I picked the house with her in mind. It's in the La Jolla Heights area, which is around ten to twenty minutes away from her dorm, depending on traffic on I-5. I really wanted to have a place on the water so we could walk out from the backyard into the ocean, but I know, with the type of business I'm in, that it would be a security nightmare. So, I selected a house in a gated community that has the best views of the ocean. It has a guest house on the one-acre plot, and I plan on telling her that Carson is renting it, as opposed to him being there to protect us. I'm not stupid enough to believe that someone from my past couldn't find out where I am. It would be easy to get retaliation on my father through me, and I won't have Gemma put in a position where she's in danger.

After having a burger, fries, and shake, we make our way to the house. The moment we pull into the gated community, Gemma starts to fidget.

"You live here?" Her voice is one of nervous amazement. "You said you sell life insurance, right?"

I can't help but smirk. I know I could brag, but that isn't something she'd like. Most women would be sucking my dick just to see what's behind the gate but not my woman. She'd prefer my time and attention most. That's another charming trait I love about her. She has money in her own right but doesn't flaunt it.

"My business does very well." I don't elaborate any more than that. The fewer lies I have to keep up with the easier to keep them straight.

I park the Maserati in the four-car garage next to my four-door, tricked-out 4x4 Jeep and my vintage 1970 SS Chevelle. She's black with two white racing stripes down her center. The first parking spot closest to the garage door that leads to the house is empty. That spot is reserved for Gemma's white convertible Mustang. Carson's ride is on the side of the house out of the way and not noticeable at all. I walk her around to the front of the house and up the path to the front door. I want her to have the full picture of the house she'll call home very soon.

"You have a beautiful home, Luca," Gemma says as she takes in the entirety of our mansion.

I'm walking her around the house and preening like a fucking peacock at her excitement of each room.

"It's just you living here?" she asks as I show her the fifth bedroom of the nine thousand square foot home.

"Just me, and now you," I add. "Carson rents the guesthouse, but you'll hardly ever see him."

After dropping her bags off in the master suite, we make our way back downstairs to the chef's kitchen. Gemma has been examining every room and for the first time, I'm nervous she doesn't like it.

"Do you cook?" She interrupts my thoughts, and I shake my head.

"There's a lady who comes and makes all the meals. I'd probably starve if it weren't for her."

"I love cooking," she says as she runs her hands across the marble counters and appliances.

"Then you're hired. I expect breakfast, lunch, and dinner every day," I order playfully. She giggles, and it's music to my ears. "Also, I can't pay in cash—only room and board for payment."

"In a house like this, that's a dream come true. I'd never want to leave."

That's the plan, baby.

I come up behind her and wrap my arms around her leaving my hands on her flat stomach. I've had so many visions of coming home from work to see her cooking dinner, pregnant with our child.

"Let's finish the tour and then have a drink out on the terrace," I suggest. If I don't get her out of here, I'm going to maul her on the island.

"Wait, you have two offices?" She looks between the rooms in the hall.

"One for you and one for me, I guess." I shrug. The house really is over the top but perfect for our soon-to-be family.

"You've got more money than sense, Luca," she mumbles in amazement.

"Let's go out on the terrace." I lead her out the French doors after grabbing a tumbler of bourbon for me and a glass of wine for her. I know she doesn't drink wine as often as those God-awful fruity drinks, but she seemed to like this particular wine while we were in Malibu this past week. Plus, I have no idea how to make a fruity drink to save my life. If she really wants, I'll hire a mixologist who can make her anything her heart desires.

The stars shine bright in a sky that is otherwise pitch-black. Gemma tries to sit down in the lounge chair next to mine but I pull her into my lap so she's straddling my hips. Her body molds to mine, and she leans over, letting her tits graze my chin as she sets her wine down.

"Thank you for bringing me here. I guess I really didn't want our bubble to be over either." She's poised above me as my legs stretch out on the lounge chair, half lying down. My mind shoots to images of her sunbathing out here naked, and my dick bites at the teeth of my zipper.

"I want you with me all the time. If I could get away with it, I'd never let you leave the house," I counter.

She smiles, thinking I'm teasing, but in reality, I'd love nothing more than to lock her away for only my eyes. She's a walking disaster that stumbles over her own feet, and it makes me a nervous wreck. Plus, I wouldn't have to share her with other people.

Her fingers play with the buttons on my shirt, then stretch out over my pecs. My body hums any time she touches me, and my heart races. *Go at her pace.* I have to repeat that mantra, so I don't flip us over and maul her. She needs to build confidence in herself and demand what she wants.

"Your body is so hard. How often do you work out?" I know she's talking about more than just my dick being hard, but I can't help where my mind goes while she's sitting on top of me in a sundress. She doesn't even seem to know it, but her hips are making small thrusts against my raging dick, and if I don't bury myself in her soon, I might burst.

"Every day." I try not to grit my teeth when I speak because I don't want to be sharp with her. "I'd love for you to join me so I can watch you sweat in a tiny little outfit."

She giggles, but it turns to a moan when my hips take on a mind of their own and thrust upward. Her head falls back, and she balls my shirt in her little fists.

"Is sex always like this? I can't seem to get enough. Jill said that most guys are only good with one round and then it takes a full four to five hours before they're ready to go again. And that it only lasts a few minutes." She starts to rock steadier on my hips. Her eyes are full of lust and wanting. "You seem to go for hours, and then you're ready to go again in only a few minutes."

"You make me that way. Your body, mind, and soul make me hard without even trying. I just think about you, and my body reacts." I palm her breasts as she pops the buttons on my shirt. That's it, baby, get me naked.

"You're a walking sex machine. How'd I get so lucky?"

"Right place at the right time, amore mio."

In no time, we're naked, and thank God I told Carson to take a hike for a few hours. He's one of my best employees, and I'd hate to have to kill him because he saw her naked.

"I still can't believe it fits in me." She nods down to my hard, throbbing dick, and he weeps at the attention she's giving him.

"Say cock, baby," I urge her. "Say it." She might love to hear me being bossy, but I want nothing more than for dirty words to come out of her pure, innocent mouth that are for my ears only.

"*Cock.* I can't believe that your *cock* fits in me."

I groan at her words. It's the most erotic sound and makes me even harder. "It fits because you were made for me." I gently guide her up by the hips and settle the tip at her entrance. "Take him, baby, take him deep," I encourage.

She moves slowly, and I almost thrust up hard to bury myself, but I find some restraint.

"That's it. All the way..." She drops down all the way to where her ass is resting on my sack. She's going to have finger bruises on her hips tomorrow, but I can't even help that I don't care. "Ride my cock, babe. Aw, that's it." I help guide her for a bit. "You feel the way your pussy grips me? How tight of a hold you have on my cock?" I watch as my dick disappears and groan at the sight when she moves upward, and I see her juices covering him. "You like that full feeling, don't you? Damn, I think you get tighter every time my cock enters your pussy."

Gemma is moving up and down, and her speed is picking up with every word out of my mouth. She has her hands firmly on my chest as she bounces on top of me. Her tits are right in my face, so I latch on to one as my other hand dives in and fingers her clit. Her moans are enough to set me off, but I hold back, wanting her to go first. My tongue laps at her nipple, and my teeth give it a nip, making her walls clamp down even firmer on my dick. She has no idea how sexy she is.

"I'm close, baby," I warn.

"Me too. Aw, oh, oh, it's coming...I'm coming." I move my hands back to her hips and guide her movements as her body stiffens. "Oh my god, I love you. Oh my god." My hips start to jackhammer up into her as her release depletes every ounce of energy she has. It takes four more thrusts, and I'm following behind her in my own release, grunting her name as cum shoots into her pussy.

Best feeling in the world.

My arms wrap tightly around her as her body lays on top of mine. I can't believe she just said that. Once she's calmed down, her body jolts up almost making my dick eject from her core.

"I…what I said…it just came out. I…" Gemma's face turns bright red, but her eyes show what she truly feels.

"I love you too, Gemma," I cut her off. "I know we've only just met, but I feel like I've known you much longer. I can't help it, but I feel the same too."

"You do?" She bites her bottom lip, and my cock stirs back to life. "You don't think it's too soon?"

"There is no measure of time that can determine my feelings. Hell, I think I loved you the first night we met." I chuckle because she thinks I'm talking about at the hotel. She has no idea that I've loved her for years.

"I can't help but get these flutters in my stomach when I'm with you, and my heart races when you look at me." She is going to turn me into the biggest pussy on this planet if she doesn't stop. I don't think it's possible to puff out my chest any more than it already is.

"Tell me again, and this time do it because you want to and not because my dick just gave you the best orgasm you've ever had." I lean in so we're nose-to-nose. My dick is hard again and still encased in her warm cunt.

"I love you, Luca." Her eyes sparkle under the stars, and my life has been given another chance. Someone has decided to give me a chance to have a happy life with the woman of my dreams.

"I love you too," I say and pick her up from the lounge chair. She wraps her legs around my hips as we walk through the house toward our bedroom. There's no going back now. She's sealed her fate the moment those words came out of her mouth. I hope she knows that nothing and no one will ever break us apart. And if she ever tries to leave, I'll lock her away until she changes her mind.

In my—our room, I kick the door shut and fall onto the bed with her under me.

"I hope coffee will help keep you awake during your classes tomorrow because I plan to keep you up all night long loving you," I say as I start to grind against her.

There's a light tap on the bedroom door that brings me out of my sex-induced sleep. I'm a light sleeper—you have to be when you've lived the mafia lifestyle. People are always trying to sneak up on you. Gio always made sure to keep me on my toes and would surprise-attack me as a training exercise.

The alarm clock shows we've only been asleep for an hour. Christ, this better be life or death. I know Carson is on the other side of the door, waiting until I open it. He wouldn't dare come in now that Gemma is in my life. I've made it perfectly clear that unless we are in any danger, he is not to approach the house anymore. The last thing I need is to have to explain who he really is or have him scare her into not staying here because she feels uncomfortable.

Our bodies are entwined together. She always has the coldest feet, and I love that she burrows them between my thighs to warm them up. Her head is on my shoulder, and I've got my arms circled around her so that half her of body is on mine. This is going to be interesting. Carefully, I untangle our limbs and wait as she mumbles something incoherent. I pack pillows around her, hoping she stays asleep. I grab for my boxers on the floor as I pad over to the door but not before making sure she's covered with the sheets.

"This had better be good to pull me from her," I demand after I softly close the bedroom door.

"Lucky's was robbed." Carson stands feet apart, hands behind his back. He was a soldier for eight years before calling it quits. Civilian life was hard for him to adapt to when he came home. He'd been homeless for six months when we met. I knew the moment I saw him that he'd make a good right-hand man to have my six. He's a no-nonsense type of guy and gets shit done when asked. He's loyal to me, and that is rare to find. He reminds me a lot of my best friend, Cassio, back home.

"What the fuck? How the hell did that happen?" I whisper-yell in disbelief as I pace away from the door so I don't wake Gemma. We have the perfect security in place to prevent robberies.

"My guess is that it's someone from the inside giving out our system details and working together with the other guy." He pauses and retrieves his phone. "Colin Benson is the guy who came in and was apprehended twenty minutes ago. We have him at the warehouse."

"Anyone hurt?" I ask. Having underground casinos has its risks, but one thing you don't want to happen is for your customers to get hurt. They bring in the cash and gamble it away. People get a little skittish if they feel unsafe at your establishment, and then there goes your money train.

Carson shakes his head. "Barged in waving a gun when a customer opened the door. Ms. Mabel was on duty and gave him the bag like we trained them to do in this situation."

That bag has a tiny tracker embedded in the lining. One thing Gio taught me was to always be ten steps ahead of everyone. Always think like a criminal in every situation so that you'll be prepared when it happens.

"I'll be down in ten minutes. Make sure the property is secure while I dress. Lock this place down until we get back and turn on the motion sensors. I want to be alerted if she gets up."

Thirty-five minutes later, we walk into the warehouse that holds all my gaming supplies. We have extra slot machines lined up along with poker tables and chairs that outfit the open space. Toward the back, I have several offices, and one in particular is soundproof for this very reason. It also has a drain in the center of the floor.

James stands in front of the door, making sure no one enters or exits. I give a nod, and he steps aside to let me in. The middle of the room holds a metal chair with Colin Benson, I presume, tied up and bleeding out of his gagged mouth.

"Mr. Benson," I start and hang my suit jacket on the hook by the door. I start to roll up my sleeves. "I hear you had an eventful night."

His head shakes from right to left, avoiding eye contact.

"Let's start here, shall we?" I pull the gag out and watch a string of blood ooze from his mouth. "I'm going to make this easy for you and save us all some wasted time." I grab his chin and force his eyes to meet mine. "Who helped you pull off your heist at my casino?"

"Please, I'm sorry. The money was returned, all of it. Please let me go—you'll never see me again, I swear," he pleads, but that doesn't answer my question. I'm dog-tired after the sexcapade Gemma and I just experienced and want to get back to bed with her for a few more hours.

"Tell me, and I'll have mercy." I grip him tighter as he struggles to be free of my bone-crushing hold. "Last chance."

He doesn't budge but continues to plead for his release. I nod over to Carson, who slides a table on the left side of his body.

"Mr. Benson, I have given you two chances to come clean with the accomplice, and you have not been forthcoming. I see that we must go a different route than I was hoping for."

Carson cuts his rope releasing his hand and stabilizes it on the wooden table at his side. James hands me my sharpened machete as all the color drains from Colin Benson.

"Okay, okay I'll tell—"

I don't even let him finish the sentence before I swiftly swing down the machete onto the table, severing half of his hand leaving his ring and pinky finger intact. Colin doesn't react at first, but when the pain finally registers, he wails. The screaming is almost unbearable, and I contemplate cutting his throat to shut him up, but I don't. I need to set a precedent for those who cross me. Word will soon get out about the man who tried to rob me and how I cut off the thief's hand, though the person who works for me and has been giving my secrets out will not meet the same fate. That traitor will be placed in a hole somewhere in the ground, never to be heard from again.

"Tell me the name, and I won't cut off your other hand, Mr. Benson" I bend down to his level.

"Doug…Doug," he blubbers.

I hand the machete back to James and wait for this pansy to calm the fuck down.

"Have Doc come by and treat the wound," I instruct James, then turn back to Colin. "I'm letting you go, but if you ever come within one hundred feet of my establishments again I'll kill your whole family while you watch, and then I'll torture you until you beg for death. Are we clear?" He jerks his head in a nod as I roll my sleeves down. It's then that I notice a spray of blood on the arm of my shirt.

I turn to Carson as I take my jacket from the hook.

"Take care of Doug, and make sure to dig deep."

"Yes, boss," Carson responds as we make our way back to the car.

We drive back home in silence as the early morning sun begins to crest. I check the monitors to see if Gemma is safe and still asleep.

"Anything else before you retire, sir?"

I shake my head as we walk through the house quietly.

"Make sure there aren't any loose ends with Doug."

"Yes, sir."

We separate in opposite directions as I make my way up the stairs and Carson heads out to the guesthouse in the back to start his search for Doug.

Quietly, I open the bedroom door and darkness meets me. Gemma hasn't moved a muscle from where I left her, and it makes me smile. *Good girl.* I lightly pad over to the shower, making sure to close the bathroom door before I turn on the water. I wash off the last hour to make sure nothing filthy will ever touch her, and once I'm satisfied everything is off, I towel dry and make my way back to bed.

Carefully, I remove the pillows and place myself under her, moving so she is back in the position where we were. My eyes are heavy, and it doesn't take long before she places her cold feet back between my warm thighs. It's weird, but that little thing makes me smile as I drift off to sleep.

CHAPTER ELEVEN

Luca

TODAY IS THE DAY GEMMA MAKES HER GRAND WALK across the stage, graduating college, and it couldn't have come fast enough. She's been working so hard to finish these last six weeks, and I couldn't be prouder. I have the biggest surprise tonight after I take her to her favorite restaurant. I feel like most of the parents here undoubtedly do, and the excitement has my knees bouncing, waiting for the ceremony to start. Gemma finished top in her class with a 4.0 GPA and a Bachelor of Science in Childhood Education with a minor in History. Over the last six weeks, I truly saw how dedicated she was to her studies and that she's going to be the perfect teacher. She's patient and kind and really cares about the kids. I can easily see her being the best mother to our brood of babies.

Last weekend, she took her state-mandated certification test to become a teacher, and I know she aced it. When she wasn't studying for her finals, she had her head in the books to pass that exam. I'm glad she's already done and finished because I've got a jam-packed summer lined up for her. Most of it involves her naked, but the rest is living the dream after my little surprise.

The ceremony gets under way with some asshole speaker

who drones about saving the earth. He's a rich prick who probably hasn't ever had to deal with missing a meal or wearing clothes that came from a second-hand store, where these poor college kids worked three jobs just to attend. After his soapbox speech on helping third-world countries, they finally start the procession of calling names to collect their diplomas. When the announcer gets to the letter B, my heart starts to pick up with excitement. I wish we had a little more time and that she'd been called with the letter F group, for Falcone—or rather Fontana.

I only finished high school because Ma would've tanned my hide if I didn't graduate. If I'd had it my way, I'd have dropped out freshman or sophomore year to start working for Pop full-time. Ma went all out with the celebration for my graduation though, inviting everyone she'd ever met to the party. Pop stayed for most of it but snuck off to do business when Ma was occupied.

"Gemma Barone," the announcer calls out, and I'm up on my feet clapping and yelling with excitement. She must not have been expecting it, because when her head turns to where the cheering is coming from, she stumbles across the stage. Thankfully, one of the staff members reaches out and grabs her by the elbow. Gemma barely catches her hat before reaching the dean for a handshake and picture. Her smile is as bright as her future, and the pink on her cheeks shows her embarrassment from the falter. Once off the stage, she returns with the other students and takes her place in her designated seat until every student's name has been called.

When the ceremony is over, trying to find her is like searching for a needle in a haystack. All the students are in their caps and gowns flooding out of the packed auditorium.

"Gemma!" I yell when I finally see her looking around into the sea of people. She hears me, and we manage our way through the crowd toward each other. "Congrats, amore mio!" I exclaim, handing her pink roses.

"Thank you." She gives a toothy smile and holds them up to

her nose. "Did you see me almost fall off the stage? I was so embarrassed." She facepalms with her free hand.

"You did great." I skim over the elephant in the room. "Did you want to hang out here for a bit or head over to the restaurant?" I check my watch and see that we've got time before our reservations.

She looks around at the people all huddled with their families, and I see her eyes sadden. I know today was a big day to share with family, just like her high school graduation, but at least I'm here with her. She tucks a lock of hair behind her ear, and it reveals the large diamond studded earrings I gave her this morning as a graduation present. Gemma knocked me over, surprised that I'd give her a gift like this. Everything I give her is met with gratitude and glee. She makes giving her things easy, and she really does appreciate even the smallest gestures—like her favorite Oreo cookie shake from the Shake Boutique down the street.

If she only knew what was in store for her in the next few days.

Wanting to turn those sad eyes happy, I decide to give her another present that I was waiting to give her over our meal, but first, I need to make this the best experience for her. Something she'll remember for the rest of her life.

"Excuse me," I grab a man walking by, "would you mind taking our picture?"

I've hired a company to photograph and capture her graduation and the big surprise I've got planned for her today. I've made it clear to make everything seem natural and not planned out. I want these photos and videos to be as organic as possible.

"Of course," he replies, taking my phone.

We take several pictures, and the photographer even encourages us to take one kissing. Gemma seems to brighten up, and those sad eyes are a thing of the past. I take that as my cue.

"Gemma Barone, you came into my life when I least expected it. I wasn't looking for love, but the moment it found me, there wasn't a single thing I could do but follow my heart. You have changed me in ways I never thought were possible. My life was dull until you came stumbling into it." Her eyes fill with tears, but I push through. "I know that this might seem sudden to you, but it feels like I've waited years to have this moment, right here. I love you more than you'll ever know, and the depth of that love could never be described in words. When I think about forever, I picture you."

I take a knee in front of her as the hired company has made sure to give us some space. A crowd has formed, and the moment I drop down gasps can be heard, but my focus is on the only person in this world that matters.

"Will you do me the honor of spending the rest of your life with me? Will you please make me the happiest man on this earth and marry me?"

Her hand now covers her mouth and her eyes have widened like saucers. Tears are spilling down her cheeks, and I can only hope she doesn't pass out before I get an answer.

We've spent every waking hour together, and she's stayed with me every night since we got back from Spring Break. Well, except for one night. It was the worst night of my life. We had our first fight, and she decided to stay at her dorm. I say 'fight' but really it was me being an asshole. I'd had one hell of a day at one of the casinos, and I snapped at her when she tripped on the hallway rug.

I walk into the house from the garage after sending Carson to deal with Mitch over at the police department. Today was a total cluster-fuck and would have landed my ass in jail if Mitch, our-on-payroll-cop didn't step in and call off the new kid fresh out of the academy looking to make a name for himself.

It smells delicious in the kitchen, and I wish I'd been here to eat it fresh when Gemma made it hours ago. I don't usually have late nights because I like to be home with her, but on the occasional nights I am late, she leaves me a plate in the microwave or warmer by the stove.

I pace down the hallway toward our offices knowing she'll be study-ing for a test she has tomorrow. I see her look up as my shoes tap against the marble flooring. She doesn't hesitate to get up from her chair and race to greet me.

Just as she gets to the hallway her foot catches on the rug, and she lurches forward but instead of going straight down, she tries to catch herself on the side table. Her hands don't find purchase, and they knock over the flower vase, shattering it into a million pieces. My legs don't get there in time, and she goes down on top of the shards.

My frustrations are already at an all-time high, and I explode, worried she hurt herself over something as inconsequential as greeting me.

"What the fuck, Gemma?!" I raise my voice more in a panic than reprimanding. "Don't you watch where you're going?" I haul her off the ground to set her on the table and check her over.

The moment the words leave my mouth, I regret them. The tone was so unnecessarily harsh that she flinched.

"I'm sorry," she whispers, trying to wipe the glass from her legs. Thankfully, there isn't a scratch on her, but I'm sure a nice little bruise will pop up overnight. "I was just so happy to see you."

"You've got to be more careful," I say as I continue to scan her from head to toe.

She maneuvers off the table and makes a wide berth around the wreckage and me as she moves up the stairs.

Not wanting her to catch a shard of glass in her foot, I go to the closet and retrieve the broom and dustpan to sweep up the broken pieces. By the time I finish and toss everything in the trash in the kitchen, Gemma is walking toward the garage. My mind is already grasping for anything I can do to make up for my outburst. She didn't deserve my wrath at all, and I need her to know that I was the one in the wrong.

"I forgot I need to go to the library for a book I'm missing for my assignment," she lies and my heart shatters like the broken vase. She wants to get away from me because I hurt her.

"Baby, it's late. Go in the morning before class starts," I suggest. Give me a chance to fix my fuck-up.

"I can't finish it until I have it." She's looking everywhere but me.

"I'm so sorry I yelled at you, baby. It was a wild day at the office, *and I never meant to lash out like that, especially not at you." I take a step toward her and notice she's got more than her backpack. What the fuck?!*

I can tell she's shut down and anything I say right now won't penetrate. So, I do the hardest thing and let her leave.

The garage door shuts, and the silence is deafening. I wish I could beat the shit out of myself.

My pop always left business at the door when he came home from work. He never involved my ma and made sure that no matter how stressed he was, she never knew he was having a bad day. Even though Pop lives a stressful life, he always says that coming home to Adele is the best part of his day. He told me once that when I finally found my wife, I needed to treat her like she was the most precious flower I'd ever find in this world. A flower that, if I didn't take care of and water, someone else would come in and do it better. Pop was all business, but when my ma called, he dropped everything to answer and find out what she needed or if she was okay.

That night, I sat in my car outside of her dorm.

The car was uncomfortable but sleeping in an empty bed without her would've been worse. I deserved the aching neck and back pain. It was my punishment for not treasuring her, for treating her poorly. She was my queen, *mia regina*, my everything, and if my pop had been there, he'd have smacked me across the back of the head for how I acted. Thankfully, I was able to make it right. I caught her the next morning as she left her dorm, heading to class.

I watch as she walks down the steps of her dorm and make my move. I'm still in the same clothes as the night before, but I don't care. She doesn't seem to have fared any better.

"I come bearing gifts, hoping you'll forgive this asshole for making the worst mistake of my life last night, speaking to you the way I did," I plead and offer her the coffee and bag of her favorite donuts.

She looks at me hesitantly. "Thanks," she says and lifts her hand to take the offerings.

"Can we sit down for a minute and talk?"

She nods and takes a sip of her coffee. Once seated, I launch into the story but instead of telling her about the illegal business, I use the insurance company inspection and how they tried to slap us with several violations. Gemma waits and listens to every lying word out of my mouth.

"Please forgive me. I promise to never take my frustrations out on you ever again," I vow. "I love you more than anything in this world, and the last thing I'd ever want to do is hurt you in any way. Please don't let this horrible lack of judgment take us backward." She seems a little skittish, so I continue, hoping she'll hear the sincerity in my voice and words. "Can we meet for lunch after your last class?"

Her pause feels like an eternity.

"Sure."

I learned a valuable lesson after that and knew that if I didn't separate my business from my home life, it would have a devastating outcome. One that I refuse to allow.

"That was so beautiful," she says with a shaky voice holding her palms to her cheeks.

"Will you?" I ask one more time, hoping she's about to say the one word that will change my life forever. I reach into my pocket and snap open the ring box that shows off her Harry Winston 5-carat oval-cut diamond ring. With thirty-six pear-shaped and round diamonds that make up bows on either side, the ring is one of a kind and has the rarest diamonds. I bought it less than a year after I moved here from Las Vegas. Of course, she doesn't need to know that.

She nods emphatically. "Yes, yes Luca. I'll marry you!" She beams, then throws her arms around my neck. There are cheers in the background, but all I can focus on is her. *She said yes.*

I waste no time sweeping her up and spinning her around.

"I love you," I say over and over as I pull her against my chest, kissing every inch of her face and not caring that we're in public.

"I love you too." She finally takes a look at the ring and looks as if she might pass out. "Oh my gosh, Luca, this is the most beautiful ring I've ever seen!"

"Only the best for you," I say as I place the ring on her left ring finger.

She looks in awe of it for a while. "Oh god, what if I lose it?" The panic in her voice has me laughing.

"Then I'll buy you a new one." It's as easy as that. I'll buy her the moon if she really wants it.

"It's so lovely, thank you." Her mouth captures mine, and I feel like I'm flying. Thank God Carson is here in the crowd, making sure we have some space as the professionals film the event.

Once we've both had a chance to come down from the high of our engagement, we take a million more photos all over the beautiful campus, then gather ourselves and head out to her favorite steakhouse. I introduced her to *Flemings* after we got back from spring break. Traffic is a nightmare with all the extra people here for graduation, but I can't complain because I've got my fiancée sitting next to me in my SS Chevelle, holding my hand. She is everything I've ever wanted, and seeing how happy she was to agree to marry me only confirms that she was meant to be mine. She hasn't stopped smiling and I find myself doing the same. This is what true happiness feels like, and I can't wait to see what the future is going to bring.

The parking is horrible at the restaurant, but we get lucky and find two vehicles pulling out at the same time. Once both have exited the small lot, I carefully pull my classic car into one of the empty spots, mindful not to get close enough for someone to ding the sides. Normally, I'd prefer a valet, but there isn't one around here tonight.

Just as I turn off the engine some lame-ass loser comes barreling in the parking lot and carelessly pulls into the empty spot next to us. Gemma leans her head out the window and looks down.

"He's on the line," she whispers, thinking the douche can hear her. She knows how much I love this car and that I only bring it out on special occasions.

I can feel my blood pressure starting to rise because I can see some kid in the car talking a little too loud on the phone and not paying attention.

Just breathe. Maybe he'll surprise me and not be careless about opening his door.

"Should I crawl over the console to get out?" Gemma asks as I mean-mug the fucker, hoping for the best.

I shake my head. No way am I going to make her climb over in her short dress. She's in a heavily beaded, crystal keyhole, sapphire cocktail dress that I bought her. I wanted something that matched her eyes, and it hit the mark. She's in silver heels and looks like she should be a model. *My model.*

"Stay put, baby girl. I got this." I give her a wink to reassure her.

Just as I open my door to step out, I hear the *bang* of a car door smacking into another door. It's enough to jolt the Chevelle a little, and I find my fingers pulling into fists. As I round the back of my car, a real-life Ken doll stands at the back of his car straightening a sweater on his shoulders. He looks ridiculous in boat shoes and short khaki shorts. Another dipshit steps out of the passenger door looking equally ridiculous.

I try not to lose my cool in front of Gemma. We just had the most amazing experience, and this pissant is not going to ruin our bubble. *Not tonight.*

"You parked a little close, don't you think?" I clench my teeth, waiting to see how this dickhead is going to respond. He looks at me as if I should be the one who takes care of his dry cleaning. "You hit my car with your door," I clarify.

He looks me up and down as if I'm beneath him. *If he only knew.* Then he looks at my car. I can tell that *Daddy* probably funds everything in his miserable little life.

He leans over and pats me on my shoulder. "Don't worry, mine's more expensive than that antique." He laughs as he and his friend walk past me toward the restaurant.

Big mistake, asshole.

I watch the prick prance off and take a step in his direction, but the sound of a car door opening stops me.

"Is everything okay?" I hear Gemma ask, but she waits to get out.

My eyes close, and I take another deep breath to loosen my muscles as I make my way over to her.

"Everything is fine, babe." I hold the door open and give her my hand so she can gracefully exit the car without popping the shithead's door.

We make our way into *Flemings* and tell the hostess our name. My mind keeps reeling back to the loser. I've never been one to let something go, and even now I've having a hard time letting the asshole get away with disrespecting me and what is mine.

The hostess walks us back to the private table I reserved, but I pause when I see the two assholes laughing at a table with other idiots dressed the same as them. Must be having a convention tonight.

I just can't let this slide.

"Baby," I place a gentle hand on Gemma's arm, stopping her and the hostess. "I forgot my phone in the car. Go ahead to the table, and I'll be there shortly. Order me water with lemon." I kiss her cheek like I always do. One thing I've learned when I'm in public is to show these other fuckers that she is mine. Short of pissing on her, it's the best way to stake my claim.

She nods, not even skipping a beat, and follows the hostess to the back of the restaurant. I love that she is naïve, without a care in the world. I know I'm going to have to teach her to be more careful, but for now, she still needs to feel like the world is a safe place.

I turn on my heels and glance back over at the table of tools, and I can't help the smirk that forms on my face. I'd never cause a scene with Gemma here, but I can do other things that will be just has effective at getting my point across. Once I'm out in the parking lot,

I check the damage the prick did to the door. The paint is scraped off where his door hit it, and there is definitely a dent. *Asshat.* One thing I love is making sure my cars are taken care of. Especially this collector. I take pride in making sure my hard-earned dollars don't go to waste, and I appreciate the things I spend my money on.

I check out the piece of shit car next to me. An Audi. Not caring if someone sees I haul my foot back and kick the side of the driver's door. As I expected, it caves easily. The sun is setting, and the lighting out here isn't the best, which means he won't likely notice it until tomorrow. Sucker. Maybe next time, he'll be a little bit more careful where he parks. As I start to walk back in, I round the back of his car, still pondering him putting his hands on my shoulder, and decide to even out the massive dent by making the other side match. With another swift kick, the passenger door crinkles and caves in just like the driver's door.

If my best friend, Cassio, were here, we'd already have the car jacked up and all the wheels off, with a pound of sugar in the gas tank. We were some mean motherfuckers back in our teenage years.

The smirk from earlier can't hold a candle to the smile on my face as I walk back into the restaurant and look over at the asshat's table. His eyes meet mine in passing, and I give him a nod and keep walking. He's lucky that's all he's getting out of this.

As I reach the table, I notice a guy hanging out next to Gemma talking to her and catch the tail end of the conversation.

"What are your plans now that you've graduated? A last hurrah summer, sewing your wild oats before entering into the real world?"

Gemma is looking over the menu and occasionally looking up at him, not showing any interest at all. Can't he see the rock on her hand? Everyone can see it sparkle from the lighting in here.

She must sense me because when she looks up and sees me approaching, her eyes flash with excitement, completely ignoring this guy.

"Leave," I calmly say, but there is an undertone to my voice as I take a seat next to her instead of across. My nose nuzzles her neck, and I plant a soft caressing kiss there. "Can't leave you alone five minutes without someone trying to take you from me."

She giggles and scrunches her nose like it's the most ludicrous thing she's ever heard.

"Did you find your phone?" She ignores my comment and plants a quick kiss on my lips.

I pat my jacket pocket, where it's been the entire time, then wrap my right arm around her shoulder, pulling her close to my side.

When it arrives, I feed her some of my meal as she starts to tell me how she ran into Jill before the ceremony began, so they didn't get to talk exceedingly long. I'm surprised the bitch had enough brain cells to graduate college.

"How was she?" I ask, not really caring.

"Fine, I guess. She asked if I was stilling seeing you, and when I told her that I was, she got all weird and cut the conversation short."

"That's strange."

"I know, right?"

I change the subject, wanting to move past that inconsiderate wench.

"Have you thought about where you'd like to teach now that you've graduated?"

She turns her body toward me and I almost place her legs over mine, but I'd hate for some joker to get a look up her dress. Her smile is so bright when she talks about her teaching career.

"Well, Professor Smith sent me several schools to apply to, but I haven't had the time to look them over."

"You could always stay home if you wanted to. I make more than enough to support us," I add, wanting to give her options. I'd love nothing more than knowing I provide for her, but I know this is one battle I'll never win. She has so much to offer kids, and I'd be putting her in a cage if she didn't teach for a living.

"Luca, we've talked about this. I want—no I need to help kids." She takes my hand, and it's like all the tension leaves my body when she touches me. "At least until we start our own family, I'd love to focus on my career. You understand, right?"

I do.

"So, once I plant my child in you, you'll quit," I state. I can't help the thump in my chest when I think of her carrying my child.

"I'd like to be a fulltime mom and maybe even homeschool when they're older, depending on how many we have. My mom stayed home with me, and I loved having her there at all my recitals and school field trips."

She just opened Pandora's box, because I plan on having her pregnant until we're fifty if she's open to it.

"I'm ready to start tonight," I joke but in reality, I've been trying to impregnate her since I broke her hymen almost two months ago.

She laughs. "I'd like to wait for at least one to two years after we're married, silly." She tosses her napkin at me. "Don't you want to enjoy the honeymoon stage of marriage before kids are in the mix?"

"Baby, I'd love for you to be pregnant right now with my kid." I place my large hand over her stomach.

Her eyes go to where my hand is, and I see them soften. I know without a doubt I could convince her to have babies sooner, but I'd never want her to regret having them too soon. She deserves to have everything in this world, and if I have to wait, then that's what I'll do.

"We haven't even talked about a wedding date! That would be crazy and the nuns at my old school would reprimand me good if I had a baby out of wedlock," she admonishes. I'd like to see them try and reprimand her. They'd be meeting their makers a lot sooner.

"Let's talk about the date another day. Tonight, let's enjoy our engagement and the surprises I have in store for you." I hold up my glass, and she follows suit. "To Gemma on an amazing accomplishment. And to our future—may we always focus on it and never look back."

We clink our crystal glasses and drink to us.

After our meal, on the drive away from the restaurant, we head in the opposite direction of our house. It takes her a while, but once we pull up to the private entrance of the airport, she starts to question.

"What are we doing here? Do you need to pick a client up?"

We pull through, and I park inside a bay that stores a jetliner.

"This is the next part of your gift and engagement surprise," I say and help her out of the car.

"But I don't have any clothes. Surely, I needed to pack an overnight bag or something."

"It's all been taken care of. Here," I help her up the steps and into the luxury jet. It has a bedroom in the back, along with a comfortable sofa and six leather chairs to relax in.

"This is crazy. Where are we going?"

"I'll tell you where, but I'm not telling you any more than that. All events are sealed tight." I make a zipping motion over my lips that earns me a giggle.

"Yes, okay! Tell me, please!"

"Hawaii."

CHAPTER TWELVE

Gemma

I WAKE TO THE SOUND OF WAVES CRASHING AS I STRETCH OUT my muscles. Light catches my ring, making it sparkle. I can't help the smile on my face. Luca is wrapped around me like a vine, as though I might sneak away during the night.

Luca and I got in yesterday evening and came straight to the quiet rental house we'll be calling home for the duration of our stay. He's being very evasive about our stay here and not budging on details.

The last two months have been a whirlwind. I met Luca during spring break, and we have been inseparable ever since. He's been so great and helpful with my last few weeks of college. He's so attentive to my needs that it's hard to take sometimes because for so long I've had to manage and navigate this world all on my own. He loves to take care of me, and I love that too. I can't even believe I'm so lucky to have met him. He truly is my rock.

As if knowing I'm awake, Luca stirs beside me. He nuzzles his nose in my neck and breathes me in.

"Too early. Sleep, beautiful," he murmurs as his grip on me tightens.

I can't help the flutters in my belly. I love this man with all my heart. I know some might think it's too soon for us to be moving this quickly, but Dr. Collins says to go with my heart and gut. She believes Luca coming into my life has been a game-changer. I'm more alive, as she likes to say. I think back to our session when I returned from Malibu and smile.

I'm sitting on Dr. Collins' sofa, my legs stretched out on the comfy cushions with my back against a pillow and armrest.

"That smile tells me spring break was good." She looks over her black-framed glasses that have little diamonds on the tips.

I'm not even sure where to start.

"It was amazing," I gush. "I met someone like you encouraged me to."

"That's great, Gemma. Tell me all about it, and don't leave anything out." She picks up her glass of water.

"Luca is everything. We had sex after I almost died," I muse and hug my favorite pillow Dr. Collins has.

Water bursts out of her mouth as she coughs and bangs her hand on her chest.

"What? What do you mean you had sex and almost died?" Her chest is heaving as she tries to control her tone. "Please tell me that you were very careful. Gemma, when I said that I wanted you to branch out and put yourself out there to meet someone new, I wasn't encouraging you to have a sex-fest. Please tell me you didn't take it that way."

I smile again, thinking about how Luca and I met and the glorious week we had together. And still are having.

"I noticed him by the pool on Saturday. He was working on his laptop, so dreamy." I can't help but swoon when I talk about him. "We met that night in person when he bought our dinner. I went over to thank him, and we talked for hours. We met up the next morning to snorkel and eat. Just getting to know each other. He's older, very sexy, and mature. Owns his own company and has tattoos that cover his body, although when he's in a dress shirt, you'd never notice it."

"That sounds wonderful. What made you open up to a stranger?

You haven't had an open conversation with your roommate that you've known for three months, but you spoke for hours with a man you just met?"

"It's hard to describe. When we talked at the bar, it was like we'd known each other for years. Almost like we almost grew up together."

"You mentioned he was older," Dr. Collins encourages.

"He's twenty-nine."

"That's quite a bit of difference in age between the two of you, don't you think?"

"He…" How can I tell her what spending time with Luca feels like? "I feel safe with him," I manage to whisper and hug the pillow tighter.

"I just want you to be careful. That is all I'm saying, dear. Some guys in this world prey on young, vulnerable girls, and I don't want you to be taken advantage of."

I nod. I know I have abandonment issues, but I hope my judgment won't lead me astray.

"He lives here in San Diego too. We've been seeing each other every day," I add.

"Well, that makes it easy to get to know each other, doesn't it? Tell me how you almost died, then had sex with this sexy mysterious man."

I tell her every little detail.

Since I'm her last appointment for the day, we extend our session. Dr. Collins is the most amazing person I've ever met, besides the nuns from my high school. She's in her mid-fifties and listens, then gives me her advice which I'm pretty sure she'd give to her children if she had any. She and her husband, Michael, couldn't conceive, so I feel like her advice is what she'd want for her own kids. She's become like a second mother to me.

"If things progress and start to take a serious turn, I'd like you to bring him into a session. I say this with not only a professional purpose but also a personal one. People come in and out of our lives for a reason, and we usually aren't sure why until much later. I'd like to get a feel if you'd let me and make sure things are as pure as this man is expressing

to you. I'm not saying that you need my approval, but I'd just like to see and speak to this man who has come into your life so quickly."

"I'll ask him when the time comes. You'll love him, I know it!" I pause before recalling my other news. "Oh, Jill moved out of the dorm."

"When did this happen? Did something happen over the trip to Malibu last week?"

I tell her all about Jill and how she left me, and Luca was there to save the week and drive me home. We discuss the importance of not blaming myself for her leaving and agree that maybe it was for the best since I was having such a hard time letting her get to know the real me.

Dr. Collins and I meet twice a week for sessions, and I've started getting excited to attend each one. The homework she's given me since then is becoming easier, and I find myself actually wanting to complete it. She's met with Luca and me on several occasions and couldn't stop raving about him when we had our one-on-one sessions. She believes he's very sincere in his feelings toward me and that he doesn't seem to have any ulterior motives.

The time change has me wide awake, even with all the activity Luca had me doing before we passed out. Three rounds of celebratory sex on top of joining the mile-high club earlier had us both barely able to move.

The covers shift, and Luca's body heat moves from my torso.

"I guess I didn't wear you out enough then." Luca climbs down my naked body and positions himself between my thighs. His chin rests on my pelvic bone as he stares up at me.

"You make me the happiest man alive."

Some of the things that come out of his mouth, I swear, come from the romance novels I read. The love from another person I've longed for so many years has been filled to the brim since he came into my life. He leaves me speechless.

"I love you so much, Luca," I whisper as my emotions erupt.

Luca lifts his head slightly and swipes his tongue on my lower lips. He pulls them apart and starts to feast on me. My head falls back at the feel of his magical attack.

"Watch me," he commands.

One thing I've learned with him since we've been together is that he likes to be in control, especially in the bedroom. He takes charge, telling me what to do once our clothes are off, and I love it. I want someone to take the reins for a change after having to make all the decisions for so long. Dr. Collins says as long as I'm comfortable with it, then nothing is wrong with that. If I have an issue, I just need to communicate that to Luca and let him know to ease up. Communicating is key. I probably communicate more than I'm supposed to, but he always says it's better than him wondering what's on my mind.

My head pops back up when he stops his assault, waiting for me to do as he says. There is nothing sexier than my man bossing me around. Once our eyes connect, he dips his head and starts to swirl his tongue on my clit. The sensation vibrates through me, and my knees box his head. A finger is inserted then another. It doesn't take long before my legs start to shake, and I know I'm about to come.

"Oh Luca," I moan as he sucks then lightly nibbles on my clit. It isn't long before wave after wave of pleasure shivers through me.

Before I have time to recover, Luca impales me with his dick. He says he loves to feel my pussy quivering against his cock.

"You. Are. So. Gorgeous. When. You. Come." He pistons his hips against me bringing my legs up to his shoulders. I love it when he's rough like this, but I love it when he makes sweet love to me too.

A light sheen of sweat starts to form on my body as it moves into overdrive at the pace he takes. I can't even believe he's able to have sex this many times in just a few hours.

"Luca, please," I begin to beg.

"I got you, baby girl." He spreads my legs wide going deeper and bottoming out at my womb. His hand comes up to my clit as his thumb circles it.

"Play with your tits."

I pluck at my nipples which quickly become overly sensitive. My eyes close as a tingle moves through my body. Luca applies more pressure to my clit, then smacks it. My body explodes into a million pieces, and I drift off. I feel him really start to thrust into me, and it isn't long before his body convulses above me. Short sharp thrusts follow as he fills me with his cum. When he's empty, his body slumps over mine, and our foreheads touch.

"I love you," he tells me, then gives me the sweetest kiss. This is something he always does after we finish having sex. He makes sure that I know he loves me.

"I love you more," I admit after he removes his lips from mine.

"Not possible."

Slowly, he eases out of me, then lies on his back, pulling me up on his chest. His wet dick smears our combined fluids on our bodies.

The sound of the ocean almost lulls me to sleep again.

"What are we doing today?" I ask as I feel my eyes growing heavy.

There's silence, and I think Luca might have fallen back asleep.

"We have a few appointments today at some shops to find you the perfect outfit for tomorrow's event."

Shopping?

"Event? Do you have a work thing while we're here?"

"No work. I'm all yours while we're here."

"Then what are we attending?"

"A wedding."

"Oh, that sounds like fun."

I've always wanted to have a beach wedding. I hope when Luca and I discuss our wedding that it's one of our options.

"Oh, it will be. You are going to love it."

"Whose wedding is it?"

I wonder if it is his secretary at his office. I've been there a few times to meet up with him for a lunch date in between classes, but I haven't been able to formally meet all his employees. His office is

large, and I think he employs over ten people who sell life insurance, along with a few secretaries.

"Ours."

My head shoots up for a second, and my neck pops at the sudden movement. I'm pretty sure I heard him wrong. Our eyes lock,
and from his facial expression, I know he's being serious.

"Wait. What?" Confusion swims around my head, and I feel
like I'm having an out-of-body experience.

"The wedding tomorrow is ours."

"Ours," I test the word out. "As in you and me?" I shake my
finger between us.

He nods but stays quiet.

"I don't understand. What do you mean?" This could be one
of my crazy dreams I have, and I'll wake soon only to laugh at all
this. "We've been engaged for less than a day."

He rolls us over so I'm on my back. He hooks his leg over both
of mine, securing me in place.

"I mean that tomorrow at sunset, we will exchange vows and
become one. We will profess our love and commitment to each other
and seal our fate together."

"But…but how?" My eyes bounce back and forth between his.
"We haven't planned a wedding. How can we have one without
going over the details? I mean, we just got engaged twelve hours ago."

"Everything will be exactly how you want it, trust me."

"This is crazy," I whisper and stare at the ceiling above his head.

"I don't want to wait anymore for our life as husband and wife
to begin. When you said yes yesterday, I wanted to scoop you up
and fly to Vegas that very moment. We are in the most beautiful
place, and I'd like for this to be where we start our journey. A place
we both love and will never forget."

"You don't think it's too soon though?"

"Baby, the moment I saw you, I knew you were going to mean
the world to me. But if I'd told you all this after almost killing you
with shellfish, you'd have gotten a restraining order against me.

That's how much I wanted you. You are it for me. For this life and the next."

His words hit deep in my soul. I know there isn't another person out there that I'd want to spend the rest of my life with, so why not jump on this and grab it with both hands? I mean, we said we loved each other after only spending a week together. Every day I fall more and more in love with him. He's proven over and over how much he loves me and wants to put me first before anyone and everyone else. I never feel as safe as I do with this man.

"Okay," I cede after mulling it over.

"Okay? As in—yes, we marry tomorrow."

"Let's do it! Let's get married here on the beach." I let out a squeal as he rolls us so that he's on top of me.

"You will never know how happy you've made me. The life I had before you was torture, hell on earth until you walked into it. I love you and will until my last breath."

This man.

"I love you too, Luca."

He kisses me until I'm breathless, then turns toward the clock on the bedside table.

"Good. We have enough time to celebrate," he says and plunges into my wet core.

"Oh, my dear girl, that one looks amazing on you," Dr. Collins gushes with tears in her words.

Luca has a driver take me to several places to find the right wedding dress. A sadness washes over me when I realize that I have to do it by myself and not with anyone, but of course, Luca is always thinking ahead, and as I walked through the upscale bridal store my phone rang with Dr. Collins on the other end to FaceTime me. We talk for a bit, and I fill her in on the past day. She was over the moon when she heard that Luca proposed but was a little shocked that we're getting married tomorrow. At the end, she told me I should go with my heart and gut, and if it felt right, then jump in with both feet.

I'm trying on my third dress, and I think I've found the one! It has a sheer bodice layered with flourishing laces and shimmering sequins. The V-neckline and shoestring straps highlight my neck and shoulders. The shimmering tulle radiates throughout the full, modern-cut ballgown skirt. The open back is to die for and I think Luca is going to love it. It's perfect.

My eyes water as the owner's assistant holds up the phone so Dr. Collins can get the full effect.

"I love it," I say to my therapist and reflection.

"Then get it. If you feel this is the one you've dreamed about for your wedding then get it. You can try on a million and one dresses, but if you know in your heart this is it, then stop right here and embrace your decision," she says with determination.

I nod, not trusting my voice. I think back to my mother and wish she could be here.

"Angela, please walk over and hug my beautiful girl," I hear Dr. Collins say.

Angela does as she's asked and embraces me in what can only be described as a motherly hug. I let out a sob, and Dr. Collins does too. She's trying to speak, but her tears are making it difficult to understand. We hold the hug for a full minute before I finally release Angela, who is my stand-in for Dr. Collins.

"You are going to make the most beautiful bride I've ever seen, my dear."

"Thank you," I say and wipe my eyes and cheeks with the tissue Angela hands me. "I wish you were here."

"Me too, dear. Make sure to have pictures taken so that you will be able to look back on this happy time."

"Luca is in charge of that part."

"I'm sure he's going to make this the best day of your life."

Once we hang up, the seamstress comes in and makes some

minor adjustments that will be taken care of today, and my dress will be delivered in the morning to our rental house. We decided on the matching anklet that loops around my second toe. Trying to walk on sand in heels would be a nightmare. Plus, I want Luca to be barefoot also, with the bottom of his suit pants rolled up. The flowers have been picked out for the bouquet, and since our background is going to be an ocean, we really didn't need to have a tremendous amount for decoration.

When I get back to our rental house, I can't help but feel like this is all a dream. How can someone like me ever have something like this happen to her? Dr. Collins says I need to embrace what is happening and not always assume the other shoe is going to drop. Even if it does, she says I'm strong enough to handle that situation. I just need to trust myself.

"Have Carson handle the Red Room situation. I'm not going to be available for a while and he is the person you contact for now. If you don't like that, then find yourself another line of work," I hear Luca sneer out on the patio by the pool that faces the ocean.

Is he talking about the Carson that lives in the guesthouse on his property?

He hangs up, but his phone buzzes again almost immediately. "Yeah?" he answers annoyed and listens for a bit. "Tell that motherfucker that if he doesn't get a handle on things, Brett isn't going to be the only one who will need medical attention. Why is it that I can't go away and not have a shitstorm as soon as I leave?" I hear a voice speaking quickly before he's laying into them again. "I expect you to handle it on your side. I'll call you tomorrow for an update." He pauses again and lets the other person speak. "Fix it and start looking for someone else to take over that area. He obviously doesn't know how to deal with the crowd."

Luca hangs up and finally stops pacing. He's looking out toward the ocean with his back to me. I take this time to walk out and wrap my arms around him. He doesn't show any surprise, and I wonder if he knew I was there.

"Everything okay?" I ask, hoping to calm him down and not have this ruin our night and wedding tomorrow. "Do you need to leave and handle something back home?"

He tugs my arms so that my body is in front of him. The sun is almost set behind the ocean, and the last of the light is shining on him.

"There is nothing more important to me than marrying you tomorrow. Wild horses couldn't keep me away." He kisses my nose and then feathers his lips over mine. "I'll always have work issues, baby, but that's the price I pay for owning my own business."

"I would understand if you needed to, though. I get it."

He smirks. "You're not getting cold feet on me, are you, baby girl?"

"You always say I have cold feet when we snuggle in bed," I counter.

We both laugh at the true statement. For some reason, my feet are always cold at night, and Luca makes a big production about it when he lets me burrow them between his thighs.

"Did you find your dress?" Luca inquires as he pulls me down on a lounge chair to watch the last of the sunset. I'm between his legs, resting against his chest. His chin is on my shoulder, and I can feel his five o'clock shadow on my cheek.

"I did."

"What does it look like?"

"I'm not telling. It's bad luck to know."

He nuzzles his nose in my neck and starts to lavish my tender skin with kisses. "Baby, we make our own luck."

I've got goose bumps as he continues, but I'm not giving in on this. I want it to be a surprise. "Not this time," I moan out. How does this man know how to play me like a fiddle? "I want to see your face when I walk down the aisle to you tomorrow," I plead as I find my resolve lowering.

"I'll grant you this one thing, but I can't promise not to tear it from your body when we're alone."

That makes me dodge his next assault on my neck. "You'd better not, Luca! I want to pass that dress down to my daughter when she finds her prince," I argue and turn to face him.

He must see my determination in my eyes because he quickly reaches for me again to settle me back into his hold. "Fine, but it better be easy to take off and not with a million buttons," he whines, and it earns a laugh from me. I love it when he pouts.

A yawn escapes me. "I think you need to hit the hay to get some rest. I can't have my bride falling asleep on me at the altar."

"The last few days have caught up to me," I answer as he pulls me up from the chair.

"I want you to be well-rested for tomorrow. I've booked you at a spa for most of the day to relax."

I pull on his arm to make him stop before we enter the house.

"I love that you always think of me and have little surprises for me all the time. I've never had someone put me first, and it makes me feel so special." My emotions start to erupt.

He pulls me into a bear hug and kisses the top of my head. "I'll do anything to keep that smile on our face. My life's goal is to make sure your needs are met."

"What did I ever do to deserve a man like you?"

"It's me that doesn't deserve you."

He ends the conversation by kissing me and leading me to the bedroom. We spend the next hour proving what we mean to each other before we fall asleep.

The next morning is bustling with activity. Luca leaves to handle the marriage license that he applied for yesterday and is ready to be picked up for the minister. He also said that he has a few last-minute stops to make and will see me at the end of the aisle this evening.

The same driver from yesterday is waiting to take me to the spa after I finish up my breakfast and dress for the relaxing day. The moment I walk into the spa at the Four Seasons Hotel, I swear my eyes are playing tricks. There, standing by the check-in counter, is Dr. Collins.

"Oh my gosh!" I scream as I run into her waiting arms. "What are you doing here?" I squeeze her tight, so thankful she's here to share this with me.

"Well, I told Michael that I couldn't sit around the house knowing my dear girl was getting married today without me there. I know this is crossing a line with the doctor-patient relationship, but I think we crossed that a long time ago. I hope it's okay for me to be here."

"Of course, it is! I was wishing you were here yesterday when we spoke. How did you get here so fast?"

"Luca called me late yesterday and invited us to come and be your witnesses for the wedding. He flew us out on a redeye private jet."

I can't believe he did that.

"I'm so glad you made it. Thank you, thank you." I hug her again as our names are called.

"Shall we?"

"Yes!"

We spend the next several hours being pampered from head to toe. Facials, massages, manicures, and pedicures. They show us private showers to rinse off the oils and get ready for hair and makeup before we are shown to the bridal suite to get ready. The dress was delivered here instead of the house, thank goodness. A photographer has shown up and started taking photos so that we'll have the entire day recorded for our wedding album.

The moment I step into my wedding dress, the room halts. Not a sound is made except for the clicking of the camera. I can't believe the woman staring back in the mirror is me. My hair is pinned to the side with curls hanging down the front. I've got a few small flowers in my hair by my neck that almost match the embroidery of my dress.

"You look gorgeous," Dr. Collins whispers as she takes me in. "This dress was made for you."

The attendants from the hotel all say the same as they make sure to fluff out the ends of the dress.

The door to the bridal suite opens, and a woman peeks her head in. "Ten minutes and the limo will be here," she announces. "My god, you look absolutely beautiful."

"Thank you." I turn back around and give myself one last look.

"One more thing before you leave," Dr. Collins says and comes over with a shopping bag.

She lifts a black velvet box from inside and presents it to me.

"Luca wanted me to give you this to wear." She opens it, and my knees buckle.

The jewelry box opens to a cushion-cut Brazilian Paraiba tourmaline center stone necklace with more than 200 brilliant, round emerald, square-cut, and pear-shaped diamonds. I can't even believe I'm holding something like this.

"It's so pretty." I'm too distracted by the necklace to see her pull another velvet box out for the matching earrings and cuff bracelet.

"He wanted you to have the best and said they matched your eyes." She smiles and helps put them on me.

Once all the jewelry is in place, I take one last look in the mirror. The photographer is clicking away in the background, but all I can do is focus on how it completes my dress. The same woman who came in earlier peeks back in and tells us the limo has arrived. Slowly, the attendants make sure we have everything from the room and follow us out toward the lobby to the waiting limo.

Several people stop us to gush about my dress or snap pictures with their phones. I feel like a celebrity getting all this attention. Dr. Collins holds my hand the entire time. Right before we exit, a little girl comes running over, away from her parents, and stops in front of me.

"Are you a princess?" she asks boldly.

I smile down at her and bend to her level. "I feel like a princess because I get to marry my prince today."

Her mother comes running over to find her daughter.

"Mommy, look a real live princess!" The girl points at me.

"I see, isn't she beautiful?" Her mother picks her up and places her on her hip.

"What's your name?" the little girl asks, her eyes never leaving mine.

I can see Luca and I having a little girl someday and know our children will probably keep us on our toes as well.

"I'm Gemma. What is your name?"

"Just like my favorite doll," she whispers as if it were supposed to be a secret. "I'm Kelly."

"What a perfect name for our next princess," I boast. "Kelly, I hope you find your prince one day and marry him and live happily ever after."

She nods and asks if we can take a picture together. I feel a little like I'm at a *Disney* park, but I love how I'm able to bring a smile to Kelly's face. She looks to be in kindergarten or about to start. I know this is the age level I'd love to teach when I start applying for jobs at the elementary schools.

We say our goodbyes and get in the waiting limo. We drive by the ocean, and I watch as the waves come in. This is really happening. I'm going to marry my prince in a few minutes. My heart is full and finally complete.

The driver comes to a stop, and Dr. Collins steps out first. Another woman is there to greet us with my bouquet and lead us down a path toward the secluded beach. I wait off to the side as Dr. Collins goes ahead to take her spot on the sand by her husband. The woman who had my flowers gives me the signal, and I start to make my way down to my forever. I can see Luca, standing with his back to me and looking out at the ocean.

The minister pats him on the shoulder to turn as a woman begins playing the harp around us. The moment he finds me, our eyes meet. He's wearing a cream-colored linen suit with a white button-down dress shirt. The top two buttons are undone, and his tattoos are peeking out. His muscled body fills the outfit that stretches across it, and I notice he's barefoot. He looks delicious.

My legs tremble slightly as I begin my walk down the aisle, but I don't even care. I know if I start to fall Luca will catch me. He does every day. My shoulders pull back, and I know in that moment that there is nowhere else in this world I'd rather be than right here with him.

Luca goes to take a step toward me, but the minister brings his hand back to Luca's shoulder halting him. He whispers something and Luca, who hasn't taken his eyes off me, gives a slight nod of acknowledgment. My heart is so full right now, it's like all the heartache and loss was worth it for this moment. Like I was meant to go through almost a decade of darkness to finally see the light at the end of the tunnel. Luca is my light, the end of the rainbow, and my happiness.

And I can't wait for our journey to begin.

CHAPTER THIRTEEN

Luca

I'VE BEEN A NERVOUS WRECK ALL DAY, BEING AWAY FROM GEMMA. A million scenarios play in my head. She could run. She could think I'm a crazy, controlling bastard and decide to leave. Or she could remember that night and realize it was me at the house.

Sometimes she has nightmares about the night I held her in the pantry. She talks in her sleep, and I hear her begging to be let go. I wish we'd met in a different way, but as I've learned over the years, you can't change the past—only pivot to have a better future. I almost called Carson to come here and follow her around to make sure she was safe and didn't run for the hills. I did, however, call the hotel manager once an hour to have a report on how she was doing. It was the best I could do, considering.

I knew Gemma was hesitant about getting married so quickly, but the controlling bastard in me couldn't wait any longer for her to be mine. The call to have Dr. Collins and her husband fly in early this morning was the right thing to do, though I was nervous that the good Doc might try and dissuade her from it. Thankfully, she was extremely happy when I told her what was happening. She has been like a mother to Gemma, and I'd do anything for the woman I love.

My feet dig deeper into the sandy beach as I gaze over the

ocean, and I can't help but look back at how I got here. Turning my back on my family was the best and worst moment of my life. The fights with Pop were always the worst. Our relationship had its ups and downs, but when the final straw broke, I decided it was time to go. Now looking back, I know that I was just looking for an excuse to leave because the longer I was away from Gemma the more I started to hate what I was doing. I resented my family, and I was getting careless, putting myself in danger along with my crew.

I left in the middle of the night. My money had already been moved to an offshore account. Millions I'd collected over the years from working in the family business. I drove straight to San Diego and started to put a plan in place where Gemma and I could casually meet and grow from there. I'd left a note for both Pop and Ma telling them that I'd contact them when I was ready but that I was going to be fine. I knew Ma would take it hard, but Pop has always been her rock, and with Alice still at home, she'd be alright.

It took a while to get my gambling business up and running, but once I found out who held the most cards in the city and greased the wheels enough, it was easy to get what I wanted. After I paid a few people off, I was sailing through. I found some trustworthy people to help me expand, and it has been a breeze ever since.

Once I got that in place, my next move was to make contact with Gemma. I'd been watching her for a while, and when I found out she and her roommate were going on a spring break trip, I knew it was time. What I didn't know was how easily we would click. She's everything to me, the half of me I didn't realize was missing. It wasn't until our first day at the beach together that the final piece of my heart had been filled. I truly thought it would take months for us to progress. She surprised me with how open and honest she is with everything. Like she was just waiting for me to make my move. I'm glad it's been easy sailing because plan B was going to involve kidnapping and being locked away until she agreed to her fate.

The harp starts to play, and the minister places a hand on my shoulder, indicating for me to turn around. I already knew she was close because I get this zing in my body when she's near. The moment I turn, our eyes meet. She looks stunning. I've never seen her look more beautiful than right now walking toward me in a white wedding dress. My angel. There's a lump in my throat, and my mouth goes dry. This is it. The moment I've waited for. Years in the making.

My feet move on their own volition and gravitate toward her, but a hand halts me on the spot.

"She's coming, be patient," the minister says, and I nod, not taking my eyes or focus from the woman who has changed me in ways she'll never know.

The smile she's wearing makes my stomach do flips. How did I get so lucky? The closer she gets, the more I notice how perfect she looks in her wedding dress. She is truly a vision in white. She has her hair pulled to one side in soft curls. The dress was made for her tight body and shows her curves. With the sun setting as the backdrop, I can already envision peeling her out of the material and ravishing her all night long as we consummate our marriage. Our future.

In the last few steps, she reaches for me, and I'm pretty sure I'd break the minister's arm if he tried pulling me back one more time. Once my hands are on hers, my heart finally slows down a notch. The fear of her leaving me is strong and something I'll never allow to happen. She passes her bouquet to Dr. Collins, and I take both of her tiny hands in mine.

"Dearly beloved," the minister begins but I'm not listening. All I can do is stare down into Gemma's eyes and think of our future. Growing old, having children, traveling—it all flashes through my mind. We have the world at our feet right now. So many possibilities are within our reach, and I just hope she never finds out the depths of my secrets. Losing her is not an option, and I'll kill anyone who tries to come between us.

A throat is cleared, and the minister's hand taps my shoulder. "Did you want to say your own vows or follow the traditional ones?" he asks, bringing me out of my haze.

With a shake of my head, to clear my thoughts I focus on my love. "Gemma, I know you may not believe this, but the moment you came into my life, you changed me forever. I never knew a love so deep until you. You are what I think about first thing in the morning and the last when we fall asleep together—and every moment in between. Fate brought you into my life, and I'm so thankful for that day. I may not have understood it at the time, but as time passed, I realized that you were my entire world. I loved you even before we met all those months ago."

I pause to take a breath. I know that if I don't, I'll end up talking about meeting her when we both were so young.

"I promise with my whole heart to honor you. In my life, there will never be another person I put before you and your needs. You are a gift I will treasure for the rest of my life."

Her eyes well with unshed tears, but I push through because I want her to know what she means to me.

"I promise to protect you. Not a day will go by that you'll have to worry about your safety. I vow that every day I'll make it my top priority to keep not only your body safe, but also your heart." I squeeze her hands. "I'll hold your hand in sickness and in health. We'll share in the good and the bad times together. We will walk through this life together in riches and stay by each other's side on our poorest days. I promise before you and our witnesses that my love, vow, and faith in us will never falter for as long as I live."

Tears are flowing down her cheeks now. My hands pull away from hers to wipe them off with my thumbs as I cup the sides of her face.

"Gemma, if you will say your vows," the minister says softly.

I take the handkerchief from my front pocket, dabbing her pink cheeks as she sniffs and clears her throat. "There was a time when I thought I'd never have another family or someone I could count on. The day we met, my entire life changed. You have shown me what it is like to be loved and cherished, and you'll never know how blessed I am for that."

A feather could push me over right now. My love for her is so intense that my heart aches. Everything I have ever gone through over the years has been worth it if it meant I'd end up right here.

"I, Gemma, take you, Luca, to be my husband. I choose you as the person with whom I will spend my life. I take you with all of your faults and with all of your strengths, just as I offer myself to you with all of my faults and strengths."

She has no idea the millions of thoughts running through my mind after saying that. If she only knew all of my faults, she'd run and never look back.

"I vow to be your faithful partner in sickness and in health. I promise to stand by your side for richer or poorer. I will love you unconditionally with my whole heart until my last breath."

Before I can stop myself, I pull her to me and crash my lips to hers. I don't even care that the minister is protesting. I need her to know that I feel and believe every word she just spoke.

"I love you," I whisper when we pull away slightly. I'm not letting her get any farther than inches. She giggles, and it's music to my ears.

"I love you too."

"The rings?" the minister interrupts, breaking our moment.

As angry as I am with him for pulling us out of our bubble, I'm also thankful. Stacking her wedding band next to her engagement ring is the telltale sign that she is mine. Everyone will know she's taken when they see those rings on her hand. *Mine.*

With both of our bands slipped on, my feet bounce impatiently for the next words to be spoken. I feel like a giddy schoolboy.

"By the power invested in me by the state of Hawaii, I now pronounce you—"

I don't even wait until he finishes the sentence before I draw Gemma up into my arms and devour her mouth. Sealing my lips over hers as we become one in the eyes of the law and our witnesses. She responds with the same fervor, locking her arms around my neck. I can't help but dip her small body backward.

She's finally mine forever!

All around us, cheering erupts but we stand meshed together as if we're the only ones on the beach. After several long moments, we pull apart to catch our breath. The look in her eyes is one of love and passion.

"We did it!" she squeals as I place her upright on her feet.

"We did." The smile I give her is one to make my face hurt.

"If I could get your signature on the marriage certificate, I'll file it first thing in the morning." The minister guides us over to the side where a table is set up next to our three-tier wedding cake. "Print your names here, then place a signature there, and I'll sign as one of the witnesses." He points out all the designated areas for us to fill out.

Gemma smiles as I pass her my *Mont Blanc* pen from the inside of my jacket. She starts to scroll her name across the official piece of paper but stops. My heart is in my throat. Did she just change her mind? A bead of sweat starts to drip down my back and more forms on my forehead.

She looks up at me and then back down at the paper. *Please don't make me have to throw you over my shoulder and kidnap you, baby. It's not beneath me to lock you away until you accept your fate with me.*

"I think there's been a mistake," she leans over and whispers in my ear so that only I can hear.

"The only mistake is if you don't sign the paper," I try my hardest to joke, but deep down it's almost a threat. My hands start to shake, and my body is buzzing, going into primal mode.

"They have the wrong last name. Do I still sign?"

Air that had built up in my lungs is expelled in a rush, and I try to lower my heart rate. My eyes scan the paper, and I see the mistake. *My mistake.* The certificate reads FALCONE as the last name instead of my alias, Fontana. *Fuck!*

After a beat, I decide the direction to go.

"I have to tell you something that I didn't think was a big deal." I grip her hands and turn her toward me. "Falcone is my legal name." I give it a beat to let that sink in. "Remember me telling you about when I left my family and went out on my own, and that I didn't want to be associated with their name? I wanted a clean slate and to make a life for myself—not what they expected of me." She nods. "I use the name Fontana as my last name for business purposes."

Her pensive eyes shift back and forth to mine.

"Why didn't you just tell me that when you told me about your family? Did you think I'd think less of you? I told you about my past and the mess with Mario and how he was a bad man. If anyone could understand, it would be me." She sounds hurt, and I hate that we are even having this conversation, much less on our wedding day.

"I'm sorry I didn't tell you. I guess I…" I pause because I need to be careful of how many stories I tell. Eventually, they come back to bite you in the ass. I've kept too much from her already and can't bring myself to feed her another lie. "Please forgive me," I beg, holding her hands tighter and hoping she will understand.

"Of course, I forgive you, babe." She reaches up and cups my cheek with a smile. "It might take me a while to adjust since I practiced signing my name as Gemma Fontana over and over in my notebooks during class," she admits with a slight blush at the confession.

"How did I ever get so lucky to find you? I don't deserve you, but I promise to work every day to show you that I'm worthy of your love and this life we're starting."

A throat is cleared as the minister comes back over after giving us some privacy.

"Is everything okay over here?" Dr. Collins comes over with her husband.

"Yes, of course!" Gemma answers, but the good doc doesn't seem convinced.

In a flourish, Gemma signs her name and passes my pen back to me. My eyes turn away from hers, and I see her name on paper. Gemma Dulce Falcone. Not letting this moment pass and giving her a chance to back out, I plant my name in the designated areas and forcefully shove the certificate at the minister. The faster he gets this filed, the better I'll feel. I watch as he and Dr. Collins sign as witnesses.

We cut into the cake and playfully smash it in each other's faces. I'll never tire of her playfulness. She brings out a new life in me that I thought had been stripped away at a young age.

"I love you so much. I almost feel like this is a dream," I say as we dance under the stars on the sandy beach. The soft music in the background and the sound of the waves crashing lull us as she snuggles closer to me. We are as close as two people could possibly be, but I want her closer.

Gemma lifts her chin and arches her back to look up at me.

"I never knew happiness until you came into my life. I know this is a whirlwind, but there isn't any part I would change."

I lean down and kiss the hell out of her. She has no idea what her words mean to me. Everything I've done to get us here has paid off. All the blood, sweat, and tears have all been worth it.

"Can we go?" she asks as she looks around. The minister left a while ago, and Dr. Collins and her husband are dancing and drinking champagne as the harpist continues to play.

"I thought you'd never ask."

We walk over and say our goodbyes to Dr. Collins and Michael. After many hugs, we climb into the waiting limo and head toward our house. The night is perfect, and I couldn't ask for a more beautiful backdrop to consummate our union. On the drive home, we fail at keeping our hands to ourselves. Our lips never separate, and even though she's covered in a lot of material, I still manage to keep my hands in contact with her soft flesh.

"Take me to bed, husband!" Gemma exclaims when the driver lets us out of the limo. My dick has been hard from the moment I saw her walking down the sandy beach toward me. I'm aching to seal our marriage.

While Gemma was at the spa all day, I had the entire house set up with rose petals and candles. I bend my knees and sweep her up bridal style as we walk past the bedrooms and out to the lanai.

I made sure to have the backyard set up to look magical. There is a king-sized canopy bed out by the pool draped with white sheets. The pool is lit with floating candles and rose petals are scattered all around with fairy lights hung on all the trees.

"It's so beautiful," she gasps as we make our way over to the bed.

"I only want the best for my wife." The moment the word wife slips from my lips, a thrill of satisfaction trips down my spine and floods my veins. She's mine. In every way.

I place her gently on her feet and step back to drink her in. There will never be another day like today. Another moment like this.

"Today is the start of our lives, and my hope is that every day is like right now." I lean back and pull out my pocketknife I never leave home without. Her eyes widen for a moment as I try to gather my thoughts. "In my family, there is a tradition of bonding us deeper. We seal our fate to one another not only in marriage but by blood." I take the knife and cut a small slash across my palm just enough to draw blood. I hold out my hand for her and wait for her to do the same.

My family has done this with all their marriages for a century. They believe that bonding your soulmate in blood will solidify you together forever.

Gemma meets my eyes, and she reaches out her hand for me. She has no idea how much my soul aches with how trusting she is, to be locked and bonded to me. I raise the knife and with care, I gently cut her palm enough to allow the smallest trickle of blood to form across her hand.

I stare into her eyes and recite the vows every man in my family has spoken to their wives.

"The world will end before something ever happens to you. Nothing in this world will ever harm you. I will lay my life down for you. My blood is your blood. My family is your family."

I place my bloodstained hand into hers and merge our blood together. Our fingers intertwine as I hold them upright in front of us. A shiver runs down my spine at the connection, and it feels euphoric. Not wanting to let this moment end, I lean down and capture her lips with mine.

"I love you more than you'll ever know. I don't deserve you, but by god, I'm going to work every day to earn you."

My arms circle around her small frame and I find the zipper to her dress. Painfully slow I pull the metal down her back as she keeps her eyes focused on mine. She's breathtaking.

"I'm nervous," she admits and it takes me a second to understand. "We've done it so many times before, but this feels different."

"You don't ever have to feel nervous around me, Vita Mia." *My life.* I softly press my lips to hers in reassurance.

Her wedding dress slips down her body, and I groan at what's underneath.

"Dr. Collins thought I needed to surprise you for our wedding night." She bites her plump lower lip, and my dick lurches in my pants.

"I think you're trying to give your husband a heart attack on his wedding night," I growl.

She's wearing a lace corset that has her large tits pushed up and cutout around them, exposing her nipples for me to see. The matching thong is nothing but a triangle covering her pussy, and as I twirl her around, the string is lost between her cheeks. *Have mercy!* She is a dream come true.

"If I'd known you were wearing this under the dress, the wedding would've been over in under five minutes," I bite clenching my teeth.

The moment she turns back around, I pounce. I drop to my knees and latch onto one nipple as my hand plays with the other. My free hand snaps the tiny string of her so-called thong and finds her clit. She's soaking wet for me, and I feel her soft hands run through my hair. My mouth swaps tits, and I devour this one with the same fervor. My hand is dripping from her arousal as she opens wider for me to plunge a finger up into her pussy. She's riding my hand like she was made for it and gripping my hair at the roots, trying to push my mouth closer.

"Aww, Luca I'm going to come!" she cries bearing down on my

hand, and her body starts to tremble. I move my mouth lower and latch on to her clit while I work my fingers in and out.

Her climax happens before I can pull back, so I let her ride it out with shaky legs and my mouth full of her juices. She almost collapses, but I catch her and lay her spent body down on the soft bed.

"You are so beautiful when you come," I say after I leave my clothes in a pile next to hers. "Pull your knees up wife. I want to see what's mine."

She does as she's asked and exposes every inch of her delectable cunt to me. Her glistening arousal is prominent, and my dick can't take much more torture. I line the head of my cock up with her entrance and nudge it forward. Even after months of sex, she's still just as small as the first time, and I go slow to let her adjust to my size. She takes him like a champ now, and the stretching isn't as painful as the first few times were.

"Let me in, baby," I coax as I rock in and out a few inches at a time.

The moment I bottom out, my body relaxes. Her walls pulse around my dick, and I try to restrain the need to fuck the shit out of her. We've had fast, rough sex, but tonight is special—even more special than our first time. Tonight, we vowed to be one for as long as we both shall live. I am hers, and she is mine. When we look back on this day, I want her to remember every detail as if it was the best day of her life. Letting the beast out to play is not what I want. She and I both need this to be romantic and memorable.

"Love me, Luca." Those words are my undoing.

My hips pull back and pump forward at a slow and steady pace. I'm hovering over her body with our noses touching. She has her legs wrapped around my hips, moving as I thrust into her. I can't tear my eyes from hers. Our whole future is in them. She holds my life in her hands, and I refuse to let it slip away from her.

I put her on top, switching positions. If possible, it feels even deeper this way. Her hands go to my chest as she bounces up and down, jacking my dick off and squeezing the shit out of it. I'm not going to last long in this position because I can feel every inch of her walls. The only sound aside from the ocean is our labored breathing and the slapping of our skin against one another. Not wanting to prolong this anymore, I strum her clit as she moves, causing her to falter. My other hand clamps down on her hip and helps her stay on course in her movements.

"You feel so good, baby. Come for me. Come all over my cock and let your juices drench me." Her moan vibrates to my core and my balls tingle. "Pop that pussy and make me come." My voice is more urgent now, and I speed up my assault on her clit. The moment I give it the smallest pinch, she detonates. I pull my finger back, place my hand around her other hip, and start to thrust hard up into her. She's still coming down from her own orgasm when my hips hit their final thrust, and I unload my cum into her. My own orgasm goes on for a while, and even after I'm empty I still thrust up into her.

Her body is laid out on my chest, but my dick has yet to soften. He's ready for round two. Once we've caught our breath, we lay there connected listening to our heartbeats and the ocean. My body has a mind of its own and flexes so that my dick is still making small movements through her pussy.

After a long sigh she asks, "Is this really how our life will be?" and starts to move at the same slow pace as my dick.

I push a strand of hair behind her ear.

"It can be whatever you want it to be. I'm at your mercy, and if you want this every day, then I will make it happen," I say with certainty.

"How did I get so lucky?" she moans, and it's all I can take.

I flip us over, driving deep into her.

"I'm the lucky one," I state.

All night long, I show her just how lucky I am.

CHAPTER FOURTEEN

Gemma

October 2022

T HE SUMMER BLEW BY. WE SPENT AN ENTIRE MONTH IN Hawaii, soaking up all the sun and activities. Our own little bubble. Luca wanted to buy the property we stayed in, but I finally convinced him not to spend the money. We could always rent it and sneak away for the weekend if we wanted. The life insurance business must be booming.

We got back from paradise, and I found a private school near our house that wanted me to come in for an interview for a kindergarten position. I was beyond excited, and a week after the interview, they offered me the position. Luca was thrilled, but I could tell he would've preferred me to stay home. I'd love to be at home when we decide to have our children, but I want to be a teacher to little ones and hopefully make a difference in their lives.

Now, two months into the beginning of the school year, I find that this is definitely what my calling is all about.

"Mrs. Falcone, Tommy took my pencil!" I hear Anabelle screech across the room.

I've decided to keep the last name Falcone instead of going by

Fontana. Our children will want to know about their grandparents one day, and I thought they deserved to be a part of that legacy.

"No, I didn't, it was mine!"

"Is not!"

"Is too!"

"Okay, you two, come here," I say, and drop to my knees as they approach. "Anabelle, what makes you think Tommy took your pencil?"

She points to the pencil. "I was using that pencil but went pee-pee, and when I came back, it was gone. He took it."

Tommy is shaking his head. "I swear this is mine. See!" He holds the pencil up, and I see his initials on it.

"Anabelle, look, this is his pencil." I show her his initials, and her eyes widen.

"But...but..."

"Did you look around the table? Maybe it fell on the floor?" I look over and, sure enough, there is a pencil right under her chair that I suspect might be the missing pencil. She turns and sees it too. "What do you think is the right thing to do right now?"

She turns to Tommy. "Sorry, Tommy."

"It's okay."

They both run off to the table and continue to work on writing the letter H.

"You have the patience of a saint," I hear from the doorway and turn to see Bianca.

Bianca just started working here about a month ago. She helps out around the school and assists the teachers when needed. When we were first introduced, she latched onto me and said we'd be friends for life. Ever since that day, she comes by my classroom on our lunch breaks and we eat together.

"We're still on for tonight, right?" she asks as she walks in and dodges the kids as they move around the room.

"Yeah, seven right?" I answer.

Bianca is great. She's easy to talk with, and we share some of the same interests.

Dr. Collins—or rather just Allison now that she has stopped being my therapist—actually said we should've stopped long before the wedding. She looks to me as a daughter and has given me the name of several other therapists. I haven't been to any since I've been back, but if I ever feel like seeing one, I know I have options.

"You sure that husband is going to let you out of his sight?" Bianca teases.

The last few times Bianca and I made plans to hang out, Luca has had a surprise planned on a special night out for us. Tonight, though, he's having some kind of work thing that will bring him home late.

I giggle. "We are a go!"

"Okay." With that, she walks out and goes down the hall to do whatever it is that she does during the day.

"Don't forget your lunch boxes. We don't want those to hang out over the weekend; they'll be growing legs by Monday morning." I cheer as the class giggles, and the bell alerts us to the end of the day. Once everyone has their gear, I walk them down to the cafeteria. "Have a great weekend, boys and girls!"

"Bye, Mrs. Falcone!"

Just as I'm turning around to head back to my classroom, I, once again, don't watch where I'm going and walk right into the door with my shoulder.

"Ahhh," I stop and rub my throbbing upper arm. That's going to leave a mark.

"Are you okay, Mrs. Falcone?" Larry, the janitor, asks as he stops mopping the floors. He's an older man who plans to retire in a few years.

"Yeah, yeah, I'm fine. You know I have a hard time walking," I joke. Everyone I work with knows I'm a clumsy disaster.

By the time I get back to my classroom, I can hear my phone dinging. He's always right on time. I check the message, and of course, it's Luca.

Husband: How was your day?

Me: Great! The kids loved planting the seeds for our garden.

Husband: That's good. I'll be home late tonight, don't forget to set the alarm.

Me: I'll remember. Bianca and I are going to dinner and drinks.

I see the three dots roaming, telling me he's texting. Then they stop before starting back up and then stop again. I know I waited until the last minute to drop this on him, but he always worries when I go out for anything, even groceries, without him.

Husband: Where are you going?

Me: Not sure. Bianca is picking me up.

Husband: I can reschedule this meeting for another time and go with you.

Me: Don't you dare! It'll be fun to have a girls' night. I'll let you know where we are going once we get there. I'll see you tonight after your meeting.

There is a long pause, so I gather up my things and make sure the room is in spotless condition before leaving. One thing I love is to come to work with a clean room. I also love to come home to a clean house. Luca has a housekeeper for our home, but I always find myself straightening up before she gets there.

Husband: Please be careful tonight

Me: I will. Love you.

Husband: Love you more

By the time I get home, I've got time to soak in the enormous bathtub and get ready for the night. I check the weather and notice it's going to be a little chilly once the sun goes down, so I text Bianca to find out what she's wearing and ask where we're going. She sends me a pic of her outfit, and I am relieved that it's not too sexy since we are apparently going to a bar. She's showing jeans and a little bit of a revealing top with heels that would break my neck if I wore them.

I find a pair of distressed medium-wash jeans with the knees cut out. They fit my legs and booty snugly and I think Luca loves them too because he can't seem to keep his hands off my butt every time I wear this brand. I grab a gray vintage Rock-n-Roll shirt with the sleeves cut off and tuck it in the front just a bit. Then I find my Gucci belt and a camouflage army zip-up jacket. I pair the outfit with a tan peep-toe bootie and make sure to cuff the bottoms of my jeans above the shoes. My hair is curled in soft waves, and my makeup is light with a smidge of lip-gloss.

I snag a pic and send it to Luca, telling him the name of the place we're heading to then place my phone in my purse. Just as I'm doing a once over in the mirror, the guard at the gate of our community informs me that Bianca has arrived. By the time I make it to the front door, her car is out front. I set the alarm and lock up before making my way to her BMW.

"Look at you! Are you sure you're not trying to snag a man tonight?" She whistles, and I feel heat rush to my face. She's always been a loud person, but it echoes off the other houses, and I'd hate for our neighbors to get the wrong idea about me.

"You're crazy. I'm happily married." I glance over at her once I'm in the car. "You're the one who's looking to hook a man in those short shorts. I thought you were wearing jeans?" I ask because this is not the outfit she sent me over text.

"Us girls change our minds." Bianca's wearing shorts that ride up high. Her top is practically see-through and exposing her black bra that pushes up her boobs. She is dressed to kill tonight, and I'm starting to worry that this might be a bad idea.

We drive to a bar called *Aero Dive Bar*, and as we walk in I see an entire wall of liquor that goes from floor to ceiling behind the bar. They have colored string lights throughout the place and large televisions on the walls. There is a jukebox playing music and pool tables lined up toward the back leading to other rooms that host games and more tables back there. It has a pilot theme to it and seems really laid back.

"You get a table and I'll grab some drinks at the bar," Bianca says over the noise of people and music.

I find us two seats at a high top in the middle of the bar. It looks like a fun place to bring friends, and I try to imagine Luca here with me. He'd love the pool tables and watching games on the big TVs. We always go out to a bar when a big game is on because it's the atmosphere that makes it so great. I've never been much into sports but going with Luca has me starting to love it too.

Bianca finds me, carrying a tray of shot glasses with amber liquid in them, a plate of limes, and a saltshaker. *Oh boy, this can't be good.*

"I've got us some appetizers before our wings and cheese fries come out. You have an allergy to fish, right?"

"Shellfish."

"Okay." She holds up two glasses and hands one to me. "To a beautiful friendship."

She clinks our glasses together and then places some salt on the top of her hand. She proceeds to lick the salt off tipping the shot back and placing the lime in her mouth to bite.

In college, I remember going to a party once and watching people do shots, but I was never one to do them. I don't mind a fruity drink, but I've never been the type to throw them back.

"Go ahead," Bianca urges and starts to sprinkle the salt on top of my hand.

"I've never done a shot before," I admit out loud, and Bianca freezes.

"What?" she shrieks. "How in the world did you survive college without doing at least one tequila shot?" She's clearly shocked.

I lift one shoulder in a shrug. "I just never did."

"Girl, this is why we're going to besties for life." She grabs another shot off the tray and sprinkles salt over her hand again. "Okay, we will do this together. All you have to do is lick, slam, then suck."

"Lick, slam, suck," I repeat and think this is a horrible idea, but then I think about Allison's advice about making new friends and trying new things. I can do this. "Okay, I think I got it."

"It's going to taste gross the first time, but you learn to love it after the fifth."

"The fifth? Why not the second or third?"

"Focus, here we go. Do what I do."

The next thing I know, my tongue is filled with salt and the liquid goes straight to the back of my mouth, making me gag at the horrible taste. Before I know what's happening, Bianca shoves the lime in my mouth and instructs me to suck the juice. Once I think the taste is completely gone, I release the lime and squint over at Bianca in disgust.

"That was horrible."

"Give it a few more, and you'll love it. Here throw one more back before our food gets here."

She hands me the next one, and I follow the leader once again, but the taste isn't getting any better.

"Ahh. Maybe we should try something else," I say as a lady covered in tattoos comes over with our food.

"You don't ever want to mix too many liquors. The hangover will kill you." Bianca bounces in her seat as she pops a few cheese fries into her mouth. "One more, then we'll pace ourselves since I'm popping your shot cherry tonight."

We do another, and I must say that the taste goes down a little easier. I feel a tingle throughout my body, but I think I'm doing good. I feel my purse buzz and know that it's probably Luca checking in. My hands are a mess with the wings, so I decide to check once we've finished our food.

"So, tell me how you met your hubby," Bianca says while we devour the wings.

I open up and tell her the whirlwind of our meeting, engagement, and wedding.

"Wow, that's crazy fast," she says in disbelief.

"I know, but it felt right."

"But how do you know that he's not some closet serial killer or mobster? That really happens and not just in the movies."

"He is the best thing that has ever happened to me. I don't know what I'd do without him," I say honestly. "It's like he was the missing piece that had been lacking in my life."

"He just seems like he wants to eat you for the meal instead of having a meal *with* you when he brings you food during your lunch break. It's a little intense."

"That's just Luca. He's always been really attentive to me and makes sure I have everything that I could ever need—before I even ask for it sometimes. He's the best." He really is a dream come true.

"I hope my husband does that for me when it comes time for marriage," she says.

"The moment you meet him, it'll all click into place." We clink glasses and shoot back another disgusting shot. "What brought you here to San Diego if you went to college in Chicago?"

She hesitates for a moment. "I followed a boyfriend here after college. I should've known when my parents *encouraged* it that it wasn't a good thing. It didn't work out, but I loved it here and wanted to stay." Bianca throws back another drink and sucks on the lime.

"Do you ever go back to Chicago to visit family?"

"To be honest, I hated it there. My parents aren't the most supportive, and I'm not really that close with them. They're so wrapped up in their business, and having a child was just a way to leverage good standing in the business world there."

"That's really sad." I can't imagine not having my memories with my mom growing up. She was always right there for me and so supportive in everything I did. "Well, I'm glad we met."

She beams back at me. "Me too."

By the time we finish our meal, Bianca and I are a laughing mess. I can't remember a time when I had this much fun with a girl in my life. I've always had a hard time making friends, but she makes it easy to be around her. We've finished all the shots on the tray and had another one brought over. I've lost count of how many I've had and am feeling really good. Tired but good. We've danced to songs on the jukebox and played a game of pool, and I *think* we attempted darts, but I can't be sure. I think the a/c went out halfway through our meal because it got really hot in the bar around that time.

"I think I'm drunk?" I slur and see two of Bianca.

"Oh, boy," I hear Bianca giggle but can't focus on her as the room spins. "I better get you home before that husband decides to bury me in the backyard."

"I need to pee?" I sway all the way and make it just in time to the toilet. I'm not sure how long I stay there because Bianca bangs on the stall door, jolting me back to focus.

"Gemma, come out before I tear the door off." I hear a slew of curses as the door opens, and Bianca helps me up and over to the sink.

"We are never having tequila shots again," she mumbles. "You're going to get me killed and labeled a bad influence on you."

"Why is it so hot in this place?"

"Good god, Gemma, where the hell is half of your outfit!" she practically yells, and it hurts my head.

That was the last thing I remember.

Luca

Do not lose your shit. Do not lose your shit. I'm pacing back and forth across the living room. Gemma hasn't responded to my text messages in over two hours, and if five more minutes pass, I'm going to head over to get her at that dive bar she's at with her little friend from her job.

"She'll be all right, Boss." Carson watches from the barstool as I pace, grabbing at my hair and pulling. "I can send one of the men over if you want."

What I really want to do is go over there and spank the shit out of her for not answering my calls or texts. Anything could happen to her. What if she has an allergic reaction to something or an asthma attack and I'm not there?

Two minutes and I'm going.

Doesn't she know I worry every second she's not in my sight? There are bad men out there who will do bad things to her before she could even wonder what was happening. I should know—my family business is what nightmares are made of.

"From now on, if our meetings can't happen before five, then they wait," I sneer.

Carson had called and told me one of our shipments of slot machines from China was coming in. The harbor manager didn't want to deal with anyone but me to let them pass through customs undetected. I had no problem with it until I learned that Gemma was going out with a friend from work on a Friday night. She texted me a pic of her outfit, and I wanted to crush my phone. She looked hot as hell in her tight jeans and concert cutoff top. I know she had a jacket, but still.

Time.

Just as I reach for my keys, the security at the gate buzzes, alerting me that a 'Bianca' is entering with Mrs. Falcone in the car.

Good.

Carson takes his leave to the guest house to give us our privacy, and I go and meet my frustrating wife and her friend out in the front yard. A BMW pulls up, but only the driver gets out. Didn't the guard say my wife was in the car too?

"I'm really sorry about this. I didn't realize what a lightweight she is." This friend, Bianca, tries to explain as she opens the passenger door. "When she told me she'd never done shots, I thought we could have a few."

"What in the holy fuck?!"

I quickly spot my wife—my naïve to the world wife—passed out in the car. My god, is she breathing? I rush over to her to check for a pulse, and it causes her to startle awake.

"Luca! Hey!" she cheers. "I love you so much and I love that thing you do with your tongue down there." She over exaggerates every motion as she points down at her pussy, and I think I might take her to the hospital for fluids to sober her ass up.

She reeks of tequila, and before I know it she's latched her lips to mine in the sloppiest kiss known to man. Christ!

"I'm so horny," she announces, and I want to bend her over the hood of the car and start her spankings. I would if her friend weren't staring at us right now.

"Let's get you in the house to drink some water, okay, babe?" I say as tenderly as I can.

"I'm really sorry about her clothes too," Bianca pleads as I hoist my horny, drunk wife in my arms.

"Clothes?" I question and look over my wife.

"I'm not sure where her jacket went, and she's missing an earring. She said she was getting hot, but I didn't expect her to start taking her clothes off. I'm really sorry and promise to never let this happen again," she says like a scolded child.

"You got that right," I snap and walk toward the house.

It's not until I walk into the kitchen and set Gemma down on the counter that I notice Bianca walked in with us. Gemma sees her and opens her arms for a hug and when her friend opens her arms in return my wife hugs her tight. Bianca hugs her back just as hard.

"I had the best time tonight," Gemma says, and it's hard for me to stay angry. My wife needs steady and true friends in her life. I know Dr. Collins worries that me being the only person in her life is not good for her. I'd like to be selfish and disagree but can't.

"Me too. Next time, we'll take the hubby and not get too wasted before ten at night." She giggles, and it sets my wife off. I pass over a bottle of water along with two pills to help with the headache she's going to have in the morning. Bianca opens it and encourages her to drink.

Gemma drinks half before putting her head down on the counter. A light snore tells us she's out for the count again.

"I really am sorry about tonight," Bianca says again, and this time I believe her. She places Gemma's purse on the counter and turns to head out the front door.

I pull my wife up into my arms and walk toward the front door to lock up behind her.

"She really is a genuinely nice girl, isn't she?" Bianca asks in wonderment.

"She is the best person I've ever met in my entire life," I state. "She's been through a lot in her short life and doesn't have a lot of life experiences."

Bianca nods then pushes a strand of hair out of Gemma's face.

"I get it now," she answers weirdly, then steps out the front door. "This won't happen again, I promise," she says with unfaltering conviction.

I stand there for a few minutes, trying to understand what she meant, but movement in my arms shifts my attention to my wife.

"Love you," I hear a faint whisper.

I press a kiss to her forehead as I walk us to our room after locking up and set the alarm for the night. Once I have her in our room, I carefully strip her down to her panties and pull the covers up her body. I make sure to place a trashcan on the side of the bed and a glass of water on the nightstand before I rid myself of my clothes down to my boxers and climb into the bed next to her. This woman is going to be the death of me, but I guess it could've been worse.

"Ahh…" I hear from the bed as I brush my teeth the next morning. "What happened to my head?"

I want to chuckle at her pain. *Welcome to trying new experiences, babe.*

"Everything okay in there?" I yell on purpose.

She moans, and I hear her plop back down on the pillow. I know she needs to have these experiences. I had them too but at a much earlier age. I never want to hinder her in anything, but she needs to do this with some type of boundaries or guidelines that won't send me to an early grave or get her harmed. I slam a few cabinet doors just for good measure and make my way to the bedroom. Gemma is sprawled out on the bed with her face covered by her arm. I opened all the curtains this morning before I went and had a workout. This is the part of her life she missed when her mom was killed and she was sent off.

"You okay, baby?" I sound concerned, as if I have no idea she drank an entire distillery.

"Mmm…my head feels like it might explode."

"Oh, you mean from the wild night you had last night, partying?" I snip.

"Oh Luca, it was so much fun, and the entire time, I kept thinking about how I wished you were there."

Sometimes she surprises me with her words and these catch me off guard. I have to remember how young she is. Changing course, I decide to use the gentle approach instead. Not wanting her to suffer anymore, I close all the curtains and slide up next to her.

"Can I do anything to make you feel better?" I ask, placing a cool washrag across her forehead. I coax her to drink the glass of water next to the bed. I shoot off a text to Carson to have our doc send one of his nurses over with an IV of fluids in about an hour for 'little miss can't hold my liquor.'

"Just hold me."

The simple request has all my frustration fizzling out. "I guess this is the 'in sickness and in health' part of the marriage, huh?" I tease as she lies across my chest and entwines her legs with mine, making sure to put her cold feet on me.

"I'll return the favor any time you need it," she sleepily agrees.

"I love you, but we will be having a discussion when you feel better about not answering your phone," I reprimand her.

"Yes, sir."

CHAPTER FIFTEEN

Gemma

May 2023

"ARE YOU HEADED HOME ALREADY?" I SPEAK INTO THE phone as I climb into my Mustang.

"I just got a call and need to head back to the office for a quick minute, then I'm heading your way. You there yet?" My husband hates it when he beats me home.

"I'm leaving the school right now. My classroom is all packed up for the summer, and I won't be returning until the middle of August. Let the summer activities begin!" I cheer.

I loved my first year as a teacher, but I'm so glad for a break. Kindergarten is not for the faint of heart, and I could tell my patience was wearing a little thin the last few days of school. I learned a lot this year, and I can't wait to see the kids that come in the fall.

"I might stop off at the grocery store on my way home though. I think we ran out of popcorn, and I plan on pulling a lot of all-nighters with Bianca over the summer. We have an entire list of shows we want to binge-watch on Netflix."

I hear a growl, and it makes me giggle. Luca loves to spend all of his time with me and hates when I'm busy with Bianca.

"Does this mean she'll be at the house all summer?" he inquires, and I can't stop my giggles. Luca may act like he dislikes Bianca, but they get along great when they see each other. She's become a permanent fixture in our life. Luca was wary of her at first, I could tell, but as time went on, he warmed up to her. He even brings her snacks when he's stopping to pick mine up on his way home and he knows she's there with me.

"Be nice, and it won't be the entire summer. We do have vacation plans coming up in Hawaii," I say, letting him know the surprise trip he planned for our anniversary has been found out.

"You weren't supposed to see that," he chastises.

"Then don't leave your notes on the kitchen counter for everyone to see," I taunt.

"Yeah, yeah whatever."

"I'll see you soon. Love you."

"Love you more, amore mio. See you soon."

The call ends, and I pull out of the parking lot. A text comes in from Bianca but will have to wait until I get home. I've got to pee so bad and home is closer than the grocery store. I'll slip in, make a list of everything I'm going to need over the next week, and then head to the store. Maybe Bianca will want to come along?

I see John, our lawn service guy, loading up the mowers and bags of grass when I pull into the garage.

"Hi, John!" I yell from the door.

"Hello, Mrs. Fontana," he responds with a wave. I still find it a little weird to hear that last name instead of Falcone, but that is how Luca would prefer it with most people. I'm used to either now since I prefer my class to call me Ms. Falcone and everyone else knows me as Gemma Fontana.

I'll never forget two months ago when my husband came home from work and found me trying to mow our yard. Poor John had gotten a call that his daughter was in a car crash and had needed to leave suddenly. I told him to leave everything here and go be with his daughter.

I thought I could be helpful by finishing the yard work to ease his stress, so I went out to see if I could do a little work around the house. I'd seen his notebook that detailed all the work he wanted to accomplish and got to work. I had thought, how hard could this really be, right?

John had left the bushwhacker-looking thing by the short bushes on the side of the house, so I thought I'd start there. The moment I tried to pick up the heavy thing, I should've known better. Big mistake. The moment it turned on, I was not prepared for the power it had, and when it jolted forward, the poor bush was cut in two. But the worst part is that I couldn't get it to turn off and took out an entire row of bushes along the side of the house.

Thank goodness for the guy, Carson, who stays in the guesthouse. He came out when I was screaming and saved me from taking out all the trees too. He was super nice but very reserved. He worked it like a pro and had it turned off in no time. By the time we took in all the damage I'd created, Luca had come home. To say he was hot under the collar is an understatement. He first made sure I wasn't hurt, then unleashed on me, exploding like a volcano.

Everyone was fired; John, Carson, me, even *John Deer*. Carson tried to calm the situation and mobilized Luca to the back of the house. After a few minutes, they came back, and he'd calmed down tremendously. It's a big joke now, and John's daughter has fully recovered. I found out later that Luca paid for her physical therapy, but John had to replant all new bushes, and I promised to never touch a piece of lawn equipment ever again. *We live and learn.*

I hurry through the house and up in the master bathroom. After doing my business, I come out and hear the downstairs door close. Luca must be home.

"Hey babe!" I call out, coming downstairs. "I still need to run to the store..." I don't even get to finish my sentence, because in the living room are six very large men standing there, waiting for me.

I'm frozen for all of five seconds before my arm reaches out and hits the silent alarm on the wall next to the stairs.

"That wasn't a smart thing to do," one of the gargantuan men says.

My eyes are bouncing all over the room for the nearest escape, but the men are blocking every exit.

"We aren't going to hurt you, sweetheart. My name is Gio, and we just need you to come with us quietly," the older man of the group says. It's odd because he looks familiar, like we've met before somewhere, but I can't place him.

The first rule Bianca and I were taught in the self-defense classes we're taking is to never go with your kidnapper. Always put up a fight or run until your lungs give out.

Fight or flight.

"She's gonna run," I hear from the back of the room. "Hundred bucks."

My chest is getting heavy, and I know I need to keep it in check. I've done really well about not needing my inhaler for a long time, but panic is starting to settle in.

"Carlo, stay back," Gio orders, and I notice he's inched up on me.

Fight it is.

I use the stair rail to kick up as high as I can, catching him off guard. He goes down like a sack of potatoes. I hear some barks of laughter and oohs, but I don't wait around for it. I take off as fast as I can through the room toward the backdoor. Maybe Carson is in the guesthouse and will save me. I only make it halfway across the room before I'm picked up around the waist from behind and feel a pinch on my neck. I fight as much as I can, kicking and screaming before I feel my body going lax.

"It's okay, sweetheart, we're going home."

It's the last thing I hear before darkness consumes me.

My head is pounding, and I feel drowsy. Did Bianca and I have another drinking night? Ahh, my mouth feels like I've swallowed cotton balls.

Slowly, my eyes open, expecting the morning sun to make the

throbbing worse, but darkness spills through the windows as I stare out them. There is a small light in the corner of the room, and I see a figure sitting in a chair next to it.

"Oh, good you're awake," Bianca says and comes over to sit next to me on the bed. "Drink this." She hands me a glass of water and pushes it to my lips.

"How much did we drink tonight?" I bring my hand up to my forehead to help relieve the throbbing. "I just had the weirdest dream."

"Gemma, I'm so sorry," Bianca pleads, grabbing my hand. The little bit of light in the room catches her face, and her eyes light up with tears in them. "Please, forgive me. I didn't want to do this after we became so close. You're my best friend."

"Bianca it's okay. We've drank way too much before, remember?" She's talking crazy. Why would she need to apologize? Maybe I'm still dreaming.

A knock on the door startles us, and that's when I get a look around the room. We aren't at home. This isn't one of my rooms at the house. I've been to Bianca's apartment, and she doesn't have a room like this one either.

"What...what's going on? Where are we, Bianca?"

The door opens, and a man I don't recognize stands in the doorway. My dream becomes reality when I stare at the man who takes up the entire doorframe.

"Mr. Falcone wants to see her now," he says, holding the door wide open and motioning for us to follow.

Bianca stands, and it leaves me confused. Why would my husband be calling for me?

"Do you know him?" I ask Bianca and push up toward the headboard, away from her.

Am I still dreaming? Wake up! Wake up!

"I'm so sorry, Gem. Please," Bianca begs.

"Mr. Falcone doesn't like to wait," he barks.

"We're coming, Bruno," Bianca snaps at him then turns to me. "It'll be okay. I promise."

She tries to reach for me, but I bat her hands away. "Stay away from me," I demand and retreat as far as I can. Something is not right here, but my brain is so foggy I can't function properly.

"You either come on your own or I'll drag you," Bruno sneers and my body starts to shake. Who is this guy?

"Shut the fuck up, Bruno." Bianca turns back to me. "You have to come, but I'll be with you the entire time. Everything will be fine."

Bianca comes over, and my trembling body starts to convulse. "Where is Luca?" I can't help the tears. "Who wants to see me?"

"He'll be here soon."

Bianca helps me get off the bed, and my shaky legs buckle. She pulls me to her, and we manage to walk out of the room and down a long hall. She's whispering reassurances, but I'm so scared I can't understand what she's saying.

Bruno knocks on one of two large wooden doors, and a voice calls out to enter. He opens the door, and we follow in behind him. The study has an old-world vibe to it with floor-to-ceiling bookshelves and a large marble globe in the corner. A map of the West Coast hangs on the wall. The large, dark, wooden desk sits in the middle of the room, and a salt-and-pepper-haired man sits behind it in a leather chair.

"Have a seat," he commands, and Bianca helps walk me over to a leather wingback chair across from him and plants me in it.

He's a large, stocky man who fills the chair out completely. The more my eyes scan over him, the more I see Luca. This must be his father. The family he left behind to start a new life.

Mr. Falcone pulls his black-rimmed glasses off his face and tosses them on the desk after closing a file. "My son has been hiding more secrets than I thought, Ms. Ricci," Mr. Falcone asserts, making me cringe at that last name. I dropped that name as fast as I could, not wanting to be associated with a horrible man.

He stands, much taller than I expected, and makes his way

slowly around his desk, leaning his backside on the edge and crossing his ankles and arms. I feel tears slide down my cheeks and use my fingers to brush them away. The movement jolts Mr. Falcone, and he snatches my left hand.

"Well, this changes things, doesn't it?" he quips snapping his neck over at Bianca who is at my left side. "I'll deal with you later, Ms. Gallo. Leave this room and go wait to be called on," he dismisses her.

I look up to Bianca and see the worry in her eyes. She places a hand on my shoulder and squeezes. She takes her leave, and I watch the last bit of support I have left walk out the door as Bruno shuts us in. I've never been more terrified in my entire life.

Aren't families supposed to welcome you with open arms? Why is he so cold to everyone?

"Tell me, what did my son say about his family?" he asks, bringing my focus back to him.

"He…" I try to swallow but my mouth is dry, and it feels like sandpaper is in my throat. "He told me that he left to start a life on his own. That he didn't want the life his family led."

"Did he now? Did he happen to tell you what this family does for a living, or did he keep more secrets?" His voice is menacing. "It seems I gave him too much freedom over the last two years. I should've kept a closer watch on him, but his mother is not a woman you want on your bad side." His eyes soften at the mention of her.

I'm not sure what he means, so I stay quiet. I notice a set of double French doors on the other side of the room, but I'm not sure I could escape with Bruno lurking by.

"My wife is going to be ecstatic to hear the good news," he says, more to himself than to me. "Tell me, Gemma, do you know what your father did before his death?"

What a strange question. How does he know about Mario? Or is he talking about my real dad who died in the military?

"You see, Gemma—"

There is a loud bang outside the room and a flurry of commotion comes from somewhere in the house.

"Aww, the prodigal son has returned." He crosses his arms over his chest. "Bruno, take the newest member of the family to the corner," he commands and stands to his fullest height. "It's time I teach my son a lesson about family loyalty."

Bruno obeys and snatches me out of the chair, forcefully latching onto my upper arm with so much strength I know I'll have a large bruise later.

Just as we make it behind Mr. Falcone and off to the side of the room, the wooden door bursts open and off the hinges. In the doorway, stands my husband. The look on his face is something I've never seen before. He looks like he could take on an army. There is a band full of men behind him as he makes his way inside, not taking his eyes off his father. It's like two bulls about to go head-to-head. The tension in the room is elevated to the extreme, and it sucks all the oxygen out. I'm not sure what's about to happen, but it can't be good. And I have a feeling in the pit of my stomach that my life is about to implode.

CHAPTER SIXTEEN

Luca

M Y SHOULDER CONNECTS WITH THE FRONT DOOR, bursting through it. I'm met with two things—silence and the barrel of a gun shoved into my face.

My entire life, I've had to deal with guns and pussy-ass wannabes who thought they could take me down. Right in front of me is the last person I'd hoped to ever see again. The one who taught me everything I know in the world I grew up in when my pop was occupied with other business.

"It's time to come home now, Prince." Giovanni Mossimo Barone's deep voice commands the room.

I take in my surroundings, knowing I don't have the option of taking him down. He'd expect it after all. Five men stand in the room behind him, waiting for instructions. These men were assigned to me years ago to make sure I survived, and they've followed my every move despite my efforts to evade them.

The house is quiet—too quiet, and that worries me. She's supposed to be home right now, but I'm hoping that, by some miracle, she went over to her friend's place or out to the grocery store. *Anywhere but here.* Why the fuck did I decide to meet up with a new guy at work instead of coming straight home to my woman.

The moment the silent alarm at the house alerted me, I blew out of the meeting to my car and raced home. That alarm was put in place in case the unthinkable were to happen. I also have cameras situated around the house, and for some reason, I couldn't access them on the way over. It was the longest twenty minutes of my life. I'm panicking inside but refuse to cower or show any sign of distress. I was brought up to not show any emotions. Even when your life is ending, you are to show no signs of weakness.

"Emotions will get you killed, Son," Pop always insisted.

"Ask me, Prince," Gio taunts, and I hate that he knows I'm hanging on by a thread. I hate that he calls me that still, to this day. It gets under my skin, and I want to rip his throat out.

In an instant, I block the gun aimed at me, knocking it out of his hands and taking him by surprise. I've got him shoved up against the wall, my forearm up against his throat with just the right amount of pressure.

"Where's my wife?" I grit out. My teeth grind and my jaw ticks.

Gio's lip twitches a fraction, knowing that I've just given him the satisfaction of showing my weakness, but I don't give a fuck. She's my world, and I'll kill a hundred bastards with my bare hands if harm is ever brought on her.

"She's on a plane headed back to Vegas," Gio informs me. "Mr. Falcone wanted to make sure your arrival was immediate. Thought this was the best way to get you there."

My body stills and a million thoughts run through my mind. Will Pop hurt her to get me back home? Does she have her EpiPen and inhaler on hand? I've always made sure all the people around her carry them, just in case something happens and they have to intervene. Did she go quietly or is she scared? Fuck!

"She put up one hell of a fight," Cassio, my best friend and right-hand man, interrupts my internal thoughts and points over to Carlo, who's sporting a swollen eye and busted lip.

"I'll gut you like a fucking fish if you laid a hand on her." I twist and pull the metal from my waistband pointing it at Carlo while still holding Gio on the wall. My voice is deadly, and there is no doubt I could drop his ass dead with a bullet between his eyes. I don't care if we were friends growing up or not. I'd get two shots off before they could restrain me, but I think better of it. They have the one possession that matters the most to me, and I need to keep a clear head and focus on her.

I go to take a step toward him, but Gio stops me, grabbing my shoulder.

"Easy, Luca. No one touched her but me. She put up a struggle, but I sedated her quickly before she could hurt herself." His words don't bring me any comfort. "She was able to get the upper hand on Carlo though." He chuckles, as do Cassio and Bosco.

"Laugh it up, fuckers," Carlo sneers as he touches his lip.

My head is about to explode. This was what I'd worked so hard to get away from, and now my two worlds have collided. I was born into one and walked away from it. But I *chose* the other and never looked back.

"Mr. Falcone said it was time to come home. Our plane is ready to board now, and all your"—Gio looks around the room before settling back on me—"things will be packed up and shipped to the house on the compound."

"I want proof she's safe," I growl.

Cassio comes over with his phone and plays a video. It shows my beautiful wife taking Carlo down. A sense of pride fills my chest as I realize those awkward and hard sessions at the gym paid off, but then rage takes over when I watch Gio sink a needle into her. Moments later, she goes limp while Gio cradles her, laying her on the living room couch. What really surprises me is the person who comes into the video—a person who's been in our house many times over the last year and who we consider a friend. They gather my wife's sedated body and leave the house, ending the video. How could I have not seen them coming? How could I have let my guard down even for a moment and allowed them to snake their way into our lives undetected?

Resigned to my fate, I mentally prepare myself to head back to Las Vegas. I'd left for good reason—to be with the one who truly became my world, the one I love more than my own life.

"If one hair is out of place or there is even a scratch on her skin, I'll torture you in the worst way before I kill you."

I kick Gio's gun out of my way and head back out the door to the waiting SUV that I hadn't noticed parked across from the house. It takes a few minutes for everyone to pile in, but once the crew is loaded, we head out in silence. It takes us twenty minutes to get to the private jet on the runway, and all I can think about is my wife.

We exit the SUV, but Gio grabs my upper arm, holding me back while the others board.

"She'll be fine Luca. Trust me."

I shrug him off. "You don't know shit!" My jaw ticks, and I really want to lay him out. He doesn't know how hard it was to get her out of her shell, to make her feel secure and safe. How my very breath depends on her. He has no idea the lion's den he's sent her into.

"I know more than you think." His eyes are hard, reminding me that he's still the same man who trained me since I was a little boy. "Mr. Falcone has known your whereabouts since the moment you left the state of Nevada." Well, shit. "Changing your last name and living a different life didn't hide you from him. He let you leave and have your fun. Now, it's time to come home and get ready to take your position in the family. Though, he has no idea you're married." Gio nods at my wedding band. "I'm sure Mrs. Falcone will be ecstatic to be adding a daughter to the family."

I brush past him, knocking shoulders, and I can't help but think about what Gio just said. Had my father truly known about where I was this entire time? Had he kept tabs on me, despite my efforts to stay off his radar? Was I deluding myself to think walking away from my family was even possible? Probably.

My wife has no idea what my family is or does for a living. She'll have a heart attack once she learns what I've done in the past. I'm clueless as to how I'm going to tell her. Will she accept me for who

I really am? Accept my family? Christ, what if Pop tells her before I have the chance to explain? She'll think I'm a monster and run.

No, I won't let her have a choice. She's mine and has been from the moment I laid claim to her. She has no other choice but to accept it. I changed for her, but deep down I always knew this day was coming. I was just hoping to have a little longer before she found out about me and my family.

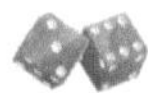

I can't believe I let Gio and my old crew get the drop on me. The shock I had when I came home rocked me, but I shouldn't have been surprised. Gio saying that Pop has known where I was all along floored me. I thought I'd done a pretty good job of wiping my tracks.

The video Cassio had on his phone of Gemma taking down Carlo was classic. She and Bianca had started taking self-defense classes right after their friendship started. I was thrilled, and it has helped her clumsiness tremendously. Don't get me wrong, she still has her moments, but they are fewer and far between.

Bianca.

That little snake is going to get a piece of my mind. Or a bullet between her eyes. After everything Gemma has been through with friends in the past, it's difficult for her to open up to anyone, and Bianca duped both of us. After this, she'll have a hard time trusting anyone again.

I'm going to be on that list, speaking of not trusting anyone again. I have yet to tell her *all* about my family. Well, the more in-depth version of my family. She knows I left because I didn't want to be a part of their business anymore, but I never told her the whole truth. I thought I'd have years before we crossed that bridge, not less than a year. I knew once we had kids, I wouldn't be able to keep them from Ma. She has been my best friend for as long as I can remember. To keep her away from her grandkids would've killed her. *Or led to her killing me.*

I climb the steps of the private jet waiting for us and take my seat toward the back. My old crew steers clear and takes their seats up front, except Gio. No, of course, he comes and sits right across from me.

"When things get back to normal, we need to talk," Gio speaks up as I take my phone out. "There are some things I need to tell you, and it might come as a shock."

"Nothing will ever be normal after today," I say, not looking up.

Before we take off from the private airport, I text Carson to get himself and two of our best guys up to Las Vegas ASAP and be on standby. I'm not sure what my father has planned, but once he took Gemma, all bets were off. Carson responds quickly that he'll get a team and be on the next flight out.

I lean back in my plush leather seat after pocketing my phone and tilt my head back. I feel a tension headache coming just thinking about how I'm going to explain this and not have her hate me and I close my eyes. I must've fallen asleep because the jolt of the jet touching down on the private runway startles me. I look around and see the sun has set. A sheen of sweat starts to form down my back. The jet takes a while to park and the bounce in my leg is making me grow even more impatient. Carlo takes a call and bounds off the aircraft into a waiting car before speeding off.

"Where'd he run off to?" Most orders come from Gio, who gets them from Pop.

"Mr. Falcone wants some time alone with Gemma before you get there. We're supposed to stall."

My hand goes immediately for my gun.

"I came willingly, but if you keep me from my wife, I'll send each and every one of you to your graves," I threaten, not caring that I grew up with all these guys.

Gio puts his hands up in surrender.

"I understand. That's why I sent Carlo ahead of the group. No detours, we will go directly to the main house," he placates.

"I fucking hate Carlo. He'd better keep his hands to himself, or he'll have more to worry about than that fat lip and black eye my wife gave him," I snap. My nerves are fried, and I can't squash the agitation.

The drive to the compound takes forever.

"Mr. Falcone had told everyone you'd gone to Italy to help oversee a new territory with your uncle," Cassio, my best friend since elementary, whispers and waits for me to respond, but I'm too busy thinking of what is happening with Gemma to care. "So, you wifed up, huh?" He nudges my arm as we're stopped at a red light. "She got a sister? Cuz she's hot as hell."

Everyone's avoided talking to me up to this point, but I should've known Cassio would be the one to break the tension in the car. I can't help but smirk for the first time since learning Gemma had been taken.

"No." I shake my head. "Only child." I raw-punch him in the upper arm. "And keep your eyes off *my* wife."

Cassio, Bosco, Carlo, and Leo all grew up together. All of their families were a part of my family's business.

"Never thought I'd see the day that you'd take on that responsibility. It suits you, man." He pauses. "I get it now, why you left and all. If there was someone out there for me, I'd do the same."

"Thanks, man."

I'd confided in Cassio and Bosco the turmoil I'd had but never gave anything away about Gemma or the very first time we met. They had known I was wanting—no, needing—to do my own thing. At least for a while.

"She'll be fine. Once Mrs. Falcone sees her and that rock on her finger, you'll be the one who has to make arrangements to spend time with your wife." He chuckles, knowing how my Ma is going to react to Gemma.

The moment is broken when we pull through the gates and up to the main house. I'm out of the car before it's come to a complete stop, storming up the steps and into the house. I hear noises coming from down toward the kitchen but keep going as I see two guards at the doors of my pop's study. I watch Bianca outside the door pacing, so I know Gemma is in there.

"You and I will talk later," I seethe, grabbing her arm with a jerk as she tries to rush past me.

"I'm sorry. I was told I had to." She's blubbering and border-line hysterical.

Cassio comes up beside me. "Not now, Luca."

I let her go and keep moving. The guards try to block my path and one of them grabs my arm, but I'm a man on a mission and all my training kicks into gear. To find and protect my wife. A fight ensues between me and the guards, but Cassio joins the action. He's always been trained to have my back no matter who or what comes up, even when I'm the one in the wrong. I've never had to ask for help from him. It's why Pop designated him as my second-in-command.

Once we've handed the guards their asses, I burst through Pop's study door, taking it off the hinges. What I find will haunt me forever.

Pop has his gun by his side with Bruno behind him holding a scared, shaking Gemma in the corner of the room. My hand imme-diately goes to my piece, pulling it out, but I leave it at my side.

"I'm glad you decided to come home, Son," Pop starts. "I was beginning to think you didn't love this family."

"You got my attention. I'm here. Now, let Gemma go and we can discuss whatever it is that has brought me back here."

"It was time for you to come home, Son. I let you have your fun and let you slack on your responsibilities, but now it's time to take your role in this family."

"I'm here, aren't I?"

"Yes, and apparently with a wife," he adds, looking over at Gemma. "Does she know about us? Does she know who you really are?" To the outside world his calm, smooth voice is inviting, but the ones who know him, know he's ready to strike out at any moment.

"Whatever you want to say, say to *me*. Don't bring her in on this. She has nothing to do with it."

"She has everything to do with it. Does she know what you've done?" He's pushing me.

"Don't do this now, Pop." I've never been one to be a nervous wreck in a hostile environment, but right now I'm sweating bullets. I need more time. She won't understand or be able to process all of this. He doesn't know her past.

"Don't do what? Tell my new daughter what you did all those years ago in her house?"

My heart sinks. I know what he is referring to. The night I killed Mario.

I take a step forward, but a hand clamps down on my shoulder. I know it's Gio holding me back. "Pop, you don't understand. Let us speak alone," I urge, not raising my voice to show him how out of control I'm feeling.

"I understand that my son kept a secret from me, and I think it's only fair to tell my new daughter the truth. We've never kept things from each other, and I'm not about to start now, Son."

My grip tightens on my gun.

"Easy, Luca," Gio whispers. He knows I'm about to lose my shit.

I notice my father's guards have come in and have taken positions around the room. Them verses us. How in the hell did we get here? Are we really about to have a shootout in his house?

My father turns to my wife, and I know there is nothing I can do short of shooting my pop to stop it.

"Darling—"

"POP!" I yell to stop him. My arm moves, and my gun now has aim toward the desk, but he doesn't even falter. I've never thought of raising my voice to Pop much less a gun, but he's provoking me.

Gemma is shaking uncontrollably now. Her breathing is elevated, and I worry about her having an asthma or panic attack. All attention has turned toward her, except for Pop's guards. They have their guns up and pointing at me and my old crew.

"Luca is the one who killed your father that night. He was the one in the house."

She gasps in shock and her face goes pale white. Her eyes pass between Pop and me. Pop turns and sees my gun pointed in his direction. His face contorts and his eyes narrow. He raises his gun but instead of aiming for me, he points it over to the corner of the room, where the love of my life is.

"I should punish you for lying to me and betraying your family. Is this how you show loyalty?" Pop threatens.

The sound of shifting clothes echoes behind me, and out of my peripheral vision, I see Cassio, Bosco, Carlo, and even Gio brandishing their guns. They have the room covered. I can see Gemma is moments away from passing out.

"Don't you dare point a gun at her!" Gio barks at Pop, surprising us all.

Never in all my life have I ever heard Gio talk to Pop that way. The tone even surprises Pop.

"This doesn't involve you, Giovanni. I suggest you put that gun down, or I might think you've switched sides on me, old friend." Pop's voice drips with venom as his best friend and second-in-command points his piece at him.

"No one will threaten *my* family and get away with it. That includes you, *old friend*." Gio meets Pop with the same force. His words again surprise us all, and for a moment I don't understand his meaning.

"Family?" Pop looks at Gemma and then back at Gio a few times. "My god."

Pop slowly lowers his gun, and Gemma's legs give out. She crumples, but Bruno hauls her up roughly by her arm and the back of her neck. She screeches as he manhandles her, and I lose my shit. I do what I should've done when I walked in and saw the situation. My finger squeezes the trigger and the sound of the bullet leaving the chamber explodes out of the gun. A mere second follows, and the body of Bruno lands on the floor in a heap. He had such a hard grip on Gemma that she falls back with him and lands on his chest.

The room descends into chaos as Pop yells for his guards to

stand down, and I make my way over to her. She's a total mess, and I'm not sure if she'll ever recover from this.

"You're okay, baby," I repeat over and over as I lift her into my arms. She fights me on instinct, but I hold her tight, not letting her see the dead man with a bullet between his eyes on the floor. "I've got you."

"Lu-ca!" She's huffing, and I know what she needs. Her breathing is worse, so I reach into my jacket pocket, pull out her inhaler, and give it a few shakes before bringing it up to her mouth. Her eyes are going wild and can't seem to focus on any one thing for long.

My hand goes to the back of her neck, and I steady her as I shove the Albuterol between her lips and pump the device. At first, her brain doesn't seem to register what is happening, so I try again, and her body takes over as it needs to, and she inhales.

"Breathe with me, amore mio," I coach, and she only has her eyes on me. Once she has her breathing back to normal, she chances a look around. The last several hours have finally caught up to her, and she passes out, going limp into my arms.

The room has gone quiet, and after I've gathered her in my arms, I turn and notice Gio, standing with his back to me, blocking everyone from viewing me and Gemma. I have a thousand questions right now, but my first priority is my wife. Cassio, Bosco, and Carlo stand side by side with Gio and make it an easy line to walk behind them to the door.

"Take her to your old room, and I'll have Dr. Fulton come by immediately. We obviously need to discuss things," Pop speaks into the silent room. He's pacing with a hand swiping through his hair.

The moment I make it out in the hall, I see Ma standing there.

"What is going on? Luca, I didn't know you were here." She takes steps toward me and bursts into tears. She goes to wrap me in her arms but belatedly registers that I'm carrying a woman and stops. "Who on earth is this? Is she okay? I heard a gunshot, and Mack wanted me into the saferoom, but I refused to come and see

what was happening down here," she explains, and I notice her tucking her gun into the pocket of her apron.

I need to get Gemma settled first, so I give Ma a quick reply.
"This is Gemma, my wife."

"Your wife?" Her delicate hand comes up to her chest in
surprise.

Just like a lightbulb turning on for the first time, Ma beams
and claps her hands together. Then her eyes dim as she looks over
to Pop's study. "What did your father do?" Her hands immediately
go to her hips.

"I love you Ma, but I need to make sure she's okay."

"Yes, of course, use your old room, and then come down here
and tell me everything." She reaches up and places a kiss on my
cheek, then does the same to Gemma. "My heart is full, baby boy."

I walk down the hall and up a flight of stairs toward my old
bedroom. I could take her to my house, but I'm not sure there is
anything there for us since I've been gone for over two years now.
I'll need to make arrangements to have the house cleaned and groceries brought in.

My room is the same as I left it when I decided to move out
almost a decade ago. The bed is still in the middle of the room, and
the door to the balcony has the same blinds. I can hear the rain
starting to come down in a rare Las Vegas storm. I hope that when
she wakes, I'll have the words to explain all this.

A knock on the door alerts me, and my hand goes to my gun.
Cassio pops his head in.

"Doc Fulton is here to have a look at Mrs. Falcone." He nods
over to my wife whom I've laid down on the bed.

"Send him in."

Moments later, an older man I've known my entire life and
who has saved me more times than I can count, comes in with his
black medical bag.

"Good to see you again, Doc." I stand and shake his hand.

"Luca, my boy, I thought I'd die before I saw you back in this state again," he answers. "And to hear you came home with a wife at that." He nods over to Gemma.

He steps around me and sets his bag on the end of the bed, then checks her pulse. Doc does a quick exam, and I fill him in on her allergies and asthma.

"Everything looks normal. She's just in a bit of shock, I'm sure. Let her rest for a while, and she'll be good as new. I'd like to get some blood work done so that if there is an incident later on, I can have it in the family file. I'll also send out for more inhalers and EpiPens to have on-hand with her security."

I nod, thankful that he always knows what we need. We walk out, and I find Cassio standing outside the door.

"Mr. and Mrs. Falcone are asking for you to come down when Dr. Fulton leaves. I'll stand guard and let you know when she wakes." I know he can see my hesitation. "I'll protect her with my life, Luca." He places his hand on my shoulder.

I retreat into the room and place a kiss on her lips before whispering, "I love you, and I'll be right back." I place pillows all around her like a baby, so she won't roll off the bed.

The door closes behind me, and I give it one last look before I turn away and Cassio moves to stand in front of it. I descend the stairs and can hear Ma's loud voice coming from the study. Gio is standing outside the door and turns when he sees me coming.

"I will tell you right now, Arturo, if you don't make this right with our new daughter, you'll be sleeping in the nearest roach motel this city has to offer! I'll make sure the guards kick your ass out and won't let you in!"

"Now wait one minute, Addy—" we hear, but Pop is cut off.

"No, you wait a minute! She is going to have our future grand-babies, and if you've put a rift in that, I'm going to make you regret it."

The brand-new door opens and Ma is crossing her arms over her chest.

"Both of you come in here," she demands, and we both hop to it.

When we walk in, I note that Bruno's body has been taken care of and there is no sign that he was ever there. Pop's men worked fast to clean and fix the door.

Pop looks like a chastised schoolboy and knocks back his amber-colored liquor as he falls into his chair, pulling his fingers through his hair. "Did you have to kill him, Luca?" Pop asks as he follows my gaze. I stand behind the chair, waiting for the conversation to start.

"Anyone who thinks they can touch my wife will be met with the same fate," I answer coolly, letting him know that the next time, I won't hesitate to kill him on the spot.

"I wasn't going to harm her. What kind of person do you take me for? She's family, for Christ's sake."

"Then why did you have Bruno hold her? Why point your gun toward her?" I seethe, trying to not let my anger get the best of me.

"I was trying to make a point. A poor one—I see now but needed you to understand the severity of your actions."

"I hear them loud and clear now." I grind my teeth.

"Arturo Falcone, I'm so mad at you right now." Ma steps in and shakes her finger. She turns back to Gio and me, then motions for us to have a seat.

Gio and I both take a seat across from Pop and wait. Ma circles around and stands off to the side of the desk. She's a firecracker when angry so everyone knows to keep a safe distance until she simmers down.

"Now that I have the full story, you men are going to answer some questions."

Pop pours himself another drink and offers us each one. We gladly take him up on it. Ma waits until the last glass is poured before she pounces. "Let's start with you first." She points over at Gio, and I watch his shoulders stiffen. "Then, I'll get to you!" She points over at me, and I feel my own muscles lock into a flex, bracing for battle.

Ma may be a loving, caring, gentle woman, but when you fire

her up, stand out of her way. And from the lashing we heard outside the door a few minutes ago, I know she'll hang us up by our toes if we don't comply.

"You've had a daughter and didn't tell us until now?" There is a bit of hurt in her voice. I know she considers Gio to be a part of our family. He's been with us since before Pop and Ma married. Hell, he was the only one there at their wedding.

Gio is Gemma's dad? How did we not know this? Why didn't he say anything? Gemma is going to be so happy to know that she still has family alive but then devastated that he never came for her.

"Mossimo Barone," I say out loud. I had an inkling in the back of my mind when Gemma was pouring her heart out to me about her biological dad dying in the military. I watch as he flinches at the name knowing what he did. "You son of a bitch!" My temper is starting to boil as I can already feel the hurt she's going to endure over all of this.

Gio throws back the bourbon, then clears his throat.

"I didn't realize she existed until she was about fifteen or sixteen. Even then, I was in denial. Her mother, Lily, and I met at a pub one night and hit it off." He pauses, as if going down memory lane. "She was beautiful, and fun, and had this presence about her. I was immediately drawn to her."

I know the feeling because that is exactly how I feel about Gemma.

"She was here at the university for an art degree. We started seeing each other almost every day. I'd told her I was in the service and was on leave. Chicks always jumped at that, and I was young and stupid back then. I thought it would impress her, but she didn't seem to care. We'd been together for about two months when I was arrested for Charlie Turner's murder. Remember, I made the plea for a two-year stint. I sent Leo a letter while I was locked up, telling him to write and tell Lily I'd been sent off overseas. We wrote back and forth a few times, but after a while, I decided to cut ties with her. I thought it wasn't fair to lie and string her along, so I told Leo to send her a letter saying I was killed and to make it look all official."

He rubs his hand up and down the back of his neck, looking ashamed.

"I had no idea she was pregnant. I would've never turned my back on her if I'd known." He sounds genuine. "She was everything to me, and I didn't want my life to touch her." He looks over at me, and I can see the sympathy in his eyes. "When we visited Mario at his house, I saw the photos of Lily, and it threw me. At the time I had no idea that Gemma was mine. I was still trying to wrap my head around the woman in the pictures being my Lily. A few days later, I started looking into Mario and his wife and confirmed that she was my Lily. I saw she'd had a daughter, but it still didn't register that she was mine until months later. By the time everything sank in, Gemma was in the guardianship of a teacher and was doing well. I thought if I tried to step in that I might screw her up or do more harm than what was already done. My lifestyle isn't the best to bring an emotional teenager into, especially after losing her mother and father figure so close together. I thought she'd be better off if she didn't know I existed."

He looks over at me.

"We've known all along that you spared her life. You can't be in this life and not know every detail that happens." He stares hard at me, and I'm shocked.

"You've known all this time?" I question, stunned.

"Yes. I noticed her coming up from the backdoor when I was upstairs retrieving Mario's laptop, but we sure as hell didn't know you were pursuing her and planning to leave the family business for her," Gio says, then leans back in his chair. "Even though I should beat you within an inch of your life for leaving a witness behind, I'm also grateful you spared her."

"Nor did we know Gio had a daughter and was keeping it from us." Pop glares at Gio. They've known each other a long time and trust one another like brothers. I can only imagine what this might do to their friendship.

"I thought by not telling you, Arturo, I was saving her, but now I can see my mistake. Our kids seem to have connected us even further and without anyone realizing it."

A figure runs across the rainy windows of the study and has us all turning to watch as it passes in a flash. My body immediately is on high alert, and I stand. Moments later, the door bursts open, and Cassio huffs out of breath. The left side of his face is red and swollen, with a cut right beside his eye.

"She ran. I heard movement, and when I peeked in, she hit me with a tennis racket and fled out the door to the balcony. When I realized what had happened, she was gone." He breathes out in a rush.

My legs spring toward the French doors that lead to where we just saw Gemma bolt. I take off in a dead run.

She's running scared. She's running from me.

CHAPTER SEVENTEEN

Luca

MY HEART IS HAMMERING IN MY CHEST AS I SURVEY THE area. It's dark, and I can hear my parents shouting to the guards for them to stand down and not spook her. Just as I'm about to take off in one direction to keep searching, the flood lights turn on and light up the entire area. It takes my eyes a few moments to adjust, but I see movement and take off at a dead sprint. I'm still in the dress pants and white button-up shirt I wore this morning for work. The shirt pulls tight across my chest and shoulders as I pump my arms to keep pace with my legs.

She's got a big head start on me, but I'm quick. Just as she makes it over the hill and almost to the wall at the perimeter, I catch her. My arms circle her middle and take her by surprise. She screams and tries to fight me off, but I hold her steady as our legs slow to a stop and we sink to the muddy ground. I'm under her, not letting her body touch the soaked ground.

"Let me go. Pl-please let me go. I-I pro-mise not to tell a single person what happened. I sw-swear." Her breathing is labored again, and I fear she's going to have another attack after all the running she just did. "Ple-please d-don't kill m-me."

Oh, baby girl.

My heart breaks that she'd think I could ever harm her in that way. Though, I might chain her to the bed after the fright she just gave me. I've finally managed to lessen my obsession with her a little by not checking in on her every hour, but now, I think having her out of my sight isn't going to happen for a long while.

"I can't let you go. Not now, not ever," I tell her as I bury my face in her neck. Doesn't she know that I'll never be able to live my life without her in it? That she is my entire world? The thought of her not being in my life makes me hold her a little tighter.

We're soaking wet with the rain coming down steadily. Her body is shaking to the point of convulsions, and she's crying hysterically now, not making any sense. I wish I could take all this hurt away. I wish I could go back and tell her about my family so this wasn't such a shock.

A dark thought crosses my mind, and I temper my blood pressure. Pop did this. If only he'd come to *me* instead, we could've avoided all this. Avoided having my wife watch me kill a man in front of her, revealing the monster hidden beneath the surface.

It only takes a short while, and her body gives out again. She struggled until her body gave out. Her heart is beating normally, so I know she's going to be fine. Once I gather her up in my arms, I make my way back to the main house, but Pop and Ma pull up in one of the utility vehicles, along with Dr. Fulton.

"Oh dear, is she okay?" Ma frets and hops out to come over. Pop is grumbling about her getting wet, but she ignores him. "Here, put this around her." Ma hands over a thick blanket when we are all seated in the vehicle.

I have Gemma in my lap, bundled up, and I'm holding her tight to me with my fingers on her wrist, checking her pulse. I've never been so scared as I was when I saw her running away from me. If it were possible, my heart would have burst out of my chest. Dr. Fulton is seated beside me checking her over.

Once we've made it up to the house, I take her up to my old room, brushing past everyone. I hear my parents calling out, both trying to talk to me at the same time, but I ignore them. I know how to take care of my wife. Pop has done enough to put a massive wedge in my marriage. The last thing I need is advice from him.

I place her on the bed as Dr. Fulton takes a needle out of his bag.

"I think she needs a little sedation to let her body relax. This should get her a few hours' rest." He administers the sedative into her arm, then continues to check her vitals.

Ma comes in with a change of clothes.

"Go get showered and wash off all the mud. I should be done by the time you get out." I nod and watch as Dr. Fulton exits the room and closes the door behind him, leaving only Ma and me.

Not wanting to waste any more time, I head to the bathroom, shuck off my dirty wet clothes, and jump into the shower. The ice-cold water shocks my body as my mind replays the image of Gemma almost making it to the wall. Dread slithers through me as I realize I might not be able to fix this, but I'll do whatever it takes to make this right with her.

I shut the water off after only a few minutes and wrap a towel around my waist, heading for the bedroom. When I open the door, we're alone, and Ma has changed Gem into some pajamas. I'm pulling on a pair of boxers when a light tap raps at my door. Placing a pillow right up against Gemma, I move to pull the door open as quietly as possible. What greets me has me almost bursting out laughing, but I stay silent to avoid startling noises that could trigger her. I know she's out, but I still don't want her to hear voices while she's sedated.

"I know you want to laugh," Cassio huffs. "Go on, get it all out now. Bosco and Leo both can't stop."

"You gonna be okay?" My voice trembles with the effort not to laugh my ass off. Both he and Carlo took a beating from my wife, and I couldn't be prouder of her assault on the men she thought were trying to harm her.

Cassio touches his swollen eye with a wince.

"I can't believe she got the upper hand on me." He shakes his head. "When the fuck did you ever play tennis? I mean, as soon as I opened the door to check on her, she pounced out of nowhere. I remember the first two hits, but God, I think she got me four times before she bolted out through the balcony door. I think I was too stunned at first to move. Doc said I'll live and gave me some pain-killers. Nothing is wrong with my sight." He shrugs. "I wanted you to know that Gio has volunteered to stand guard tonight, and I'll be back first thing in the morning."

I nod.

As the next in line to take over as the head of our family, I've come to know that there is never a moment when I'm not being guarded. I'm not surprised it's Gio doing the watching after every-thing that just came out, but I think we all panicked when we watched Gemma try to escape from us.

Movement catches my eye as Gio climbs the stairs and makes his way down the hall toward us. He nods to Cassio, who takes the hint and leaves. "I'll be on watch tonight. Garrett and Luis will be posted outside on your balcony. Everyone on the compound has orders to stand down if Gemma takes off again and to approach her with caution."

"She's going to have a lot of questions."

"I know, and that's why I wanted to stand guard tonight. I've got a lot of soul searching to do to try and find the answers that will help her understand—or at least make the most sense to her."

"She may want nothing to do with you," I clip. "If that's the case, you'll need to accept that because what she says and what she wants supersedes what you want. I won't let you be a dark cloud around her."

"I understand that," he grits. "I'll take whatever she is willing to give me right now and hope for the best."

"I've got some people coming in from San Diego that will be a part of my team. They've been vetted and will make the crew stronger."

He nods, and I turn away, effectively dismissing him to be with my wife. "See you in the morning."

I close the door and lock it. I have no desire to sleep, but if I do fall asleep, I want to be able to hear if she tries to leave me again. She won't get as far as she did before.

With the covers pulled back, I remove the pillows and crawl into my old bed next to her. She whimpers when the pillow is missing but stops when I pull her to my body and entwine our legs making sure to put her cold feet between my thighs. Gemma snuggles closer until she's practically on top of me.

The morning light wakes me, and I try to shake the horrible dream I had. My body is primed and ready to start my morning between my wife's legs, but I don't feel the warmth of her body. Panic sets in, and I jackknife from my position. My eyes are a bit blurry from only a few short hours of sleep. They settle on the tiny figure at the edge of the bed by the headboard. The events from the day before come rushing back, and I'm reminded of the shit show that really happened and that my dream was actually reality.

Thank God she didn't run again.

Gemma is hunched down with her arms wrapped around her legs and pulled up to her chest.

"Morning, amore mio," I greet trying to slow my heart rate. I shift toward her, and she watches my every movement like a hawk.

She doesn't answer.

"I know you must be completely confused right now, but if you'll just hear me out, I promise everything will be just fine."

Her body is stiff and unmoving.

"You must have a million questions," I push, hoping for some kind of verbal response. When she doesn't, I continue, "Remember me telling you about my family? That I wanted out and to branch off on my own."

She still doesn't make a single sound and she doesn't move. The only relief I get is watching her chest rise and fall.

"My family isn't like a normal Italian-American family. We dabble in—"

"I-I won't say anything. I pr-omise," she stutters.

"No, that's not it." She's not understanding, and I'm afraid that too much has happened for her to have an open mind. "No one is going to hurt you. I know what happened yesterday scared you, but please know that nothing and no one will ever hurt you, not here." I inch closer to her because if I can get her to feel me and have her in my arms, she'll melt into me, and I'll be able to explain everything to her. "My pop is a little over the top making points, and I'm so sorry he had his men grab you from our home." Another inch. She doesn't seem to notice that I've moved closer. "I should've told you the entire truth about my family. I was worried that you'd never give me a chance if you knew."

She blinks, so I know she's hearing me. I'm so close now.

"Wh-ho are you people?" It's so low I almost don't hear her.

"Baby—" I reach out for her with my arms, sweeping from underneath to place her in my lap and secure her to me, but the door bursts open startling both of us.

Gemma leaps off the bed and backs up against the balcony door.

"It is true!" says a voice from over my shoulder.

I'd know that voice from anywhere.

Alice.

"OMG!! I finally have a sister!" Alice squeals barging into the room further. "When Ma said you'd come home, I was excited, but when she said you'd brought back a wife, I didn't believe it. It's like Christmas morning!"

Alice has always been over the top. If it wasn't such a security nightmare, she'd probably do well as an actress.

I slowly get off the bed so as not to spook Gemma any further and turn toward my sister.

"I'm here, Sis," I say, and she comes barreling into my chest. I circle her tiny frame, and she reminds me of how little Gem is. My cheek rests on the top of her head as I keep my eyes on my wife. She hasn't moved, but I can tell she is thinking about trying the door to the balcony again.

"How'd you get in here, Alice?" I ask, remembering I locked the door last night.

She looks sheepishly around.

"I distracted Garrett and used my key." She holds up the offending item, then puts it back in her back pocket. "Oh, Luca don't you ever leave for that long again!"

Alice backs up and tries to punch me in my gut. She then turns her attention to her new sister-in-law. "She's beautiful," Alice states like she's looking at a piece of artwork.

"Gemma, I'd like to introduce you to my little sister, Alice. Alice, this is my wife, Gemma." I can't help the pride I feel when I say that word out loud. It's been almost a full year, and I don't think I'll ever tire of saying it.

Alice wastes no time pushing past me to bounce over to Gemma and engulf her in the biggest hug. She has no boundaries and never has. Gemma's arms are at her side as Alice crushes her. "We are going to be the bestest of friends!!" my sister exclaims, placing her hands on Gemma's shoulders.

"Oh, good lord in heaven! Alice, I told you not to disturb them, and look what you've done," Ma says from the doorway. "Give the poor girl a chance to breathe this morning before you smother her."

"Morning, Ma," I say as she comes in and gives me a hug.

"Morning, baby boy." She smiles up at me, beaming. Ma always loved having all her chicks under one roof. "Now, let me have a turn to introduce myself."

She shoves past me and walks over to Alice and Gemma. My wife is just looking back and forth from my sister to Ma. I'm sure this is still a shock and so overwhelming to her.

"Oh my, you are the prettiest little darling. I'm Adele, Luca and Alice's mother. You must be Gemma."

She finally nods, still not saying a word.

"She isn't a mute, is she?" Alice busts out.

"Alice!" Ma and I both yell at her at the same time.

"What? If she is, that's fine. I'm sure we can have an instructor to come and teach us all sign language."

"Alice, go and find some clothes for Gemma for the next few days. She seems to be around your size," Ma instructs, dismissing her.

My over-the-top sis huffs but complies. "I'LL SEE YOU SOON!" Alice shouts out as if Gemma is deaf after grabbing her for another hug. I can't help but roll my eyes. It'd be funny if it were any other situation.

"I'm very sorry for my children; you'd think I raised them in a circus," Ma jokes. She reaches out very slowly and caresses Gemma's hands in hers. "I know yesterday was a whirlwind and there are a lot of questions that need to be addressed, but I want you to know that you can come to me for anything. We take being in this family very seriously around here. I've been so worried about Luca, and to find out he added to our family with you has made my heart full. I hope, over time, you will be able to accept us as your family too. And to not judge us all on the actions of a few." She cuts her eyes over to me.

Again, Gemma only nods.

"My husband has some apologizing to do, so please make him grovel a little before you fully forgive him." I watch my ma wink at my wife. "And to this guy." She elbows me in the ribs. "We need to keep these husbands on their toes."

"Ma," I groan, knowing I'm already in the doghouse.

The tension in Gemma's shoulders has relaxed slightly, but she's still wound up tight like a spring.

"Here you go!" Alice bounces back into the room with an armful of clothes and sets them on the end of the bed.

"Breakfast is ready when you two want to come down, but I'd suggest having Rosa bring up your meals so you two can have some discussions. Let Bart know; he's on duty today."

"Thanks, Ma."

She smiles at me before turning back to Gemma. "I know this is overwhelming, but please give us a chance to right our wrongs." Ma hugs her again, then leaves with Alice by her side, closing the door behind her. Just before she closes it, she gives me the look that says, *'Make this right.'*

The silence is deafening after the door clicks shut. Gemma is looking down at her feet, and I can't form any words to make a coherent sentence. Where am I supposed to start? Do I tell her everything and risk rejection? Shit!

"Can I use the bathroom?" Her voice is timid, and I hate that she's lost her confidence.

"You don't have to ask permission, Gem," I say as I take a step to her. She winces, and my heart cracks. "Please, don't do that. I'd never lay a hurtful hand on you. I love you so much." I place a finger under her chin so I can see her eyes. My hand cups her cheek. "I love you more than my own life. I know that your trust in me is shaken, but I swear I'll tell you everything and explain it. Give me a chance to fix this. Don't shut down on me or push me away."

She stares at me, and I know I need to give her time and a little space to process everything. I hate that we can't just go about our day like normal. Our life was perfect before yesterday.

"Why don't you take a shower and get dressed? I've got a few phone calls to make, and then we can have breakfast and talk. I'll answer any questions you have, okay?"

She finally nods, and I lean in and kiss her forehead. I'll take what I can get at this point. I watch as she gathers some of Alice's clothes and walks into the bathroom. My heart cracks even more when I hear the lock on the door set into place.

Give her time, my mind keeps chanting.

A deep sigh leaves my lungs as I ponder my next moves. I grab my pants from last night and make a call. It rings three times before they pick up. "Shit has hit the fan. I'm in Las Vegas, and I need you here."

CHAPTER EIGHTEEN

Gemma

S*NICK!*

The sound of the lock puts my racing heart more at ease even though I know for a fact Luca could shoulder through this door in one try. At least I have a barrier between us to think. He's always given me space if needed during our time together. My mind flashes over the past twenty-four hours and I can't help letting a whimper creep out. I throw my hand over my mouth to silence the noise. My free hand finds the light switch and illuminates the bathroom. I can hear Luca talking to someone, so I quickly move to the shower and turn it on.

I can't believe that yesterday I was having my last day of school with my kids and now I'm...shit, where the hell am I?

My head starts to pound, so I drop my clothes and jump into the steaming water. It pelts against my skin, and I stay under the deluge for as long as I can, trying to waste time before I have to face what's on the other side of the door again.

What is going to happen to me? Are they going to keep me here forever and never let me go? Do I try to make another run for it? Why does everyone have guns if they're all family? Should I play the perfect wife and gain their trust until I can find help? Do I get a phone call? Who the hell are these people?

Knock! Knock!

"Breakfast is here!" I hear Luca call over the water.

Shit! Am I ready to face him? I have so many questions racing through my mind that I can't focus on just one. His dad said he killed Mario. Is that true? Was he the one who was at the house that night? Did Luca threaten to kill me in that pantry?

My eyes stare at the closed door for a beat as I mentally prepare my big girl panties to take control of this. *Right!?* I reach for the knob, turn off the water, and catch a glimpse of myself in the mirror. Holy hell, I look worse than I feel.

After another ten minutes of trying to make myself look less frightened and adding more questions to my already overflowing list, I slowly unlock the door and carefully peek out.

Luca is typing on his phone but snaps his neck toward me upon hearing the door open.

"Hey, baby girl, I've got all your favorites this morning." He motions to the balcony where I tried to escape last night after clobbering that guy. I'm about to tell him in my most confident voice to shove the food where the sun don't shine, but my body becomes my biggest traitor and my stomach growls.

Thanks a lot, stupid stomach.

So, instead of giving him my attitude, I decide to hold off for a bit and let him lead me out the door onto the balcony where a table and two chairs have been magically placed—because I swear they weren't there last night or I'd have definitely tripped over them.

Luca, with his impeccable manners, pulls my chair out and helps me slide it closer to the table. *Geesh! Why does he make it so hard to not swoon over him? Focus, Gem, stick to the game plan. We are furious with this man and need answers!*

"You look beautiful this morning," he compliments as he sits down and starts plating food for us. I'd normally find it endearing that he'd want to take care of me, but today I find it annoying and unnecessary.

"Hmm," is all I give him, but when I look up at his face, I see him frown at my reaction. A knot twists in my chest. "Thank you," I quickly add.

After Luca plates himself a large assortment of food, we eat in silence and let the tension build. Out of the corner of my eye, in the distance, I notice men walking the large property.

"I know you must have a million questions. Please talk to me. I can't handle this silent treatment."

"I'm not even sure where to begin," I answer after a beat. "You killed Mario?" I blurt out. "You were the one that threatened me in the pantry?"

"How about you ask me who my family is? And then we'll go from there, and I'll walk you through every step." He eases forward and lays the gentlest hand on mine.

I feel like my entire world is about to be blown up, just like the day I found out my mom had been killed.

You can do this, Gemma! Let's test out our big girl panties and all those years in therapy.

With my spine straight, I square my shoulders, "Okay, who are you, and what kind of freaking family do you come from?"

There is a slight smirk on his face when I say 'freaking' instead of the cuss word. Being a teacher limits your vocabulary, and my brain is still in school mode.

"This isn't the time to be funny, Luca!" I try to pull my hand back, but he keeps me in his grasp.

"I'm sorry, Gem. I know it isn't. I can only imagine what you must think of me and this entire situation, but please know I love you with all my heart, and everything that has been done on my side has been because you're my whole world."

"Well!"

When Luca releases my hands and promptly stands, it surprises the hell out of me. I expect him to start pacing or leave the patio, but instead, he scrapes his chair over to my side, and turns my chair to face him so that we are knee-to-knee and eye-to-eye. He catches both my hands in a tight grip again. "There's no easy way to put this, so here goes. My family is in the mafia."

Of all the things he could've said…

Before I can contain it, I burst out a giggle. *This man!*

"Luca, stop this right now and tell me what is really happening here," I demand.

His face is so serious that the hairs on the back of my neck stand. *Oh, no.*

"You're serious?" My eyes bounce back and forth between his eyes looking for any trace of humor.

"I wouldn't joke about this. I promised to be honest with you, and I'll tell you everything you need to know to understand about me and my—no, *our* family."

Mafia? Is that still a thing? I look around at our surroundings and pause.

"Where are we?" This doesn't look like New York or Chicago.

"Las Vegas, Nevada."

"But I thought the mob was in Chicago or New York?"

He tries but fails to stifle a chuckle. "Baby girl, you and Bianca watch way too many gangster movies."

I frown at the mention of Bianca and his expression slowly dissolves to match mine. My head is treading just barely above water with all this, and I forgot about her. "Did you—"

"I had no idea she was working for my father," he answers before I finish my sentence. "Had I known, she wouldn't have gotten within five-hundred yards of you."

Betrayal.

Again.

Just when I think I've gotten my life on the right track and have the family I've always wanted, the rug is pulled out from under me again. Why can't I ever have a stable life where I'm not thrown a curveball at every turn?

Luca reaches for my chin and cups my cheek.

"I'm going to make this right. I'll earn your trust in me again," he promises, but I'm not so sure. I feel like our entire relationship is one big, fat lie. How do you come back from that?

He starts telling me all about his family and the dynamics of their business. He tells me all about the five families that run Vegas and the rundown of each of their dealings. From there, he recalls our meeting in Mario's house, my childhood home.

"So, it was you? This entire time, you were the one who threatened and terrorized me that night." I whimper, recalling how scared I was. "Do you have any idea what I went through? Every night, I barricaded my door and window at school, terrified that the person who held me in that pantry would come find me and kill me like I found Mario that night."

I shove the chair back and stand, letting it fall over behind me as I start to pace away from Luca. He must think I'm about to bolt down the stairs located near us because he rushes over to me, righting my chair before matching my steps the length of the balcony.

"Meeting you at the pool wasn't a coincidence, was it? You've been stalking me," I accuse. My mind is starting to clear, and the events of our entire relationship are coming into focus.

"I wouldn't say I've been stalking you. I've kept tabs on you over the years since the Mario drama. I tried to leave you alone. I truly did, but there was this pull you had on me. I couldn't shake it." His eyes are pleading with me to believe him, but right now I can't trust myself to think clearly or objectively.

"I can't believe this." I run my fingers through my hair and pull at the roots, trying to wrap my mind around everything he's told me so far. Somehow, I don't think we've even touched the surface of the entire situation. "What else have you done that put you on my radar since Malibu?"

Luca huffs, pulling at his own hair and letting me know I'm not going to like what he has to say next.

When he finishes telling me every little detail about our time together up until yesterday, my body is shaking. I feel stupid for being so naïve about everything and disgusted that I had no clue as to what was happening right under my nose. Carson was living on our property as protection. Luca's real job is underground gambling.

"This whole time, my life has been one big lie. You've—"

"No," he rushes over, crowding me. "My love for you has never been and will never be a lie. I've loved you for so long. Please don't say that. Yes, our meeting might not have been as random as you thought, but everything that has happened between us since we met and our feelings have been true. We can't fake that."

"I wasn't given that chance to pick you or any of this!" I yell in his face, breaking down. "You orchestrated and manipulated everything! You must think I'm the stupidest person on the planet. Poor little lost, foolish Gemma, who didn't have anyone, is finally shown some attention and fell right into your trap. I can't believe I fell for all of your bullshit." I can't keep the sarcasm out of my tone. "You say you love me, but this isn't love! It's control and obsession. I didn't get a choice in how I wanted to live. You stole that from me!"

Before I can register what my body is doing, my hand snaps out and makes contact with Luca's cheek. My heart starts to pound against my ribcage. Holy shit! My hand stings, and I bring it up to my mouth in shock. What did I just do? Oh my gosh! I've never erupted like that before.

"I-I didn't mean to do that. Oh my god! I'm so—"

He doesn't take his eyes off of me, "I deserve that and much more. If you need to do it again to make yourself feel better, then do it." He steps closer to me using his hands to rub my upper arms. "What I can't take is you leaving me."

"Leaving? Do I even have a say in the matter?"

He shakes his head as his jaw ticks. My stomach drops at the thought of him not being in my life.

"I've been without you, and that is not something I'm willing to go back to. You could leave, but I'd find you. The best and safest place for you is by my side. Being in the mafia is hard, but you'll get used to it."

By the time he finishes telling me about being the next in line to take over for his father, my body feels as though I've swum over a hundred laps in a pool. The sun is high in the sky, and several hours have passed. My head hurts from all the information, and he has answered every one of my questions and then some. My hope of escaping dims more and more.

"How does Gio fit into all this? Is he my biological dad—the one my mom spoke about dying in the military?"

"Gio was never in the military here, and I think that's a conversation you should have with him. I was given a very brief run-down last night before you fled and I don't have those answers. If you want, I'll be with you when you're ready to speak with him."

A rush of air leaves my body, and I sink back into my chair. My muscles are tight and aching from all the tension. "I don't know if I'm ready to even have a conversation right now on that subject," I say honestly.

Luca squeezes my hands. "I know this is a lot to digest."

Understatement of the year.

There is a knock on the French doors of his room's patio and Luca stands to answer it. Just as I'm rubbing my fingers over my temples, I hear a familiar voice that brings a fresh flood of tears. "Honey, are you okay?" Allison comes rushing over, and another sob bursts out of me. She holds me tight, and I fall limply into her. "Let's get you inside so we can talk."

I lean on her as we head back into Luca's room. She helps me sit up against the headboard as she makes herself comfortable on the side of the bed. When I look around, I see Luca is nowhere to be found.

"I thought it might be better if it was just the two of us for a while," she assures me.

"How did you get here?" I whisper, afraid that this might be a test and Luca might have the room bugged listening in on our conversation.

"Luca called me this morning and briefly told me that you needed me here. He set up transportation for me to fly here as soon as possible."

I look around the room as I lean in to speak. "You have to help me get out of here. I'm not sure it's safe for you to even be here."

"Tell me what's going on first and then we can figure out safety. I'm almost a hundred percent certain Luca would never knowingly put you in any type of danger."

"You don't know him, Allison. He isn't what I thought. I've been set up."

"Set up? For what?" she questions.

"He's been stalking me."

Allison takes one of my hands and holds it in hers. "Why don't you start from the beginning and tell me what is going on?"

I start from the beginning but leave out some details, not wanting to involve her too much in this mess. This way, she can't be implicated and called as a witness if something happens.

As I'm telling her about Luca knowing me the entire time and how our meeting wasn't an accident, I notice that she doesn't seem to be shocked. She's calm—too calm—for my liking.

I pull my hand from her.

"Wait, did you know about this? Do you know Luca and his family?" My voice goes up an octave, hoping I'm wrong. Is she a part of all this like Bianca?

"Gemma, what I can tell you is that Luca came to see me shortly after your return from Malibu as a patient."

What the hell?

"What I can tell you is that if I thought you were in any type of danger from him, I'd one hundred percent tell you to run and never look back. Remember all those sessions where I encouraged you to ask more about his family or be more involved in his business? You needed to make those decisions on your own. You'd come such a long way, and I was only there to be a tool for you to use."

"You knew?" The accusation is bitter in my belly. Is there a single person in my life who hasn't been keeping something from me?

I feel as though I'm a puppet, following along with the script of someone else's show. How did I not know that all these people in my life didn't meet organically? That they were placed to sway me in a certain direction. Like a herded sheep.

"You were thriving, Gemma. You'd opened up and were living your life like I'd never seen you do when you came back from Malibu. When Luca told me who he was and that he left this life behind to have you, I made it perfectly clear that you were my main priority. If I'd thought he was going to hinder any part of your life, I would've told you. He knew this and promised me that he would die before anything from his past would touch you. We spoke about his life here, but we mainly spoke about what he could do as your man to make you the happiest."

She pauses briefly and I try to absorb everything she just told me.

"I'm sorry I didn't tell you, honey, but I truly believe that he loves you and wants to give you the world. Did he keep a huge chunk of his family history from you? Yes. Did he keep his true identity from you and only give you a small piece of who he is? Yes. Are you two going to have to work on building that trust back? Yes. But, Gemma, can you honestly say that this is something the two of you can't work through once you've had some time to think it over and talk to each other about it? Are you truly going to walk away because he couldn't help being born into his family? Are you proud of the man you thought was your father? You don't talk about or tell anyone about that time or mention your name change that often, if at all."

She leaves the questions floating in the air, but all I can think about right now is getting away from this crazy house I feel trapped in. "I want to leave this place," I admit. "I want to go home." I feel like no one is listening to me or understanding the situation.

Do I even have a home? I moved in with Luca shortly after meeting him.

"Then leave. Get up and walk right out the door," she states easily. "I can guarantee you that you are not a prisoner here."

Did she not hear me telling her what happened last night when I tried to escape?

A knock on the door cuts off any reply I might have come up with. Adele walks in and takes in the room with a friendly smile on her face. "I just wanted to come and see how you were and if you'd like to go out for a late lunch in the city? I think a girls' day seems to be much needed."

Adele seems like the most nurturing woman on the planet other than Allison. If we'd met under different circumstances, I might have wished to get to know her better. As it is, I'm planning on leaving and not being involved in any mafia-related situations.

"I think that sounds lovely, don't you, Gemma?" Allison answers, then looks over at me for my response.

"Sure," I offer. My mind is working overtime at the thought of leaving the house.

Adele brings her hands together in a clap. "Wonderful! I'll make the arrangements." She takes her leave just as Luca taps on the doorframe.

"Hi," he says quietly, almost unsure if that is the right word to say to me. He stays outside the room, filling the entire doorway. "Dr. Fulton is here to check you over and to restock your inhaler."

I watch as Allison nods and stands from the bed.

"I'll go and help Adele with the lunch plans," Allison says to the room, then turns toward me, bending down. "Offer Luca mercy and grace. He might not have gone about your relationship the correct way, but I do believe that he has your best interest at heart. If after you have thought about everything and see it through his eyes, and you still can't cope or handle it, then I'll help you in whatever you'd like to do." She cups my cheek, giving me a soft smile before taking her leave, but not before halting at the doorframe and speaking with Luca in a low conversation that I can't hear. His body tenses and his spine straightens.

When she steps out, Luca closes the door and turns around to face me. He looks like a man ready for battle standing there.

"What'd she say?" I ask, wondering if he'll really tell me or just change the subject.

"She told me that if I don't turn this around and bring back her happy and loving girl, she'll personally make sure that she helps you run and hide where no one will find you."

I can't help the tiny smirk that forms. I've never seen anyone stand up to Luca the entire time we've been together. Everyone always seems so afraid of him, but not her.

There's another knock, and an older gentleman walks into the room, holding a black medical bag. This must be Dr. Fulton.

"We meet again, sweetheart! I'm just glad you're awake this time."

My eyebrows lift in confusion.

"Last night, you passed out from shock, and this one was ready to come out of his skin." He chuckles. "Can't say I've ever seen him like that before."

I watch as he sets out a blood pressure cuff and stethoscope on the nightstand.

"You've known Luca a while?" I find myself asking. It's hard to find people who know him well since we were only around each other in California.

He lets out a chuckle. "I've known this boy since he was in diapers, wreaking havoc on the entire staff. He'd run through the halls setting off alarms in the middle of the night after he somehow snuck out of his crib." He continues to chuckle with a wetness forming in the corners of his eyes. "His teenage years weren't much better. Luca was always up to something."

My eyes move over to the end of the bed where Luca stands,

watching us. He has a smirk on his face and is shaking his head as though trying not to laugh. "I did have a few rough years, huh."

"A few? My boy, they set up my office down the hall from your room because you never went a day without hurling yourself into something or needing stitches."

"I wasn't that bad."

"Not that bad?" Dr. Fulton gasped as if that were the craziest thing he'd ever heard. Turning back to face me, he says, "One time, he managed to find the roof access and proceeded to jump off the roof into the pool. I thought heads were going to roll that day because Mrs. Falcone had to make a short trip into the city, leaving him in the care of his father and Gio. Of course, he was an angel around his ma—it was only when others were watching him that his mischief came into play. I always knew when Mrs. Falcone was away that I'd be needed onsite."

Luca laughed, and it was the first time since all this began that I saw a glimpse of *my* Luca. It even forced a smile out of me without realizing it.

"Ok, sweetheart, let's get the tough stuff out of the way," Dr. Fulton said bringing his attention back to me. "I'll just need to take some vitals to have on file and to ask a few questions so that I can better assist you if you should ever need it."

"You mean in case I'm shot like the man last night…"

"Baby," Luca tries to cut in, but Dr. Fulton speaks.

"Well, that was an unfortunate situation." He sighs as though it was a normal event that plays out regularly around here. "I'm sure that will never happen in your presence again."

He takes my wrist and places the cuff around it before pushing the button and moving my arm across my heart. Just before the pressure releases against my wrist, I have the worst thought. I saw vials and needles in his pocket.

"Wait, how do I know if you're really going to help me and not inject me with something that will kill me?" I start to panic as I realize I've just let a stranger get this close to me and didn't question any of this. Isn't this how I got into this ordeal in the first place? By not questioning more?

"Baby, I'd never let anyone hurt you. You and Bianca watch way too many crime shows," Luca tries. "Besides if you were going to be injected with anything it would've been last night when Doc took your blood while you were passed out." He points down at the crease of my elbow and that's when I notice a flesh-colored bandaid on my right arm.

Dr. Fulton turns to Luca, "You guys did a number on this poor girl in the last twenty-four hours." He bites before turning back to me. "Sweetheart, I swear I'm not going to harm you in any way. I know you've been through a lot over the last day or so, but I can promise that I'm here to help. Medically speaking," he's quick to say.

I finally nod and let him finish his exam. Once he is finished looking in my ears and eyes, he taps my leg and gives a soft smile. "I'm here anytime you need me. I'll text you my number shortly so that you can call me whenever you need it. Also, here are some extra inhalers to keep around here for you. Please call if you continue to have attacks, there might be something else going on if it continues and we'll need to do a more thorough check."

Once Dr. Fulton cleans and picks up his things, he leans over and presses a light kiss to my forehead. Behind him I hear a low growl, and as much as I don't want to feel any which way at this very moment, I feel warmth spread across my chest. It doesn't matter where we are, if someone of the opposite sex ever even looks in my direction, Luca's possessive side comes out.

"Call if you need anything, sweetheart, and don't let this young man keep you locked up in the castle too much. Enjoy what Las Vegas has to offer."

Dr. Fulton retreats out the door, leaving me here with Luca. He quickly makes his way over and starts to examine my wrist and arm where the bandage is.

"It wasn't painful, was it?" His thumb gently slides over my wrist and brings it up to his lips, pressing a kiss to the slightly red area.

"I'm fine. It's not like I've never had trips to the emergency room before, remember?" I can't help the edge in my voice and pull my arm out of his reach.

"You're still mad?"

Thank you, Captain Obvious!

Why do men always think we should be over it and move on from a conversation after they explain themselves? Just because you explain doesn't mean I'm done and over it. I get to process it!

"I'm a lot of things, Luca! I'm angry, hurt, sad, but mostly con-fused." My hands cover my face to try to hold off the headache I know is coming from everything that has happened and is still hap-pening. "You have no idea the chaos that is running through my head right now. I don't know which way is up or down or if this is some sick and twisted joke that someone decided to play on me. I'm ques-tioning everything and everyone. All these conversations have me thinking that maybe they're just feeding me more bullshit. And it's a total mindfuck! What I thought was the most stable and happy time of my entire life has been one enormous lie, and the person I thought was my rock has been not only lying to me for the past year but has been stalking me for years. You threatened to kill me if I told anyone about that night."

"I know it's been a lot to digest, but baby, everything with us has been true and real. There is no faking what we have. I've wanted to tell you so many times, but I was scared. Afraid you'd look at me as though I'm not the husband that hung the moon with you. The thought of you thinking I was anything but perfect for you was like swallowing a cactus. You deserve the best that life has to offer, and I wanted to make sure to give that to you."

"I don't need perfect, Luca!" I yell. "I need someone who is completely honest with me. Someone who won't hide things and make me question everything. Trusting that when you say you're going into the office to handle a paperwork mix-up that's really what you're doing. How am I ever going to *not* question you?" I'm getting worked up again. "We haven't even talked about how your dad treated me."

Luca grasps both of my cheeks in his hands, forcing me to look into his eyes.

"I'm never going to keep anything from you ever again. I swear on my life. I will tell you every single thing and never hold back. You want to know if those jeans make your ass look big? I'm going to tell you. You want to know where I'm going if Carson calls? I'll tell you exactly what I plan to do when I get there. I know once trust is broken, it takes time to get it back, and I promise to spend the rest of my life proving to you that you'll never have to question whether I'm telling you the truth. Every day. Just promise me you won't give up on me or us," he pleads, wanting this to be a quick fix. "As for Pop, he'll make it right. One thing he loves more than business is his family. Last night was about me and he got carried away. It's not an excuse, but he'll prove himself to you."

Before I can answer, Adele and Allison come in. "Ready to go, Gemma?" Mrs. Falcone asks.

I nod, turning my attention back to Luca who is pleading with his eyes for me to answer him. I'm not even sure I have an answer right now. I need time to think about everything before I can even think about my next move.

Swiftly, I move around Luca and make my way over to them. "Yeah, sure, let's go."

And for the first time since being with Luca, I leave without kissing him goodbye.

CHAPTER NINETEEN

Gemma

I FLED.

    Oh.

    My.

God.

When Adele, Allison, and I went to lunch, I snuck out using the excuse of having to use the restroom. I grabbed Allison's wallet from her purse when she wasn't looking and slid it into the back of my pants. We had an army of men guarding us, and I had to be very careful as I went through the kitchen and out of the delivery bay.

Now, the Strip isn't far, so after walking for what feels like forever in this heat, I duck into a hotel and casino called *Hearts* and check in to lay low until I figure out my next move. It hits me hard when I realize I have nothing—no ID, money, clothes, or phone. Nothing. Thank goodness the hotel uses a kiosk to check in instead of doing it face-to-face. I'm able to use her credit card and scan her license, all on a machine without being noticed or questioned. *Thanks, advanced technology.*

After the kiosk spits out a key and I hurry to find my room, I bolt the lock and finally let my tired body rest. I've devised a plan to find a bus station and get back to the house in San Diego after

I take a short nap. When I get there, I can get my wallet and pack some clothes before getting the hell out of dodge and away from all of these lunatics who think it's normal to kidnap people like it's just another day at the office. When my head finally hits the pillow, I'm out.

Just as it felt like I was floating into unconsciousness, a pounding noise jolts me awake, and I can hear someone yelling my name. The hammering on the door sounds as if it's about to come off the hinges.

Luca.

I should've known he'd find me. I take my sweet time getting to the door and peek through the hole. Sure enough, Luca is on the other side, beating on the heavy door and calling my name, making a scene in the hall.

"I know you're in there, Gemma. Open the door."

"Go away!" I yell.

"I can't."

After a few minutes of silence, he starts up again with the banging.

"Ahh." I give in and crack the door slightly. "What do you want?"

He must notice the poor shape I'm in because his hard features soften. "You scared me."

"Well, the feeling is mutual!"

He looks as though I've shocked him. "Can I come in?" he asks since I haven't made any attempt to open the door any wider.

"No. I want some time to think without everyone breathing down my neck."

"I thought we—"

"You thought that once you explained all your lies and deceit that I'd, what? I'd be okay with all of this? Continue on as if nothing happened?" He's still standing there stiff as a board, not moving. I can see a few guys down the hall trying to blend in with the wallpaper. "That I'd pretend you didn't mold and maneuver me to fit into this little life you've had planned out for the last six years."

"That's not—"

"Oh, go suck a lemon, Luca! You knew all about me before we even met that night at the hotel. You planned everything out. You don't get to manipulate my life and hide things from me. I might've let you take the lead in our relationship with my head in the clouds but no more. I'm not going to let you bulldoze me." I'm getting worked up again, and something inside of me ignites with fury. "I need time to breathe and think. Away from you and all the craziness that comes with you." I just need some space to work all of this out in my head.

"I get it. I'll give you the space, but please don't try to leave. Can we try to talk this out? Can you give me the chance to make this right?"

I stare at him, wondering if I want to work this out with him or if I want to leave and never look back. There is so much to process, and I can't wrap my head around everything that's been happening. Plus, my bio dad is really alive. Talk about having my emotional tank overflowing.

"That's just it. I don't know what I want. I haven't been given the chance to just sit down and think."

His shoulders slump in defeat, obviously not liking my answer. "I'll do whatever you want." He places a hand on the door jam. "The only thing I request is that if you do decide to leave your room, please let your guards know so you'll be protected. I know that you don't want to see me, but please know that being a Falcone makes you a very valuable person."

His other hand goes to the back of his waistband and pulls out a bag. It's my purse. The purse that was left at our house in San Diego. The purse that has all of my things like money, cards, and my ID. Once he's placed it in my hands, he pulls out a phone from his suit pocket and hands it to me.

"I've programmed all the numbers to your security in the favorites so that you can get to them easily."

I take my phone but hold it like a bomb. "Thanks."

"I…" he starts but stops and takes a step back. His mouth is turned into a frown. "I know you feel betrayed and think what we have is a lie, but it's not. What we have is once in a lifetime."

He rubs his chest where his heart is, and I feel like breaking down in a fit of tears.

"Before I go, can I hold you?" he asks. I'm not sure why I agree, but it feels right. I allow the door to open enough for me to step into the doorway, and he steps into me and engulfs me in his strong arms and body. "I love you with my whole heart," he whispers, and the dam breaks. I cry into his chest as my body shakes. I'm not sure how long we stand there, but he doesn't let me go until I make a move to back away and grip the door.

"If you need me, I'll be here. No matter the time," Luca says and steps back into the hallway.

I nod and wipe my face.

"Allison is at the store picking up clothes for both of you and all the other things you girls need. She'll call you in a little while."

I nod again because I don't trust my voice.

Luca stares at me for a long moment. "Close the door and use the deadbolt," he says with a nod to the door.

I take a step back away from him as I grip the door, ready to close it. There is so much I want to say, but I hold it in. A few days to think is what I need, then I'll talk to him. With a clear head to process everything and a plan in place.

The deadbolt echoes in the empty room, and it sounds exactly like I feel on the inside. Empty. After tossing my purse on the small table by the window and chair, I launch myself onto the bed. My phone lights up, and the screen displays a picture of us on our wedding day at the beach. We're feeding each other cake and have the biggest smiles on our faces. The tears start to flow as I remember our one-year anniversary is slowly approaching. A guttural wail escapes my throat, and I lose the battle and let myself feel the devastation of everything.

Over the next few days, I wallow and eat my fill of room service.

The hotel manager tries to give me a room upgrade, probably at Luca's request, but I refuse.

Allison takes up residence in my room, and we hang out every day. We've made spa appointments daily to relax and hang by the pool. At night, we go down to one of the many restaurants to eat. During the day, we laugh and cry as we discuss my situation, and what I want out of life. It's hard, and even though Allison is motherly, I still ask her to help me and put on her therapist hat when we talk about Luca. She'd like for me to see someone here and include Luca in the sessions, but I don't want to talk to anyone else about this. I'd love to talk with Bianca, but I'm still reeling from that punch in the gut.

I journal a lot over the next several days, and I think it helps my mind to unclog from all the mess pinging around up there. Some pages are longer than others, but I feel like I've got a small grip on all this chaos. Luca sends me breakfast every morning through room service with handwritten notes. Back home in San Diego, every morning before I left for school, I'd find a sticky note on my steering wheel with a phrase or sentence wishing me to have a good day. The ones I get now are memories of our time over the last year. He's even included pictures or ticket stubs from our dates.

It's hard because I miss him so much, but I know I need this time. Once I decide what to do, I'll speak to him.

Luca

When I got the call that she'd gone missing during their girls' day lunch, I lost my shit. I thought someone had taken her again, and it was like my heart left my body. It took two hours to finally locate her, and all I wanted to do was tan her ass for putting me through all of this. Once we found out that Allison's wallet was missing, we were able to find her within twenty minutes. Thank God she was at Bobby Dawson's casino, Hearts, and not any other of the three families' properties. Mr. Dawson and Pop have a good working business relationship and are close. His son, Wyatt, and I know each other very well since our dads are the heads of our mafia families and we used to hang out a lot before I left to pursue Gemma.

I called Wyatt right away, and he'd met us over at the casino. We talked for a while, waiting for the receptionist to get us the room number. Allison had told us to wait, let her settle in, and give her some space, but I wanted to see with my own eyes that she was okay. Wyatt and I went to the bar and had a few drinks before my impatience got the better of me. I gave Wyatt the rundown, and after we spoke, he also said to let her cool down for a bit.

I was a nervous wreck pounding on her door. When she didn't answer right away, I panicked and was about to plow through it, but Cassio and Wyatt encouraged me to hold off.

My heart sank into my stomach when she wouldn't let me in, but I understood. I needed to let her deal with all of this and wait for her to come around. I couldn't push, or she might regret staying and run off when I wasn't on alert. Her crying into my chest almost broke me. I'm not much of a crier, but it was hard to stand there and hear it coming from her. I'm sure Cassio and Wyatt thought I was the biggest pussy as they stood down the hall, trying to be out of sight and not draw any attention from other guests.

When I made it to the elevator after hearing her lock the deadbolt, I paced the hall for a while as her wails turned to whimpers, and then she finally quieted down.

"Here," Wyatt hands me three room keys.

"What are these for?" I take them with a raised eyebrow.

"These are the rooms on either side of her, and one across the hall from her. Thought you'd want her protected. Three guys at the most or Dad might think you don't trust his security." He smirks.

"Thanks, man." Relief rushes through my body. "I owe you for this."

"I'm sure you'll be saving me with my woman in the future."

We exit the elevator and go our separate ways as I pull out my phone to call Allison. "She's safe, and I'll text you the hotel and room number," I inform her.

"Give her some time to process. Try not to crowd her, and let her come to you," she offers. "I tried to warn you that this might happen when you came to see me in my office. Gemma needs stability in her life after losing both parents at an early age, but she doesn't need to be kept in the dark. If you'd told her more about your family and past, this wouldn't be such a shock to her. She's a very forgiving person, but we all have our limits, Luca. I'd suggest you both start seeing someone here in Vegas."

"Easy for you to say," I mumble as Cassio goes to pull the car up. "I've got rooms and men that will be here to watch over her."

"Okay, I'm going to give her a few more hours before I head over. She needs this. If she doesn't resolve this on her terms, there will always be a lingering voice in the back of her mind. She is strong and will get through this, but just know that if she wants out, then I'll help her do whatever it is that she wants. You need to respect that." Her tone is harsh, but I hear her loud and clear.

"There isn't any other option than us being together," I growl. "I'll do whatever it takes to make sure of that."

We end the call, and I'm miserable the rest of the day. I really hope I'm doing the right thing in giving her the space she needs because once she decides to come back to me, I'm never letting her out of my sight again.

CHAPTER TWENTY

Gemma

NINE DAYS.

That's how long it's been since learning my life wasn't a fairytale.

Nine days since I last talked with Luca.

He's not here when I go to sleep or wake up. The pillow smells of him, and I'm pretty sure Luca has given the housekeeping his cologne to spray the room to smell like him. My body seeks his as it clings to the pillow, but we haven't spoken. I've asked Mrs. Falcone—Adele, as she insists on me calling her. That or Ma—about him when she comes for lunch or dinner with me and Allison. She said he's out with Gio and Arturo, dealing with a pest who thinks it's okay to move product and cause problems on our turf. And by turf, she's referring to the Falcone district here in Las Vegas. I'm not sure what 'product' she's referring to, but I'm sure Luca will fill me in when we actually see each other face to face.

Despite what I thought at first, I'm not a prisoner here. I'm able to come and go as I please, but the stipulation is that we have guards with us at all times. After going with Adele and Allison the first day, I realized the type of danger we could be in if we're not protected. Adele travels with no less than five guards when she's by herself, and that has certainly doubled now that I'm here. Todd and Sam, my personal guards, are now attached to my hip anytime I step out of the door to go anywhere.

Yesterday, all the women went shopping. All day. Allison, Adele, Alice, and I hit every store within ten miles of the Strip. As much as I didn't want to admit it, I was having a good time, but in the back of my mind, Bianca kept creeping in. She's an entirely other headache I want to avoid until I have to, but I miss her. I miss my best friend.

I was also shown pictures of Luca's home which is not far from the main house and still on the compound. It's beautiful, like our home in San Diego, but it definitely needs a woman's touch. Our conversation from last night has me yearning for a big family.

"What if I decide that I don't want this and can't get my trust in Luca back?" I ask over coffee. Allison and I are at this little coffee shop in town after dinner with the girls.

"But what if you can? You've always wanted to have a big family because you grew up alone. This might be your chance at that family. I'm not saying that you have to jump in with both feet—I know everyone understands the situation that you've been put through and is giving you some breathing room. I'm just asking that you keep an open mind and not push away what's right in front of you because you're scared to open back up. Weren't you and Luca wanting to start trying to expand your family?"

I wince at the mention. Luca and I had been wanting to try for a baby for the last two months. I'd gone off the pill, and we were having fun until eight days ago. Summer break was going to our little love fest of baby-making. Is that something I still want? With him?

"It's hard to even think about all of that right now until I can figure out how to navigate everything. I don't want to make a hasty decision when I feel like I'm not even on stable ground."

"My advice is to go back to journaling like you did when we first started seeing each other. Put your feelings down, do a pro and con list, or just write about the blue sky. If you need an outlet, then use that. I

know Bianca is another issue, and I really wish I could be here for that when you speak with her, but I know you can do this." She grips my hands over the table, squeezing them. "You've come a long way from the young girl who moved away all on her own to become the beautiful, smart woman you are now."

I know I've come a long way. I was scared of my own shadow when I first arrived in San Diego to start college. Allison helped me overcome so many things.

"I know what you're thinking over there and you need to stop right now. I didn't fix you; I only gave you the tools, and you did all the rest. The most important part is to believe in yourself. Follow your gut and your heart, and you'll be just fine."

"Are you listening to me?" Allison nudges me as we head toward a deli downtown.

"Sorry, my mind continues to drift lately." I shrug off my thoughts and focus on her as Todd drives us with Sam in the passenger seat. There is also another SUV behind us with a couple more guards. I don't think I'll ever get used to having someone follow me around everywhere.

"Just don't stay in your head for too long. Assess the situation, make the decision, and then move on with whichever you choose. Doubt can get you caught up in the what-ifs. Nothing good ever comes from that. Smart, educated decisions."

I smile. "Got it."

Todd eases up to the curb while Sam gets the door for us, and we slide out as the other men from the SUV behind us gather around. We walk into the deli and before we can even speak to a hostess, my entourage is ushering us to a booth in the back.

"I think we were supposed to wait for the hostess, Sam," I whisper as everyone starts to stare.

"We called ahead, Mrs. Falcone," Sam states. His eyes never come in contact with mine. He's always looking around at our surroundings.

"Gemma," I say, and for the first time, Sam looks down at me with a raised eyebrow. "My name is Gemma. You can call me that," I suggest, feeling weird to be called something so formal.

Despite being a teacher whose students call me by that name every day, coming from someone older than me feels awkward.

"That is how Mr. Falcone would prefer us to address you, ma'am."

Ma'am?

"Oh, I guess if my father-in-law wants that—"

"No, ma'am, not that Mr. Falcone. Your husband," Sam clarifies.

Why the heck would Luca want these men to refer to me as Mrs. Falcone?

"I'm pretty sure it's a respect thing, honey," Allison says as we take our seats with the men seated at a small table in front of ours. Their backs are toward the solid wall.

The young waitress comes over to our table after nearly being strip-searched by the men and takes our orders. "Here are your cups. The drink station is over there by the counter." She bounces to the next table to take another order.

Just as I'm getting up to get our drinks, Sam is there reaching for our glasses.

"What would you ladies like to drink?" he offers.

"Oh, um I'll take a Coke," I offer and sit down as Allison asks for tea.

We sit for a while talking about the summer and Michael, her husband, until our food arrives and we dig in.

Allison is leaving today, and I'm going to miss her so much.

"You know you can always visit, right? Or stay with me. If you truly wanted to leave Luca and walk away, there is always a place for you," Allison says sincerely. "Gemma, you are like a daughter to me, and I want you to be happy and healthy."

"Thank you, I appreciate that."

Halfway through our meal, we both run out of drinks, so I pick them up and head over to the drink station before Sam has a chance to take over. As I'm filling them up someone comes up behind me. Normally, it wouldn't be a big deal, but the stranger is crowding me. So close that I can feel their breath on the back of my neck. I try not to make it too obvious as I slide a step over, forgetting the ice for my cup and reaching to place it under the nozzle for the dark liquid to come out.

"Hello, gorgeous, can I help you with something?" A deep slimy voice with a thick Spanish accent says from behind me. The hairs on the back of my neck rise. "Aren't you a pretty little thing?"

At this point, I forgo the soda, hoping Sam will refill it for me, and a take large side step toward the tea dispenser to escape, but as luck would have it, it doesn't seem to deter him.

"Ahh, don't run away, sweetie. I'm just making conversation."

My eyes cut over and come face to face with a man who looks like pure evil. He has jet-black hair and eyes such a light shade of brown they almost look yellow. He's wearing a button-down white shirt with the sleeves rolled up his forearms. His black slacks are creased down the center without a wrinkle in sight, along with polished black loafers. He's got a scar on the left side of his face from his eye toward his chin, and his smirk makes him look even more sinister.

He takes another step forward, and the sound of chairs scraping the floor echoes through the room. Just as he reaches out with his hand to touch a strand of my hair, I'm yanked back.

"Cat got your tongue, Mrs. Falcone?"

"Get the fuck out of here unless you want trouble," Sam's voice is low, but I swear I could fall over dead from the venom behind it.

The air in the room is chilly and tense. Everyone seems suddenly on high alert.

"Now, now is that any way to speak to your future boss?" The evil man's voice gets deeper. "I was only trying to get to know the pretty little thing that has the Prince twisted in knots and hiding her like a treasured gem. Damn, if she isn't a looker. How do you boys watch her all day without wanting a little taste?" I almost vomit over his words. My hands seek the back of Sam's suit jacket and dig in.

"She isn't any of your concern, and I'd watch my mouth when you speak about Mrs. Falcone if I were you."

I peek slightly around Sam just as the door opens, and several men storm in with their hands inside their jacket pockets. My breathing starts to pick up because I swear Bianca and I have seen enough gangster movies to know what is about to happen next, and it isn't going to be good.

Hands grab my upper arms, and I'm shoved behind every one of my guards with all of their guns drawn. There's a lot of commotion and gasping from other patrons eating their meals.

"This is your last chance to walk out of here alive," Sam states calmly. How in the hell is he so calm while I'm barely able to hold myself up? Allison is now by my side, shielding me in a bear hug.

"There's no need to get your panties in a wad. I was only trying to say hello. Tell Mr. Falcone and the little Prince that I'll be in touch soon. Very soon." He turns on his heels and heads out, but not before he takes one last look in my direction. His men all circle around him as he moves for the door.

I'll never forget the way he looked at me and mouthed, 'See you soon.' Chills run down my body, and I shiver enough that Allison rubs my arms with her hands to help calm me.

As soon as the last man walks out the door, our guards are moving. Every one of them holsters their guns inside their jackets and pulls out their phones. Every one of them. Sam stalks over to me but continues to give me his back as he speaks to someone.

"Sir, we have a situation…Yes, sir…the package is secure…Yes, sir…No, sir, he didn't. He got close but we managed to intercept before…There were ten, sir, and a black SUV…Yes, sir…"

I have no idea what is being said, but then Sam turns and hands me the phone. "Mr. Falcone would like to speak to you."

"Hello?" I say into the phone expecting to hear from Arturo Falcone as Sam turns to watch the activity in the deli.

"Baby," the unexpected sound of Luca's voice after nine days of avoiding him cracks the dam. Tears I didn't know I had in me start to flow and I can't stop them.

"Oh god, Luca," I sob.

What the hell just went down? Was that guy going to do something to me? The tension is still high as a line of men blocks me from everyone else in the room.

"It's going to be okay. I'm on my way right now. I'm forty minutes away, but I'm coming. Nothing is going to happen to you, I swear. Sam will kill anyone who looks at you funny. I need you to stay calm and don't leave his side. I'll be at the airport soon to pick you up after you see Allison off."

I can't talk. I can't even form words.

"Baby girl, I need you to talk to me, so I know you are okay. Sam has an inhaler in his jacket pocket, and so does Todd if you need it. Tell me you understand."

"I—"

"Take a deep breath in your nose, then out your mouth." I do, and it helps the sobs. "That's my good girl. I love you so much."

"Okay. I'm o-okay," I finally say after I've repeated it a few times. Allison is rubbing my back, trying to soothe me.

"Good. Hand the phone back to Sam, baby."

I do, and Sam gives one more, "Yes, sir," before ending the call.

"Do you need your inhaler, Mrs. Falcone?" Sam gently asks, holding one out from his pocket.

I shake my head as I start to feel my breathing normalize. "I think we need to get out of here and to the airport," Allison urges, but I'm not sure who she's talking to.

After a few minutes, our cars are pulled up to the curb, and we are safely settled in the back seats of our SUV with two additional vehicles added to our convoy. It doesn't take long for me to get my bearings, and all I can think about is what the hell just happened back there. Who was that guy? Why did he want to talk to me? Was he going to do something back there with his men at the deli?

"Gemma, your phone has gone off twice now," Allison says as she gently shakes me out of my thoughts.

"What?"

"Your phone's been vibrating, honey. Someone is trying to get ahold of you."

Oh.

Checking the screen, I see two notifications, both from Dr. Fulton. Strange, I wonder what he could be calling about. I press the call-back button and put the phone up to my ear, waiting for him to answer.

"Sweetheart, how are you doing?" he answers right away.

"Fine." I don't elaborate, because what would that do?

Am I really though? Did I just witness a modern-day stand-off like they did in the old days of a Western movie? Has my life become that insane?

"That's good. I just received your results from the bloodwork I drew last week and wanted to tell you the findings. Are you sitting down?"

"Uh-huh."

The SUV pulls up to the private jet hangar, and all the men get out, surveying our surroundings. Allison opens her door while gathering up her belongings. I hold up a finger, letting her know I'll be right behind her in just a second. She nods and gives me some privacy as she makes her way to the steps of the jet and hands over a bag.

"Sweetheart, when I sent your blood off to be tested, I went ahead and had the lab do a full workup—blood count, vitamin deficiencies, cholesterol, the works. I wasn't expecting the results I just received and wanted to tell you as soon as I was made aware." I can hear him shuffling papers in the background. "You're pregnant."

"What?" I swear, I don't think he just spoke English.

"Sweetheart, I said you're pregnant. In fact, the numbers are pretty high, which means you might be further along than four to six weeks."

"Pregnant?"

"Yes."

"Me?"

"Yes."

Holy shit. I'm pregnant. Oh my gosh. Pregnant. Me. I'm going to have a baby.

"I'll get with my good friend at the hospital, who is an excellent obstetrician to schedule an appointment ASAP."

"Okay?" I'm shocked. I feel like I'm not done processing what happened earlier, and now I'm hit with this.

A knock on my window lets me know that I'm needed, and I quickly get off the phone. I can't believe it—I'm going to be a mom. The door to the SUV opens, and I see Allison waiting by the steps of the plane and talking on the phone.

"Okay, honey, I'll be home soon. Love you too," she says with a smile, then hangs up before looking at me. "What's wrong, Gemma? You're white as a ghost. What did the doctor say to you?"

I shake my head to clear the shock. I can't believe that one minute I thought I was going to be kidnapped or in a shootout, and the next, I'm told I'm going to be a mom.

"Ma'am, we have to leave now if we are going to be on time to make the departure. They have a tight window for us to fly out before the next plane is scheduled to go," the pilot calls from the top of the stairs.

Allison nods then turns back to me. She sees my face and her mouth curves into a frown. She knows something isn't right.

"Come with me. Right now, get on the plane with me, and come back to San Diego. Leave all this stress behind and come with me. Leave, Gemma, right now," she pleads. "We'll take some time away and figure this out."

"What?"

"Something isn't right, and I don't like what just happened. It doesn't have to be forever; just until you've made your decision. I know it seems selfish, but I hate leaving you here after what just happened and then whatever that phone call was about. Oh, honey, I hate to leave you like this. As a therapist, I'm supposed to give you some options, let you make the choices, and let you figure it all out, but as someone who sees you as a daughter who's hurting, I want to wrap you up and take you with me. You need more time to process this away from all this chaos." Allison wraps her arms around me in a crushing hug. "Let Michael and I take care of you for a bit and get some fresh air at the beach to clear your head. I don't want to leave you like this."

The pilot yells that the doors have to close in the next two minutes, or the jet can't take off. Allison looks back at me and sticks her hand out, inviting me to take it and come with her. Away from what happened today and the last nine days.

"Come," she urges. "Take my hand and walk away."

I look at her hand one more time and take one second to think before I slip my hand into hers. I take a step forward to make the biggest decision of my life and the life of my baby growing inside of me.

CHAPTER TWENTY-ONE

Luca

Gᴏᴅ, I ꜰᴏʀɢᴏᴛ ʜᴏᴡ ꜱᴀᴛɪꜱꜰʏɪɴɢ ɪᴛ ɪꜱ ᴛᴏ ʙᴇᴀᴛ ᴛʜᴇ ꜱʜɪᴛ out of someone when you're stressed. That's what it's been like for the last nine days. Ass whoopings are being handed out like popsicles on a hot summer day. It's been a good stress reliever for sure after everything that's happened. I'm doing my best to give Gemma the space she needs and time to heal after what's been thrown at her. I know her world has been shaken and it's going to take a while for her to find her footing again, but damn, I'm feeling lost without her.

After being away from her the first night, I had housekeeping spray my cologne in her room every day when they cleaned. I need her to continue to remember me—all the good times we've had and all the wonderful memories we've made along the way. I want to go to her every morning, but I don't think I could handle her rejection right now. So, I settle for sending her breakfast and little memories of us. She doesn't know it, but I sleep in the room next door. I'm gone long before she wakes, but I can't be away from her all day and not be as close as I can at night. This relationship not working out is not an option. Her not being by my side until we are old and gray on our rocking chairs is not even in the realm of possibility. We are meant to be together, and come hell or high water, we will be—even if I have to chain her to the bed until she sees reason.

I'm an asshole for keeping the biggest part of my life from her, but she was too innocent to handle this side of my life. Why taint her if there was no need to? Why dim the bright light of the most amazing human being God ever created? She believes, even after everything she's been through, that there is good in everyone. I'll make sure to gain her trust again, and then we can continue with our lives. If she wants me to tell her every gory detail of my day or how many times I take a piss, I'll do it. I'm not sure how she's going to feel about being here in Vegas instead of San Diego, but that's another bridge we'll cross when we come to it.

Pop wants me here to run things and it makes sense. If I'm honest with myself, this life is what I want. I left because Pop was pushing for an arranged marriage and the thought of being with anyone but Gemma repulsed me. I tried all different options on the legit side of the law when I arrived in San Diego but was drawn right back to where my roots were. It's what I crave. I was born to run the family business and have missed it. I'll have to find a way to make both my marriage and my job work, like Pop has, but will that make Gemma happy? Her happiness is all that matters to me, and I'll do anything to make sure she doesn't go a day without that gorgeous smile on her beautiful face.

Her job is another bridge we'll have to cross when the time comes. As much as I want her to be at home full-time, I know she loves teaching. She has such a passion for those kids, and even though I'm a bastard and want her all to myself, I love her even more that she wants to make an impact on their lives. It's what's going to make her the best mother for our children.

"You paying attention back there?" Gio's voice brings me out of my thoughts.

The last few days, we've been on a mission to eradicate the prick who thinks he can come into our territory and push drugs and guns on our streets without any repercussions. But this guy is smart, I'll give him that. He's accumulated quite an army of followers. He goes by the name of Lorenzo 'Enzo' Perez. He's a slick young bastard who continues to slip through our fingers. And from the photos we have of him, he looks the creepy part too. He's got someone rich and powerful bankrolling him to take us out, but we haven't figured that part of it out yet. He came in strong on our territory and has taken quite a few of our men out.

"I'm here," I reply. "This fucker has some loyal assholes."

We've been on a wild goose chase at every turn. Every tip we've managed to punish out of a poor bastard from his crew has come up dry. The guy is like a ghost, but I know he'll show himself soon. They always do.

Just as we see a sign letting us know we're back in Las Vegas, all our phones start buzzing, and everyone tenses before answering. This is never a good sign.

"Yeah," I say to Sam. "Is everything alright?" He's out with Gemma and Allison at lunch before Allison goes to the airport to head back home.

"Sir, we have a situation," he says, and before I can question any further, Gio is relaying what went down at lunch with Gemma.

That little fucker thought he could show just how big his balls are by getting close to my wife. He already has a death wish, but now I'll take pleasure in making it a slow death.

"Is he gone?" I demand.

"Yes, sir,"

"What about Gemma? Is she safe?" My thoughts are running wild. We just got things calm, and she was doing so well with Ma and Alice being around. I don't want her to regress after another incident.

"The package is secure."

"Did he touch her?"

"No, sir, he didn't. He got close but we managed to intercept before."

"How many did he have with him and what did they leave in?"

"There were ten, sir, and a black SUV."

"Text me the details and see if you can get me the camera footage of the surrounding businesses to see if we can get any other details that will lead us to the fucker." I pull at my hair, wishing the car would magically place us with Gemma and not on the other side of the city. My nerves are severed at this point, and I don't care how I sound. "Hand my wife the phone."

"Yes, sir."

"Hello?" I can hear how scared she is with the tremble in her voice. God, why did this have to happen right now? I needed a little longer to ease her into this lifestyle before she had to deal with this shit being in her face again.

"Baby," I lower my voice to the gentle tone that she's used to hearing from me. The comforting side that only she gets.

"Oh god, Luca," Her voice cracks, and I can hear her sob so hard. This right here is why I never wanted her to be introduced to this life. Why I tried to keep her separate from my family. It crushes me that I'm partly to blame for her distress.

"It's going to be okay. I'm on my way right now. I'm forty minutes away, but I'm coming. Nothing is going to happen to you, I swear. Sam will kill anyone who looks at you funny. I need you to stay calm and don't leave his side. I'll be at the airport soon to pick you up after you see Allison off." I try to give her words of reassurance that everything will be fine. That prick Lorenzo will pay with flesh for every tear she's shed today. I can hear the gasping and know she's trying her hardest not to panic, but it's not working.

"Baby girl, I need you to talk to me, so I know you are okay. Sam has an inhaler in his jacket pocket, and so does Todd if you need it. Tell me you understand."

"I—"

"Take a deep breath in your nose, then out your mouth." I mimic the actions over the phone, and it seems to help with the sobs. "That's my good girl. I love you so much."

"Okay. I'm o-okay," she finally says. There's a pang in my chest that she doesn't say those words back to me.

"Good. Hand the phone back to Sam, baby." My hand is balled up, ready to punch a hole through the car door.

My teeth clench and grind. "Get my wife out of there and safely into the SUV. We'll meet you at the airport soon. Make sure you watch for an asthma attack, and nothing else better happen or I'll kill the entire team!"

I hang up before he can respond because I'm hanging on by a thread at this point. My teeth are clenched so tight, any more pressure and they'll crack.

"That motherfucker!" I punch the back of the seat and jolt Cassio forward. "When I get my hands on him—"

"Easy, Luca, now is not the time to lose your cool. We're headed to Gemma, and you'll see she's okay. Once we get home, we'll regroup and take action," Gio says from the driver's seat. "Carson was able to find three abandoned buildings Lorenzo has used recently. I say we hit them hard and draw him out."

"I want the city burned down and leveled."

Gio's hands are pure white from the grip he has on the steering wheel. His shoulders are tight, and his face shows one that I only see when he's about to kill someone. I know this must be hard on him not being able to speak to Gemma, but he's the one who boxed himself in. He had ample opportunity to make that connection with her years ago and didn't take it.

We sit in silence the rest of the way to the private airfield. My knee bounces with anticipation, wanting to see Gemma. I've seen her from a distance but have given her nine days of space. I've resorted to calling Allison and Sam for updates about her. It's killing me, and I'm not sure I can keep this up much longer. My phone buzzes and I send it to voicemail. Dr. Fulton will have to wait until after I've seen and held Gemma.

My phone rings again just as we turn down the street to the

private airstrip and a cold sweat skims across my flesh. "Yeah," I answer when I see it's Sam.

"We lost her, sir."

I almost drop the phone. "What the fuck do you mean, you lost her? How in the fuck can you lose something when your eyes are to never leave her? She's five-foot-nothing, you dipshit!"

We enter the private airfield, and Gio seems to understand the conversation, so I place it on speaker as he races over to the hangar and parks right outside the doors.

"I needed to take a piss and went around the side of the building; told Ronny to keep an eye out. The hangar is surrounded by our men, so only the jet was in there. When I got back, she and Dr. Collins weren't there."

Gio skids to a halt, and we all jump out, rushing over to Sam and the team. The hangar is now empty.

"Where the fuck is she?" I yell at the team, and they each look just as troubled.

"Sir, we think she must've gotten on the plane with Dr. Collins. We wanted to give her some privacy because of what had happened at the restaurant. So, we stayed back and kept a lookout around the building."

I'm going to murder everyone on this team. "Call the pilot and have him return right now!" I scream at Sam.

"Sir, it's just taking off." Sam points at the jet as it zooms down the runway.

My heart sinks at the thought of Gemma leaving. Leaving me. Does she think I won't find her?

Just as the jet lifts off the tarmac, a loud boom sounds and the jet is engulfed in flames, slamming down on the hard pavement. In slow motion, we watch the jet burn. The entire aircraft has been blown to pieces, and billowing flames consume every inch of it.

Right away my weight sinks to my feet. No, this can't be happening. That can't be her jet. No, no, no! I hear myself screaming as I stare at the ball of flames in the distance. My ears start ringing, and all I can think about is getting to her. To save her. Several sets of hands come around me as I take off at a dead sprint toward the flames. I try with all my might to fight them off. When I get halfway there, I'm pushed down on the concrete and feel the weight of the world pressed against my chest. I hear screaming from a distance and continue to fight to get back up. My throat starts to hurt, and I realize I'm the one doing the screaming. My eyes never leave the ball of flames that held my life. I move to my knees rocking back and forth as my hands go to my hair. My heart starts to physically hurt in my chest, and I try to rub it away. I'm having a hard time breathing as the fire trucks arrive and start pouring water onto the now destroyed aircraft.

I try one more time to stand, to race over, but my body gives out and I think my heart is slowly stopping. Both hands are now on my chest over my heart as an ache I've never experienced before takes over. The last thing I see before I welcome the darkness is Cassio.

"Hold on brother." I hear the sorrow in his voice, and it burns all the way to my soul.

At least I'll be joining Gemma soon.

CHAPTER TWENTY-TWO

Luca

"He's going to be okay, Addy, give him some space like Doc mentioned," I hear Pop in the distance but I'm finding it hard to open my eyes.

Oh god, why am I still here? Why couldn't I just be with Gemma now and not feel hollow inside?

"I'll give him some space when he opens his eyes! You can't make me before I'm ready, Arturo, and if you try I'll shoot you before you get close enough."

If I weren't dead inside, I might laugh. Ma always panics when one of her kids is injured. Especially me. I don't brag about it, but I am the favorite. Although, if you ask Alice, she'd say she's the favorite because she's the only girl.

I hear a sigh from Pop, knowing it's a losing battle.

"Ahh," I groan as my body aches like it's been bouncing off semi-trucks when I try to move.

I faintly hear a constant beeping noise, and it's starting to annoy the shit out of me. Can't everyone just leave me alone to try to wrap my head around what's happened? To try and make sense of all of this.

Slowly, I move my eyes back and forth, opening my lids. There are lights everywhere in the room, and I notice we're not at the airfield any longer but in Doc's office back at the house. He has his own section of the house due to the nature of our business. It's a mini hospital, loaded with everything a doctor could need for surgery.

"There you go, my boy, open those eyes for us. Try and stay as calm as possible, I'm going to raise the bed slightly," Doc says as the bed starts to move.

The room starts to come into clear view, and I see all the faces. All except the one I truly want. My heart hurts that I won't ever see her face again, and it makes my chest tighten even harder. My parents and Doc are around the bed, and Cassio is standing over by the door with Sam, while Gio is in a chair with his hands covering his face leaning forward. His shoulders sag, and I can tell he's in bad shape.

I know the feeling.

"All right, let's get a good look at you," Doc says and starts checking my eyes with a light. "Squeeze my hands." He checks my feet next. He's got a bag of fluids hooked up to me along with a heart monitor.

"Everything okay?" Ma asks anxiously when he's done checking me.

"He's going to be just fine. No sign of heart attack or stroke. I'm sure his body went into shock and shut down a bit. No reason for alarm or worry."

"Get this thing out of me." I go to remove the IV, but Ma stops me.

"Just a little longer, baby. I've been so worried since they brought you in," she pleads in that way that makes it hard to say no. "We'll get you out of here soon, and then we can process everything." She places the gentlest touch against my face. Any other time, I'd relish my Ma's touch, but I don't want it now. My head hurts as I try to process a life without the one person who is my reason for living.

"How long have I been out?"

"Not long," Pop says. "I've got a team at the airfield getting answers. They should be calling with a report soon."

"I want to go there." I move to get off the bed, but hands and arms push me back down. "I need to see for myself. She could need help, or maybe it wasn't our plane." I try to reason.

"It was ours, Son."

"No," I try. "No, it can't be. We had plans," I gasp as my chest starts to throb.

"I'm so sorry, baby," Ma starts to tear up again.

"We wanted to start a family, to have a houseful of kids." Every word out of my mouth is a list of reasons why Gemma can't be gone.

I turn my head toward the window to keep my emotions in check. I can't break down right now. I need anger to fuel me until I can kill the motherfucker responsible. My anger has always gotten me in trouble in the past before Gemma. It's been lying in wait just below the surface waiting to come out to play, and right now I feel it clawing to be set free. To snap and retaliate against anyone who dares step in front of me. My tender side that only Gemma sees starts to dim, and the beast is ripping at my flesh to be released.

Dr. Fulton comes over and continues to check me over, watching the monitors.

"You called me earlier. Why?" I ask, trying to quiet the static in my head.

He opens and closes his mouth several times. He looks at me with such pity, and I hate it.

"It doesn't matter anymore. She's gone, and it will only bring more pain," he says, almost to himself.

I grab his arm, and the movement pulls on my IV. "Tell me." Doc never calls out of the blue, so it must've been important.

He brings his hand up to the back of his neck and starts rubbing it. "I'd gotten the results of Gemma's blood tests back and found a surprise in the report." He pauses, then cuts his eyes over to Pop before meeting mine again.

"And?"

"The hCG levels were extremely high."

"I have no idea what that means. Is it bad?" I ask, but I hear Ma gasp and cover her mouth with her hands.

Gio stands abruptly and looks white as a ghost, as does Pop.

"It means that Gemma was—"

"Doc…" Pop interrupts, cutting him off before he can tell me what it all means. Was Gemma sick?

"Just say it!" I demand, and Dr. Fulton comes over to the bedrail and places his hands there.

"It means that Gemma was pregnant."

The words continue to echo over and over as I stare at him.

Pregnant?

Pregnant.

"Gemma, my wife, was pregnant?"

Was. She *was* pregnant.

"Yes."

I vaguely register him stepping back from the bed before I explode. An anger I've never felt before rushes through my entire body. It's like I'm watching it all play out from the other side of a movie screen.

"This is why I didn't bring her here! So this life would never touch her!" I aim my aggression at Pop, and the room freezes. "Why did you have to do this? We were so happy. I finally had built a life I truly wanted, not what I was *told* to have! You've ruined everything good in my life! All for what? She wasn't ready for this life. I needed more time to explain everything. I was coming back to fulfill my duties and take over as head of the business, but I wanted to live my life outside of all this before having to put her in a gilded cage of armed bodyguards and threats against the family." I run my hand through my hair and then hit my chest hard to dull the pain ripping my heart in two…again.

"I'd never thought I deserved anything of my own until Gemma came into my life and gave me a reason to live. My entire being begins and ends with her. She makes every piece of me whole. She washes away all the dirt that has stained my soul. And you just couldn't let me have it! You kidnapped her and scared the ever-loving shit out of her. She hated me, and now she's dead, and I'll never be able to make it right. To tell her how much I loved her and how sorry I was for hiding the truth from her."

"Son, I'm…" He stops, at a loss for words judging by the shock on his face. I can see the anguish. Pop is rarely sorry and doesn't have a lot of regrets in his life, but you can tell by the way his body sags that he is feeling it now. He never shows weakness unless Ma is having a go at him.

Cassio jumps from the buzzing of his phone and steps out into the hall. I can't take all these faces watching me anymore. I need to be alone. I need to punch something or kill someone, and if I don't get out of here, I might not be able to stop the fire I have inside of me toward Pop.

At the same time as I rip out my IV, Cassio reaches into the room and snaps a fist full of Sam's shirt, pulling him out into the hall. Voices downstairs erupt, and chaos has everyone on their feet moving. We keep Ma and Doc in the room as we all haul ass down the stairs where the shouting is coming from. Cassio, Sam, and Bosco are all in a heated exchange with Todd and a few guys from the team who were on duty for my wife. As we get closer, we're able to make out a few words.

"How in the hell did you not know? You had one job, dipshit!" Cassio berates them. He is holding a guy up against a marble column, his feet dangling off the floor.

"Did you notice any of it?" Sam grabs ahold of Todd and lifts him up like Cassio has the other guy but without a column as Bosco lunges for another guy standing there. What the hell is going on, and why are they being so aggressive toward our own men?

"What the hell is going on here?" Pop bellows.

"Sir, we've got—"

Just as Cassio is about to say something, movement draws my eyes toward the formal living room, and we all stop. My eyes must be playing tricks on me, or Doc injected me with something, because what I think I see and what I actually see can't possibly be the same thing.

There, in all her glory, stands my wife. My beautiful, loving, pregnant wife. She looks as though she's confused with all the yelling and men dangling off the floor as if the world didn't just end an hour ago. There is a look of relief and love when she stares back at me.

Can I see dead people now?

I waste no time rushing to her and taking her into my arms, holding her as tightly as I can. If this is a hallucination, it's a damn good one. What's even crazier is she holds on just as tight, as if needing me just as much. I hear crying in the background and know Ma has made her way down from the room upstairs. She's never one to take orders from anybody.

"What are you doing here? I thought—" I can't even say the words out loud.

Gemma buries her face in my neck and holds onto me tighter. She's mumbling into my skin, and I can't make out any of her words. I realize that my cheeks are damp from my own relief and continue to hold her in place. I whisper into her hair all the apologies she deserves and say all the words I'll tell her for the rest of our lives. I thank God for giving me another chance to make this right and swear to do better this time.

"I love you so much, baby."

She pulls her head back and shakes her head, looking right into my eyes. It's as if I'm looking at them for the first time again. I can't help it and I don't think twice as I smash my lips to hers. She's shocked at first but then reciprocates. My tongue touches the seam of her lips, and she opens to accept me as our tongues dance together. Her legs that were dangling come around my hips automatically, like we've always greeted each other after a long day, and my dick ignites. We haven't had sex in so long, and my body is demanding that be rectified right now. My brain is on overload and really can't comprehend how she's here and not dead, but I don't care as long as she's still breathing. I need to feel her, all of her, and make sure this is really my wife. A moan leaves her as I...

"Umm, maybe you should take this up to your room or maybe

even your own home," Pop's voice echoes in the entryway startling us, but I don't let her go even when she tries to release me. I've got my hands on her, and after what happened earlier, I don't see that changing for a while. She blushes as I block her from leaving my arms and tell her that I'm not letting her go.

I nuzzle her neck, placing kisses on every inch of skin I can reach when she whispers, "I need to talk to you." Her breathless voice is confirmation enough that she is truly my wife. Only she could make those sounds when I've got her pinned to me.

I have a very good idea of what she wants to say, and I'll let her be the one to announce our baby, but for now, I just want to hold her until my arms give out.

"I love you, anima mia." *My soul.* I see her eyes have softened some and aren't saddened like they have been for the last nine long days.

"What's going on? Why did we get left at the hangar?" Allison finally makes herself known from behind Gemma. Her hands are on her hips as she looks around the people in the foyer of the house. "I'd rather not be a witness to Sam or Cassio killing someone and be called to testify." She nods over at Todd, who is turning blue.

"That's what we'd all like to know," Pop demands, looking over at Sam's team, his patience is running thin if the vein pulsing in his forehead is any indication. He comes over and wraps an awkward arm around Gemma, with me still holding onto her. "Good to see you, *cara*. And in one piece." *Dear.*

"Let's go sit down and talk in there," Ma suggests just as Alice comes through the door with shopping bags in hand and her guards carrying even more. She's completely oblivious to the last few hours.

Gemma holds me back from the group outside the formal living room. Her eyes are sparkling like they did before we ever came to Vegas. She's absolutely gorgeous and tiny in my arms as I hold her at eye level. I'll need to get our cook to start making her meals more often to put some weight on her now that she's carrying our baby.

"I need to tell you now because I can't wait any longer. I could burst with this news," she exclaims as if we haven't been avoiding each other. It's as if we are back to our nighttime routine of discussing how our days were. We'd sit out on the balcony with a drink and the ocean in the background and just talk. Her excitement banishes the pain in my chest and throughout my body. Her joy is my joy.

"Then tell me, baby girl." I'm holding her around the waist with our fronts touching.

"We have a peanut." She bites her lip. That same plump lip that drives me wild.

I pause for a second to let the news of the life we created wash over me again. Hearing it from Doc was entirely different than hearing those words come from my wife. So pure, and I want to cherish this moment forever.

She leans in as if she's telling me the most prized secret of all time. "I'm pregnant."

My eyes close, and my face breaks into the biggest smile as I lean down and place my lips to hers. This time, we go soft and slow, relishing the moment. Celebrating. I've imagined and waited for those words to come out of her mouth for almost a year.

"You make me the happiest man in the world. I can't imagine a more perfect and amazing woman to be my wife and carry all my babies." I cup her cheek and rub my nose along hers. "You make me want to be the best version of myself, Gemma, and there won't be a day in our lives that I won't strive to make you feel loved and happy. You're my whole heart, baby, and I love you more than my own life."

"I love you too, Luca. Please don't do this to me ever again." She looks directly into my soul, and I know I'll never take her or this chance for granted.

"Never again," I vow.

"Are we going to have to watch this soft porn much longer, or can we find out how the women are here?" Cassio interrupts as we hear muffled chuckles from the other room.

With regret, I place Gemma down at my side as we make our

way over to a seat. I've got her practically in my lap and don't plan on letting her go let alone out of my sight any time soon.

Once everyone is situated, all eyes fall on Gemma and Allison as they retell what happened.

"Come," Allison urges. "Take my hand and walk away."

I look at her hand one more time and take one second to think before I slip my hand into hers. I take a step forward to make the biggest decision of my life and the life of my baby growing inside of me… but then I stop.

"I can't. My life is with Luca, wherever that might be. I know it's going to be hard, but I can't imagine my life without him in it." I pull her into a tight hug.

"Are you sure, honey?"

I smile and place my free hand over my stomach. "I'm pregnant."

Her mouth opens. "What? Oh my goodness, honey! Really?"

I nod, no longer able to contain my emotions. "We'll be okay, I promise. I might have him sleeping on the couch for a while or on diaper duty for the first three months, but he's it for me. I don't feel safe unless he's here with me."

"Oh, honey, I'm so happy for you." She pulls me in for another hug and holds me.

"Times up, doors are closing," the pilot says.

"Stay a few more days. Help me navigate this with Luca. I'd like to speak with Gio too, and I really need you there for that. Please," I beg.

"Well, when you put it like that." Allison giggles as she waves the pilot off and grabs her bag from the steps.

"I really could use a bathroom. My stomach isn't feeling well," I say as we move away from the jet. I notice the guards are scattered around the outside of the hanger with their backs to us.

Over in the far corner of the large, oversized hangar, we enter the bathroom. After we both finish and wash our hands, a loud boom echoes off the walls. We huddle down on the floor, waiting for some sort of impact. When nothing else happens, Allison suggests we wait for the guards to come and give us the okay before we exit. The seconds extend to minutes, and after twenty minutes, we pop our heads out of the bathroom to see what is happening. We decide to wait a bit longer, assuming the guards will come when the coast is clear.

"By the time we came out of the bathroom and out of the hangar, all the SUVs had left, and emergency vehicles were almost done putting the fire out at the end of the tarmac," she explains. "I'd left my phone in the car, and I didn't have Sam's number, so we booked an Uber with Allison's phone to come pick us up and bring us back here."

My mind is on extreme overload at the moment. She holds nothing back, even when I don't want to think that she might've considered getting on that plane and leaving me. She's such an over-sharer that her telling me all her thoughts has the acid in my stomach threatening to spill up my throat.

"Ma'am, I'd like to say how sorry I am about—" Sam starts, but Pop cuts him off quickly.

"Not now, Sam! I want your team in the back garage within the next ten minutes."

"Yes, sir." Sam nods, his back straight as he turns from the room, phone in hand.

"You look pale, Luca," Gemma whispers. I've got her across my lap in a strong hold and didn't realize I'd shifted her. I'm not sure if I'm more relieved or angry. Relieved she's unharmed, but furious Allison wanted her to leave me. I get she's on Gemma's side, but I brought her here to help me get Gemma to forgive me and have a neutral party as a sounding board.

"It's nothing, baby."

"So, is someone going to tell us why our plane exploded?" Allison pipes up, and if I could shoot daggers out of my eyes, I'd impale her. "It was our plane, correct?"

Gemma's body tenses and whips her head to mine. "What? Was that our jet?" I could strangle Allison. So much for keeping

Gemma relaxed. Maybe it's time for the good doctor to head home. On a commercial flight. In coach…or the cargo hold.

"Darling, we aren't sure what happened. We've got a team down there with the investigators looking into it," Pop answers diplomatically. He's always been so good with words. "Could've been an engine failure or something with the pilot. It'll take several days before we'll know anything." He's had decades of experience with Ma and knows when all the details need to be given. "We're just glad that you weren't persuaded to leave us and you weren't on that plane." Most people don't catch it, but I do. He didn't mention Allison in that sentence, but I have a feeling we're on the same page when it comes to her. Pop will protect each and every member of his family and will take on anyone who dares to come between us. Allison needs to tread lightly with him, especially with the guilt he feels for causing Gemma so much distress.

It must placate Gemma because she nods and nestles against my chest. A tired yawn surfaces from her, and I know she's about to crash. This has been a long day, and she needs to relax and enjoy the little miracle we created.

"Let's get you up to bed." She nods as I stand with her cradled in my arms, and I turn my head toward Pop, "Give me twenty, and I'll meet you in the garage."

He nods and I head up the stairs to my old bedroom.

"We're going to have to get our home put together soon so the baby can come home to their own room, you know. As much as I love my parents, I'd like to have our naked Sundays back."

"I was thinking we could start working on it together."

Any other time, I'd try to find a way to get out of decorating or doing any kind of household duties, but the fact that I've got my woman back means I'll bend over backward to help pick colors or fabric for the rest of my life if it means she stays with me. Hell, I'll be on diaper duty the entire first year. When I thought Gemma was gone, I prayed for more time with her, and I'm not going to waste a single opportunity.

"I'd love nothing more."

We reach the bed, and I lay her down gently, slipping off her shoes and working her jeans down her legs. Her blouse is the next to go, and the sight of her in just her bra and panties has my dick thumping against my zipper. My eyes train on her still-flat stomach and an overwhelming sense of pride has me bending down and kissing her there.

Mine.

"I love you so much," I whisper to both my wife and baby. Fingers thread through my hair and her touch sends me over the edge.

"I love you too. We love you." Moisture gathers in the corners of my eyes at today's events, and I can't hold back. The thought of Gemma not in my life could bring me to my knees and slay me.

I crawl up her body until we're nose to nose. She moves her thighs until they are around my hips, opening up to me. God, she's perfect. Slowly, our lips move with one another as our mouths open and our tongues caress. My hips buck forward trying to search for friction to help the ache I feel in my dick. Gemma meets me in the rhythm, and a wetness starts to form on the front of her panties as I slip my hand from the side of her neck down to my most treasured spot.

"Please, Luca," she begs as soon as my fingers brush against her clit.

"You never have to beg me, baby," I say as I sit up and roll her panties down her legs before tossing them somewhere behind me.

The sight in front of me almost sends me over the edge. This is the longest dry spell we've had since we met over a year ago. She's open for me, and my mouth waters. Changing direction, I crouch down and dive into her folds. My tongue swipes her slick slit just as her hips buck up. Her moan is almost too much for me, but I continue to assault her hard nub with the tip of my tongue while, as gently as possible, holding her hips still. My hips fuck the mattress to ease the pressure building.

"Aww, Luca," she mewls as I add a finger into her pussy and find her favorite spot.

"You like that, baby, huh?"

"Yes, yes," she chants as I add another. "I'm so close."

"I know you are. I can feel you quivering. Who do you belong to, Gemma?" I demand.

"You."

I return my mouth to her perfect pussy and lick her until her legs begin to shake. Her fingers tighten their hold on my hair, and I continue to thrust my hips against the mattress to try to relieve the pain in my dick.

"Luca!" she yells out as her orgasm takes over, and she rides my face to completion.

"I love the way you fall apart on my mouth, but right now I need you to do it again on my cock," I growl and sit back to remove my clothes. "Lose the bra, baby."

Once I'm naked, I climb up her satisfied body, marking kisses along my way and, paying special attention to her stomach where my baby rests safe and sound.

"You gonna be a good girl and come again on my dick?" I say when I reach her mouth. I'm notched at her pulsing entranced.

She nods and leans in to kiss me, likely tasting herself. Her velvety folds caress the crown of my cock. It's been far too long, and I'm not a patient man, so in one smooth thrust, I'm buried to the hilt. Planted right where I belong.

"You feel so good, baby." I moan as my eyes roll back. "Feel what you do to me." Her walls are crushing me as I pull back slowly, then push back in.

My hips tilt up at an angle, hitting the spot that has her gasping. When she starts to meet me thrust for thrust, I pick up my speed, knowing she likes a faster rhythm. Her hands go to my shoulders as she pushes me at the pace she wants, and it turns me on even more. I love the way she's getting what she wants, but this time I need it for me.

"Gonna take over, babe." I grunt as I punch my hips a few more times. She feels too good, and it's been so long since my cock released that I'm not going to last much longer.

Flipping her over as carefully as possible, I position her on her hands and knees. The sight alone could make me bust a nut.

"Ready to ride?" I don't give her a chance to respond before I slam into her.

"Aww, yes!" she calls out as I start rutting away.

Her head goes down on the bed along with her shoulders as I place one hand at the base of her neck, holding her in place while the other has a tight grip on her hip. Our skin slapping echoes off the walls in the room, and the sound of my grunts along with her gasps is all I can hear.

"You always feel so fucking good. I love the way your pussy takes my cock." I thrust in and out.

"I've missed it soooo much!"

My balls start to tighten at her words, and I know I'm about to come. "Play with yourself now!" I demand getting her there with me as I focus on not coming too soon. I've never gone before her, and I'm not going to start now.

Her pants pick up and she's groaning. I can feel her walls clamping down around my cock fluttering to hold me in place.

"Here it comes, baby." I pick up my pace and thrust even deeper. A slight worry that I might bruise her ass from my thrusts crosses my mind, but it passes just as quickly when her pussy clamps down harder on my dick.

"Luca!" she yells into the mattress, and her body jolts as wave after wave of her orgasm rockets through me.

I pump three more times, riding out her pleasure before I plant my cock in as far as it can go and drain all the cum from my balls. Moments later, I'm still pulsing, dropping every bit into her until I'm dry.

God, I needed that.

I turn us as I pull out so she's lying completely on my chest.

"I love you," I whisper against her forehead.

She turns slightly, shifting her body to my side, and drapes a leg over my thighs. I can feel the mixture of our release coming from her movement. My hand goes to her belly.

"I love you too, Luca. These last nine days have been so hard. You're my person and all I have. The thought that we wouldn't—"

I place a finger across her lips, not wanting her to finish that sentence, because even though I'd never let her leave me, it's still hard to hear. "I know, and I'll do whatever it takes to get us back on track, but you better never think about leaving me again."

I'm not using a threatening tone, but the truth is, I'd burn down the entire world looking for her. I'd find her and lock her away if she ever tried to leave me.

"We have a lot to discuss and work through. I don't want any more secrets, Luca. If I find out that you're keeping things from me, then we are done. I won't be in a relationship where I'm not an equal partner." She looks me dead in the eyes.

"I'll tell you everything you want to know. No holding back this time."

"Good. I've got an entire journal full of questions that need answers."

I almost laugh, because of course, she does. Gemma loves to be thorough when having meetings.

"I'll answer every one of them." She must be satisfied with my response because that's all that is said.

We're silent for a bit with her head resting on my shoulder.

"Why did the plane catch fire? Do you know?" she asks, looking up into my eyes.

This could go either way, so I need to be very careful with my words. "I don't know, but I'm going to find out. Pop had a few men on the jet that were headed to San Diego with Allison to check on things, so I don't know why it happened. I'm just glad you didn't get on that jet."

"Me too. I'm trying not to think about Allison being on that plane." She shivers, and I hold her tighter.

"Everything worked out, so try not to dwell on it. We've got a lot of prepping to do with this little one on the way. I want all of your attention and focus on that. Let's get the house ready for our family." I place my large hand on her belly and softly rub where my child is safe.

"So, we're never going back home?"

I've thought about that same question. Life was so much easier there. I know when I take over for Pop I'll have to be here. She has a lot of bad memories here, and I know it'll be hard for her, but I'm hoping we'll make new memories at our house and be able to turn it into a home where she can thrive and be happy.

"We can go visit as much as you want, but for now I'm needed here. At least until we can get the situation under control."

"You mean with that man who approached me?"

"Yeah, Lorenzo Perez is his name. He also goes by Enzo," I tell her, so if she ever sees him again, she'll know his name.

Another yawn escapes her, and I know she'll be out in a matter of minutes. She never takes long to go into a deep sleep. When her breathing evens out, I gently position her in the bed, hugging my pillow closely to her body. She shifts as I ease out of the bed but doesn't stir.

After getting my clothes on, I check on her one more time before heading out to meet up with Pop. We need to get this over with so I can come back here and be with my woman. I've missed her so much these last nine days that it seems like months, and we need to reconnect and get back on solid ground again.

Going out the back doors of the house, I find one of the UTVs and climb in. The 'garage' isn't near the house. We don't need the family hearing or seeing what happens there. We only ever use this building if something happens on our compound and we don't want to transport it to one of our warehouses.

I see a few of Pop's men standing outside by the door and know things have already started. The moment I walk in, I notice the tarp on the floor and men standing around the edge of the room while Pop has three men lined up in the center.

"Someone got laid," Cassio says under his breath when I go and stand next to him. "Your buttons are off."

I glare at him, trying not to give him the satisfaction of imagining my woman getting it good, but his comment makes me look down at my buttoned shirt. As I inspect it, a snort leaves his mouth which causes Pop to look our way. Knowing I've been busted, I shoulder-check him before making my way over to the center of the room to Pop's side.

"She get settled?" Pop murmurs.

I nod, not wanting everyone to know our conversation. The squint of his eyes gives me my acknowledgment, and he continues with his tirade. I know Pop can be a hard ass, but he really does care about his family. He's been trying to make up for causing so much stress to Gemma. And after my own tirade from earlier, he'll most likely want to make up for every event that has caused Gemma pain since being here.

"She is my daughter, my family, and you let her out of your sight," he continues. He's not asking for a reply at all, and if anyone tries, they just might eat a bullet. The redness around his collar shows just how mad he is. "When you were assigned family protection, you were trained in all situations to be everywhere at all times."

He draws back quick as a snake and punches Todd across the face before anyone realized it was coming, snapping his head in the opposite direction. Most people don't think Pop does his own dirty work, but that is far from the truth. When it comes to his girls like Ma or Alice, he doles out punishment every time. Now that Gemma is a part of our family, she is now under his wing of protection, and he won't hesitate to remind his soldiers of that.

"When you took over as our wives' protection, it was the most important job you could've ever taken on in this organization." He moves over to Ronny. There's a shift in his body, and we can see he's bracing for the attack.

According to Sam, Ronny was the one who was on 'Little Bird' duty while he went over to the side of the building to take a leak. Sam has already gotten his punishment from Pop if the shiner forming on his right eye and his bruised jaw say anything.

Pop pulls out his gun from the holster inside of his jacket and points it right at Ronny. All the spines in the room go straight, and their shoulders tense at attention.

"I will not tolerate laziness in my organization. I will not let my girls be put in vulnerable situations. Period," he demands. His voice is deadly, and the thought of anything happening to my wife sets my blood to boil all over again. Pop shoots Ronny between the eyes and then knocks Mark, standing next to him, upside the head with his gun. "Do I make myself clear?" he booms to a silent room. All the men are on high alert now.

"Yes, sir!" echoes off the walls.

"Get to your posts and out of my face."

Sam signals to a few guys to help clean up the body as Pop and I walk out the door.

"Have Sam double the number of men on the girls. We'll go back down to the normal number of guards once this Lorenzo threat is taken care of. I want the girls to know they are to not go out without their guards."

"I'm going to leave that talk with Alice to you since she thinks the guards are optional and are only there to carry her shopping bags."

He chuckles. "I told your mother when we found out our last baby was going to be a girl, that she'd be the one to give me gray hairs and not you." We climb in the UTV and take off back toward the house. "You were such a handful growing up, but your sister has made me lose a lot of sleep over the years. Let's hope this new baby will go easy on the both of us."

I smile at the thought.

I can't wait.

CHAPTER TWENTY-THREE

Gemma

"Mrs. Falcone, you have a delivery," Ernie states from the kitchen. His name is Ernesto, but it's the name I gave him when he refused to call me Gemma.

"Thank you, Ernie." I leave the cookies cooling on the kitchen island in our home and head toward the front of the house to the door.

I step out the front door and see Sam speaking with two delivery men from the furniture store. He is patting them down and having the box truck thoroughly checked before they put a foot through the front door. Today, we're getting the dining room table that seats eighteen people along with furniture for the living room, guest bedroom, and my study. We've gotten everything else delivered. Our bedroom furniture was the first to be delivered, and I think Luca made some calls to get it here sooner because he was tired of living under the same roof as his parents. He said we needed more alone time and hated sharing me every second when he got home from work. Adele has really stepped in as a mother figure since Allison left as well.

"Mrs. Falcone, a Bianca Gallo is here to see you. She's at the gate." Sam pulls the phone from his ear and looks at me for confirmation. I nod and head back into the kitchen as he confirms it to the person on the other end.

Movement by the doorway brings me out of my thoughts as Bianca walks in hesitantly. She looks so uncertain and out of place when usually she'd barrel in with a hug and make herself right at home. We grew as close as sisters over my time teaching, and I wonder if any of it was real.

"Hi," I break the tension and offer her one of my chocolate chip cookies from the island.

"Hi," she replies, and her voice shakes. I've never known Bianca to falter—she'd always been so sure and confident. She's got tears in her eyes, and I can see the hurt and remorse in her face.

I grab the plate and walk over to the small sitting area in the kitchen that overlooks the backyard and pool. Bianca follows close behind, and as I sit down, I see Ernie just outside the room, standing in the hallway. I know Luca has made it clear that when someone is with me, I'm to be guarded at all times if he isn't present, but this hovering is going to drive me insane.

"I'm sorry," Bianca bursts out right as our butts hit the cushion. She looks as though she might fall to her knees and beg. I go to open my mouth, but she holds up a hand to stop me. "Give me a chance to explain and plead my case, please." Her voice is shaky and quivering. "If afterward you don't want anything to do with me, I'll understand, but please let me tell you the position I was in."

"Okay." I truly believe everyone deserves to be heard and to be allowed to tell their truth. Even when it's hard to hear.

Bianca starts to pick at the skin around her nails, a nervous tick. "I've lived my entire life under the thumb of my parents. I was told how to dress, what to eat, and when to speak. I knew what my family was at an early age; they never hid it. But I never thought it would follow me once I was an adult." She kicks off her sandals and pulls her legs crisscrossed. "When I finished my degree in photography, my father called me home. My mom had this elaborate graduation party for me. It was one of the best days I'd ever had until that night. My dad had us meet in his office and my stomach plummeted. Nothing good ever happened for me when I was called in there. I knew things were going to change, and my hopes of being a photographer were for nothing."

I knew Bianca loved photography. She always had a camera with her, like it was an extension of herself. Most of Luca's and my framed photos are ones she's taken.

"I grew up right outside of Chicago as the daughter of an underboss. I knew what was expected of me from a young age, but I'd have hoped that, since I was allowed to attend college, maybe Dad had changed his mind and would let me live my own life. A life outside of organized crime." She looks so heartbroken, and my own heart hurts for her. "In the study, Dad told me that he'd received a call, and I was to insert myself into the life of the son of the head of the mafia family here. I had no idea who he was talking about. I'd been told the eldest son had left to get some space and I was to implant myself in his life in California."

"Like a spy?" I ask interrupting.

"Kind of." She pauses and cuts her eyes away. "I was to report back to Mr. Falcone every once in a while. I had no idea who Luca was or what he even looked like. When I was shipped to San Diego, I got the biggest surprise of my life. I had no idea he was already going to be married. You were the biggest surprise of all. And I was sure Mr. Falcone didn't have a clue that Luca had gotten married either. I didn't know what to do. So, I followed you around for a while, hoping to give myself some extra time to be alone. I got the job with the school and made friends with you. I never in a million years thought we'd end up best friends. I swear it on my life, Gem, please believe me. I thought it was a sham marriage at first, but then I got to know you and saw what a truly amazing person you are, and I didn't want to ruin it. Luca was just as enamored with you, and I didn't know what to do. I've always had a hard time making friends because of who my dad was back home, and you were like a breath of fresh air. You were kind and didn't judge me. You accepted me for me."

"I don't know what to think. We knew each other for a year, Bianca! You knew about everything I went through making friends myself, and you played me. I thought I'd finally found someone I could trust."

"I am, Gemma, I promise," she cries. "You are like a sister to me. When we were together, you got the real me. The me that could be herself and have a friend who didn't judge me for who my dad was or only be my friend so that your parents could get promoted. You're my sister, and I swear, besides not telling you why we met, I never lied to you."

We both have tears leaking from our wet eyes. My hormones are all over the place these days.

"I was told that he and I would be married when he came back to take over as the head of the family. That our marriage would unite our organizations," Bianca says after wiping her eyes and nose.

"What?" I gasped. "What do you mean—that you'd marry Luca?"

"That is how it's usually done in our world, cara." *Dear.*

Our heads whip over to a man's voice in the doorway. Arturo and Luca are both standing there. My husband doesn't look happy at all, which tells me he's heard our entire conversation. It's low, but I hear a growl come from Luca's throat. Crying or upsetting me in any way equals an ass beating for someone.

"I had planned to unite our families through marriage. In our world, we make allies to become stronger. Bonding through arranged marriages is the simplest way. This is how it has been done for decades. I also thought it would persuade my son to come home once he settled down with a family of his own," Arturo explains.

Bianca tenses beside me when the men step into the kitchen but stay close to the doorway.

"Bianca's father and I arranged for our children to marry, and that would've given us a foothold in Chicago." He glances over at

Bianca. "Ms. Gallo kept quite a few details to herself and didn't report the pertinent information clearly or I'd have called off the arrangement and found another avenue. I'd also have gone about getting my son here differently had I known the woman who was brought here was now part of my family and carrying our family heir." Arturo glares toward Bianca, and I can see her wilt inward.

Arturo doesn't wait for Bianca to respond before turning on his heels and leaving the kitchen. Luca walks over with a glass of milk and hands it to me. He puckers his lips in a smooch, which is usually reserved for the bedroom while rubbing my belly, then leaves the kitchen without a backward glance.

Bianca notices Luca's hand on my oversized sundress, and her eyes bulge.

"You're pregnant?! How far along are you? What are you having?" Bianca squeals. "Oh, Gem, I'm so happy for you! You're going to be the best mom ever." She moves to hug me but then stops, remembering herself. I hate that we can't be like we were. I miss my best friend so much.

"Thank you, Bianca. I'm seven months now and this little peanut won't let us take a peek to reveal the gender." I rub my ever growing belly.

"You have to know that once I found out how genuinely nice and sincere you were, I stopped reporting anything to Mr. Falcone. I swear it. You were so nice to me and really wanted to be my friend, and I hated that I couldn't tell you. I regret not saying anything, but I know I'll have to live with my decisions. I'm just really sorry for betraying your trust. I'm not even sure if I'm going to be shipped back to Chicago or not at this point. Mr. Falcone said he'd make a decision soon regarding my future."

"I'm sure everything will work out."

"Are you going to be teaching after the baby is born? Or has Luca finally talked you into staying home?"

We both giggle. Luca was always trying to get me to quit this last year and be a housewife. We went round for round about me not needing to work since he made enough to support us. It was truly the biggest fight in our marriage. I see now why he was pushing so hard, but I wanted to follow my own dreams, and he finally let up on the topic.

"I think I want to stay home with the baby for a while before returning to work. Especially since I'm in a new city. I want to soak up all the moments I can before this little one grows up."

There is also the issue of the psycho running around the city causing problems for our family. I'd never want to put anyone in my classroom at risk either, so I think staying home and being with my little one for a while is the best option.

"Can you imagine if the baby is a girl? Luca is going to be bald and have bars on all the windows and doors!" We fall into more fits of giggles again, and a feeling of peace settles in my chest. "Let's hope you stop him when he wants to put an ankle monitor on her if she ever goes on a date! Or has one of the men sit in between her and her date at the movies!"

This is how we've always been. Bianca says some of the craziest things, and we end up laughing all night while watching our shows. I've missed her so much.

With my mind made up, I get up from my chair and pull her up with me, wrapping my arms around her in the tightest embrace. I need her in my life. I need normalcy, and my baby will need it too.

"I forgive you." I squeeze her a little tighter. "Please don't keep things from me again."

She pulls back slightly not wanting to lose our connection.

"Oh, Gem, I promise on my life I'll never keep a single thing from you ever again," she swears.

We talk a little bit longer, then she heads out with the promise of seeing each other in two days for movie night. I told her to pack a bag so we could catch up on some of our shows since we've got six months to make up for. I'm sure Luca is going to have a field day when I tell him she's coming to camp out like the good ole days. I didn't realize it at the time, but I'd decorated the guest room with her in mind.

With a thought swirling in my mind, I turn on my heels after shutting the front door and head for my husband's office, on a mission. Without knocking, I barge in while Luca and Arturo sit on the matching sofas, facing each other with amber-colored drinks in their hands. Good lord, it's early afternoon, and these guys are already drinking. I swear, it must be a requirement to drink alcohol with morning coffee in the mob. Or something bad is happening. I try not to focus on the negative and push for my agenda.

"Baby, you alright?" Luca goes to stand and come to me, but I hold up my hands to stop him in his tracks. Worry is immediately etched on his face that he can't touch me, but I've been working on this speech in my head all the way down the hall. If he comes near me, I'll forget.

Before I can speak my first word, a wave of emotion about Bianca leaving me to go back to Chicago comes out of nowhere, and tears overflow down my cheeks. "I-I want Bianca to stay with me," I blubber with my hands pleading, and I'm pretty sure my words were unintelligible.

"Baby girl, I'm not sure what's…"

"Gemma, darling, it's a little complicated right now with her father's organization. We've not come to another arrangement, and she'll need to head—" Arturo stands, his voice calm, and kind. After our first encounter, he has always used a soothing tone like he does with Adele.

"I WANT HER HERE WITH ME!" I weep while yelling like a toddler. All the books I've read over the months talk about a hormonal shift, but sometimes I feel like I'm a completely different person. "I haven't asked for anything since I was taken from the safety of my home. You interrupted my life and stole me." I point to him. "My baby could've had severe health issues with all the drugs that were dumped into me when you had your thugs break into my home and kidnap me! You told me that if I ever needed anything, to come to you and you'd make it happen—well, I'm here to tell you that she's with me." My eyes narrow to slits. "She's my best friend, and I don't want her to be shipped back to her horrible parents."

Then I do something I know will get me what I want. I've learned a thing or two since coming into this family because Adele has all the best advice. Arturo is all about family, especially us girls. I place both hands on my round belly and start to rub. Baby Falcone starts to kick right on cue.

Both of their eyes follow my hands, and Luca bolts over to me with one hand on my belly and the other around my waist, pulling me into his side. Arturo looks me over and comes close. My tears are still streaming down like a faucet. Once they start, it's hard to make them stop these days.

"I'll make sure Bianca is here to stay, darling. I'm sorry to upset you."

I nod triumphantly, turning to face Luca.

"And I want to go to the grocery store!" I demand, looking right into his eyes.

"Why?" Luca looks confused as if I've grown two heads. "Mrs. Harris takes care of the shopping and cooking for us. We don't need to do the shopping," he says like the notion is the most ridiculous thing he's ever heard.

"Son—" Arturo tries to get Luca's attention, but he's focused on me.

"Why? *Why?* It's not normal to be locked away every day with nothing to do. I can only read so many dirty romance novels before I lose my mind! There's nothing for me to do here! And I want to go and pick out my own fruit and snacks!" *What in the hell has gotten into me?* "And if you didn't want to take care of me and my needs, which by the way includes grocery shopping, then you shouldn't have knocked me up!" I poke his hard chest.

"Baby girl, calm down..." He tries to rub a soothing hand down my back.

Calm down? I wonder how many pregnant wives that actually works on.

"Son, don't—"

"Calm down?" I say it out loud, wondering if it will magically come true. Yep, that didn't work. I let it sink in for a millisecond before I step out of his reach which surprises him. I can hear Arturo swearing under his breath and telling Luca to shut the fuck up. At hearing the cuss word, my brain goes in a different direction. "And I want everyone to start watching their mouths! This baby's first word better not be a curse word, or there will be hell to pay!"

My thoughts are all over the place, and I need to collect myself, so I brush past them both. I hear Luca call after me as Arturo interrupts him as I make my way into the hallway and up the stairs toward our room. Calm down…we'll see how calm he is when I decide to lock him out of the bedroom for a few nights, or maybe I'll just…

A knock on the bedroom door breaks me from my thoughts, and I turn to see Luca standing in the doorway with his hands in the pockets of his slacks shoulders slightly hunched. It blows my mind that I keep forgetting that a locked door is never going to keep my husband from getting to me. He apparently learned the lock-picking trick at the age of four.

"Can I come in?" he asks, not moving from the door. If it were any other time, I'd burst out laughing that he'd have to ask permission to come into *our* bedroom.

"Do I need to calm down first?" I sass. He looks gorgeous as ever in that *keep your daughters locked up bad boy* kinda way.

"I'm sorry I suggested that. It was incredibly stupid according to Pop. I just didn't want you to get your blood pressure up or get you any more upset."

"Well, how did that work out?" I snip, crossing my arms over my chest and lifting my chin. I've never been so snippy in my life, but this baby has brought out a side of me that I don't even recognize sometimes.

"According to Pop, I'm lucky you didn't grab the nearest sharp object and stab me with it. Baby girl, I have a lot to learn and am going to say a lot of stupid things. Please forgive me. I love you and the baby and want the best for you both." He rubs the area over his heart where he had my name tattooed.

I'm softening with every word he spouts and can feel myself starting to tire. Who knew cooking a human was so exhausting?

"Why don't we lie down, and I make it up to you with my mouth? Then we can take a nap before we head to the grocery store. I'm sure we need some bananas and popsicles."

I can't even hide the smile as my body reacts to his words. Right now, my body craves two things, and it wants them on tap—peanut butter banana sandwiches and Luca's body.

Not one to let him win so easily I say, "I guess a nap sounds good," before pulling the sundress over my head and lying back on the bed. Luca doesn't hesitate before striding over to the bed while dropping articles of clothing along the way. One rule we've always had since being married is sleeping naked.

I'm in the middle of the bed, where I always sleep, as Luca stops at the end of the bed. He's licking his lips as his eyes roam over my entire body. When he reaches my chest, he gives a disapproving grunt letting me know I need to remove my bra. With our unspoken conversation, I lie there completely naked, squirming at his heated gaze. Fatigue is now a thing of the past, and I'm ready to get this party started. As his eyes do another sweep of my body, he leans down ever so slightly, placing a knee on the mattress. Luca slides his hands under my thighs until he has two handfuls of my butt cheeks. His eyes lock with mine, and I'm hypnotized.

"Spread," he demands, and my body obeys like a good girl.

CHAPTER TWENTY-FOUR

Gemma

TODAY IS GOING TO BE A GOOD DAY, I JUST KNOW IT! THE smile I had when I woke up hasn't left my face. I've been preparing mentally and emotionally for months and it's finally here. Today I'm speaking with Gio. My dad, the man who didn't die in the military like my mom thought and who lived in the same city as me my entire life until college.

I'd been wanting to do it for a while now, but every time my dang hormones got the better of me and I turned into a blubbering mess. Every time, Luca would put his foot down and stop the meeting. He didn't want any undue stress on me or the baby. So now at thirty-seven weeks pregnant, I'm finally going to have a conversation with the man who is my biological father.

"Mrs. Harris has lunch ready," I hear from my husband, standing in the doorway of our closet.

He always looks so sexy.

"Is Gio here yet?" I know my voice sounds shaky.

Luca arches an eyebrow and comes over to me as I try to clasp the necklace he gave me for our first wedding anniversary. He brushes my hair over one shoulder, then takes both ends and finishes hooking it for me. He leans down and kisses the nape of my neck as his hands rub down my arms and settle on my round stomach.

"Maybe we should wait until after the baby comes before we talk with Gio. I don't want you getting upset and dealing with any more stress."

I turn in his arms and have to take a step back to accommodate my large belly.

"I've wanted to do it for some time now and definitely before the baby comes. I have questions, and when I'm up at night, all I can think about is sitting down with him and getting answers."

"You could always write your questions down and I could give them to him, or I could just print up his background check for you."

"That's not what I want. I want to be able to see him at your parents' house and not get this ball in my throat. I want to try to understand his reasons. I need it so I can move on before the baby gets here and so I can put all my focus on our family," I plead for him the understand.

He nods. "Ok, let's go down and wait for him in the kitchen. I think Mrs. Harris made some pasta for lunch."

My nose scrunches like it does when I smell coffee. I can't stomach the thought of pasta at the moment. Brownies, on the other hand, I could eat all day.

We exit our room, and Luca helps me down the curved staircase. His phone starts to buzz, and when he looks down, I see Arturo is calling.

"Take that, and I'll see you soon." I shoo him away. He looks reluctant to take the call, but I reach up and kiss his lips to silence him.

He starts toward his office at the back of the house when an idea comes to mind.

Quickly, I pull out my phone and text Gio.

Gemma: Change of plans.

Just as I'm about to take a seat in the formal living room, I hear Ernie talking to Sam about Gio being here. Not wanting to miss my chance, I stand up and walk as quickly as I can toward the door. Once I've brushed past Ernie, I make my way down the steps to where Sam and Gio are talking. My belly is so large it bumps Gio as I come to stand next to them.

"I thought we could go and get some food," I say, slightly out of breath. I give a glance over my shoulder and decide to keep my momentum going down toward the car. It's now or never!

"Where did you have in mind?" Gio asks as we pull out onto the road from the compound.

Just as I'm about to tell him *Sweet Spots* is a good place to grab some treats, my phone rings. I chuckle, rolling my eyes as I stuff my hand into my purse and pull it out. It took him longer than I thought to find out I left.

"Hey, babe!" I exclaim as if I haven't seen or spoken with him today.

I can hear Luca's breathing from the other side of the phone as he makes a dramatic pause that I guess is supposed to alert me that I'm in trouble.

"I'm going to paddle your ass when you get home, baby girl! I hope those treats are worth it. I told you yesterday after the doctor's visit that I wanted you to stay close to home and I'd send Sam or Ernesto out to get you anything you wanted. Or I'd have left and gotten it for you. Why in the hell did you leave and not tell me?"

"Oh! I didn't realize you didn't hear me say that." I play up an absent-minded pregnancy moment, hoping to turn the tables around and make him seem like the one who's forgetting things these days. "Well, since we're already on the road, we might as well stop in for a treat, don't you think? I've been craving those brownies something awful. I swear, it's all the baby can survive on these days."

I listen a little longer as his delicious threats turn me on even further, and now I'm wondering if brownies are what I'm craving or if it's Luca's punishments. I'm humming, lost in fantasies of all the things my husband could do when he gets my attention.

"Baby, put Gio on the phone, and stop daydreaming about my dick." A small gasp leaves me, and I hear him chuckle at having busted me. "Don't worry, I'll make sure to save the best treat for last."

I give one more hum that could almost pass as a moan, then hold the phone up for Gio to take. I flush red when I remember I'm not alone and that my father is the one next to me.

"It's Gio," he speaks into the phone, then switches ears so I'm unable to hear their conversation. I really hope Luca doesn't make Gio turn around. I'd like to talk with it being just the two of us. Luca is so protective of me, and I love that, but I want to be able to show emotions and not have to end the talk before we're able to finish everything that needs to be said.

"Sure thing. Are you sending Sam or the others our way?" I hear Gio ask. Ugh, I really hate that Enzo guy for being such a pain in the ass. I wish they'd find him or come to some agreement so I can stop being cooped up in the house all the time. When the baby comes, I want to be able to take short trips to the zoo or the park without the fear that this maniac is going to try something. I'd also like to not have a team of twenty follow us around.

He hangs up with a sigh as we pull into the bakery parking lot.

"Whew! Dodged a bullet on that one," I chuckle to myself.

"You know, I don't think Luca would deny you anything."

"I like to keep him on his toes." I can't help the smile.

Luca must've told him where I wanted to go because he doesn't ask for directions. As soon as we pull into the parking spot, I'm out of the car with my mouth watering for some brownies.

After ordering six different types of brownies, a ham and cheese sandwich, and a large chocolate shake, we find a spot over in a quiet corner of the shop. When we're settled and the excitement of sneaking out past Luca has subsided, reality sets in. Now

I'm face to face with the only other person on this planet who shares my DNA.

You can do this, Gemma! Just ask him everything and find out why he ghosted!

"So," I pause and take a deep breath trying to figure out where I want to start. "You're my dad. My biological dad, who my mom thought was dead."

There, that wasn't so hard!

"I am," Gio announces and seems a little startled as I put him on the spot. "There aren't any excuses I can give you to make what I did right, but I hope that if I tell you what I was going through, you might be able to understand where my head was at the time."

Over the next ten to fifteen minutes, he tells me how he and Mom met. The way he describes her is like a schoolboy with the biggest crush on the popular girl in class. He speaks about all the adventures they had together for those few short months, and when he describes Mom, it's like I'm remembering her from when she was alive with me. I can't help but smile at Gio, appreciating that someone else was able to experience her love other than me.

"Lily was young and had a free spirit that drew people to her. She was fun and never seemed to let things dampen the light that shined. She was here at the university for an art degree. We started seeing each other almost every day. I'd told her that I was in the service and was on leave. I thought it would impress her, but she didn't seem to care. Lily wanted *me*. Not what I could give her or what she could gain from me." We both laughed because it's true. Mom was never impressed by wealth or status. She only cared that the person had a good heart and good intentions.

I also realize some of the places he's describing are places Mom took me to when I was young. I'd thought she was showing me places connected to her and Mario's adventures together, but now I realize those stories were about Gio instead.

"Mom used to take me to Lake Meade all the time and to

that canyon too. I think she was trying to recreate those moments for me."

"I'm glad she was able to move on and be happy."

Gio then told me all about the way he grew up, how his life in the mafia was dark, and that he hadn't wanted to taint mom with it.

"I never thought I'd ever want a family. Never thought this life was family friendly, to be honest. I watched my best friend deal with all the threats and attempts on his family's lives for years and didn't think I'd be able to handle it. Arturo is one of the strongest men I've ever known, and I'd lay my life down for him and his family, but I just never thought I'd be able to balance it. I knew the longer I was with Lily, the less likely I'd be able to walk away. There was no way I was leaving this life, and I wasn't sure if she could handle the dark shadows that came with being saddled to this lifestyle. Sure, she'd never want for anything, but the constant threat of being killed or kidnapped lurked in the background. So, I did what any other idiot would do and broke things off. A clean break. I organized for her to receive a letter saying I'd been killed in action. Cowardly, I know, but I didn't want her to waste her life waiting for me or to see the look on her face when she learned I'd lied to her about who I really was."

It's hard to hear how devastated Gio was, and I can tell that it weighed heavily on him to decide to cut himself out of Mom's life with a clean break. I'd be so broken if Luca left me, and I'm sure a piece of my mom's heart died the day she got his letter.

He shifts the conversation to when he found out about me and our moment begins to sour.

"Never in a million years did the idea of getting her pregnant cross my mind. Sure, I'd let my mind briefly go there in the long game, but it was never something I thought would happen for me. Had I known, I'd never have let her go. I'd have bound her to me and made sure she'd never leave my side."

He starts to sound a lot like Luca, and I wonder if it's a trait all mafia men have.

"When we went over to kill Mario, it was like seeing a ghost. I saw photos of Lily with a young girl, and I blanked out. I thought surely I was seeing things because there was no way my girl would end up with someone as slimy as Mario Ricci. I'd always wondered what had happened to her, but once I let her go, I promised myself I'd leave her alone. I knew I'd be tempted to steal her away from all the dreams she'd wanted to accomplish. While Luca was downstairs dealing with Mario, I went through the entire upstairs on a mission, trying to determine if the woman in the pictures was my Lily. I'd found a few things but wanted to have our IT guy look into it."

Gio looks so haunted retelling the horrific night that seems to have changed more than just my life.

"It took our IT guy eight days to get back to me with the full report. It took a week after that for me to come to terms with what I read and absorb all the information. Lily was dead and left behind our beautiful little girl. I never knew Lily had money. She never put out that vibe, as if it would've mattered, but she'd made sure that her—our—daughter, would be fine and continue on with whatever dreams she wanted to chase. I can't prove it, but from what I've read over in the files, I have a sneaking suspicion that Mario might've had a hand in the car crash that killed Lily."

A gasp leaves my mouth. "What? Do you really think that?"

"I don't have any solid proof, but a few leads certainly point in that direction. I wish we could go back to that night at Mario's house and have a do-over with him. Maybe prolong his misery and get a few answers to those questions. It seemed Mario had gotten himself in a little bit of a bind and was in need of money to pay off a debt he had accrued with a bookie in the Slater Organization here in Vegas. Victor Slater is the head of his organization, and one of the five families that run the Las Vegas territory, alongside ours. He's a slimy fucker who doesn't get along with anyone in the other families, which makes my job harder sometimes."

"Oh my gosh! I don't understand how someone could do something like that to the person they're married to," I say and twist my hands in my lap. Mario might've killed my mom over money. "Is it bad that I wish he'd suffered?" I whisper, voicing my inner thoughts aloud and hoping that doesn't make me a completely horrible person for wanting another person to die a slow, painful death for taking my mom away from me.

"No, sweetheart, it's not." He gives me a sympathetic look. "Luckily, Lily had already filed for divorce and had switched over all of her accounts and put all of her assets into a trust for you, making one of the nuns at your private school your guardian until came of age. It makes me think she knew something wasn't right and wanted to protect you."

I start to tear up learning all this new information, but I want to hear the rest.

"What else?"

"We can hold off until another time, sweetheart. I don't want you to get your blood pressure up too high."

My blood pressure has been slightly elevated lately, and the doctor wants me to keep my stress levels down. I'm pretty sure this would not be recommended, but I need to know everything now.

"No, I want to hear this. I have to know," I plead.

Gio nods, then goes on. "After learning all this out from our IT guy, I had you followed when you were in high school. I made several trips a month up there to watch you. You seemed so well-adjusted and happy, and I didn't want to disrupt your life. What could I offer my beautiful daughter except a life of being caged and guarded? You'd have come to hate me eventually, and I wanted to give you the world."

"Wait. So, you knew this whole time that I was your daughter, and you didn't come for me?" I'm more hurt than angry.

"I—"

"You let me believe that I was alone in this world rather than claim me? I was an orphan teenager who had not only lost her mom but found out that the man who had helped raised her was a sicko who did bad things to children. And you didn't think that I needed some kind of support emotionally?"

"Gemma—"

"I kinda wish you'd lied and told me you'd just found out right before you kidnapped me. At least then I could understand why you'd leave me all alone with no one in my corner." I can't help the tears that start to run down my face. "You have no idea the mental and emotional pain I went through in high school when it was parent's weekend. I had no one to share my successes with or my failures." Sobs wrack my chest.

He knew where I was, and he didn't come for me.

"I'm so sorry if you felt alone. I thought you'd be better off without me in your life. Look what I do for a living. You'd never have had the freedom to go and explore college or travel the world. You seemed so happy at private school and then at college. I honestly thought you didn't need me tainting your life. I've never lived a safe and boring lifestyle, as you can see." He reaches over and places his calloused, scarred hand over mine. "Just like with your mom, I fucked up royally. I just hope one day you'll be able to look at me and not see me as a man who abandoned you but rather someone who was truly trying to put you first. Even if it was the second biggest mistake of my life."

I can't help but swallow back my sobs and pull my hand away to wipe my tears.

"What is it with mob men and stalking?" These men are a different breed. Whatever happened to the white and shining knights who presented themselves before saving the damsel? Not this group who waits in the shadows and conquers the world before they pull you into their dark world of guns and bodyguards.

The air shifts, and Gio tenses, something dark and callous

glazing over his eyes. His soft gentle side is now gone, and a hard, tough-as-nails person has replaced him.

"Gemma, listen to me," his tone has changed, and it makes my entire body lock up. "Get up right now and hurry to the back of the store. Go out to the alley and call Luca for help, I'm outnumbered and need to know that you aren't in the crosshairs."

"I—" Something bad is about to happen. I can feel it. Gone is the laid-back, cheerful man that spoke so lovingly about my mom a short while ago. My belly twitches and tightens.

"Go now and don't look back. Get somewhere safe and wait for Luca or Arturo."

He doesn't say another word but stands and brushes past me. I knew if I was going to get out of this safely with no harm to my baby, I need to do as Gio says.

Without another moment of hesitation, I stand with my purse in hand and make a quick escape behind the counter, passing a few cowering employees as I follow the exit signs. As I reach the back door, I'm already dialing Luca.

"Hey, baby girl, you didn't eat too many brownies, did you?" His calm playful voice is the opposite of what I'm feeling at the moment.

"Help," is all I can get out before he's firing off a thousand questions. None of which I can answer.

The moment I stepped out the door, I spotted two giant men in black attire standing there, waiting.

"They have me," I scream before one of them grabs my phone.

I might be heavily pregnant, but I'm not going down without a fight. They're both taken off-guard when I whip my foot around and nail the other giant in the knee, just like my instructor showed me and Bianca in self-defense class.

"Jesus!" Giant Number Two yells as he tries to stay upright, but the surprise attack leaves him off balance and he topples down onto one knee. I slip by him but don't make it far before Giant Number One hauls me back by my upper arm.

I start to scream and yell, but when he flashes his gun to my head, I stop and start looking for other ways to get away. Once Giant Number Two is able to stand again, they both hold me by the upper arm and march me back to the door at *Sweet Spots*.

"You don't want to do this, please," I beg when I realize I'm out of options.

"Don't worry, the boss will take excellent care of you." They both laugh, and a sickening feeling forms as my heart plummets into my stomach when another squeeze comes from my abdomen.

Hold on, little one. Daddy will save us.

As we make our way into the shop, the two men holding me tell the two employees to beat it. When they bring me around the counter I notice the business is empty except for Enzo and his men who are surrounding Gio. I see blood pouring out of his nose, and I can't help but whimper at the sight.

Don't hurt him. He's all I have left.

"Gemma! I'm so glad to see you again," Enzo exclaims. "I hope you didn't hurt yourself in your condition. I was just giving Giovanni an offer he couldn't refuse, but it seems the Falcone men aren't the brightest. I've got one spot on my team left, and he has regretfully declined. Such a shame."

He takes a step over to me to brush a strand of hair from my face when Gio lunges at him. He snatches his wrist but is met with one of the guards swinging their gun to his knee and taking him down to the ground, making Gio lose his grip on Enzo's wrist.

Three guards jump on Gio and start to kick him. He doesn't stand a chance against four giants.

"Please, don't!" I scream at them to stop as I try to shrug off my two guards, but it's no use. My limited capabilities are no match for these men holding me.

"That's enough, boys." Enzo holds a hand up to stop the beating. His eyes gleam with a dark, cruel look. "Princess Gemma has asked so nicely." He chuckles, and the wicked tone he used has the hairs on the back of my neck rising.

I try to think of something to spare us some time before Luca and the guys get here. My mind is mush though, as I watch a helpless Gio bleed from his nose, mouth, and forehead. *Why can't my brain function when I need it to?* I only hope backup will arrive shortly.

"I think it's time for us to part ways now, Giovanni. Gemma will be a much better conversationalist to have under my care since you turned me down."

"I'll go! Take me!" Gio shouts not caring that he's a bloody mess. I can hear the panic in his voice, and it breaks my heart to hear him plead. He tries to get up but is shoved down by one of the guards.

"Sorry, but we only have room for one, remember?"

Enzo gives the most horrifying smile then pulls out a gun from his suit jacket. Lifting it, he aims right at Gio. His body jerks as three shots ring out in the bakery. Gio grunts and exhales harshly. Red blood immediately starts to soak his shirt, and I can't stop my screams as his body goes limp.

"DAD!" I scream over and over. "No!"

CHAPTER TWENTY-FIVE

Gemma

I YANK MY ARMS HARD OUT OF THE GUARDS' HANDS AND FALL to the ground where Gio is lifeless.

"Please don't die, please stay with me." My vision is blurry as I try to cover his wounds with my hands. "HELP! Somebody help me!"

I feel an arm sweep under my underarms and pull me up to my feet. My legs buckle but whoever has me has a tight grip that holds me firm. I'm grateful that they are being mindful of my belly.

"Let's go, boys," Enzo says as he turns on his heels and makes his way to the door.

"HELP!" I continue to scream as my body is lifted so that my feet don't drag as we make our way out on the sidewalk.

"Keep her quiet," Enzo orders as all the men come together at the curb to form a semi-circle around Enzo and myself.

I feel the snap as I'm backhanded, and it shocks me mute. There's a white-hot pain on my cheek as my sight comes back into focus. I'm quiet now, but the tears are still streaming down my face. I try to turn my head to look into the window for Gio, but the sound of popping catches my attention.

The arm that was around me vanishes, and my knees drop hard

onto the concrete curb. Several more guys hit the ground with sickening thuds as I start to crawl back toward the bakery door. The window bursts above my head, sending shards of glass everywhere. I hunker down into a semi-fetal position and stay still, waiting for this to end.

In the distance, I hear the sound of screeching tires as several cars converge on the scene.

"Don't move, Enzo, you cocksucker, or I'll blow your brains all over the pavement!" I hear my husband shout, and I've never been more relieved. "You're blocked in from all sides."

I peek up from where I'm on the ground and see a flash of blond hair hovering over me.

"Oh my god, Gem, are you okay?" My eyes and mouth are having a hard time functioning, and it feels like I can't make my brain work properly.

Bianca kneels at my side and starts to brush off all the glass that's piled on me. She has splatters of blood on her face, neck, and shirt.

A single shot rings out, making us jump as the sound of someone hitting the curb fills my ears.

"If you try to make a move toward her, I'll keep cutting you down," Luca's voice is getting closer as Bianca tries to help me up from the glass-covered ground. She's shielding my body from any potential threats.

"Are you hurt?" She brings my eyes to focus on her and not Enzo who is currently cradling his knee.

Bianca has her hands all over me. I must look a fright with all the blood spattered on me.

Gio.

"Dad!" I finally start to lose the haze from my mind and try to take a step in the direction of the bakery, but strong arms lift me and the familiar smell I've woken up to every morning fills my nose. I'm lightheaded and starting to sway as my adrenaline begins to recede.

"Easy, baby."

I wiggle to be let go but his grip is firm. I grab his collar and force him to hear me.

"Dad was shot. He's in there. We need to help," I say frantically.

"The guys have him and are already headed to the hospital."

Luca takes me to the side of the building and gently sets me down with Bianca right beside him, helping to keep me balanced. In the distance, I can hear Enzo shouting, but Bianca blocks my view as I try to see what all the new commotion is about. Luca has his hands in my hair, pressing my scalp with his fingers.

"Does this hurt? Do you hurt anywhere?" He's firing questions as he examines me from head to toe, but I can't think of anything other than what is happening with Gio.

"I'm fine. We need to head to the hospital. I need to see if Gio is okay."

I go to move around them both, but a sharp pain hits me right in the stomach, causing me to clutch my belly and bend over.

"Ugh!"

"What's wrong?" I hear the panic in Luca's voice as his face comes into view when he squats down in front of me.

Just then a gush of liquid rushes down my legs and onto the pavement.

"Oh, shit!" I faintly hear Bianca's voice.

"ERNESTO!" Luca yells, and somehow he appears from around the corner.

"Sir."

"Pull the car around now." Luca is barking orders as his men form a line to block the street from my view.

Another sharp pain hits my stomach, and I let out a cry. This one hurts more than the last.

"Sam, take Enzo to the warehouse and make sure to have a dozen men there to stand guard. Call and get this place cleaned up now."

Luca stands from the crouched position, but his eyes never leave mine as he gives orders.

"Everything is going to be fine, baby. Just breathe through it, and we'll be at the hospital in no time."

I hear a car come to a stop, then I'm gently lifted off my feet. Bianca has the door to the car open as Luca places me carefully in the back seat, then runs around to the other side.

Once all the doors are shut, Ernie starts the journey down the streets. Luca is on the phone with Dr. Fulton, letting him know what's happening.

"He'll be at the hospital waiting for us, Gemma. He wants us to time your contractions until we get there." He maneuvers my legs across his and reaches out to hold my hands.

"I'm scared," I confess and look down at my belly. "It's too early for this. Our baby is too small. What if something happens? What if what happened out there caused our baby harm? What if—" I gasp as I take in the blood stains on my dress, arms, and legs.

"We'll get you cleaned up once we get in the room. Dr. Fulton is bringing us in through the back of the hospital. Everything is going to be just fine. Dr. Fulton is going to make sure our baby is perfect and that everything goes smoothly."

"He shot Gio…I couldn't do anything." My voice is quivering, and all of my extremities are starting to shake. "I can't lose him."

"There are blankets behind your seat, Luca," Bianca says from the passenger seat. She's turned her body around to me. "Focus on your breathing, and let the doctors focus on Gio." She moves her hand and starts to rub my thigh as another contraction starts. Luca and I have gone to the classes, and Bianca has watched all the videos on breathing through the pain.

"Almost there, baby. Breathe and focus on me. Look at me, and let's do this together." Luca's voice is calm and soothing as I grit my teeth and breathe through it. "Good, you're doing so good, baby. Lean back and relax now."

"How did you get to me so fast?" I ask Bianca, panting through the contractions.

"Adele, Alice, and I were planning to surprise you with a small baby shower tomorrow. I was in charge of the sweets and know how you've been craving these brownies," she explains. "I was one store over buying you an outfit when I heard the gunshots. When I saw you being dragged out I pulled my gun out and shot the guy who had his arm around you."

"Thank God those training sessions involved weapons training," Luca says, "but next time, call for backup. You could've been killed. You were outnumbered ten to one."

She nods looking a little chastised, and I reach for her hand and give a thankful squeeze.

"Thank you."

The car comes to a stop, and both Bianca and Luca exit the car. My door is finally opened by a nurse with a wheelchair, and Luca practically pushes the nurse out of the way before he bends over to lift me from the car and place me in the wheelchair. Once we enter the hospital, we are whisked to an elevator and moved to a floor that looks more like a five-star hotel. Dr. Fulton is there waiting with a friendly smile.

"Sweetheart, I hear we're having a baby today." He claps once and I want to punch the cheerful grin off his face.

If he notices the blood covering me, he doesn't mention or react to it. I'm sure he's used to seeing Luca and all the men in a far worse state. I'm wheeled into a room where two more nurses are setting things up. There are men stationed along the hall and two in the room, watching over the nurses. Luca tells them to wait outside as he wheels me over to the edge of the hospital bed.

"Oh dear, let's get you cleaned up with a shower, then we can get you settled. The anesthesiologist will be in shortly for your epidural as soon as you are ready."

Things are happening so fast my head is swimming. I feel like I'm a spectator watching from above as everyone moves around me.

"I'll be giving her a shower." Luca closes the door on the nurses as we enter the bathroom.

"That was rude," I mumble as I feel another contraction coming.

"Ohh!" I grab the counter with one hand and cradle my belly with the other. "It's starting to hurt more."

Luca wraps me in his arms as we breathe through the pain together. When it's over, he turns on the large shower and starts to help me undress. Once I'm under the spray, he divests himself of clothes and joins me. He takes his time as he washes off every bit of blood and dirt from my body. I vaguely register that he's using the same body wash I have at home, along with my shampoo and conditioner. We both are quiet as he gently washes me twice to make sure every trace of the earlier incident is gone.

After I'm all cleaned up, I'm put in a hospital gown and led out to the room where everything is set up and ready for us to have our precious baby. Adele and Arturo are in the room when we walk out, and they jump up from the couch when they see us.

"Darling girl, how are you feeling? Dr. Smith is waiting out in the hall to prep you for the epidural," Arturo tells us as Luca is buttoning a new shirt that seems to have appeared out of thin air.

"How is Gio? Has anyone checked on him? Can we see him?" I ask as the nurse leads me over to the bed.

"Gio is still in surgery. The surgeon has informed me that he is doing well and should be in recovery within the next hour. You let us worry about Gio, and you focus on bringing our grandbaby safely into this world."

Adele stays on the other side of the bed and holds my hand as my contractions continue.

"Sweet girl, I'd love nothing more than to help bring this little one the world, but would you rather Bianca be in here?" Adele asks as she dabs the cool washcloth over my sweaty forehead. "She's in the next room over cleaning up."

She must have noticed my eyes checking over by the door for something. I've never had any extended family since my mom died, and I'd like to bring this baby into the world with as many loved ones as possible.

"I want you here with me, Adele. Can Bianca come in and be

here too? I know they limit the number of people in a room, but I want this little one to be surrounded with all the love."

"Maybe everyone else, but not you, baby girl. If you want ten or even a hundred in here then that is what is going to happen," Luca cuts in from beside me. He hasn't let go of my hand since I got in bed.

"Let me go out and let her know she can come in. I'll go and check on Gio for you also." Arturo stands from his chair in the corner and walks out. Not even a minute later, Bianca comes barreling in and sets up shop at the foot of the bed. She's freshly showered and has her camera in hand.

Over the next hour, I'm hooked up to IVs and my epidural is placed. Now we just wait for me to dilate to ten so I can start pushing. Arturo came in ten minutes ago with an update that Gio pulled through surgery and is in recovery down the hall.

"Who is ready to bring this little bundle of joy into the world?" Dr. Fulton asks as he checks me. Everyone has a designated place in the room so that they don't interfere with Dr. Fulton and the nurses.

Since getting my epidural, I've not had a single bit of pain except for my strong, surly husband who has been bugging the nurses every few minutes about my vitals when there is a slight increase on the screen. Over the next few minutes, there is a flurry of movement as everyone gets into place. Adele is holding my leg, and Bianca is up by my head, holding my hand. Luca is on the other side, holding me as though I might bolt off the bed.

"Ok, sweetheart, on this next contraction, I want you to start pushing. Bare down and when I'm done counting, you stop." We continue this for what seems like forever.

"Oh my!" Adele exclaims as I rest for a bit in between pushes. "Baby's crowning."

"On this next one, I want you to give me a really big push, Gemma, and when I say stop, you stop. I see the head."

When I get the green light, I do as I'm told and stare into the eyes of my husband. "I love you so much," I say.

"There are no words in this world that can describe what I feel for you, baby. You breathe life into me and give me everything to live for."

Tears well up in my eyes as he leans in and gives me the gentlest kiss.

The sound of a tiny cry rings out in the room. My baby is quickly laid on my chest as the nurse tries to reach over Luca to rub our little bundle of purple and blue with a towel.

"Would the Papa like to cut the cord?" Dr. Fulton stands with a pair of surgical scissors.

I turn my attention away from the most perfect baby I've ever seen in my life and catch sight of my man. He's looking down at our baby with such awe that I'm afraid he might be in shock. Our eyes meet, and for a quick moment, he has unshed tears filling his eyes. Bianca has her camera out and appears to be catching everything.

Luca hesitantly reaches over and snips the umbilical cord where Dr. Fulton points. He stares down at me and the baby with an intense look that I can't decipher. His large hand engulfs the baby's back as he leans down close to our faces.

"The world will end before anything ever happens to you. Nothing in this world will ever harm you again. I will lay my life down for you both. My blood is your blood; my family is your family."

A rush of emotions overtakes me as he recites the same vows he spoke on our wedding night. I place my hand over Luca's hand where our beautiful baby lays.

"The world will end before anything ever happens to you. Nothing in this world will ever harm you. I will lay my life down for you both. My blood is your blood; my family is your family," I promise as I look between my husband and our baby.

We stare at each other, caught in our own little bubble as the world around us moves. Something in me shifts, and all the past secrets and mistakes that still weighed in the deepest parts of my mind disappear. If there was ever a thought in my mind causing me to question being with Luca or his family, it dissipates in an instant and a renewed perspective comes to the forefront. This is my family, and I'll do whatever it takes to keep them all safe and in my life, no matter what.

"So, are we going to find out the gender?" Bianca asks from across the room where she and Adele are videoing and snapping pictures.

It's in that moment that we both realize we didn't even check or ask when Dr. Fulton laid our baby on my chest. In every scan, the baby had refused to be in a position to show us, and Dr. Fulton would always comment on how this is definitely Luca's child.

Slowly and carefully, I turn the baby over in my arms and smile. Luca's face lights up. He leans down and places a kiss on my forehead before doing the same to our baby. He lifts then cradles the baby in the crook of his arm like it's the most natural thing and he's been doing it for years.

"We have a baby boy!"

Cheers ring out loudly in the room, causing Sam and Ernie to come rushing in to make sure everything is okay. Thank goodness Dr. Fulton is finished with me and has me covered back up, or that would've been horrifying. Arturo follows in behind them, having gone to check on Gio.

"I missed it?" His disappointment makes me giggle.

"Pop, come meet your grandson."

"A little boy?" Arturo rubs his chest right above his heart where Luca rubs his own when he's having a moment.

Luca carries our boy over to his grandparents as they take a seat on the couch. Bianca follows our baby, snapping pictures with his grandparents. After a few minutes, he starts to fuss and my own emotions intensify in response.

"Let's give the new parents some time with the baby. We also need Gemma to start breastfeeding, and we need to weigh the little guy," Dr. Fulton says, ignoring the death glares from Arturo and Adele.

Luca is over there in a split second, scooping up our son. He takes him over to the corner of the room where Dr. Fulton and a nurse measure and weigh him before they finish cleaning him up. Luca never leaves his side, and it makes my heart skip a beat.

After a while, the room has been cleared out, and our boy has taken to the breast. The nurse showed us everything we needed to know, and it's just the three of us now in our room. Luca has his shirt off, waiting as patiently as possible to burp our son skin-to-skin.

"Do you think he'll want to share those?" Luca asks seriously as he watches our son suckle my breast.

"He looks like you," I say dreamily, ignoring Luca's comment as I stroke his cheek and his eyes flutter closed. "I always hear that the mom does all the heavy lifting and carries the baby for nine months, only to have the baby not look even remotely like them." I can't help but chuckle. "Don't you think the guy should be put through some of the pain and suffering that goes along with birth?"

"Baby, guys do suffer." I raise an eyebrow, wondering what he's talking about. "The moment we find out about having a kid on the way, our entire world changes. We are up at all hours of the night, playing every scenario known to man of what could happen to our wife and baby. Then there's all the planning to make sure you both are comfortable and healthy. Not to mention all the mood swings you women have."

I pop him on the arm, jostling our baby and disturbing his meal. Luca laughs and pretends to rub the spot where I popped him.

"All I'm saying is that you take on the front-end part, while I take care of the behind-the-scenes part." I roll my eyes as I hand over our now sleeping newborn to his daddy to burp and snuggle while pulling up my gown to cover myself.

"Do we have a name for our little guy?" Luca asked.

We had spent the last few months trying to decide on a name, but since we hadn't known the gender, we struggled with pinpointing one.

"Should we keep it in the family?" I ask.

"What are you thinking?" He continues to pat our boy on the back while doing a light bounce.

"What do you think about Dante Mossimo Falcone?" I offer. Arturo's middle name is Dante, and Gio's middle name is Mossimo.

Luca seems to think on it for a minute, and then it dawns on him. Something clicks. His face tilts toward our son's head as he whispers.

"What do you think? You like Dante Mossimo?" Luca continues to rub his back just as our baby boy lets out the most adorable burp I've ever heard. "I think that settles it then."

The smile on Luca's face doesn't budge for the next hour as he refuses to put his son down in the bassinet. Just as I'm about to ask for an update on Gio, the door slowly opens, and Arturo pops his head in.

"Hey," he looks around making sure he's not interrupting something, "I wanted to let you know Gio is awake and was asking about you."

"Can I see him?" I look to Luca. I've been up and moving a little bit, but I'm not sure if I'm allowed to truck it down the hall yet. I've gotten the feeling back in my legs and the catheter out but am being told to take it nice and slow when moving around.

Luca thinks it over for a minute, probably going through a million different scenarios. "Let me get you a wheelchair and have a nurse accompany us." He comes over and places a sleeping Dante in my waiting arms.

He heads out to the nurses' station where our four private nurses and Dr. Fulton have been waiting.

"How's everything going?" Arturo comes over to the side of the bed, leans down, and places a kiss on my forehead before running a pointer finger down Dante's puffy little cheek.

"Everything is going great. I can't believe he's finally here. I feel like I've waited an eternity to hold him."

"Time is a thief. Soak it all in, even on the days when you want to pull your hair out. They are worth every second of the ups and downs."

"Would you like to hold him again? I've got to use the bathroom."

"You'll never hear me turn down a chance to spend time with this little one."

My heart squeezes as I hand Dante over to his grandfather. Just as I'm about to close the door to the bathroom, I turn and stare at Arturo. To the outside world, he is this ruthless, terrifying man who takes no prisoners, but to his family, he is the gentlest man who loves them and will do anything for them.

"Did Luca tell you the name we picked out?"

Arturo shakes his head, not taking his eyes off Dante as he walks by the couch.

"I'd like you to meet Dante Mossimo Falcone."

Arturo stops walking and carefully takes a seat on the couch. His eyes find mine, and a flurry of emotions cross his face.

"Dante," I hear him whisper.

"I thought it only fitting that our son be named after his two grandfathers."

Even though Gio and I have more to work on, I know in my heart that we'll eventually be very close. After today, I can't even think about him not being in my life.

As I close the door to give Arturo some time with his grandson, I hear a faint sniffle and know he might need a few moments after the big reveal. Just as I'm washing my hands, the bathroom door opens, and a very concerned Luca stands in the doorway.

"Why didn't you wait for me? What if you fell?" he chastises. Oh, brother, here we go. "The button on the side of the bed is there for a reason."

"I don't need someone to hold my hand while I pee, Luca. Besides, your dad is right there if I need something." I go to roll my eyes but stop at the look Luca is giving me.

"You might've had our son a few hours ago, but it won't stop the spanking you'll get if something happens to you because you're being stubborn." He turns and rolls the wheelchair into the bathroom, helping me get situated. "They said Gio can see you, but only for a little bit because he needs his rest."

As he pushes the chair into the hospital room Arturo and Adele discreetly wipe their eyes.

"What's wrong?" Luca immediately goes into panic mode, and he moves to where they are holding Dante.

"Nothing, Son. We are just so happy for you and our family," Arturo says as he passes Dante over to Adele. He comes over to Luca and gives him a crushing hug. "You'll never know how proud I am of you. I may not have expressed it often when you were younger, but you have become everything I could ever want in a son, and my hope is that Dante will do the same for you."

"Pop," Luca chokes and tugs his dad back into a hug. They stay like that for a while before they gather themselves, and Adele hands me Dante as we all make our way down the hall to Gio's room.

The hall is lined with our men, and no one is batting an eye at the host of them, all strapped to the teeth with guns and ammo. Gio is five doors down and has a full staff looking after him as well.

"Darling, please try not to get upset when you see him. He is alive, and he's going to make it. He has tubes and machines everywhere, okay?" Arturo advises.

I nod though I'm not sure I can keep that promise.

We push through his door, and now I know why Arturo tried to warn me. Gio is so very pale, his face is swollen from the beating he took before he was shot, and his chest is exposed with a gruesome line of stitches from his chest to his abdomen. If I didn't already know that this was him, I'd have a hard time believing the man in that hospital bed is my dad.

The noise of the door closing makes him pop an eye open.

"Hey, kiddo." His voice is gravelly.

Luca helps me stand up from the wheelchair, and I move to the side of the bed to hold his cold hand.

"I'd like for you to meet someone." I lean over to make sure he can hear me. His eyes try to focus, but I know he must be exhausted after the long surgery. "Meet your grandson, Dante Mossimo Falcone."

I hold the swaddled little boy upright so that Gio doesn't have to move an inch to see his perfect little face. When I look up from Dante, I see tears spilling from the corners of his eyes.

"Thank you, Gemma. Thank you for giving me something to live for." His heart rate spikes a little, and a nurse comes in to let us know he needs rest. Much to Gio's protest, we leave him with the promise of coming back tomorrow for a visit.

Once I'm settled back in my room, I think the day has finally taken its toll on me. I feed Dante again and snuggle into the plush bed for a nap. Bianca went home and brought back my overnight bag. She and Adele also went shopping and bought out all the little boy outfits.

"Baby," I hear just as I close my eyes.

"Yeah," I open an eye and see Luca hasn't put Dante down yet after his burping.

"I've got to go and handle some things. I'll only be a few hours, but I didn't want you to wake without me here."

"Go? Where do you need to go?"

"Enzo needs to be dealt with." He leans in and presses his lips to mine. "Bianca and Ma are here to watch Dante while you rest."

My energy is completely drained, and I don't even try to put up a fight.

"Okay, but be careful. Love you."

"Love you more."

My mind goes blank, and I fall fast asleep before he even has a chance to walk out the door.

CHAPTER TWENTY-SIX

Luca

I HOLD DANTE FOR A MINUTE LONGER, INHALING HIS PURE baby smell, then pass him over to Bianca. I know that he and Gemma will be in the best hands with her and Ma watching out for them. I turn back toward the bed and see Gemma is already sound asleep. She is exhausted mentally and physically, but she's the epitome of strength after having to endure what she did today. I know the conversation with Gio had been taxing on her emotionally, and though I tried my best to prolong their conversation, wanting her to be in the right mindset, I knew it was futile. Then, to almost be kidnapped while watching her dad be shot a few feet away from her had to have been devastating. I'm used to the violence of this world, and I try my hardest to ensure that she's shielded from it, but she had a front-row seat in the action today.

With one last kiss on her forehead and a whisper in her ear, she relaxes even further into the bed.

"Take care of them," I quietly say as I walk around the bed toward the door.

"With my life," Ma states, and I know she means it.

Out in the hall, Pop is already speaking to a few of our men. We have twelve guards split between Gio's and Gemma's rooms, along with others who are spread out within the hospital. Hell, even Dr. Fulton carries a gun and will get into the action if necessary.

"Everything situated, Son?" Pop asks as I approach.

"She's fast asleep with Ma and Bianca with her and Dante," I respond.

"After today, we need to sit down and have a discussion about Bianca's arrangement to stay here. I've put her father off as long as I can."

"Do you have someone in mind?" I have some thoughts on it but want to see what he's thinking.

Pop turns toward Cassio, my second, who is approaching in his tactical gear, and gives him a hard stare.

"What are your thoughts on tying *him* to Bianca?"

I let out a chuckle and shake my head. "It really is scary how we are almost always on the same page, Pop," I say as Cassio comes to a stop and takes his stance, hands behind his back with both feet shoulder-width apart. A true soldier stance. Little does he know that I'm pretty sure he's got it bad for Bianca but hasn't acted on it.

"And this is why I know, when I decide to retire, that our family and organization will continue to thrive, Son." He places a firm hand on my shoulder, giving it a slight squeeze. "This should solve our problem with Chicago, and it'll make my daughter happy." My heart clenches when he refers to Gemma as his daughter. She's always wanted a family, and she couldn't have asked for a more loyal one. I know it was really rocky at the beginning, and I thought I'd lost her, but everything has worked out better than I could've imagined. Pop would do anything for her—all she has to do is ask. And now that she's given him his first grandson, I can only imagine what he'd do for her.

"Sir," Cassio addresses Pop, "the team is ready and in place."

"Good, let's head out."

As we load up in the SUVs, I hand my phone over to Cassio to show him a few pictures of Dante.

"Log into the cameras and set me up so I can check in on them," I say when he's done swiping through the dozens of photos.

Cassio begins quickly tapping away on the phone bringing up the hospital cameras. I watch for a beat as Bianca goes to put Dante in the bassinet, but Ma intercepts them. At this rate, Dante will be in kindergarten by the time he learns to walk with the way no one wants to put him down.

"Your Ma is the happiest I've seen her since we brought you and Alice home from the hospital," Pop speaks into the silent car. "Did she tell you that she had contractors come and take out my closet so Dante could have his nursery as close to us as possible? She moved all my stuff across the hall. Now, every morning I have to walk in my boxers across the hall. Heaven forbid she share any of her closet with me." He shakes his head, but there is no anger or resentment behind his words. "She had them make a door into the sitting room that's connected and turned it into a baby's indoor dream playground. I think she broke me on all the soft play equipment." He continues to chuckle as he shows me the progress pictures. "It's supposed to be a surprise, so be sure you act accordingly."

"Yes, sir," I say trying not to laugh at the thought of what would happen if Ma found out he ruined her surprise. His closet might be moved to the garage.

"Oh, and Alice has decided to have an area for our newest addition in her own room. She had the contractors add a little area on her side of the house."

"You do know that it might be a while before we let him out of our sight, right?" I say, not wanting anyone to get their feelings hurt.

"I'll let you tell your Ma that."

As the SUV turns off the highway into a remote area where we have warehouses, the atmosphere in the car changes. Everyone seems a little more tense as we get into business mode.

Right before we come to a stop, Pop addresses Cassio. "I'm arranging a marriage for you and Bianca." Pop stares at Cassio daring him to challenge his authority.

"Sir?" If this weren't a serious moment, I'd have laughed my ass off at the expression on Cassio's face right now. I've never seen him look so stunned. I bite my lip hard to keep from howling out.

"You will marry her. My daughter wants her to stay, and for that to happen, she'll need to be married to one of our top men."

Cassio looks like a fish out of water, and I'm a horrible person for enjoying this moment. He's probably waiting for someone to jump out and tell him it's a joke. Eventually, he recovers and gives a slight nod. "Yes, sir." His voice goes up an octave, but he quickly shakes his head and clears his throat. "Yes, Sir."

"Also, I'm giving you two months. No one is to know about this arrangement. My daughter can't find out about this, so whatever you have to do to woo Bianca, make it happen and make it as real as possible. This is good for both of our families in creating an alliance and getting a foothold in Chicago."

With that, we step out of the vehicle and walk into the musky building that houses a man who has been a thorn in our sides for months. Enzo is strapped to a chair that is bolted down to the concrete floor. Our men are circled around him even though there's no way for him to escape.

"Oh Enzo, I do hope you've had a comfortable stay with my men." Pop and I approach flanked by even more of our men. We've lost a lot of guys because of this bastard, and our men are chomping at the bit to have a go with him.

Of course, Enzo has a gag in his mouth, so all the muffled words are unrecognizable. Pop rips the gag off. "What was that?"

"If you think this war is over, then you're an even bigger fool than I thought!" he spits.

I take that as my opportunity to throw my right fist and smash his nose. The crunch I feel under my knuckles is so satisfying.

"Enlighten us, then," Pop pokes.

Enzo shakes his head and refuses to talk.

"Let's light him up, boys!" I cheer as we all line up around him and start taking shots.

After a few minutes, Pop holds his hand up for us to stop. Enzo looks like he went ten rounds with a boxer. One of our men produces a bucket of water and splashes him to get his attention.

"You might've been able to evade us for months, but you aren't the brains or the money source behind the mission to take our territory. Who are you working for? Who helped hide you?"

Pop pulls out his 9mm from his suit jacket.

Enzo looks past Pop, right into my eyes. "How's that pretty little lady doing? I can almost taste her on my tongue. He said I could have her after she dumped that kid out of her," he taunts me.

A shot rings out, and Enzo lets out a scream as Pop blows a bullet into Enzo's other kneecap. The one I took out on the curb by *Sweet Treats* has someone's belt tied above the wound to staunch the bleeding, prolonging his miserable death.

"My family is none of your concern." Pop gets in his face gripping his chin to get his eyes focused on him. "It would be in your best interest to say something useful, or I might have to bring in the good ole doc to keep you alive so we can torture you for weeks on end."

"I won't talk," Enzo sneers, trying to breathe through the pain.

"So be it," Pop says and backs up. "String him up."

Over the next few hours, the man hanging from the hook attached to the rafters looks nothing like the man who was dragged into the warehouse. Enzo has chunks of flesh seared out off of him, broken ribs, and his body is turning purple from where we've used him for a punching bag. He's really surprised me by not folding or giving the names of the people who orchestrated this takeover.

Pop comes over with a heavy-duty power drill and I almost cringe, thinking about where this might be going.

"Last chance to get a swift death before Doc is called."

Pop revs up the drill and moves toward Enzo's balls. Our men all take a step back, and my body wants to flinch and grip my own sack to take cover.

Enzo tries to swing away and starts to holler. "WAIT, wait,

wait!" What little strength he has left seeps out of him in defeat. "I'll tell you, but you have—"

A zing whizzes past my right ear, and Enzo's head explodes like a busted watermelon. I jump over to Pop and throw him down as his guards cover his body. Our men and I take cover looking for the shooter and waiting for another attack. Luis, who has been patrolling the perimeter, comes in from the side.

"Sniper," he states. "Has to be—no one has been on the property, and all alarms are intact."

"Fucking shit!" I yell. "Clean this up." I wave over to what's left of Enzo.

"Depending on his skill level he might've been almost a mile away from here. Finding him might be like a needle in a haystack." Cassio comes over to Pop and me.

"I'm going to make some calls to the other families and see if they've had any issues recently. I know the Dawson's were dealing with something a while ago," Pop tells me. "Knowing that a threat is still out there means the same level of protection for our family, Luca. I want at least two for Dante. Don't stress Gemma out with this news. She needs to feel secure and safe when she brings our little one home. Wait until we know more if you choose to tell her anything. Keep it basic."

He knows how I feel about keeping things from Gemma after what we've finally overcome. We promised to be open and honest like Ma and Pop are. She doesn't need the gory details about torture and eye gouging, but letting her know that this particular threat has been eliminated is fine.

We leave the warehouse on full alert as we drive to one of Pop's offices to get cleaned up and changed before heading back to the hospital and our family.

As we pile into the SUVs, Cassio turns from the front seat with an amused look on his face. This fucker is about to agitate the shit out of me. My arms cross over my chest as I lean back, in case I need the room to strike out and whack the shit out of him.

"So, Luca, what present did you get Gemma?" His eyes glow, which makes my nose scrunch up. He knows I'm terrible at this shit.

"Present? What are you talking about?"

Out of the corner of my eye, I see Sam in the driver's seat shaking his head. I'm not sure if it's for me or Cassio, but I'm confused.

"You know, a push present," Cassio says as if I've lost my mind.

"Sam, stop off at the jewelers," Pop instructs, and Sam speaks into his radio to tell the other soldiers we're making a pit stop.

"Do you know what that is?" I ask Pop.

"Yes, Son. Did you read the book I gave you months ago?" His tone is flat as if bored and exhausted speaking about this. I guess this is just another thing to add to the list of things I screwed up with this pregnancy.

"I read most of it. Just tell me what it is, and I'll make sure to get it." God, there were like a million different books on pregnancy.

"A push present is what the husband gets the wife after pushing the baby out. Hence, push present," Cassio answers in a taunting tone.

"That's really a thing?" I swear some of this stuff has to be made up. "Isn't having a baby celebration enough?" I ponder.

"You have so much to learn, my friend." Cassio chimes in with a smirk.

"I wouldn't be gloating if you want any help with Bianca."

His face pales slightly, and he turns to face front again, staying out of the rest of the conversation. This is going to be an exciting two months to watch as he fumbles his way around wooing Bianca.

"I ordered a few things last month for Gemma in thanks for delivering our first grandbaby, so we can see if there is anything there you can get for her. I really should've asked when I ordered if you'd been in yet to see Raj. I keep forgetting you haven't the slightest clue how all this works."

We arrive at our jeweler and are buzzed into the store with Raj waiting behind the counter.

"Mr. Falcone, I'm so glad you called. We just finished the last piece about an hour ago. We are polishing it up for you now to take with you," Raj informs Pop.

"Luca needs something special for Gemma." Pop never gives too much information out because any little bit might be used against him. I've learned this over the years, but now it's really hitting home.

"What about something like this?" Cassio points out a beautiful diamond necklace.

It's beautiful, that's for sure, and I'm sure it's ridiculously expensive, but Gemma wouldn't wear it. She'd be too afraid of losing it. She's so practical and loves homemade ideas or things that would benefit others.

A thought crosses my mind, and I whip out my phone. After looking over several sites, I execute my plan and hear the ding of the confirmation email in my inbox. Smiling like the Cheshire cat, I head back over to Pop and Cassio when something catches my eye. In the glass enclosure sits a pair of dainty diamond earrings. She has a second piercing in her ears, and they would be perfect. With the baby, I know she'll want to keep the jewelry to a minimum so it won't scratch Dante, and these would be perfect.

"Are you sure I can't interest you in a matching necklace or bracelet?" Raj pushes as he rings us up.

"This is all I need for now."

"Wow, maybe I should've sent you a link of ideas other men have bought for their baby mommas."

"What other stuff could you give?"

I hear Pop chuckle as he checks his phone as we pass through traffic.

"Cars, boats, condos, trips, shopping sprees—you name it," Cassio lists off.

"Just wait, I'm pretty sure my gifts are going to win me brownie points for the rest of the year," I boast.

As we walk through the hospital and up to our floor, I see Ernesto pacing outside Gemma's door. He pulls his phone out, and within a second my phone rings. The hairs on the back of my neck lift, and I pick up my pace.

"What?" I shout instead of answering his call.

A look of relief flashes over his face. "Sir, Miss Falcone brought in a photographer to capture the baby's newborn pictures, and they've seemed to upset Mrs. Falcone—eh, Ms. Gemma. Bianca and Mrs. Falcone are trying to calm her, but it doesn't seem to be working."

Pop and I don't wait for any further explanation and barge into the room. Gemma is crying in the recliner with Dante trying to latch onto her breast as Ma and Bianca try to console her. Alice and some other female are on the opposite side of the room having a quiet conversation.

"What the hell is going on?" I rush over to where my woman is seated.

"Oh, Luca," Gemma seems to cry harder as Dante continues to do the same. His little cry is more of a pathetic whimper that breaks my heart.

"Alice just flew in and thought she would surprise you guys with a newborn photoshoot for memories," Ma starts to explain. "Everything was going fine, but then I think Dante became overly stimulated. Gemma's hormones are all over the place, and she's having a hard time not crying when Dante starts to cry. I spoke with Dr. Fulton, and he assures us that this is normal."

"I need for everyone to leave right the fuck now!"

There are too many people here, and I think Gemma might be overwhelmed. After everyone is out of the room, I surprise my wife by picking her up with Dante in her arms and settle in the recliner with her in my lap.

"I love you," I whisper with my arms around her, using my pointer finger to lightly stroke Dante's cheek near her breast. He lets out a frustrated grunt then snaps his face into her boob and latches, suckling like his life depends on it. His little red face starts to calm, and Gemma's shudders start to subside.

"Talk to me, baby girl."

She sniffs and wipes her face with the hand that isn't securing Dante on the half-moon pillow that fits around her stomach so that breastfeeding is easier.

"I…I was taking a shower with Bianca's help when I heard Dante start to cry, and we came out Alice was here with that lady—who is very nice, so don't do anything," she adds quickly. "But I guess the sight of Dante being touched and moved around by a stranger made me upset, and I started crying. She wasn't harming him, but he was crying, and it was like he was calling to me. I started crying and scooped him up. Adele suggested the photographer come back at a different time because maybe Dante was hungry, but Alice thought just a few more pictures wouldn't hurt."

"I see. Did Alice say why she brought a photographer when Bianca is doing all of our photos?" I question.

Alice had gone away for the weekend with some friends to Disneyland, having thought we still had a few more weeks before the baby came. I know she's probably devastated for missing out. I'm sure she thought it was a good idea, but I'll have to remind her to check with me before allowing a stranger near our baby, especially with the threat still out there.

I slowly rock my wife and baby. Gem snuggles down in my arms, and I place a protective hand on Dante's back holding them close. Once Dante is fed and burped, I place her back in bed and crawl in beside her with Dante on my bare chest. His breath tickles the few hairs I have as I gently tap his back.

Pop cracks the door open, not coming fully into the room. "Everyone okay?" His voice is full of concern.

"They're good now."

"Your mother wants to stay overnight, but I told her the three of you need to be alone. We'll be back early in the morning." I can only imagine what that is going to cost—him telling Ma no. "Expect her before the sun comes up though."

His movements are quiet as he comes over and kisses Gemma's

forehead, then does the same with Dante. "We'll check in on Gio on our way out."

I nod and he leaves just as quietly.

After the nurse comes in one more time to check on everyone, I settle down and pull the bassinet next to me by the bed. With skills I didn't know I had, I place him in it without waking him and watch over him until my body gives in to sleep.

What a day from hell but also the second-best day of my life. Somehow, I met this woman, and she loves me enough to have a family of our own. I'm not the easiest to live with, I'm sure, but she's here and I couldn't be happier. Our relationship might've started out a little differently than most couples, but I wouldn't trade it for the world.

CHAPTER TWENTY-SEVEN

Luca

MY BOY IS SIX MONTHS OLD TODAY, AND LIKE EVERY month, the women in my life have to celebrate with a small cake, balloons, presents, and pictures to document this month's occasion. To be honest, I don't mind it at all. The fact we even get to celebrate my boy being here is enough for me. Things could've gone the other way six months ago, and the thought stays at the forefront of my mind often. I never take for granted the time I get with them.

"We'll have to finish this meeting quick so we're not late for the party," Pop interrupts my thoughts as Sam drives us to meet up with Bobby Dawson, the head of another mafia family here in Las Vegas, and his son Wyatt. We have a closer business relationship with their family than the other three families here. "Your mother will start without me, and I'll never hear the end of it." Pop chuckles, but I secretly think he enjoys these parties. He's the one who won't put Dante down and is in every video and picture. If an outsider didn't know…they might think Pop was the dad with how proud and boastful he is.

"I'll set an alarm, sir, to signal when the time is close," Sam speaks up. *The suck up.*

Pop nods then turns toward me.

"I'm giving you five years."

"Five years? For what, exactly?" I ask, confused as to how he's able to ping so quickly to a completely different conversation.

"I plan to retire in five years. Really, I'd planned to do it sooner, but now that Dante has come, I want you to be able to soak up as much time with him and his future siblings as possible before taking over the business."

I'm shocked and speechless. I've always known I'd be taking over, but it was always in a more nebulous future sense.

"Your Ma and I never had the chance to enjoy our time with you and your sister before being thrown into this business. I want you to be able to sit back and cherish this time with Gemma and the baby. Go stay in San Diego for a week or take them on vacations."

"Pop…" I don't know what to say.

My father is tough, never showing his soft side except to his girls.

"Adele and I have been talking, and I know I pushed you hard while you were growing up, but it was because this life isn't for everyone. You show these fools the slightest bit of weakness, and they'll pounce. I wanted you strong so that nothing could ever be used against you. I should've known the perfect woman would worm her way into your life, just like your Ma did to me. When you took off, I knew I'd pushed too hard. I never imagined you'd found your better half. She makes you happy and is your perfect balance. We may not deserve such a pure soul, with what we do for a living, but we do try to earn it every day."

I drop my head and look at my hands resting on my knees. I don't deserve my wife, but there's no way on this earth I'd let her go. Pop's right—she is my better half. My redemption, the purest soul that lets me, for just a little while, think that every good thing I've done will balance out the blood I've shed.

"That's why I want you to know that I'm waiting to hand the reins over to you. I want you to have this time with them and not have to worry. I've got you covered, but you will take this business over. And one day, you'll be having this same conversation with Dante."

My mind can't even wrap around the fact that he is my future. I'm just in the zone of him finally sleeping through the night in his own room. Gemma has been very adamant about not having any hired help with Dante, so we do all the nighttime stuff, like feedings and walks up and down the hall that put him back to sleep. I've worn a path in the rugs with my pacing. One time, the guards caught me carrying a pillow around instead of Dante late one night, exhausted out of my mind.

"Thanks, Pop. I may not have always shown it, but I am grateful for everything you've done for me growing up. I think until you're in the other's shoes, you really can't appreciate all that a parent does for their kids."

The SUV slows, alerting us that we've arrived. Our men are already stationed around and throughout the restaurant. Sam gets out and opens the door for Pop as Cassio opens mine for me, and they lead us through the back door.

"Mr. Dawson and his son are in the private room," Cassio announces.

Cassio has pursued Bianca for the last six months, but they haven't made it down the aisle to the altar yet. She's got a ring on her finger but refused to settle on a wedding date. The deal was made with Bianca's father, and as long as she marries into our organization, she gets to stay here. As far as I know, she and Gemma don't know Pop arranged for Cassio to woo and marry her in order to keep her here. She's been a little hot and cold lately. Gem says I need to stay out of it and won't mention anything the two of them talk about. Bianca finally got a place of her own not far from us, and as far as I know, Cassio still has his place. He's been tightlipped about their relationship when I pry, so I leave it alone, opting to stay out of their business. Gemma says there should only be two people in a relationship, and it needs to stay that way—even though I know she and Bianca gossip about everything, including Bianca's relationship with Cassio.

We enter the room and both sets of our men line the walls, on alert.

"Bobby, good to see you again. How's Mary?" Pop greets and asks about his wife.

"She's wonderful and wants to have Adele and that grandson over as soon as possible. I think she's getting a little baby fever." Mr. Dawson cuts his eyes over to his son, Wyatt, with a pointed look but then focuses back on Pop and me. "Good to see you again, Luca. You look way too rested for a guy who has an infant at home," he jokes.

If he only knew how few hours of sleep my body is used to at this point. Even when Dante sleeps through the night, I'm up a handful of times to check. Gemma bought the best cameras that allow us to monitor and view him from different angles, but I need to physically touch him to know he's okay.

After shaking hands with Pop, Wyatt comes over, and we shake, leaving our fathers to continue their conversation about their wives.

"How are things going?" I ask.

The thing with the Dawson's is that there isn't a rivalry between our families. Yes, we both are mafia families, but Vegas is big enough. We have our own territories, and we each keep to it. If there is a problem, we meet and solve it like men. The other families aren't as civil but do try to keep the peace. Every now and then, we have a setback with other families overstepping, but it hasn't been anything to wage a full-on war over.

"Things are good. Busy as usual." Wyatt is in the same position as I am. He's going to be taking over for his father when Mr. Dawson decides to retire. Although, I'm not sure anyone actually retires from this gig unless it's in a body bag.

"I heard it through the grapevine that a certain guy has his head turned upside down over a cute little thing visiting Vegas for the summer."

Wyatt narrows his eyes.

"She's…" He pauses, and I chuckle.

"I've been there, man. Just know that fighting it will only make things worse. If she's the one, then go full speed ahead, and don't let anything stop you."

"She drives me crazy." He scratches at his jawline. "I can't focus or say the right things around her."

Don't I know it. When you lock in on the love of your life, there's no turning back. Even if you try your hardest.

Our dads signal us over, and we sit down to talk about the threat still plaguing us. It seems to have spread over into the Dawson's territory and has been hitting them just as hard. Pop and Mr. Dawson have always tried to work together to keep the peace, but now someone is targeting both of our families. With our forces pulled together, I think we should be able to snuff out the bastard who's behind all of this.

"The shipment last week was intercepted, and all the guns were gone with three of my guys dead," Mr. Dawson explains.

"We've had a few attempts, but our soldiers killed them all and left no one alive for us to question," Pop adds. "Do you think we need to call a meeting with the other families?"

"I hate involving the others. It makes it look as though we're not strong enough to keep the peace in our own territories," Mr. Dawson admits.

"Whoever is behind this is coming for our territory and needs to be stopped. He might be targeting the others as well," I say.

"Or it could be one of the other families doing this." Wyatt voices what none of us have been willing to say out loud.

"If it is, then they're starting a war," Pop states, and Mr. Dawson nods. "Blood would coat the streets of Vegas."

The next half hour is spent brainstorming ways to draw out our guy. Victor Slater's name keeps popping up and it doesn't sit well with me. Not too long after this, Sam signals to Pop and we wrap up our meeting with the plan to meet up again soon and discuss further investigations of both situations.

As we are leaving, I walk out with Wyatt, and we head to the back door.

"If you're serious about this woman, let's double up for dinner and drinks. I could use some adult time with my wife," I offer, even though I hate the idea of sharing her time with other people.

A smile beams across his face. "That'd be perfect. I'll call you this week. You sure you can find a babysitter in time?" There's a gleam in his eyes as he taunts me.

"If Adele could, she'd kidnap Dante and never give him back," Pop interrupts with a proud grandpa smirk.

"Let the young go out, and we'll come over and meet this grandson Mary is dying to snuggle," Mr. Dawson offers.

"Sounds like a plan. I'll call with the details or have Adele phone Mary."

We head to our SUVs with our men and head back to the compound. We arrive with ten minutes to spare. Pop pats Sam on the shoulder in a rewarding gesture, and it makes me chuckle. I know I'm now in the same boat, not wanting to ever be on the receiving end of an upset wife.

"You made it!" Ma praises as she holds a happy Dante on her hip.

"Of course, my love." Pop swoops in and steals Dante just as he reaches out for him.

I let Pop steal Dante's attention as I slide over toward my woman, who is setting out the forks and plates for the cake. My arms encircle her waist from behind as I lean down with my lips on her ear.

"Want to sneak away for a while?"

"Luca," she shivers, and it ignites a need in me. "Your parents are here, and we have Dante's six-month cake celebration right now."

"Babe, Dante doesn't know the difference between now and an hour from now. I'm pretty sure he's never even going to remember this." She turns in my arms and tries to swat me in my chest, but I latch onto her wrist and guide her out in the hall and down toward my office.

"Luca!" she whisper-yells, but it only makes her sexier and my dick harder. My knees bend, and I put my upper body against her stomach, hauling her over my shoulder.

I kick my office door shut and lock it before striding over to my desk and gently setting her down. I attack her neck, loving her soft skin, and work my way up to her ear. Her moan and her fingers digging into my sides are all the encouragement I need to continue my trek to her petal-soft lips. Devouring her is my favorite pastime. Our tongues dance and swirl as we work each other. I push her knee-length dress up to expose her black lacy panties.

"I'm the luckiest bastard," I murmur as I whip the entire dress off her body. It lands somewhere along with my shirt as Gemma tugs at my clothes, just as desperate as I am.

Not giving a shit, I rip her panties at the crotch into two pieces. She's already undone my belt and pushed my suit pants over my hips. A haze overtakes my vision as I thrust forward without hesitation and bring her hips to meet mine. Her pussy encases my hard dick, and I have to take a pause. She's hot, wet, and tight—exactly how I love her to be. A while back, Gemma and Bianca went to some classes, learning how to strengthen their vaginal walls, and I damn sure gave those bastards a donation after a week of training sessions. My wife hasn't changed in size since Dante was born, but my God, she can clamp down now and take my breath away when she flexes.

"We have to be quick, Luca," she encourages as she moves her hips slightly, trying to get me to move.

I growl at the thought of not savoring our time, but my dick wants to rut in her tightness, not caring that I'm the one in control.

"You'll take what I give you, baby girl." I start to thrust palming one of her plump breasts that have grown since Dante came into the world. She's still breastfeeding, and I devour them when she's not pumping for his nutrition.

Her head sinks back, enjoying the ride as I work her over. Her moans spur me on as her eyes lock on mine. The glint in her eyes tells me I'm about to blow my load. She squeezes her pussy muscles around my dick and brings her legs around my waist, locking me in. I'm a goner for her. With the knowledge of having less than a dozen pumps left before I come, I move a hand down to her clit and start circling her tight little button. She's slick and pulsing. I angle my hips to change our position slightly, hitting her right where she loves it.

Gemma brings her hands from my sides to the edge of the desk, bracing herself as she falls over the cliff, calling my name. I'll never tire of hearing her call out for me as her orgasm crashes into her. She locks down on me and pulses against my cock, allowing me only a few more thrusts before I erupt into her waiting womb.

My free hand reaches for the tissues on the corner of my desk as I clean her up before helping her onto her feet, and she goes in search of her clothes, sans panties.

A knock at the door brings me out of my trance as she bends over to retrieve her dress. My cock perks up at the thought of her splayed out across my desk again. Hmm.

"Luca, Mrs. Falcone has sent us to locate you."

Of course she has.

I don't respond but watch as my beautiful wife tugs on her dress, not even realizing how amazing she is. She asks for nothing, yet I want to give her everything.

"Are you going to start attending the meetings at the school regularly or just quarterly?" I ask as I pull my pants up and fix my belt.

"I'd like to be more active on a weekly basis, but something has come up recently where I'm not sure you'll let me."

Six months ago, as a push present, I donated a hundred thousand dollars to a local elementary school in Gemma's name. She loves children and wants to better their education for them. The school was so thankful that she is now helping with administration when she can. Every time she comes home from a visit, she's excited and thinking of other ways to improve the school and learning for the kids. The new playground is now complete, and the plans for the pool are underway. During the school year, every class will take time out of their schedule to learn how to swim. So many kids every year drown because they are never taught, and Gemma thought it would also give the kids extra P.E. time to get the wiggles out of their system and be able to focus on bookwork. She already has the lifeguards lined up and the instructors ready to go when it's all finished. I couldn't be prouder of her.

She comes over and pushes my shoulders down so that I'm seated in my chair. Once she lifts herself back up on the desk, it takes all my willpower to focus on what she's saying and not what we just did across my desk.

"What…I'm not sure I'd want you away from Dante for long periods of time, but why couldn't you be more active?" My eyes focus on hers.

"Well, I'm not one hundred percent sure, but I think you've impregnated me again."

My mind ticks a few beats with her words. I'm sure my expression is one of confusion because I swear, I was just starting to plot how to get her pregnant again, and then *bam*, she's saying these words.

"Really?" I can hear the disbelief in my voice. "I only just started trying." I let that out instead of keeping my crazy thoughts to myself.

She giggles and narrows her eyes at me. "Well, when we have sex and don't use protection, babies tend to happen, Luca. And you seem to have a big appetite."

"Because you are the sexiest woman on this planet." *Duh.*

"I was going to call Dr. Fulton later today and see if he could work us in this week."

"I'll message him now. We'll head over after Dante's cake. Ma can put him down for his nap," I rattle off.

My fingers swipe through the text, letting Dr. Fulton know we'll be there in the next two hours.

"You can't just demand to be seen, Luca. He might have a

full schedule." She exhales deeply, still not understanding how the dynamics work.

I place my palm on her flat stomach which bounced back too quickly for my liking. I loved her curves and round belly. All that's left to show she was pregnant is her large, lush tits and a few of the tiniest stretch marks that I love to trace with my tongue, lips, and fingers. I miss seeing her body heavy with my child. Now the possibility of her being pregnant again is on the table, and I'll savor every moment of her growing body.

"I can do whatever the hell I want. Dr. Fulton is on our payroll and has been since I was born. He'll always make time for us, especially for you since you've seemed to worm your way into another man's heart." I grunt at the last sentence.

Gemma has become a favorite amongst our crew. I take that back. She's a favorite of anyone she meets. It's as if she has them all spellbound, a beacon of light in our rather dark lifestyle. She's always baking the men cookies or sending home treats for the wives. She now holds a family picnic once a month here on the compound. Everyone is dazzled by her. Gemma has really fallen into this role nicely, and I think she's going to make the perfect queen when it's our turn to take the reins of our organization.

Another knock on the door signals that our time is up. If we don't go out now, I can be certain Ma will be the next to bang on the door.

"Let's go celebrate our boy before they send in the big guns." I stand and hold my hand out for Gemma, snatching her wrist when she extends her hand and yanking her into my chest. Her body is flush with mine. "I can't wait to celebrate later tonight with the newest little addition to our family."

"We don't even know if I'm pregnant or not. I'm only a few days late."

I look down deep into her eyes. "You are. I should've realized it when your taste sweetened on me." I give her a salacious smile. She has gotten sweeter, and her breasts are a lot more sensitive this last week. Breastfeeding has made her tender, but she's been different, just like when she was first pregnant with Dante.

"What are you going to give me this time, baby girl? Another little boy like Dante or a sweet gentle baby girl like you?"

"I think you already determined that during conception, honey." She giggles, setting my heart ablaze.

"I love you, vita mia." *My life.* I lean down, and with the lightest touch, I place my lips to hers. "Thank you for giving me this life."

We make our way down the hall and back into the kitchen where everyone is waiting for us.

"Da da da," I hear Dante chant as we draw closer to the group.

"It's not fair that I carried him for nine months and you get to be the superstar," Gemma huffs. "This next one better be *my* sidekick," she says offhandedly but loud enough that the room goes still and quiet.

"What did you say?" Ma questions as everyone's attention lands on us. *So much for keeping it under wraps.*

Gio is the first one to reach Gemma. He wraps her in his arms. "Oh, sweetheart, that's wonderful news."

Gio has been on the mend for the last six months and is on Dante duty with Pop. They seem to manage to go into the office for a few hours, only to end up coming to play with and watch Dante the rest of the day. When they have to leave the compound, they dress him in a mini suit to match them before we head out to family events. Gemma and Gio are as close as Pop and I and I couldn't be happier for them. I was worried it was going to be hard for her to trust Gio after feeling abandoned by him, but she shocked us all once Gio came home after being shot. She moved him into a guest room in our house to recover. She wouldn't hear of anyone watching over him besides her. They talked every day during his recovery, and the bond they share now is unbreakable.

"Thanks, Dad, but we don't know for sure. Dr. Fulton is going to check us after Dante's celebration.

"We'll keep him overnight so you two can celebrate afterward,"

Ma offers, as though she hadn't planned to steal him after this anyway.

"Did you hear that, big boy?! You're going to be a big brother!" Pop bounces Dante in his arms which causes a giggling fit.

"Ba ba ba," Dante starts to babble.

My eyes scan the room, watching our family in such a surreal moment. I never thought having a family would be this rewarding. I'd always seen my parents and wished I'd find someone who filled my heart that way.

"What are you thinking so hard about?" Her voice is a balm to any storm.

"Just thanking my many blessings that you loved me and all my flaws."

"There was never any doubt, Luca."

"Love you, baby girl."

"Love you more."

"Impossible."

EPILOGUE

M Y CAR PULLS UP TO THE HOTEL, AND I LET MY MEN HOLD the door as I make my way into the casino. I stay toward the outskirts of the room so I won't be recognized by anyone. My men flank me as I approach the elevators and punch the up button with urgency. I shouldn't be here doing this, but it's the only way to solve this need. The elevator arrives, and we step on, waving my keycard at the scanner to take me to the penthouse. A room that is meant for only me. A place to unwind and hide from everything that is dark. My home on the compound is a place that is pure and full of light. Darkness can never touch our home. I won't let it. So, I come here to release that darkness before going home to my beautiful family.

The ding of the elevator signals we've reached the top. My men span out in the hall to keep watch and stay until I'm ready to leave, once I've had my fill.

I swipe my card, and the door unlatches as I step into the foyer. It's decorated with dark accents, from the curtains to the couches and rugs. I need this place to take the edge off from dealing with the scum of the earth after being named head of our organization a few years ago. Things are different now, and to keep my sanity, I always come here to be with *her* before going home to my family. I keep this shit separate. I kill men, bad men, so that this town is safe and not turned into a funnel of anarchy and killers who rape or steal women and children.

I never understood how Pop was able to dissociate this life from his family life, but I know now. He too had a place to leave all the bad behind.

My feet take me into the massive bedroom, where I see the curtains drawn, and the only light on is the one in the corner of the room. In the middle of the bed, lies the woman who will take all of this dark and twisted from me. She allows me to be the man who can be around his kids and not think of all the bad happening around them.

"You're late," the sweet voice says as I approach the bed, shedding all the layers of clothing in my wake.

"I'm never late," I growl, hating to be called out.

She's lying there in a corset that pushes her tits up and the tiniest pair of crotchless panties. She pushes up onto her elbows and watches me stalk toward her. She knows the score and is happy to help on the hard days. Today was especially bad.

Without another word, I grab her knees, haul her to the end of the bed, and impale her on my pulsing cock. There is nothing better than this heat surrounding my dick. She lets out a loud groan that spurs me to speed up my thrust. Her tits bounce with every thrust, causing them to rush up to her neck. My hand releases from her knee, and I place it on her slender shoulder to hold her in place.

"You like that?" I grit my teeth as I plunge in harder, and she moans.

"Yes, yes!"

She tries to reach up and touch me, but I know if she does this will all be over too soon. I drop her other knee and step back. In one quick motion, I've got her flipped onto her stomach, and my dick is driving back into heaven. She's pinned under me with my weight over her back making it impossible for her to go anywhere.

"Can you take it?" I'm drilling into her tight, wet pussy not caring that the headboard is beating against the wall.

"Please don't stop." Her walls are starting to flutter, and I know her impending orgasm is quickly approaching. "I'm coming!" she shouts. "Yes! Yes!" she chants as I pound into her, not holding anything back.

Over the years, I've learned not to hold back. I've got needs that only she can meet, and I don't want to hide those anymore. I wrap a hand around the front of her throat to feel her erratic heartbeat. She loves being manhandled, and I love that I get to do it. I know the moment she peaks. Her body tenses as her pussy tightens around my cock, strangling it, and her muscles go lax, enjoying the ride as she's thrown into ecstasy. Her walls squeeze the life out of my dick as I thrust three more times, then finish off in her pussy. My cum coats her to the brim, so much that it's gushing out of her. We both lie there for a beat, catching our breaths before I pull out and stare down at the mess I made.

"You didn't use protection," she chastises as she tries to crawl up the bed toward the pillows and turns to face me.

I didn't. I know I should've, but I didn't.

I shrug, turning on my heels as I walk over to the ensuite and gather a washcloth, dousing it in warm water before going back to the bed. I take my time and clean her up, just like I do every time I've met her here. I feel like I need to be gentle after being so rough during sex.

"I'll deal with it if something comes of it," I say off-handedly watching as more of my cum leaks out.

"Deal with *it?* When did possibly knocking me up become an 'it?'"

"Sorry, not what I meant." I let out a frustrated sigh. I lean back so my back is up against the headboard. I had a vasectomy a little more than a week ago, and though I'd been told to wear a condom during sex until my sperm count came back clear, I haven't. I won't have a barrier between me and my love.

"How'd it go today?"

I hate talking about business with her, but she's the only one who listens and doesn't judge what I have to do. What I go through to keep the peace in our territory.

I lean my head back and think about everyone waiting for me at home.

"Luca, you can't shoulder this alone. I'm here, let me in to help."

I know she's right, but I hate tarnishing her bright beautiful world. I pull her close to me and cling to her as I let all the darkness wash away and get my head out of the work I did today.

"I know, baby girl. I just hate for you to hear the horrible details."

"Was little Tommy right?"

Gemma has continued to be involved with the elementary school I donated to in her name a decade ago. She's made so many improvements to the school and the lives of each of those kids over the years that I can't keep up. Every time we go out in public to eat or to an event someone from the school or a former student always recognizes her, stealing my time with her. At first, it annoyed the hell out of me, but over time I've learned that she is who she is. Someone who needs to do good in the world for others. Someone who thinks about the children who are left behind and overlooked.

She came to me yesterday because a little boy named Tommy in kindergarten had bruises on his arms and legs. He normally wore long sleeves and pants out in this Vegas heat, but last week he'd scrunched them up on the playground, and Gemma had seen the deep purple and blue marks all over him. She'd asked what had happened, and he was hesitant to say. Every day she went and played with Tommy until yesterday when he finally let some things slip, and she'd told me about their conversation. Tommy's dad and uncle were making and running drugs out of their house. His dad and uncle would try a batch, and that is when the beatings would start. Tommy has two younger siblings who aren't in school yet, and Gemma was scared they were being abused too. She told me that Tommy looked underweight, and his clothes were always dirty.

Of course, she wanted to go over there right after school like she was the police, but I shut that shit down quickly. We've always talked about me handling the bad and she was to dish out the good. She gets so fired up that sometimes it takes holding her down in a bear hug for twenty minutes before she calms enough to speak.

"They can't defend themselves, Luca. It's not right. Someone needs to give these people a taste of their own medicine." She'd said that years ago when she started volunteering at the school. It's heart-breaking, watching as children are starved or hurt because an adult was neglectful. But that is where I come in. I may have done and still do a lot of bad things, but hurting children has never been one of them. So, I gather the info and take care of the problems that Gemma comes home with.

"We paid Tommy's house a visit." I look down at her as she rests her head on me, giving me her full attention. "It was bad, babe." I let out a breath, not wanting to tell her the horrors of what we saw. "Cassio and I entered, and it was like we'd walked into a scene of *Breaking Bad*. They had music turned up so loud you couldn't hear your own thoughts, much less the crying babies in the back rooms." She gasps, and I can already see the tears welling in her eyes. "The dad and uncle were passed out on the couches. They've been living in squalor. Bugs everywhere and not a clean dish in the place. When we went to the back of the house, we found the babies. Babe, they had horrible sores on their skin from their dirty diapers."

"No!" she cries, and it tears my heart up. "Did you get them to safety?"

"Of course. I called Ma's shelter and let them know what I'd found. She's going to have someone come to the school and pick up Tommy and take him to be with his siblings."

"Good, good." She grips my hand in hers and looks me straight in the eyes. "They won't hurt them again or come after them, will they?" I know what she's asking, so I give her the PG version instead.

"They will never be able to hurt anyone again, let alone a child," I state with conviction.

She nods, and that's good enough for her.

What I don't tell her is that we hauled them both to our warehouse in the middle of the desert and tortured the shit out of them. Slowly. We cut every finger off their hands and blowtorched their skin. When they passed out, we shot them full of adrenaline to wake them up and started the entire process over again. It went on for hours until their hearts gave out. The guys took them out into the desert and buried them where they will never be found.

"You ready to get home?" I ask and bring her up to straddle my lap. "I didn't hurt you, did I?" My hands massage her shoulders.

We'd started doing this years before my father retired. The kids were getting older, and it was getting harder to find hiding spots in the house to spend time alone with each other. She was the one who thought of all of this. She has really come into her own, sexually. What really threw me was when she turned up here one time as a redhead. I'm pretty sure that is how we conceived our third baby. We try to make this time all about us, but sometimes I just need to escape from all the ugly in the world, and being inside of my wife's pussy is the best way to do that.

"You didn't hurt a hair on my head. Although, next time I'll bring a paddle or riding crop to play with." She teases.

I twist us, flipping her over onto her back, and plant myself between her thighs.

"I guess the kids can have a little longer to play at Ma and Pop's house."

Two hours later, we walk through our front door, hearing the chatter of little voices throughout the house. We have an army of little ones, and I wouldn't have it any other way. I'm hoping I just impregnated Gemma with baby number six this evening.

"Daddy's home!" I call out, just like I do every day when I get home from work.

The thunder of many little feet on the floor make it sound like a stampede. I brace for impact as Dante is always the first one to reach me. He's the oldest at almost ten and follows his grandpas around, soaking all of their time up.

Our second child, Alessandro Felix, who is nine, is stuck to Gemma's side at all times. He still sneaks into our room at night to sleep next to her. He's the only one to rush over to her first to welcome her home. He has a kind soul, just like his mother, and I hope this world never breaks his spirit.

Our third and oldest baby girl is Liliana 'Lily' Adele, named after her grandmothers. The hospital room was a sobbing mess when I suggested we name our first girl after our moms. Gemma had named our son after our fathers, and I saw it as only fitting we honor our moms the same way. She came a little later and is now six. I'm pretty sure she's going to be an artist because every time I turn around, there is a new drawing on the wall somewhere in the house.

Another son and our fourth child came two years later, and Gemma was adamant that we have one of our sons named after me. Luca Mateo is now four and is every bit as stubborn as his father. The things that boy does give me a run for my money. Dr. Fulton, who retired after Mateo—as we call him—was born, always said I'd have one just like me, and he was right. He's had more stitches than all of our other kids combined and he's fearless. He's going to be the one that keeps me up at all hours of the night when he's older.

And last but not least is our fifth and precious baby girl Annabella Alice who just turned two. She toddles in screeching as Ma and Pop follow behind. She is the spitting image of Gemma, and I know I'm going to have to assign several guards to her to keep boys away. She has the looks of an angel, and her heart is so loving.

The kids bound into the room, and I act as though they knock me down. They cheer, and I'll never grow tired of hearing those voices or giggles. Time is a thief—as Pop once told me—and if there was a way to stop and hold on to this, I would. I might have long hard days, but coming home to my wife and the kids make it all worth it.

"Dinner will be ready in ten minutes, Mrs. Falcone," Rosa announces from the other side of the room.

"Thank you, Rosa."

The kids start to wander off, but Annabella doesn't move. She's got her stuffed dog tucked under her arm and is waiting for her moment. We just started doing this last week, and I know it makes Gemma nervous, but I wouldn't let any harm come to her.

I stay on my back and give Annabella a wink that she takes as our signal and climbs on my stomach. I lift her with my hands at her hips, and she thrusts out her dog in a superman position. Barely bending my elbows, I bounce her up, making her feel like I've tossed her in the air. She squeals yelling, "Abain, abain!" We do that a handful of times before one of her siblings yells to gain her attention, and then she's off to the next adventure with Ma on her tail.

"You good?" Gemma asks as she helps me up from the floor.

I wrap my arms around her, listening to all the kids in the background.

"There is no other place I'd rather be." I lean down and kiss the woman who changed my life. A woman who has stayed by me even when I didn't deserve it. "Love you, baby girl."

THE END

Thank you for reading my debut novel! I hope you loved it and will leave a review on all platforms.

What's Coming Next?

Hidden Queen: Dawson Family
Las Vegas Mafia Series

Kendall Drake defies her family and sneaks off to Las Vegas for a summer internship with her roommate at a prestigious company. What was supposed to be a summer of learning and opportunity turns out to be a host of revelations that she wasn't prepared for. She meets a handsome, arrogant guy named Wyatt and her internship plans take a turn. Being associated with his family throws her life into a tailspin when she learns of their dark ties to the mafia. Will Kendall turn to her family for help when she's put in a compromising position, or will she try to fight her way out of the mess she's tangled in?

ACKNOWLEDGMENTS

They say it takes a village to raise a child and that is true, but also to write and publish a book. There are so many people that come in at different seasons of your life and you never understand it until you have time to look back and appreciate the bigger picture. Sometimes you can't understand the whys or whats until you later find that it's because of certain moments like these.

Kevin, thank you for your endless support not only in writing but also in life. My world would be complete chaos without you. We have seen our share of ups and downs over the recent years and I'm so glad to have you as my rock. I love you and thank you!

Mom and Dad, thank you for teaching me that I don't have to fit the status quo to find happiness. The lessons you taught me over the years have shaped me into the person I am today. Thank you for supporting all my crazy adventures.

Erica Marselas, Paula Donovan, your advice and feedback on this book has been invaluable. Thank you for responding to every text, email, and phone call giving your opinion on every aspect along the way.

Kristen Portillo, thank you for taking your time analyzing the first draft. It was a complete mess and your advice and direction helped me navigate in cleaning it up and creating a final product. You are truly a miracle worker! My debut book wouldn't be so perfect without your help.

Christi Price, thank you for edits and proofreading. You have an eye for looking over and making sure all the little mistakes are corrected and the words make sense. Thank you for your time and detail.

To the readers, thank you for taking a chance with a new author. I hope it's as enjoyable as it was to write. Thank you for following me on this journey!

Lastly, thank you to FanFiction readers. I never would've thought in a million years to write a book, but your love and support helped make this day come true. Thank you to everyone who read my first entries back in 2015 and gave me the courage to continue to write and publish a book.

ABOUT THE AUTHOR

Amber Allee is a brand-new author with her debut novel *The Prince* out in early 2024. She started writing in 2015 but finally pulled the trigger to publish recently. Amber loves to write about romance, drama, and suspense along with hot alpha heroes.

She lives in the great state of Texas in the same town she grew up in. She lives there with her husband and two kids. When she isn't writing, Amber can be found under blankets reading or playing games with her family. She loves to travel and shop. She is the lover of wearing animal print and everything bling!